He held her hands close against his chest, then pressed his lips caressingly against her palm. Jeanine shivered, a flood of warmth shooting through her. She was on fire.

"Please," she whispered, "I have to go . . . you mustn't . . ."

But he wouldn't release her. He took her face in both his hands and gazed at her hungrily. As his eyes devoured her, something strangely exciting passed between them that she couldn't explain. It felt wildly wonderful, delightful yet terrifying, and she wanted it never to end.

"You can't go," he murmured breathlessly, his lips almost touching hers. "Not yet." And his mouth came down on hers, soft and yielding at first, then demanding more . . . more. . . .

BELOVED TRAITOR

Great Reading from SIGNET

BELOVED TRAITOR

by

June Lund Shiplett

A SIGNET BOOK

NEW AMERICAN LIBRARY

SIGNET TRADEMARK REG. U.S. PAT. OFF. AND FOREIGN COUNTRIES
REGISTERED TRADEMARK—MARCA REGISTRADA
HECHO EN CHICAGO. U.S.A.

SIGNET, SIGNET CLASSIC, MENTOR, PLUME, MERIDIAN AND NAL BOOKS
are published by New American Library,
1633 Broadway, New York, New York 10019

First Printing, September, 1985

1 2 3 4 5 6 7 8 9

PRINTED IN THE UNITED STATES OF AMERICA

This book is dedicated to my sisters, Rena Groth, in Burton, Ohio; Ruth Olsen in Tampa, Florida; Reta Rann in Wadsworth, Ohio; and to my brother, Jack B. Lund, in Valley Station, Kentucky. The years have put many miles between us, I know, and we don't see each other too often anymore, but the memories of growing up together are still there for me, and will never be forgotten. We fought, we laughed, we teased, we cried, but most of all we loved through all the good and bad times, and I'll cherish them always no matter how far apart life takes us. I love you all!

Prologue

Jeanine's blue eyes flashed angrily as she straightened the hat on her blond curls, then stared at the uniformed officer sitting at his desk across the sparsely furnished room from her. He looked tired and weary, but she didn't care. It wasn't fair. She'd given four years of her life to the government. They had to owe her something.

"I'm sorry," General Sheridan apologized, his jaw tightening. "But there's nothing more we can do, Jeanine."

"Why not?"

He shook his head, straightening some papers on his desk self-consciously, wishing he could have avoided this scene with her.

"You know as well as I do, why not," he said slowly. "Lee surrendered, yes, and the war's over as far as the military is concerned, but politics being what they are, and now with President Lincoln's death, and sentiment in the South so strong against us . . . we wouldn't dare make the kind of statement you want."

"Just a few lines," she begged, hoping to sway him. "It wouldn't hurt anyone. Just so my friends know I'm not a Southern sympathizer. That I didn't switch sides because the South was losing." She pursed her lips. "You don't know what it's like having to face their silence and ostracism. Even the children taunt me." Her eyes hardened. "I can't even earn a decent living. If it weren't for one of my uncles, I'd have starved months ago. But I can't live off him for the rest of my life. Besides, his wife doesn't know he's helping me, and if she suspected anything . . ."

"Surely there's something," he insisted.

She laughed. "Oh yes, there's something. There's always something," she replied bitterly, then lowered her voice. "Of course it has its shortcomings too, General. Prostitutes aren't any more welcome in my town than spies." His face reddened and she went on. "All I ask," she said, "is that the government acknowledge that I acted out of loyalty to the Union cause. That when I traveled through the South entertaining Confederate soldiers, I did so at the request of the United States government, and was working as a Union spy. The South already had a price on my head long before the end of the war, and from what I hear, there are still some who are willing to pay it, so what does it matter if the whole world knows it!"

The general sighed. "I know how you feel, Jeanine," he said. "But it's just something . . . You knew—I explained at the start that if you were discovered, we could help only so far. That we could never officially sanction what you were doing."

"I thought maybe now that the war was over . . ."

He shook his head, trying to make her understand. "I'm afraid not. Our policy is still the same. There are hundreds of unsung heroes just like you, my dear, some even gave their lives, and every Union soldier whose life was spared because of people like you will bless you a thousand times over, but that doesn't change things." He straightened behind the desk, eyes unwavering. "There'll be no statement in the papers, Jeanine!"

She stared at him long and hard, the sudden silence in the small dingy office vibrant with emotion, and he stared back, seeing not the woman she'd grown into over the past four years, but the young girl he'd met that evening in Chicago.

It had been New Year's Day, 1861, and that night was to complete her holiday engagement at the Rialto Theater. She was leaving the next morning for New Orleans, where she was booked into the LeGrand. Everyone in theater circles was talking about Jeannie Gray, the girl with the golden voice. She had been eighteen then, and on her own, her parents having died some years before. Not only was she pretty and could sing, dance, and play the piano, but she could act too. This, coupled with the fact that she was headed South, was what had brought her to his attention.

She hadn't wanted to accept his offer at first, and he'd argued for hours, but she'd finally given in. Now he stared at her, concerned. The blue eyes were no longer innocent, but held a depth of feeling that sometimes frightened him with their intensity, and her mouth curved sensuously, even in anger. She had changed in those years. Ripened into a beautiful woman, but a woman whose feelings, except for the anger she now felt, were all but dead. She had pushed her own feelings aside and served her country, and now all she wanted was for her country to acknowledge what she'd done, so she could go back to living, but it was impossible. There was nothing he could do . . . unless . . .

He made a quick decision, and she watched coldly as he opened one of the desk drawers and drew out a sheet of paper; then he brushed aside the other papers on top of his desk and began to write. The scratching of his pen echoed loudly in the quiet room, grating on her nerves as she watched him, yet she held back the words that itched to leap from her tongue. After a few minutes he looked up into her hostile face, setting the pen aside, blowing the words on the paper dry.

She eyed him curiously, then took a deep breath. "What's that?" she finally asked, tucking a stray strand of hair back beneath her worn straw bonnet.

He glanced at her for a moment, then back to the paper. "How would you like to go West?" he asked.

She stared at him in disbelief. "West?"

He pushed back his chair and stood up, walking toward her from behind the desk. "You could lose yourself in the West, Jeanine," he explained, handing her the sheet of paper. "Here, read this."

She took it from him gingerly, her eyes scanning the paper. "But I'm not a teacher."

"I know." His eyes narrowed shrewdly. "But you're a smart woman, Jeanine, and Raintree, Texas, is far enough out on the frontier they were probably too busy fighting Indians to know there was a war going on back here."

Her brows knit together as she stared at the paper in her hands. Maybe it would work. After all, Texas was a long way from Ohio, and Richmond, and . . . She read the letter again, then inhaled deeply, her eyes lifting to the general's.

"That reference letter is all I can do for you, Jeanine," he said softly. "I wish it could be more."

Her face was grim as she reluctantly folded it, and he handed her an envelope to put it in. "It isn't much for four years of a person's life, is it?" she said, and he flushed, embarrassed as she shoved the envelope into her handbag.

"No, it isn't," he agreed. "But it's the best I can do."

"When do I leave?"

"I'll have to make arrangements. It'll take a little time. Can you bear with your uncle for another month or so?"

"I guess I haven't much choice, have I?" she answered, fingering the frayed edges of her handbag, and he flinched.

They talked a little longer while he explained who the people were. "I'll let you know as soon as I get word," he said when there seemed little more to say.

She moved toward the door. "Well, I guess that's that, for what it's worth," she said abruptly.

"Jeanine?"

She turned, her icy blue eyes hardening.

"Good luck!" he said, unable to think of anything more appropriate.

She didn't answer. Instead, her mouth tightened stubbornly, and she took a deep breath, then turned and walked out, leaving only the faint rustle of faded silk in her wake.

1

It was late afternoon when the stage rattled into Raintree, a small settlement on the frontier, just north of the Brazos River and about fifty miles from the Red River, the borderline of Texas. Inside, Jeanine pushed the wire-rim glasses up on her nose as she stared out the window. Her curly flaxen hair was pulled back tightly and twisted into a bun at the nape of her neck, and with no lip rouge and the dowdy brown suit she was wearing, her whole appearance was changed.

Across the seat from her, the only other passenger, a paunchy well-dressed man with his hat pulled down over his face, leaving only bristly whiskers sticking out, had been sleeping, and he began to stir, sputtering, pushing the hat back on his head as the stage slowed, then came to an abrupt stop in front of the Empire Hotel. The man hadn't spoken a word to Jeanine during the long ride from Dallas, and it seemed he wasn't about to now either as he cleared his throat, swept the dust from the front of his brocade vest, then took out a pocket watch, checking the time.

The stage door flew open and the driver reached in. "Help you down, ma'am?" he asked hurriedly.

Jeanine accepted his offer. She was stiff and sore from the ride, and climbed down slowly, followed closely by the bristly man, who, after checking his watch again, spotted a young man walking toward them leading two horses, and quickly called to him. The two men exchanged a few words as the older man mounted one of the horses; then while Jeanine stood watching, they spurred their horses into a gallop and disappeared around one of the buildings, she assumed leaving town by a side road.

"Here's your bags," called the driver as he tossed them from the top of the stage, and she turned quickly, forgetting the two riders while she retrieved her baggage, disgusted with the reckless way the driver was handling it. Posters at the stage office had advertised courteous service. She'd be more than glad to dispute that statement.

She dragged the suitcases out of the dirt road and set them on the boardwalk, while the driver hurried to the door of the hotel and called inside. When no one came out, he returned to the stage, climbed aboard, grabbed the reins and flicked them, yelling to the team, and Jeanine quickly covered her face with her hand, listening to the creak of leather and squeak of metal against wood as the stage rolled out of town, leaving her standing alone in front of the hotel with a cloud of dust surrounding her.

Jeanine kept her eyes closed, letting the dust settle, then opened them again, brushing off her clothes, looking around. Raintree was far different from what she'd expected. It had the usual facaded stores, a bank, jail, livery, blacksmith, and one building that looked like a combination church, school, and meeting hall rolled into one, and all of them were in sad need of paint and repair, except the two saloons that were sporting newly painted signs, although the rest of both buildings proved they'd been there for some years. A newly established newspaper, with its fresh paint and new wood, looked out of place among them, while houses, some newer than others, were scattered here and there.

Since it was late afternoon, only a few people were moseying about, and none of them seemed to be paying much attention to Jeanine. She took a handkerchief from her reticule, wiped the dust off her glasses, then set them back in place, pushing them up on her nose, hoping she'd soon get used to them, then straightened her worn straw bonnet and turned back toward the Empire Hotel.

According to the stage driver, it was the only hotel in Raintree, at least the only one worth staying in. She glanced up at the sign with some of the paint chipped off its lettering. Well, she was here, and there was no going back. And she couldn't stand out here in the street all day. With a sigh, she squared her shoulders and headed for the open door of the hotel.

It was just as hot in the hotel as it had been outside, and Jeanine brushed a fly away from her face as she stepped into the lobby, adjusting her eyes, now that she was out of the bright sunlight. The lobby was small and unpretentious, with a few chairs here and there, spittoons at strategic places, and a flowered carpet that would have been impressive if it hadn't been so faded and worn. On the far wall hung what looked like a well-kept Confederate flag, and as she stood staring at it, a chill suddenly shot through her.

"May I help you, ma'am?" a deep voice asked from behind a desk at the inside wall near the stairs.

She turned, swallowing hard, forcing the apprehension that had begun to grip her into the pit of her stomach, where it joined the rest of her misgivings, and stepped over to the desk.

"I'm afraid I have a bit of a problem," she said, trying to ignore the flag that seemed to dominate the room. "Someone was to meet me, but I'm a day early."

He frowned, staring at her. "Who was to meet you?"

"I don't really know who," she answered. "But I'm to go to a place called Trail's End."

"The Heywood ranch?" His eyebrows arched, then dipped thoughtfully as he scratched his bald head. "I guess you do have a problem, ma'am," he replied. "Trail's End's a long way out."

"Maybe I could hire someone?"

"Not likely this time of day."

"I saw you have a livery in town. Perhaps I could drive myself."

"You could, but it ain't really safe, what with Indians roamin' about."

She frowned.

"You could stay here though," he suggested. "Since you're sure they'll send someone to fetch you tomorrow."

She hated the thought of dragging her baggage upstairs, then trying to while away the time till they decided to come after her. Besides, she was tired and weary, and the last thing she wanted to do if she could help it was hang around an empty hotel room.

"There's no way?" she pleaded.

The clerk started to shake his head as he studied her thoughtfully, then suddenly stopped, his eyes lighting up. "I just remembered," he said hopefully. "Cinnamon and some of the crew were in earlier today for supplies, and I remember my boy Jasper, here"—and he nodded toward a young boy sitting on a chair behind him, whittling—"I remember him tellin' me one of the hosses throwed a shoe. They just might be in town yet, gettin' it fixed." He saw the puzzled look on her face. "Cinnamon works at Trail's End," he explained quickly. "If you want, I could run over to the blacksmith's and see."

"Would you?" she asked. "I am rather anxious."

"You'd have to ride a buckboard."

She sighed. "I'd ride a horse, if that's all they had."

He smiled, turning to his son, instructing him to watch things while he was gone; then he left hurriedly, while she waited. When he returned a few minutes later, he was out of breath.

"They're on their way over," he said as he poked his head through the doorway. "I caught them just as they was pullin' out."

She was relieved, and walked over to the front window, glancing out in time to see a buckboard pull up out front. An elderly black man was driving the buckboard, and it was flanked by four horsemen. The desk clerk disappeared from the doorway again, and she followed him outside, watching as he headed for her suitcases.

"These yours?" he asked.

She nodded, then watched as the black man climbed down and helped the clerk heft her luggage onto the wagon, while the men on horseback sat quietly in their saddles studying her. Jeanine glanced at them surreptitiously. They were a strange lot, their faces so weathered it was hard to guess their ages. They looked coarse and rough, and she flushed self-consciously, hoping they hadn't noticed her looking them over.

"This here's Cinnamon," the hotel clerk said, introducing the black man as they came back around to the front of the wagon where she was standing.

"Cinnamon?" she greeted him pleasantly. "I'm Miss Grayson."

He nodded, smiling through a gray beard, then took off his straw hat to reveal hair peppered with the same gray. "I figured as much," he said. "I know you wasn't due till tomorrow, but you're welcome to ride out with us."

"I'm much obliged," she answered, then thanked the desk clerk for his help before letting Cinnamon help her climb onto the buckboard, conscious all the while of the four horsemen watching her intently. When she was finally seated beside Cinnamon, he glanced about, realizing the men were staring.

"This here's some of the boys, Miss Grayson," he said as he gestured toward the first man. "That's Spider."

He was long and lanky with piercing topaz eyes and sandy hair, his features sharp, reminding her more of a fox. She learned later that his name was really James Spider.

"That's Luke."

Luke sat his horse easily, his big square frame hunched comfortably in the saddle, as if he were a permanent part of it.

"Dustin."

The next man tipped his hat and smiled, showing crooked yellow teeth and brown eyes shining beneath heavy dark brows.

"An' the Kid."

The Kid's pale blue eyes glistened proudly as he straight-

ened, trying to look as tall in the saddle as the other men.
It was obvious he was still in his teens, with a scraggly bit
of fuzz trying to gather together across his upper lip into a
sorry excuse for a mustache.

She nodded hello to all of them, then watched Cinnamon flick the reins and edge the buckboard away from the
hotel and on down the dusty street, heading out of town,
with Luke and Spider in the lead, and the other two
bringing up the rear.

"They's gonna be s'prised you comin' today," Cinnamon said as they rambled along, and he glanced at her
furtively, watching as she adjusted the glasses on her nose
with her index finger.

"I imagine they will," she answered, then asked, "How
far is it?"

"Oh . . ." He thought a minute. "Never paid much
attention. I know it takes 'bout three hours in the buckboard, and two on horseback, if you keep a good pace."
He frowned, glancing at the narrow brim on her little straw
hat. She was squinting, with one hand over her eyes,
trying to keep out the sun. "Say, miss, I don't mean to be
bossy or nothin'," he said, "but if you want somethin' to
keep the sun out of your eyes, they's an old umbrella
behind the seat. It's got a few holes in it, but it'll keep you
from gettin' burned."

She reached around behind the seat and dragged out an
old black umbrella, shook off the dust, then thanked him
as she opened it. He was right. It was full of holes, but
would do nicely.

As they rode along, Cinnamon answered all her questions readily, and she soon realized he was exceptionally
fond of Garfield Heywood, the young boy who was to be
her charge. Gar, as he called him.

"Yep," he said, his dark eyes sparkling beneath the
floppy straw hat as they moved along in the hot afternoon
sun. "Me an' my brother, Venable, think the world and all
of that boy, and you won't find nobody nicer'n Mr. Griff."

"Griff?"

"Yas'm, that's what folks calls Mr. Heywood."

"He's Gar's father?"

"Yas'm."

"And Mrs. Heywood?"

His eyes narrowed slightly. "Oh . . ." He cleared his throat, shifting uncomfortably on the seat beside her. "It ain't rightly my place to say, since she ain't no blood Heywood," he answered reluctantly, surprising Jeanine, and he quickly changed the subject, telling her about the rest of the people she'd be meeting.

"Mrs. Brandt's the housekeeper," he explained. "Then they's Crystal Eaton an' her gals."

Cinnamon told her that Crystal had been eighteen when some Indians captured her, and by the time she was rescued, she'd been passed around by the Indian braves and was some months along with a baby. Her family wouldn't take her back, so the Heywoods took her in. A short while later, she had twin girls.

"Beth and Peggy looks more Injun than white," he offered. "They's 'bout fifteen now and he'p wif the house chores, whilst their ma does the cookin'. Then they's some twenty-five or thirty ranch hands, give or take a few, Cory McBride, the foreman, and Mrs. Heywood's brother."

"Sounds like quite a crew."

He grinned. "Yas'm." And he went on talking, telling her some of the history of the place.

The ride was long and tiring as well as unmercifully hot. The umbrella helped, but not enough, and by the time Cinnamon pulled off the main road, maneuvering the buckboard between a row of tall sycamores, she was relieved when he told her the ranch house was only about half a mile up the drive. Their escort had left them a few minutes earlier, disappearing down another well-used drive that Cinnamon explained was the back drive that led to the stables, bunkhouse, and barns.

"But I'd best take you to the front door," he said, and flicked the reins, urging the horses out from beneath the shade of the sycamores, and Jeanine got her first glimpse of the place.

"That's the house?" she gasped in disbelief as it came into view.

Cinnamon nodded. "Yas'm." Jeanine stared in awe as they pulled away from the line of trees.

Cinnamon had told her that the ranch house at Trail's End was the largest in the area, but she hadn't expected to see a rough-hewn log house measuring some two hundred feet or more across the front, with five chimneys peeking above a gabled roof. It was nestled in a lush green valley, with a number of outbuildings scattered about. But as they rode closer, she could see signs of neglect that made her start wondering.

Cinnamon drove the buckboard up to the front door, got down, then came around and helped her down.

"I'll take your things around back," he said as he climbed back to his place on the wagon seat, and Jeanine watched as Cinnamon and the wagon disappeared around the side of the house; then she turned toward the front door, aware of a face at one of the curtains at the small window beside it. She took a deep breath and started up the walk, once more hitching the glasses farther up onto her nose with her index finger.

The door opened before she reached it, and she was confronted by a young girl with dark sloe eyes, wearing a pale blue dress that brought out the blue-black highlights of her waist-length hair. She would have been pretty except for the flat, wide bridge of her nose that showed she was part Indian.

"Yes, ma'am?" she asked as Jeanine slowed for a second, then continued on into the house.

"I'm Miss Grayson," Jeanine announced, her eyes quickly taking in everything.

She was standing in a large foyer with two sets of stairs, one on each side, and a balcony across the back and down each side. Dark, highly polished wood gleamed everywhere, and delicately flowered paper covered the walls, while a chandelier, resembling a wagon wheel, hung from the high ceiling, with a round table placed directly beneath it. A vase of varied flowers in hues from pink to red was on the table, lending a dash of brilliant color to the room, which, except for the deep blue worn carpeting, was devoid of any other furniture. The effect was striking.

Jeanine turned to the girl expectantly.

"Follow me, please," the girl said timidly, and Jeanine followed her into a hallway that started at the foot of the stairs, to the right of the door.

The house was huge, and the library the girl led her to traversed it from front to back, with two fireplaces on the inside wall and a set of French doors at the far end, a flower garden visible through the sheer curtains that covered them.

"You'll have to wait here," the girl said abruptly. "I'll tell Mrs. Brandt," and she left, going back the way they'd come, leaving Jeanine standing alone in the middle of the room.

Jeanine shuffled her feet nervously. Since her first sight of the house, her stomach had been fluttering wildly with apprehension, and she began to wonder if she could really get away with pretending to be a teacher. Granted, she was smart enough, but there was more to teaching than just knowing the facts, and she'd had very little chance ever to be with young children. What if the boy didn't like her? This was almost as frightening as some of the assignments she'd had during the war. Well, she certainly couldn't change her mind now.

She set her jaw stubbornly and began to look around the room. It was warm and comfortable, the furniture well used, but as the sun continued lowering itself below the horizon, shadows began filtering into the corners, making grotesque patterns on the wall, only adding to her uneasiness.

The general had said Raintree was too far west to really feel the effects of the war. Well, if that was so, why the Confederate flag in the lobby at the hotel? And she'd seen more than one remnant of gray uniform on some of the men in town. It seems the general had been wrong, far wrong, and she had the sneaking suspicion that she just might possibly have landed smack dab in the middle of what looked like a town full of diehard rebels. The thought was unsettling.

She'd been looking out one of the windows, daydreaming, when a slight noise made her turn to find herself staring back at a rather tall, stern-looking woman dressed completely in black. Her thick gray hair was braided into a coronet atop her head, and her pale brown eyes were studying Jeanine intensely. Jeanine wondered how long she'd been watching her.

"You're a day early, Miss Grayson," the woman said curtly, her thin lips pursed. "We were expecting you tomorrow."

"We made better time than expected, and there was no way to let anyone know."

The woman scowled, then walked over, lighting a lamp on the desk in the far corner of the room. "Well, let's get a good look at you," she said. "You sound a bit young for a teacher," and she turned, her eyes on Jeanine again, as if to get a better look now that the light from the lamp was beginning to brighten the room. "You are young," she concluded. "Younger than what I'd expected."

"But capable," Jeanine said quickly, a little irritated by the woman's unfriendliness.

"I was hoping for someone a bit older," the woman mused, as she seemed to take in every detail of Jeanine's appearance. "But as you say, perhaps you're capable. We'll see." She paused to take a deep breath. "Oh yes, I didn't introduce myself. I'm Mrs. Brandt, the housekeeper."

Jeanine dug into her reticule. "Then I guess this is for you," she said quickly, and pulled out the envelope with the letter in it given to her by General Sheridan some months before.

Mrs. Brandt was hesitant as she reached for it, then suddenly seemed to make a quick decision and opened it briskly, reading it to herself.

Jeanine watched the look on her face as she read it, but the woman's expression never changed.

When she finally looked up, her topaz eyes were sparking dangerously. "I'm going to have to extract a promise from you, Miss Grayson," she said abruptly as she fingered the letter uneasily. "You will mention nothing to any of the other members of this household that General Sheridan recommended you. Is that understood?"

Jeanine was startled. "If that's what you want," she answered hesitantly.

"It is," Mrs. Brandt replied, and for a moment the harshness left her voice. "As you have no doubt observed," she said, her voice hushed, as if afraid of being overheard, "this part of the country, and the people in this house, fought for the Confederacy during the war, and General Philip Sheridan's name isn't spoken of in these parts. If anyone asks, just tell them you were recommended by a friend of mine. That's all they need to know."

"Yes, ma'am," Jeanine answered, and she began to wonder just what she was getting herself into.

Mrs. Brandt folded the letter, put it back in the envelope, and slipped it into the pocket of her dress. "Good," she said, then straightened, more self-assured again. "Luckily, we have your room all ready, so if you'll follow me," and she started for the door.

Jeanine followed close at her heels, while Mrs. Brandt kept talking.

"I'll take you upstairs to your room and you can freshen up a bit before dinner, but remember, dinner's promptly at seven." They reached the foyer and Jeanine followed the woman up the stairs to the right of the door. "You'll be expected to take dinner with the family every evening, Miss Grayson, unless otherwise instructed," Mrs. Brandt went on. "Our cook, Crystal, will see to it that you and Gar get breakfast in the morning, but you won't have to worry about the boy, he dresses himself. You'll eat lunch at the same time every day with the rest of the family, but evenings after dinner will be your own, as well as weekends and holidays, unless an emergency arises that would necessitate us asking you to watch him outside of school hours."

When they reached the top of the stairs, Mrs. Brandt

gestured toward a door in the middle of the balcony that ran across from one staircase to the other. "That's the master bedroom," she explained matter-of-factly, then pointed off to the left. "The servants' bedrooms are in that wing of the house. Your bedroom is this way," and she turned to her right, moving along the side balcony, then went down a hall that extended through the middle of this side of the house, and stopped at the first door on the left, opening it. "Here we are," she continued briskly, and stood back, waiting for Jeanine to go in ahead of her.

Jeanine stepped into the room and stopped, staring. All of her suitcases were open on the bed, and the young dark-haired Eaton girl was busy putting things away. The girl stopped what she was doing and stared back at Jeanine, a pile of underclothes in her hands.

"I hope you don't mind," Mrs. Brandt said in a way that told Jeanine she'd better not mind. "We knew you'd be tired, so Peggy's putting things away."

Jeanine watched the girl fold the underclothes she was holding, and set them neatly in the drawer, while Mrs. Brandt walked into the room, and moved past Jeanine, across to the French doors on the far wall, pushing them open farther as she kept on talking.

"I'm sure you'll like the room," she said. "There's a balcony here overlooking the gardens, and the furnishings should please you." She came back and stood at the foot of the bed, staring at the open suitcases for a moment as if she was going to say something else, then turned abruptly toward Jeanine. "I'll send someone up with warm water so you can wash up." She was sharp again, her voice demanding. "And remember, Miss Grayson, we'll expect you downstairs for dinner at seven," and with that she left the room, closing the door firmly behind her.

A long silence hung in the room for some minutes after the housekeeper left, while Jeanine stared at the closed door; then suddenly she sighed and slowly turned to the young Eaton girl, who had stopped unpacking again and was watching her closely.

"Is she always like that?" Jeanine asked as she walked

over and set her reticule on the dresser, then took off her
hat, setting it down beside the handbag.

"You'll get used to her," the girl said. "She's really
not too bad, just a little bossy, that's all."

"You're the girl who let me in, aren't you?" Jeanine
said, but the girl smiled, her eyes crinkling.

"No, ma'am," she answered. "That was my sister,
Beth."

"I thought . . . How do they tell you apart?"

"They don't." Her smile broadened. "At least not
unless we're wearin' our ribbons." She reached up, touching the ribbon in her hair. "I'm Peggy, so I wear a pink
ribbon. Beth's ribbon is always blue."

"That's the only way?"

"Yes, ma'am." She cocked her head, looking at Jeanine curiously. "You know, we never had a governess
before," she said, then went on unpacking Jeanine's things,
examining the various dresses, especially her scarlet ball
gown. It was the only fancy dress Jeanine owned, and the
only one that didn't show signs of wear. "We had a few
crabby nurses for Gar when he was a baby," Peggy went
on as she lifted the ball gown out of the suitcase, shaking
it out. "But it was hard getting anyone during the war, so
we've all just been raising him ourselves the past few
years." She held the dress up, examining it, running her
fingers carefully over the tucked bodice. "Ain't none of
the nurses had a dress like this," she said. "But Mrs.
Heywood does." She held the dress in front of her, then
twirled in circles as if dancing, her eyes drooping dreamily.

"That's the only fancy dress I have," Jeanine said,
watching her.

Peggy stopped. "It's a beautiful dress." Then she smiled
sheepishly at Jeanine, and walked over, hanging the dress
in the armoire. "If you'd like to change before dinner, I'll
press one of the dresses for you," she added, glancing at
Jeanine hesitantly. "That suit you're wearin' must be
scorchin' in this heat."

The girl was right. The suit was sticking to her. Jeanine
searched through the clothes and found a pink-and-white-

checked gingham with short puff sleeves and lace around the low, scooped neckline. It was faded, with a mend at the bottom, near the hem, but would have to do.

"This one should be cooler," she said, handing it to the girl.

Peggy started out the door with it, almost bumping into Beth on her way in with a pitcher of hot water. As Peggy disappeared down the hall, Beth shut the door, then walked over, setting the pitcher on the dry sink next to the dresser.

"There's towels here in the top drawer," she said, opening it; then she glanced at the open suitcases. "Don't worry, we'll finish the unpackin' and iron your dresses whilst you're eatin'," she said. "Is that all right?"

Jeanine was pleased. She thought she'd have to take care of her own things. "It's fine with me," she agreed. "But if you want to, you can go on unpacking now, while I freshen up."

"You don't mind?"

"Not at all." She began to unfasten the buttons down the front of her brown suit. "It won't take me long to wash, and I'm sure you've seen ladies in camisoles before."

Beth smiled, nodding, and went back to the unpacking, while Jeanine took off her glasses and set them on the dresser, poured hot water into the basin on the dry sink, and began washing.

The room was quiet for a few minutes, the only sound that of the washcloth in the basin as Jeanine wrung it out, splashing some water; then suddenly Beth stopped what she was doing and glanced over at Jeanine.

"Miss Grayson, may I ask you something?" she said hesitantly.

Jeanine turned, continuing to wash. "What's that?"

"Well . . ." Beth's face reddened. "When Peggy and I were little, Mrs. Brandt started teaching us how to read and write, but then after Mr. Griff got married, well . . . I was wondering, if you had a little spare time when you aren't in the schoolroom with Gar, do you think maybe you could teach us a few things while you're here?"

Jeanine stared at the girl, frowning, and Beth's flush deepened.

"I sure would like to learn, but I wouldn't want you to go to any extra trouble or anything," she went on hurriedly.

"You mean you and your sister don't know how to read or write?" Jeanine asked, the washcloth slowing its vigorous strokes on her soapy arm.

"That's right, ma'am," she answered. "It's too far for us to go to school, and Ma never learned, so when Mrs. Brandt quit, there just wasn't nobody else to teach us."

Jeanine stared at her thoughtfully for a minute, then turned back to the washbasin, rinsed out the washcloth, wiped the soap from her arm, and began to dry herself off. "I'll tell you what I'll do," she said as she finally turned back toward the girl again. "If it's all right with Mr. Heywood, I'll teach the two of you right along with the boy—that is, if it won't interfere with your work. I can't see where there'd be any harm in it, and it'd probably make it more interesting for him. How's that?"

Beth grinned. "I don't believe it," she said happily; then her grin began to fade. "But what if he says no?"

"Do you think he will?"

"I don't know, it all depends. Mr. Griff went to school back east awhile, and when they decided to get a teacher for Gar, I heard him say how he thought book learnin' was important, but if he listens to Rhetta . . ."

"Rhetta?"

"Mrs. Heywood." Beth frowned. "Before she married Mr. Griff, she went to some convent school someplace near San Antone, but never got to finish, and I think she's afraid we might learn more'n she did, 'cause she's the one who made Mrs. Brandt quit teachin' us in the first place. She told her there wasn't time for such nonsense."

"And Mr. Heywood agreed?"

"He must have, because nothin' more was said about it, and if he listens to her again . . ." She looked disgusted as she sat on the edge of the bed, absentmindedly fidgeting with one of Jeanine's scarves she was unpacking. "And it'd be just like her to say somethin', too."

"You can't be sure."

Beth sneered. "I can tell you ain't met her yet."

Jeanine was still holding the towel, and she eyed the girl curiously. First Cinnamon, now Beth. "What is she, some kind of an ogre?" she asked.

"Might as well be," Beth answered. "She never did like Peggy and me, and the fact that our pa was some Injun just makes it worse. But then, she hates all kids."

"What about her son?"

"Gar?" The girl shrugged. "I guess she likes him all right, much as she can, but Ma says it's probably good she can't have no more, 'cause she probably wouldn't want 'em anyway. Too bad she's not more like her brother. He loves kids."

"Oh yes. Cinnamon told me her brother lives here too."

"Yes'm, he came here when they kicked him out of the army."

Jeanine hesitated, her stomach suddenly tightening as an uneasy prickling shot down her spine. Her hands gripped the towel tighter, holding it to her breast as she stared at the girl. Oh, Lord!

"He was in the army?" she asked, trying to keep her voice steady.

"Yes'm. Rhetta's folks was killed, leavin' her and her brother to run their small spread, but shortly after she married Mr. Griff, her brother lost the place gamblin', and a few weeks later he took off. Nobody saw hide nor hair of him for years," she explained. "Then one day, a few months after the war broke out, he showed up in town in an officer's uniform, only it didn't last too long. He was kicked out before the war was over, because of his drinkin', and Zeb took him in."

"I thought Mr. Heywood's father Zebediah was dead?"

"He is. But he only died about five months ago."

"I see." Jeanine turned slowly and set the towel on the dry sink, staring at it absentmindedly. Cinnamon hadn't mentioned anything about Mrs. Heywood's brother having been in the army, and from what Mrs. Brandt said earlier, it had to have been the Confederate Army. Great! Well, all she could do was hope he'd never heard of Jeanine Gray, or seen her perform, and most of all, she'd pray that in case he had, he'd never recognize her with the glasses, no makeup, and her hair like this. She ran a hand over her head, smoothing back a few damp strands of curly hair that had loosened while she washed.

"Is something wrong, Miss Grayson?" Beth asked from behind her.

Jeanine took a deep breath and turned quickly, then picked her glasses up from the dresser, putting them back on. She began to straighten her petticoat, making sure it lay right, since she no longer wore a hoop beneath it.

"No, nothing's wrong," she answered. "I guess I'm just a little nervous, never having met the Heywoods, and not knowing what to expect."

"I hope Mr. Griff says it's all right for us to learn with Gar," Beth said anxiously. "But what if he doesn't?"

"Then I'll teach you on my own, like you asked at first. Mrs. Brandt said evenings and weekends will be my own, so no one should mind."

Beth flushed self-consciously. "You ain't gonna tell Mrs. Heywood what I said about her, are you?" she asked warily.

"Heavens no!" Jeanine assured her, and both of them glanced over as the door opened and Peggy called in that Jeanine's dress was ready.

It took Jeanine only a few minutes to put the dress on and fasten some pearl earrings in her pierced ears before addressing both girls.

"Now, if one of you'll show me the way to the dining room," she said. "It must be close to seven by now, and Mrs. Brandt was quite clear that I be on time."

Beth stayed in Jeanine's room, continuing to unpack, while Peggy showed Jeanine where the dining room was, downstairs, off the foyer. The arched doorway to it was at the back, beneath the set of stairs to the left of the front door.

"I think Mrs. Heywood's waiting for you," Peggy said

as she left Jeanine just outside the archway and started to
walk away. "I'll go back up now and finish helping
Beth," and she disappeared back upstairs.

Jeanine straightened, smoothing the skirt of her dress,
and stepped under the arch, unprepared for the room she'd
walked into. It was every bit as large as the library, with a
table that could easily seat thirty or more people; however,
only one end was set, the place settings delicately trimmed
with gold and resting on a fancy linen-and-lace tablecloth.
At the far end of the room, overlooking the front drive,
and below a row of huge windows, was a built-in window
seat, the plush velvet burgundy cushions on it comple-
menting the ornate table, chairs, and buffet, with matching
drapes at the windows, and the stark white walls, decorated with fancy paintings, were softened only by the intri-
cate gold design in the red flowered carpet. It was a
flamboyant room, its extravagance characterized by a crystal chandelier above the table, highly polished and glistening from the flames of a dozen kerosene lights.

A young boy wearing a crisp brown suit sat on the
window seat, one foot curled beneath him, eyes gazing out
toward the drive, a finger easing its way between the
starched collar of the white shirt he had on and his tanned
neck, where a slight redness showed it had been rubbing.

Beside him stood a woman. Her back was to Jeanine,
but Jeanine could see that her hair, soft and lustrous, and
the color of black coffee, was pulled up from creamy
white shoulders and piled in curls above the nape of her
neck, and her small waist, able to be spanned by a man's
hands, was covered by turquoise satin that billowed over
starched crinolines, making her waist seem all the smaller.
The dress was prewar Paris, faded but elegant.

"Do you think he'll be home in time?" the boy asked
his mother, and Jeanine heard the woman's quick intake of
breath as she spoke.

"I doubt it," she snapped. "You know he pays little
attention to time." Then suddenly the woman whirled
around as Jeanine cleared her throat, making her presence
known, and Jeanine was taken completely by surprise.

If this was Rhetta Heywood, she was absolutely lovely. Her features were classic. A small tapered nose, dark long-lashed eyes, high cheekbones, full lips that moved provocatively as she spoke.

"Miss Grayson?" she questioned crisply.

Jeanine nodded. "Yes, ma'am, and you're Mrs. Heywood?"

Rhetta Heywood stared at her but didn't answer, her dark eyes studying the plain young woman who was across the room staring back at her. Their eyes locked, and Rhetta suddenly had the feeling that she too was being scrutinized, a thought that was irritating. Her eyes hardened, and she tensed, drawing them away from Jeanine's gaze, turning to her young son.

"Stand up, Gar," she ordered firmly, and the boy reluctantly left the window seat to stand in front of his mother, face flushing uncomfortably. "Gar, this is Miss Grayson," his mother said as she introduced the boy, and Jeanine couldn't help the annoyance that crept into her eyes.

The boy was definitely uncomfortable, shyness apparent in the way his eyes were focused on the floor rather than Jeanine. His lips pursed, then slowly his eyes lifted, and he looked at Jeanine, hesitantly at first; then the hesitancy was replaced by curiosity as he stared into her brilliant blue eyes that were watching him from behind the wire-rim glasses.

"How do you do, Miss Grayson," he said stiffly, his voice almost lost in the large room.

Jeanine smiled. "I'm pleased to meet you, Master Garfield, and I do hope we'll get along."

His freckled face began to show interest as he gazed up, warming to her friendly smile. "You're the lady who's going to teach me numbers and reading, aren't you?" he asked timidly.

"And writing and geography," Jeanine added as she studied the boy. He looked much like his mother, only his eyes were hazel and devoid of the hard demanding arrogance Jeanine had seen in his mother's dark eyes. "We'll have a lovely time," she assured him.

Rhetta's eyes flashed. "Don't deceive the boy, Miss Grayson," she interrupted arrogantly. "School is work, and I never saw a child yet who liked it."

"Mrs. Heywood!"

"Do I shock you?" She laughed, her laughter bitter. "You might as well know, young lady, this whole thing was my husband's idea, not mine," she said. "If I had my way, Gar'd be in a boarding school back east, where he'd get a proper education, instead of depending on one person to know enough to teach him properly. He's a rebellious child with a mind of his own, and how my husband expects a mousy little thing like you to handle him's beyond me. I thought you were supposed to be older."

Jeanine glanced quickly at Gar, whose face was crimson, his mouth twitching nervously; then she looked up again at his mother, frowning. "Age doesn't really matter, Mrs. Heywood," she answered. "I don't see why your son can't learn from me as well as someone else."

"Hmph!" Rhetta wasn't convinced. "That'll have to be proved." A slight drawl took some of the sting from her words, but they were still cutting. "Until then, however, I guess I'll have to put up with it, just like everything else around here lately."

At that moment a door at the far end of the dining room behind Jeanine opened.

"Ah, I see you've met," Mrs. Brandt said as Jeanine turned abruptly, and Mrs. Brandt let the door swing shut behind her. The housekeeper stopped, her hands resting on the back of the chair at the head of the table. "I'm glad to see you're prompt, Miss Grayson," she said, then looked at Rhetta. "There's no use waiting any longer for Griff," she informed her. "There's no sign of him yet, so I told Crystal to start serving."

"Not again!" Rhetta was more than just annoyed. "He knows we eat at seven." She tried to keep the flush from her face as Jeanine turned toward her. "You'll have to excuse my husband, Miss Grayson," she apologized curtly.

"I'm afraid he pays little attention to regular hours." She put a hand on her son's shoulder. "Go sit down, Gar." She looked at Jeanine. "You'll sit beside him, Miss Grayson," and she motioned toward the far end of the table, where Gar was pulling out one of the chairs.

Rhetta walked around to the other side of the table and sat opposite her son, with Mrs. Brandt next to her, and Mrs. Brandt leaned back, tugging on the bell pull for the cook to start.

The chair at the head of the table, where Jeanine assumed Griffin Heywood usually sat, stayed empty during the whole meal, and Jeanine was sure it was this fact that made the meal so uncomfortable. Mrs. Heywood's foul mood got worse, and poor Gar was caught in the middle. He tried to please his mother in every way, and yet get to know Jeanine better at the same time, and the result only seemed to grate on Rhetta's nerves, making matters worse. If it hadn't been for Mrs. Brandt's firm interruptions, the meal would have been a complete disaster. As it was, although the food was delicious, more was left than consumed, and Jeanine's stomach was still fluttering nervously as they left their dessert half-finished, at Mrs. Heywood's insistence, and went into the parlor.

The parlor was directly beneath the master bedroom at the back of the house, and was decorated in different shades of blue, with ruffled white curtains beneath heavy blue draperies. A fireplace graced the back wall, and to its right were French doors that opened onto the flower garden Jeanine had seen earlier while standing in the library. It was the same garden she could look down onto from the balcony off her bedroom. Jeanine was surprised at the grandeur of the furnishings in the parlor, yet very aware that most of it was well worn and quite out-of-date.

When they'd first entered the parlor, she had tried to ignore a piano on the inside wall near the door; now she turned back toward it as Gar spoke.

"Do you play?" he asked eagerly.

She smiled, caught by the anxiety in his eyes. "Would you like me to?"

"Oh, do," he begged.

Rhetta glanced down at her son, then walked over and sat on the pale blue velvet sofa, reaching into a sewing basket beside it. "Yes, do, Miss Grayson," she said as she took out some embroidery. "That is, if you know how. I'm sure we could do with some entertainment," and she settled back smugly, her eyes on the new governess.

Jeanine stared at the piano for a minute, reluctant to touch the keys. She hadn't really wanted anyone to know she could play, but the eagerness in young Gar's face and the self-satisfied gleam in his mother's eyes were enough to challenge anyone. Recklessly throwing caution to the wind, she walked over, pulled out the piano bench, and sat down, letting Gar climb up beside her.

While he sat entranced, listening as she played one song after another, although it looked like she was lost in the music, in reality her mind was wandering far from what she was playing. All through dinner, and even now as her fingertips moved deftly over the keys, she kept wondering apprehensively just what kind of a man Griffin Heywood could be. Over and over again she kept asking herself: what kind of man could be in love with this cold, calculating woman who was sitting across the room from her on the sofa, staring at her so intently? And she was very wary of what the answer would be.

2

It had been dark for well over an hour as Griffin Heywood and his foreman, Cory McBride, reined their horses out from among the trees that edged the pasture, and headed toward the ranch buildings below in the valley. They were side by side now, with Griff riding closest to the fence, his tall frame tensing as his eyes searched the darkness around them for anything that might be out of place. Today's happenings had made him extra cautious, and although he knew the lay of the land, he slowed his sorrel to a leisurely walk while his thoughts wandered.

Twenty longhorns dead. Why? Such a senseless waste. They'd fenced in the water hole, put up signs, and made sure all the cattle were moved until it ran pure again, then posted guards at every other water hole on the ten thousand acres so it couldn't happen again. But why had it happened in the first place? It didn't make sense.

He and Cory had arrived home a few months back, right after the end of the war, only to discover that his father'd died about a month before, and Mrs. Brandt was trying to run the place all by herself, with little help from Rhetta. However, even though she'd been there for years, Mrs. Brandt knew nothing about ranching, and things were only going from bad to worse. So he'd plunged right in and taken over, trying to salvage some of what had been lost.

The war had taken its toll on everything in the South,

including Trail's End, leaving him with too many debts and a run-down ranch that hadn't really been a working ranch since the tides of war had changed so drastically. The cattle had roamed far and wide with only a skeleton crew to ride herd on them, and the ranch buildings had slowly begun to crumble.

Even the old copper mine near the north ridge was played out. There was still good timber in the hills, if he could get it out, but he'd been to Dallas just last week trying to talk the railroad into bringing a spur west. They weren't buying. They listened, all right, and said he had a good idea that would work someday, but not now. Money was needed to build railroads, and there just wasn't any money. The bottom had dropped out of everything in the South. Even longhorns were selling for only three to four dollars a head in Texas, and he'd already seen some of the other ranchers give up and move out.

Well, he wasn't about to. His intense blue eyes hardened. He'd found the perfect solution. He'd decided to round up and brand every stray and maverick he could, and run a herd north, to Abilene, where he heard cattle were selling for thirty dollars a head. No one had ever done it before, and most folks thought he was crazy, but he had to give it a try. Only the cattle had been running wild for so long that it was going to take until spring to get things organized, and it was time he wished he didn't have to take. Now this.

He thought back over the past few months since he'd been home. Gar was really growing up. He'd barely been out of diapers when he'd left for the war; now he was in long pants, and it was time to start his schooling. Thank God he'd gotten home in time to keep Rhetta from sending him to some school back east. He knew she'd do almost anything to keep him out of her hair, and he cursed softly to himself, clenching his teeth angrily as he thought of her.

Dear, sweet, beautiful Rhetta, and he remembered his homecoming with a bitter taste in his mouth. What had she expected, a change of heart? She'd made her bargain, and he'd stuck to it, just like he promised, but he'd promised no more, and four years away from her hadn't changed his mind. He remembered the way she'd looked at him when she'd come into the bedroom that first night he was home. The seductive tilt to her head, the way her nightgown clung to her figure, showing off every soft curve. Damn her anyway! What made her think it'd be any different now?

He straightened in the saddle, muscles rippling beneath his buckskin jacket, the cool night air invading its warmth and making him shiver as much as the unsettling thoughts of his wife did. Shoving the thoughts of Rhetta aside, he glanced over at Cory.

"Got any ideas?" he asked.

Cory shifted his weight in the saddle, his big red mustache hiding the uncertain curve of his upper lip. "Maybe."

"Seems somebody doesn't want us to make that drive."

"Maybe."

"You startin' that again, Cory?" he asked, glancing over at this big burly redhead who was his friend as well as his foreman.

"I ain't startin' nothin'," Cory answered, pulling his hat down a little farther over his intense brown eyes. "But it seems mighty strange to me that you were supposed to come back from the line shack tomorrow morning like you do every month at this time, and would've stopped for water at that particular water hole too—that is, if you hadn't changed your mind and decided to come back a few days early because that schoolteacher's comin' tomorrow. And we'd never knowed the water hole was poisoned if those strays hadn't wandered in. The cattle haven't used that water hole for years. Only ones ever usin' it are you and the hands comin' and goin' to the line shacks."

"Coincidence, that's all."

"What about the payroll?"

"What about it?"

"You got a short memory, Griff." Cory glanced at Griff as they rode along, and his mouth was grim. "Everybody knows you were supposed to be haulin' that payroll, and the man who took your place got him three bullet holes in the back for his trouble." He straightened stubbornly in the saddle as he gazed out ahead of them into the valley, where the lights from the buildings were dotting the darkness. "And how about Jake Harper last month?" he went on. "You were supposed to be at the line shack, not Jake. I still say someone mistook him for you in the dark."

Griff frowned. "Hell, Cory, who'd want to kill me?" He shook his head. "No, whoever's doing this is trying to keep me from making that drive, that's all. They're hoping I'll sell out like everyone else, and we both know who it is."

"Don't be so sure," Cory answered. "Just because they missed again . . ."

"You're daydreaming."

"Am I?" Cory's eyes hardened. "Somebody's mad you came back from the war, Griff, and if I were you, I'd be just a mite more careful about where I went and who I took with me."

Griff studied Cory's huge six-foot-four frame, hunkered onto the saddle, barely visible in the dark. He'd have paid little attention to a warning from anyone else, but coming from Cory, maybe . . .

"All right," he conceded. "I'll keep my eyes and ears open, but I still think you're wrong," and he reined his horse a little to the left as they reached the end of the pasture fence and headed toward the barn at a slow canter.

No one was about as they dismounted, then walked their horses inside, the familiar scent of hay and manure mixing with the pungent odor of sweating horses. Each man moved to a stall and began unsaddling, when Cinnamon's brother, Venable, shuffled in, his squat body swaying from side to side. He was shorter and fatter than his brother, with completely white hair, but the facial features were so alike they could never deny they were kin.

"Crystal say the missus was right upset 'cause you wasn't here for supper tonight," he drawled as he stared at Griff, watching him unsaddle his horse, while the flickering light from a lantern hanging near the horse's stall cast vague shadows about the huge barn.

"What else did Crystal say to tell me?" Griff asked.

"She say supper's warm like usual, and that the school-teacher got here a day early."

"She's here already?"

"Yep, Cinnamon brung her out in the buckboard."

Griff glanced over to Cory. "Looks like Cinnamon saved us a trip to town."

"Good," said Cory. "Only I bet she didn't relish ridin' in Cinnamon's buckboard. The springs on that thing are shot to hell."

Griff watched Cory set his saddle aside and begin rubbing down his horse; then he hefted his gunbelt more comfortably on his hips before heading for the barn door, while Venable picked up a brush and started currying his horse for him.

"Guess I better go make sure she lived through it," Griff called back to Cory. "I'll catch you later."

"Remember what I said," Cory reminded him.

Griff nodded, waving as he left the barn and headed toward the house.

Crystal was at the sink with her back to him when he walked in, and he stood for a minute watching her. She was still a good-looking woman at thirty-five. Her gold-flecked brown hair, almost waist-length, was piled atop her head, and she had misty green eyes that mirrored the sadness she'd endured over the years. A few extra pounds had been added to her figure lately, but on her it looked good. She'd always been more like a big sister to Griff than the cook, and the familiar sight of her took some of the edge off his unrest.

"Sit down," she said, sensing his presence, and he slipped off his buckskin jacket, giving it a toss behind the door, where it caught on a hook, tossed his hat on top of it, then began to roll up his sleeves as she turned to face him. "Your plate's still at the dining-room table."

He nodded toward the kitchen table. "Bring it in here."

She grabbed the front of her apron and began wiping her

hands as she left to get his plate while he washed up at the sink. By the time she returned, he was finished and rolling his sleeves back down. He sat at the table while she dished up his food.

"Was it bad?" she asked, setting the plate in front of him.

He sighed. "Worse than I'd hoped. We lost twenty head."

"That many?"

"If the men hadn't discovered it when they did, we'd have lost more." He reached for a slice of bread. "I can't understand anybody who'd poison cattle."

"Maybe they weren't after the cattle."

"You too? Cory said the same thing."

"Well, it is logical, Griff. Why would anyone want to kill the cattle? That wouldn't stop your drive, but with you out of the way . . . I don't think there's another rancher around with the guts to lead a drive like that."

"And without the drive, not only do the ranchers who've thrown in with me go under, but Trail's End would be in jeopardy too, and if Rhetta inherited, they'd force her into selling for sure." He thought for a minute. "I don't know, maybe you and Cory are right." He shook his head. "But who'd believe us?"

She shrugged and went back to the dishes.

"Did Venable tell you about Miss Grayson?" she asked over her shoulder while working at the sink.

"Hmm." He pushed a chunk of bread into his cheek. "I suppose Gar's scared of her."

"She ain't the scary type."

"No? That's a surprise. I thought she'd have beady eyes, a wart on her chin . . ."

Crystal was rinsing the last pan and set it aside, then turned to face him. "She's a strange one, Griff," she said, frowning, and grabbed the front of her apron again.

"Strange how?"

She walked over to the table, wiping her hands on the way. "It's hard to explain, but . . . she's younger than we thought she was gonna be, and real plain, only . . ."

"Only what?"

"There's somethin' about her eyes." She pondered her last words. "It isn't just that she wears glasses, it's . . . well, at first glance she gives the impression of bein' real subdued and timid-like, but when I was servin' dinner, I noticed she not only handled Gar real well, but her eyes seemed so intense. I swear she didn't miss a thing goin' on at the table."

He stared at Crystal. "You said she was young?"

"Not more'n twenty-five at the most."

He frowned. "I was hoping she'd be older."

"I know. Oh, she might be, but I doubt it. 'Course, I could be wrong. It's hard to tell, since she don't fix herself up much." She let the apron drop from her dried hands and walked over, pulling the ironing board out of the wall, securing it, then put a flatiron on the stove to heat. "One thing for sure, though, I don't think you'll have to worry about Gar not likin' her. He seems to be fascinated. When she looks at him with those big blue eyes, he can't seem to resist."

"That's surprising. He was all set to hate her."

Crystal smiled, her pale green eyes studying him curiously. "I assume the description you gave before—beady eyes and a wart—was his?"

"How'd you guess?"

"Well, it sure don't fit her." She turned toward the door. "I'll be right back. I told the girls I'd help bring her dresses down to be ironed." She started to leave, then turned back, nodding toward his plate. "There's more where that came from if you want it. If not, just leave the plate, I'll be back down in a few minutes."

"Crystal?" he called as she started out the door, and she turned back again, watching his eyes harden. "Tell Rhetta I'm home," he said roughly.

She nodded and left.

Rhetta was sitting on the sofa, her sewing in her lap, her eyes intent on this young woman who'd been hired to be her son's teacher. They rested on her pale gold hair, then traveled to her hands, so seemingly at home on the piano keys. Her piano playing made Rhetta's look sick in comparison, and Rhetta's eyes narrowed jealously. Why did she have to be so accomplished? Bad enough she could play like that, but she'd been singing for Gar too, and Rhetta was forced to admit the woman's voice was far more than just pleasing. Unlike her own voice, which was high and slightly nasal, Miss Grayson's voice was rich and full, like a finely tuned instrument, and as Rhetta stared at her, a feeling of bitter envy settled over her.

Suddenly Jeanine stopped playing as Crystal poked her head in, interrupting from the doorway.

"Mr. Griff's home, ma'am," Crystal said, and watched curiously as Rhetta drew her eyes from her perusal of the new governess, to answer her.

"Is he in the dining room?" she asked.

"No, ma'am, the kitchen."

Rhetta looked annoyed. "Well, just tell him to come in when he's through, will you please?"

Crystal nodded. "Yes, ma'am." Then she left, heading upstairs.

"Pa's home!" Gar cried enthusiastically, and looked up at Jeanine beside him on the piano bench. "Is it all right if I go get him?" he asked.

Jeanine was hesitant as she glanced down at him, then saw the way his eyes were shining, and sensed his eagerness. "I . . . well, yes . . . I guess it's all right. Why not?" she said, and he quickly slid from the piano bench, then halted his hurried flight toward the door as his mother's harsh voice stopped him.

"Gar, just where do you think you're going?" she asked.

He turned apprehensively, eyes protesting, and stared at her. His body was poised, ready to take off again at a second's notice, yet he didn't answer.

Rhetta's eyes demanded a response, and her voice sharpened even more. "Did I say you could leave?"

He took a deep breath. "No, ma'am, but . . ."

Rhetta continued to stare at him, fingers flexing nervously on her sewing as she saw the familiar curve of his mouth tilt down stubbornly. He was looking more like his father every day, and a twinge of regret suddenly seized her.

"Next time, ask my permission. Do you understand?" she said.

He nodded. "Yes, ma'am. Now," he asked, anxious, "may I go?"

She straightened authoritatively. "If you must." She watched as he fled the room, leaving a deadly silence in his wake.

Jeanine was still sitting on the piano bench, and Rhetta stared at her hard, anger building as the seconds went by.

"Just what did you think you were doing, young woman?" Rhetta finally asked as Jeanine shifted her seat on the piano bench.

Jeanine turned to her, all too aware of what Mrs. Heywood felt she had done.

"I beg your pardon?" she said, feigning innocence.

"Miss Grayson," the boy's mother demanded, her eyes flashing, "Gar is my son, not yours, and you'll do well to remember that, do you understand?" Her jaw tightened. "You had no right just now to tell him he could go bring his father."

"I'm sorry. I didn't think—"

"That's just it. You people never think." Her chin tilted haughtily. "You, Miss Grayson, are a servant. Gar's schooling, and only his schooling, is your responsibility."

"But I thought—"

"I don't care what you thought. You were hired as a governess, and only a governess, not a substitute for me, and I expect you to keep your place. Do I make myself clear?"

Jeanine had all she could do to hold back her anger. She had come up against some strange people over the years, but never had she run into anyone quite like this. The woman was impossible. All she had done was try to be nice to the boy. Oh, this was great. She had two choices. She could tell Mrs. Heywood what she really thought of her and catch the next stage back to Ohio, or swallow her pride and keep pretending to be as meek and unpretentious as she was trying to appear. The struggle between the two decisions was a hard one, and only the remembrance of how degrading it had been trying to exist in the world she'd left behind gave her the strength to do what she knew she had to do.

Her eyes lowered, and she shook her head reluctantly, forcing herself to play the role she'd chosen, her hands resting submissively in her lap.

"Mrs. Heywood, I didn't mean to overstep your authority," she apologized, then lifted her eyes again. "It was just that the boy looked so anxious—"

"Well, see it doesn't happen again!" Rhetta's eyes caught Jeanine's, and as they locked in combat, a strange friction sparked between them. Rhetta Heywood was the first to look away. "Just remember what I said if you intend to keep your job here, Miss Grayson," she said viciously, and picked up her sewing again as Gar suddenly burst into the room, dragging his father along behind him.

Outwardly Jeanine tried to look docile, but inside she was still seething from Rhetta Heywood's blistering attack, and although her eyes were half-hidden behind the wire-rim glasses, they glinted vibrantly with pent-up emotion. She tried not to let the incident spoil her rapport with young Gar, and glanced toward the doorway where the boy stood with his father, and was suddenly jolted by another surprise as she found herself looking directly into a pair of deep-set eyes as startlingly blue as her own. They were set in a ruggedly tanned face beneath a shock of honey-blond hair that waved close against the collar of a faded red shirt, and as she gazed into them, they seemed to devour her with their intensity, making her tingle all over.

"Here's Pa!" Gar exclaimed proudly, then smiled shyly as he began pulling his father across the room with him.

Jeanine could only stare awkwardly as Gar hurried his father over to meet her. The hilt of a knife protruded from a sheath attached to the gunbelt that hung on Griffin Heywood's slim hips, and he moved in an easy gait alongside Gar's small frame. He stopped before Jeanine, the faint scent of horseflesh emitting from the buckskin pants and vest he wore, his heeled boots making him seem taller than his actual six feet.

Jeanine fought hard to take her eyes from him and look at the boy, but it wasn't easy. There was something magnetically intriguing about the man. He wasn't extremely handsome, but there was a rugged masculinity about him that Jeanine had never encountered before in a man. He was staring down at her, and she could feel an unexpected flush spreading from the tips of her ears to her face.

"I told you she was pretty," Gar said quickly as both father and son stared at her, and the flush deepened even more.

"You're embarrassing Miss Grayson, son," Griff said as he let go of the boy's hand and held his hand out for Jeanine to take. "Miss Grayson, how do you do, I'm Griffin Heywood. You'll have to excuse my late appearance, but business always comes before pleasure."

Jeanine reached out demurely and they shook hands. His fingers were sinewy and firm as they closed around hers, the strength of them sending pulsating currents of warmth clear through her.

"Mr. Heywood?" She heard her voice crack unsteadily in the middle of his name.

"Stay there at the piano," he said, suddenly sensing her wish to run. He released her hand. "Gar says you play well. I'd like to hear."

"If you wish," she said timidly, and forced her eyes from his compelling gaze, turning again to face the keys.

Small frown lines creased Griffin Heywood's forehead, and he felt a sudden sense of loss as Miss Grayson's blue eyes left his, and he found himself staring at the back of her head. He straightened instinctively, suddenly aware that he'd been staring at her a little too hard, and not quite able to understand why, except that he'd seen something in her eyes he'd never seen before in a woman's eyes. Something that seemed to reach down deep inside him with the same intoxicating effect as if he'd had a glass of heady wine. The sensation was unnerving, and he fought to pull

his wayward emotions back together again as he drew his
eyes from the sleek smoothness of her pale hair and glanced
toward Rhetta, all too aware that she'd been sitting on the
sofa watching him.

"Rhetta." He nodded toward her. "Sorry we couldn't
make it back in time, but it was worse than we thought."

"Isn't it always."

His jaw tightened at her sarcasm, and he fought the urge
to retaliate. "We'll talk about it later," he said calmly,
and turned back toward the piano as Gar once more climbed
onto the bench, then gazed back up at him.

"She's been teachin' me a song, Pa," he said hopefully. "Can we sing it for you?"

"If I can join in."

"Oh, do!" His face was beaming as he looked at Jeanine. " 'Oh! Susanna!' " he half-whispered to her, and
Jeanine smiled at him, unable to resist the open warmth in
his eyes.

Her fingers ran over the keys, then quickly picked up
the melody, and they began to sing. Their voices filled the
room, Gar's loud and sometimes off-key, his father's deep
and resonant, blending with Jeanine's as he soon fell into
the harmony.

But all the while they were singing, Jeanine had a hard
time concentrating on what she was doing. She could feel
Griffin Heywood's eyes studying the back of her head, and
his nearness was unnerving her as much as his low husky
voice that seemed to vibrate clear through her. Nothing
like this had ever happened before, and it was frightening.
She wished she could run somewhere and hide, far away
from the unsettling emotions that were surfacing inside
her. Emotions she'd always been able to control before,
but which now were wreaking havoc on her self-control.
She'd been wondering all evening what Griffin Heywood
would be like, but had never expected anything like this.
How on earth was she going to work for a man whose very
presence threw her feelings into such turmoil? She should
stop playing and run like hell, but knew that was impossible. Instead, as the song ended, she sat stiffly, her hands

still on the keys, unable to turn around just yet, trying to muster the courage to face him again.

As soon as the music stopped, Gar jumped off the piano bench and ran to his mother. "Didn't we do good, Mama?" he asked anxiously.

Rhetta was staring at the governess and her husband. Neither had moved since the music stopped, and she watched as Griff continued to stare at the back of Miss Grayson's head.

"Yes, dear," Rhetta said placatingly. "It was nice, very nice."

Rhetta's answer invaded Griff's thoughts, and he realized he'd been staring again. What was it about this young woman that seemed to intrigue him? He tried to put his finger on it, but couldn't, and straightened, shoving the unwanted notions aside, turning toward Gar and Rhetta. He smiled at Gar.

"It certainly didn't take you long to learn that song," he said.

Gar grinned sheepishly, pleased with himself. "I knew most of the words already."

"I figured as much." Griff stooped, holding his arms out, and Gar ran into them, giving his father a big hug. "But it's way past your bedtime, young man," he said. Griff stood up again and ruffled Gar's hair as he looked down at him. "What say I go tuck you in now that I'm home?"

Gar hesitated. "If you don't mind, Pa," he said self-consciously, "could Miss Grayson take me up tonight?" He glanced over to Jeanine, who had finally turned and was watching him. "I'd like her to."

"I'd love to take him up, if it's all right with you, sir," Jeanine said quickly.

Griff glanced at her. Once more their eyes met, and he was captivated by the blush that tinted her cheeks and the warm glow flooding her eyes that the glasses she was wearing couldn't seem to hide.

"Why don't you both take him up?" Rhetta said sarcastically as she watched her husband staring at the governess, and Jeanine felt a chill run down her spine.

If Griffin Heywood sensed his wife's irritability, he didn't let on, just said, "Since I have to go see Cory at the bunkhouse, I'll let you have full honors tonight, Miss Grayson," and he drew his eyes from Jeanine's and looked down at Gar to say good night.

Jeanine was relieved, because besides her anxiety over her own reaction to Gar's father, she'd realized Gar's father had been staring at her far more intently than was normal, and her imagination had really begun to run wild. She knew very little about Griffin Heywood or how he'd spent the past few years. What if he'd been in the army? And what if he'd seen her perform as Jeannie Gray? Maybe he could see through her disguise, and knew who she was. She hadn't met him personally, she knew that for certain. If she had, she'd have never forgotten, but there'd been so many soldiers during the war. What if he'd been among those she'd entertained? And she'd been fool enough to let him know she could play the piano and sing. Was that why he'd been watching her so closely?

She kept her eyes on him surreptitiously, his muscular body moving beneath the buckskins as he leaned down to kiss Gar, and suddenly she had a strange feeling she shouldn't have taken this job.

After the kiss from his father, Gar hurried over, kissed his mother, then came back to Jeanine, who had stood up and was waiting for him. He took her hand.

"I'm ready," he said enthusiastically, and Jeanine smiled at him, then hastily excused the two of them and they left the room.

Griff started to follow, then stopped as Rhetta called him back.

"What is it?" he asked.

"We have to talk."

"About Miss Grayson?"

She put her sewing aside and stood up. "Griff, the woman's impossible," she said. "She's been here only a few hours, and already she's tried to undermine my authority with Gar."

"How?"

"Every way she can. Already he's asking her permission to do things, instead of mine."

"Is that so bad?"

"Don't be ludicrous. She doesn't know her place, Griff," she went on angrily. "She's a servant, not my equal. Besides, she's far too young to manage a boy like Gar. She was supposed to be older, much older."

"Rhetta, we agreed before we sent for her that she wasn't to be treated as an ordinary servant." He watched her full lips tightening stubbornly. "You aren't supposed to order her about like you do everyone else around here, remember? And as far as her age, I can't see where it makes much difference how old she is as long as Gar likes her."

"You mean I'm just going to have to put up with it?"

"Well, I don't intend to send her packing."

"This is ridiculous." The lines slowly began to soften about Rhetta's mouth, and her eyes caught Griff's, warming instinctively. "Griff, there's something strange about that young woman," she said huskily. "It's not just her attitude, it's something else I can't quite explain, but her quiet manner puts a lie to the hard, cynical look in her eyes. I don't think she's as innocent as she lets on. I have a feeling she's hiding something."

"For heaven's sake, Rhetta, give her a chance," he pleaded. "Please, for the boy's sake."

"The boy's sake?"

"All right, for my sake, then. I want him here with me, not back east in some school with a bunch of strangers."

She reached up to touch the collar of his shirt, to smooth it down against his shoulder. "You won't change your mind?"

His hand covered hers, and he lifted it from his shoulder, holding it momentarily as he gazed into her dark eyes. "Hardly, and I don't know why you even bothered to ask."

He stared at her for a minute, their eyes fighting a clash of wills, then he dropped her hand and started to leave. Suddenly he turned back. "And remember, she's not a servant, so don't ride herd on her!"

Rhetta watched him leave, wishing she could strike out at something, anything, but there was nothing to vent her anger on, so instead, she took a deep breath, straightened a wayward curl from her forehead, and returned to her sewing. She didn't like this young woman invading her home, and most of all, she hadn't liked the way Griff had looked at her, and even though Miss Grayson wasn't very attractive, Rhetta was more determined now than ever to prove her husband wrong. Nothing was going to spoil things for her. Nothing and no one.

Gar led Jeanine down the upstairs hall past her bedroom, and stopped at the first door past hers on the left.

"Here we are," he said, his voice echoing in the quiet hall.

He turned the knob, swung the door open, and Jeanine followed him inside, then suddenly stopped, staring at her surroundings. Crossed tomahawks hung over the head of the bed, along with Indian ceremonial masks and beaded tapestries, and the bedspread on it was a colorful hand-woven Indian blanket. On the floor beside the bed was a huge buffalo-hide rug, and at the other side of the room stood a small replica of a tepee, its sides painted in bright colors with birds, snakes, and animal designs.

"Well, this is quite a room," she said, closing the door behind them.

"I get undressed in the tepee," he said proudly. "Peggy and Beth make sure my bedclothes are there for me every night."

He headed for the tepee, and she moved toward the bed.

"I'll pull back the covers." She glanced up distastefully at the tomahawks as she folded back the Indian blanket and fluffed up his pillow. "You must really like Indians," she said curiously.

His voice was partially muffled as he answered from

inside the tent. "I do. Pa used to live with them, and he tells me about them all the time."

His answer surprised her.

"They called him Tosi Nuit. That means White Wind in Comanche."

She straightened, looking around once more at all the Indian artifacts, studying them a little more closely this time. "Your father lived with the Indians?"

"Yes, ma'am. He was captured when he was about eleven, and his pa had to trade rifles to the Indians to get him back, but that wasn't till he was almost growed. Chief Horseback of the Comanche let his sister have him, and he was made one of the tribe. They said he could run fast as the wind." Gar emerged from the tepee in his nightshirt. "I like when he tells me about it, but Mama gets mad. She don't like Indians. Are you afraid of Indians?" he asked.

"I never met one."

"If you did, would you be afraid?"

"Probably."

"Just like a girl," he said seriously. When his mother wasn't around, he talked more freely. "Pa says Indians aren't really bad, but that sometimes people take things from them and they fight back, like in a war. He knows all about Indians."

"I'm sure he does."

Gar folded his hands and dropped to his knees beside the bed, closing his eyes, then opened them again for a second and gazed up at her. "Can I put you in my prayers tonight too?" he asked.

She smiled. "I'd like that."

His eyes closed again, and his lips moved soundlessly. She watched him closely, studying him, a prayer of thanks on her own lips, because although looking very much like his mother, he seemed to have inherited none of her personality. He was likable and easy to get along with, and she was pleased. At least this part of her job looked like it would work; it was the rest of the household that bothered her now. Well, she'd just have to wait and see, and she tried not to look too worried as she tucked him in, then left the room. But once downstairs, her frown deepened as she neared the parlor again.

Rhetta Heywood was yelling about something, and for a minute she wasn't sure she should go in. But it was too late to back away from the doorway again as Griffin Heywood caught sight of her and interrupted his wife's tirade.

"Come in, Miss Grayson," he said quickly, ignoring the disgusted look on Rhetta's face as she whirled toward the doorway. "You might as well get in on this, since it concerns you. We were discussing the Eaton girls."

"Oh yes." Jeanine's voice wavered slightly as she came into the parlor, fighting the urge to forget she was supposed to be quiet and unassuming. "I . . . I meant to ask you about them before, but forgot," she explained hesitantly.

"I happened to overhear them in the kitchen a few minutes ago, so they told me."

"But you might as well forget it," added Rhetta. "There's no way I'm going to let those girls spoil Gar's schooling."

"They won't spoil it, Mrs. Heywood," Jeanine said, Griffin Heywood's presence giving her courage she'd almost forgotten she had. "In fact, it'd probably help him, having others to compete with."

Rhetta sneered. "Don't be ridiculous. How could those girls possibly compete with my son?"

"My wife thinks it's a waste."

"A waste to teach someone to read and write?"

"If you could teach them!" Rhetta's dark eyes narrowed. "But they're savages, Miss Grayson. Their father was an Indian. A stupid, ignorant Indian, and everyone knows you can't teach Indians anything."

"Everyone, who?"

Rhetta's mouth pursed angrily. "Are you contradicting me?"

"For heaven's sake, Rhetta, leave her alone." Griff's eyes darkened. "It won't hurt to give it a try. Besides, I think it's a good idea. I should have thought of it myself."

Rhetta's voice lowered, and she glared at him. "You're making a mistake, Griff. A big one," she said furiously.

"She's only going to be wasting her time, and Gar's too. She'll never be able to cram anything into those girls' empty heads."

"Don't you like them, Mrs. Heywood?" Jeanine asked curiously as she felt the hatred emanating from Rhetta Heywood.

"What I do or don't feel for the girls is beside the point, Miss Grayson," Rhetta answered. "Facts are facts. Their father was a stupid, ignorant savage." She glanced at Griff. "But since my husband already seems to have made up his mind on the subject, I'll be anxious to see just how much their mindless brains can absorb. I wish you luck— you're going to need it." Her chin tilted stubbornly as she stuffed her sewing into the sewing basket beside her, then stood up. "Now, if you'll excuse me, I have some things to do before retiring," and she swirled the skirt of her dress dramatically as she left the room, carrying her sewing basket with her.

Jeanine felt uneasy. She didn't like being left alone with Griffin Heywood. She glanced at him uncomfortably. "I'm sorry, Mr. Heywood," she said. "I didn't mean to antagonize your wife."

"No need to apologize, Miss Grayson. Instead, I apologize, but you see," he tried to explain, "Rhetta's parents were killed by Indians and she's still resentful. I'm afraid she can't bring herself to accept them the way I do."

"Because you lived with them?"

He looked puzzled for a moment; then his eyes softened as he realized what she meant. "Aha, Gar's room. He told you?" he asked.

"I hope you don't mind."

"Not at all. It's common knowledge." His eyes caught hers for an unguarded moment, and Jeanine trembled. "I lived with them for six years, until I was seventeen," he said. "Then I was sent back east to school so I could catch up with the rest of the world." His eyes grew hard again. "My wife wishes I'd forget that part of my life, but it's not all that easy. She's been understanding about Gar's room, though, although she rarely goes into it."

"I guess that's only normal, under the circumstances."

"I suppose." He sighed. "I was hoping she'd mellow some by now, but I'm afraid she still hates them."

"Have you ever gone back to see the Indians you lived with?" she asked.

"Our paths have crossed a few times over the past thirteen years, but our worlds aren't the same anymore."

"What was their world like?" she asked. "Or would you rather not talk about it?"

"On the contrary," he answered. "I don't mind at all," and for the next half-hour or so, while he slowly drank a glass of brandy from a decanter on one of the stands, and Jeanine sat on the sofa listening intently, he told her some of what it had been like living with the Comanche.

He had just finished a lengthy answer to one of her many questions when Crystal suddenly bustled into the room, heading toward the open French doors. She glanced over quickly to Jeanine. "Oh, I thought you'd gone up already too," she said, surprised, then closed the French doors, locking them.

"We've been talking," Griff answered. He frowned. "Did Rhetta go up?"

"Yup. Said to remind you about the early appointment in town tomorrow morning."

"I'm sorry." Jeanine stood up. "I've kept you up."

"Nonsense." He straightened, stretching slightly. "I'm the one who's kept you up. You must be exhausted after the long stage ride, then the ride out here this afternoon. Come"—he walked over, taking her elbow—"I'll see you upstairs."

At first she was going to pull away, but then his fingers felt good on her arm and she let him usher her from the room. It wasn't until they reached the stairway to the right of the front door that he relinquished her arm, turning back, and she went on up the first few steps alone.

"You turning in, Crystal?" he asked.

"Got a few things left to do in the kitchen." She locked the front door. "Don't worry, I'll be up for a while yet."

He nodded, as if there was an understanding between

them about something; then he joined Jeanine on the stairs and they continued up them, stopping on the landing in front of the master bedroom. A kerosene lamp on a stand beside the bedroom door was flickering low, and Griff reached for it.

"I'll see you to your room."

"There's no need, really," she said, hoping to discourage him. "Mrs. Brandt showed me the way earlier."

"But the hallway's dark."

"Not completely. I can see fine."

He was still holding the lamp, and looked down at her, studying her face, wondering why she once more looked as if she wanted to run as she had earlier in the parlor. He knew he should probably have cleaned up before meeting her, but didn't think he looked that bad. Of course his buckskins weren't any too clean, and he could use a shave. He reached up, rubbing a hand across his chin. But Gar had been so anxious. He must be a sight. His eyes held hers, and again that strange elusive heady sensation flooded through him, and suddenly he found himself wondering what she'd look like without the glasses on and with her hair falling loose about her shoulders.

He swallowed hard, forcing words to his lips, his stomach tightening defensively. "Then I'll bid you good night, Miss Grayson," he said. "But do be careful. If you get up during the night, we leave only this light burning low."

Jeanine tore her eyes from his penetrating gaze. "Good night," she said, and turned abruptly, willing her knees to quit trembling and hold her, at least until she could reach her room, and with his eyes following, she fled hurriedly along the balcony, disappearing down the hall toward her room.

Once in the hall where she knew he couldn't see her anymore, she slowed, leaning against the wall for a brief moment, then mustered enough strength again to reach her bedroom door. She hurried inside, closed the door, then leaned back against it, breathing heavily, her heart pounding from the sheer strength of the look that had passed between them.

There was no mistaking that look in his eyes. They had talked to her as surely as if the words had been spoken aloud, and what they'd said was disturbing, because it was the first time that look had ever brought an answering response from her. She took a deep breath, straightened, then sighed.

She lit the lamp on the dresser, and stood trembling for a moment, collecting herself. When her knees finally felt secure, she walked over to the open French doors and stepped out onto the balcony, breathing in the fresh air.

The light went on in the master bedroom across the way, and she felt uneasy as she wondered whether Rhetta had been asleep or not, and what they might be talking about. What a strange pair. She frowned. And what a strange man. She shivered.

Turning abruptly, she went back into her room, leaving the French doors open, and undressed for bed, suddenly realizing how tired she was. She didn't even bother to take down her hair, but slipped into her nightgown and set her glasses on the dresser, then blew out the lamp. But as she climbed into bed, pulling the covers up, hoping to erase the sight of Griffin Heywood's blue eyes looking deeply into hers, she knew it'd be no use—they were even going to haunt her dreams; and she vowed vehemently that since she had no recourse but to stay, she was going to avoid the man as much as possible. And as the moon climbed above the trees, filtering into the room, bathing it with a soft light, she finally relaxed some and was able to drop off to sleep.

3

It was later, sometime during the middle of the night and still dark out, when Jeanine slowly opened her eyes, her mind quickly alert to the fact that something was wrong. The moon was low in the sky now, casting weird shadows, and she lay watching them play about the room. She had no idea what had awakened her, then suddenly heard a scuffling noise. Raising onto her elbows, she listened for a few seconds, then slipped from the bed as the noise grew louder. Tiptoeing to the door, she leaned against it and listened closely. Someone or something was in the hall.

She crept back to the chair by the bed, picked up her wrapper and put it on, then groped for her glasses on the dresser. She had to remember not to be seen without them, even in the middle of the night. Making sure they were secure, she went back to the door, opened it quietly, and slipped from the room, closing the door firmly behind her.

The hallway was pitch dark. Evidently the lamp by the master bedroom had gone out. She'd barely taken a step when there was a weird grunting noise, and scuffling right in front of her, and suddenly a body pressed hard against hers. She gasped a startled shriek, and a pair of hands shot out clumsily, attempting to cover her mouth, only to knock her glasses aside instead. Grabbing for them with one hand, she tried to fend off whoever it was with the other, the rest of the scream frozen in her throat.

As she grappled unsuccessfully with the intruder, making no headway at all, the hallway suddenly began to get lighter. Someone was coming from the main balcony, carrying a freshly lit lamp. She began focusing her eyes quickly, and as the light grew brighter, she found herself face to face with a man who, if he hadn't been so intoxicated, would have been quite dashing.

His thick dark hair was disheveled, and a lock of it had fallen onto his forehead, dangling above a pair of very bloodshot amber eyes that were squinting only inches from her face.

"Jeannie?" His breath smelled of stale whiskey, and his voice was slow and slurred as he stared at her. "Jeannie? Ish that you, Jeannie Gray?" he asked drunkenly.

Jeanine's face went white as she realized she was staring into the glazed eyes of an ex-lieutenant who had carried an important dispatch from General Lee to General Jackson during the war, regarding the arrival of ammunition, supplies, and reinforcements. A dispatch whose contents was known by the enemy long before reaching the general, thanks to Jeanine.

Her hand shot back to her face, making sure the glasses were set back in place, and she pulled her head back, looking down her nose at him, trying to remember what his name was, and figure out what the devil he was doing here, and hoping he hadn't really recognized her. She'd have to bluff it through. He was so drunk it just might work.

"I beg your pardon, sir!" she gasped breathlessly. "If you'll kindly take your hands off me!"

He was holding her shoulders, staring into her face. "No . . . no . . . you're not her." He scowled, shaking his head. "Where ish Jeannie? D'you know wha' she did . . . d'you know?"

"Warren!" Griff's voice was like a pistol shot interrupting him.

He leaned sideways against the wall, loosening his grip

on her, and shut one eye, cocking his head to look back at Griff, who was holding the lamp.

"Know who he ish?" he half-whispered, turning back to her like a little boy sharing a secret. "Thash my brother-in-law. Good ol' Griff . . . eh, boy?"

Oh my God, she thought as Griff closed the gap between them, and the realization was stunning. He was Rhetta's brother, and now she remembered his name. It was Granger. Warren Granger.

"Come on, Warren," Griff said solicitously. "It's two in the morning. You'll have the whole household awake."

A half-sob caught in Warren's throat. "Hell, somebody turned out the lamp, Griff. It was dark . . ."

Griff opened the door opposite Jeanine's room. "You've frightened Miss Grayson enough for one night," he said, then grabbed Warren's arm. "Come on, I'll help you," but Warren wrenched free of him and straightened stubbornly, fighting to keep his balance.

"I'll get there myself," he insisted, and aimed for the open doorway.

Jeanine held her breath, watching as he lurched forward, just missing the doorjamb, and stumbled into the bedroom, and as Griff held the lamp up so they could see better, they watched him collapse on the bed, falling across it sideways, out cold.

"You'll have to forgive my brother-in-law, Miss Grayson," Griff said apologetically. "He's not really a bad sort. It's just that liquor and self-pity don't mix. I'm only sorry you had to see him like this."

She smoothed some strands of loose hair back absentmindedly as she stared at the inert body sprawled across the bed, her breathing still erratic from the unexpected encounter.

"I'm sorry too," she said breathlessly, trying to keep her voice from trembling. "But don't worry, I'll be discreet."

He glanced down at her, aware that she was shaken more than she was admitting, but not wanting to embarrass

her further. "No need for discretion," he said calmly.
"Warren's binges are no secret to the folks in Raintree."

"Oh . . ."

"But don't let it concern you," he said quickly. "Now,
if you'll excuse me, maybe I can make him a little more
comfortable."

"Will you need help?" she asked hesitantly, still staring
at the man lying across the bed.

"I'm sure I can manage," he answered, then reached
out and opened her bedroom door.

She forced her eyes away from Warren's limp body and
looked up into Griffin Heywood's worried face.

"You're sure you're all right?" he asked, concerned.

She nodded. "Just a little shaky yet," she said. "I
hadn't expected . . ."

"I know." He straightened. "Now, why don't you try
to get back to sleep again. I'll take care of Warren."

She nodded, her thoughts still racing in a limbo of
uncertainty as she stepped back into her bedroom and let
him shut the door behind her.

She stood for a minute just inside the door, staring
across the darkened bedroom toward the open French doors,
trying to adjust to the full reality of what had just happened. It was impossible, yet . . . A sick feeling swept
over her, and she swallowed hard, wishing she could die.
Of all people, Warren Granger!

How long ago had it been? Two years? Slowly she
walked past the bed to the French doors and leaned against
the doorframe, staring out into the night. Richmond in the
spring. It had been warm and beautiful then, even with the
war going on. He'd been so dashing and romantic, without
the slightest suspicion that she'd had a special reason for
singling him out from all the other men.

She took off her glasses and sighed. Strange she should
remember Warren so well after all this time. But then, of
all the men she'd deceived during those years, her betrayal
of Warren had been performed with deep regret. She'd
liked Warren. He'd seemed so much more sincere than the
other men she'd met, and the three days they'd spent

together had been really unusual compared to most of her assignments. They'd taken long rides in the country, and had a quiet walk in the moonlight. It was on that long moonlit walk, the last evening they were together, that Warren had proposed to her. She had turned him down gracefully, of course, trying to make him understand that three days wasn't long enough to fall in love, but it hadn't been easy, especially since she was planning to complete her assignment that evening and it depended partly on his cooperation. But she had convinced him somehow. Then, the next day, before he had a chance even to suspect she had betrayed him, she'd moved on to another city and another theater, promising not to forget him, yet knowing she'd probably never see him again.

It was her usual procedure when a job was completed, to just move on, and most of the men she left behind had been easy to say good-bye to because with the majority of them she'd been only a brief interlude in their lives. Someone to have fun with and try to forget there was a war going on. Many of them were married or had sweethearts at home, and their betrayal of the women they supposedly loved helped relieve some of the guilt she felt at her own betrayal of them, but Warren had been different. He'd told her he didn't have a sweetheart back home, and he'd seemed so naive when it came to women. Three days out of his life. Had she made that much of an impression on him?

She remembered his pitiful, searching words a few moments ago out in the hall when he'd first looked into her face, and she shuddered.

She straightened and turned, walking back toward the dresser, set her glasses down, took off her wrapper, then sat on the edge of the bed, suddenly wondering if he had really recognized her or if it was only the ramblings of a mind clouded from alcohol. She reached around, plumped the pillow up, then lay down on her back, pulling the covers up to her chin, and stared toward the ceiling, even though she couldn't see it in the darkness.

And what of tomorrow? Would he recognize her in the

morning, or was she going to be able to go on pretending to be something she wasn't? After all, Jeannie Grayson looked nothing like the glamorous Jeanine Gray he had met. She had seen to that. But was it enough to keep on fooling Warren in the light of day when he was sober?

She turned onto her side, her eyes settling on the crack of light shining from beneath her bedroom door, and tried not to think of the disastrous repercussions she might have to face in the morning. Then, as she heard the door to Warren's room close, and listened to Griffin Heywood's footsteps fading down the hall, the crack of light beneath her door disappearing, she prayed with all her might that Warren had been so drunk that when morning came he'd never even remember their encounter in the hall, and sometime within the next hour, after a dozen more desperate prayers, she was finally able to drop off to sleep again.

It was early the next morning, the sun barely tipping the horizon, when Jeanine finally relaxed a little at the kitchen table with a cup of black coffee and a slice of toast, watching Crystal scurrying about fixing breakfast for the rest of the family. Jeanine hadn't slept well, and the first few sprinklings of morning light had pulled her reluctantly from the bed. With heavy eyes, and her insides trembling, she had made up her mind that if she was to face the day and get through it, regardless of what might happen, she could do it better with a clear head, a good hot bath, and fortified with a cup of strong coffee.

Now, cleaned and refreshed, she nursed the black coffee, wondering how long it would be before Warren would make an appearance. She had learned from Crystal that Griffin Heywood had left for town while she was taking her bath in the small room off the kitchen, and everyone else was still asleep. She watched Crystal take three loaves of bread from the oven, then start assembling the ingredients for some pies.

"Griff told me you met Warren last night," Crystal said as she set the things she was going to use at the other end of the table from Jeanine. "I was hoping I'd be up yet when he came home, but he was a little later than usual." She opened a canister with flour in it and began measuring and sifting as she talked. "Too bad you couldn't have met under better circumstances," she went on. "He's not really all that bad. Just can't hold his liquor too well, once he gets started."

Jeanine stared apprehensively at Crystal. "Has he been that way long?"

"Oh, he always liked gamblin' and women, I guess, but he wasn't much for drinkin' till he went into the army." She began cutting the shortening into the flour. "He don't get drunk all the time, mind you. Only when he's tryin' to forget, which is usually on Friday and Saturday nights."

"He must have a lot to forget."

"From what Griff learned when he got home, I guess it has to do with somethin' that happened to him durin' the war. He was a lieutenant then, one of them couriers, and we thought he was doin' real well. Then one day about a year ago he showed up at the front door with no money, and so drunk it took us two days to sober him up. All the while, he kept rantin' and ravin' about some woman messin' up his life, and how he let himself be took in, and how his superior officers didn't believe him." She started rolling the dough. "Griff said all's he can figure is that Warren must of got mixed up with that woman spy all the papers was writin' about. I guess they never did catch her. Too bad." Crystal shook her head. "She sure made a mess out of him, that's for sure."

Jeanine had a hard time swallowing the coffee. "Maybe you shouldn't have told me," she said, her voice hushed.

"Nonsense." Crystal laid the crusts out neatly in the pie tins, then began filling them with slices of apple she'd peeled and cored earlier. "It's probably best you hear it out here than in town—at least you'll hear the version closest to the truth. Warren never talks about it when he's sober, and when he's drunk it never comes out the same twice in the tellin'. But I'd say he's told Griff more'n he's told anyone else."

"I see." Jeanine managed to finish her coffee, but knew

she'd never be able to eat the toast. "Well, I'm glad he only gets like that on weekends," she said. "I'm just sorry to hear that something like that could happen."

"Aren't we all. But don't worry." Crystal fluted the edges of the pies. "He shouldn't bother you none. He rides with the men durin' the week, helpin' round up the cattle. Besides . . ." Crystal flushed. "Excuse me for sayin' so," she said, "but you ain't much his type. He's more at home with the gals in town at the saloons. Said he always knows what they're after, and there ain't no strings attached."

Jeanine stood up, her face turning crimson.

"Now, like I said before," Crystal went on, hoping she hadn't embarrassed the young governess too much, "if you want to look over the schoolroom, it's right beneath the stairs the other side of the house, opposite the dinin'-room doorway. It's all cleaned and ready to use. Even some books left over from when Griff and his brother used it years ago."

Jeanine frowned. "His brother?"

"Yes, ma'am. Garfield Heywood. He was younger than Mr. Griff. Been dead about eight years now. He's young Gar's namesake."

"I see." Jeanine smoothed the skirt of her dark blue cotton and readjusted the high ruffled collar that felt as if it was choking her. The material was faded but sturdy. Her only wish was that it didn't have long sleeves, because the day was already promising to be warm. She slid the chair in. "If anyone wants me, tell them I'm in the schoolroom," she said, and started to leave.

"Miss Grayson?"

Jeanine turned back to Crystal, who'd picked up a pie, ready to take it to the oven. Crystal nodded toward Jeanine's empty coffee cup with the piece of toast untouched beside it. "You didn't eat your toast."

"I guess I'm not as hungry as I thought," Jeanine apologized. "I'm sorry, I shouldn't have put you to so much trouble."

"Oh, no trouble at all," Crystal said. "One of the

girls'll probably eat it. I just don't want you to go hungry. But I 'spect you're a bit at loose ends over the long trip out here, and all. Can't blame you myself, and then Warren scarin' you the way he did last night . . . Oh yes, and while I'm at it, I want to thank you for sayin' you'll teach my girls along with Gar. I really appreciate that, miss. But I want you to remember, now, if they don't do their schoolwork or give you any trouble, you just let me know.''

"I'm sure I won't have to worry about them, Crystal," she assured her. "They're too eager to learn. Now, if you'll excuse me." She turned back toward the swinging door that led to the dining room, hoping Crystal hadn't seen the way her mouth was trembling and the guilt that surely must have shown in her face, because although they were no longer talking about Warren, she was still nursing her guilty feelings over the part she'd played in his troubled past.

Crystal frowned as she stared after Jeanine. Funny one, the new young governess. Almost looked like she was ready to cry. She shrugged. "Oh well," she muttered, "maybe she's homesick already," and she was shaking her head as she pulled the oven door open and started putting the pies in to bake.

Jeanine sat at the scarred desk in the schoolroom, her thoughts far from the neat rows of books stacked in front of her and the tables and chairs to be used in place of desks for her pupils. She was hunched over, her elbows planted firmly, hands holding up her chin as she stared toward the windows across the back of the room where the early-morning sun was streaming in, baking the bare wood floor.

She had spent the past hour sorting through books and supplies, trying to keep her mind off her conversation with Crystal, but now, with nothing more to distract her, and unwilling to leave the schoolroom in the fear that she might run into him, her thoughts had turned full circle again to Warren and what she had done to him, and she began wondering how many more lives her actions during the war might have affected. If only she hadn't accepted

General Sheridan's offer that night in Chicago, then there'd be no Warrens to look back on with regret, and no Homer Beacons to worry about either.

She straightened and stood up, leaving the desk, walking toward the windows at the back of the room. It had been a long time since she'd thought of Homer. He'd been an agent long before the war started, and the general had assigned him to work with her, masquerading as her manager and booking agent. They had worked well together, and he'd tried hard to keep suspicion from her, but as time went on, she'd taken one too many chances. Homer had been her mainstay then, the only person she could really call a friend, and without his help she'd never have made it back across the Union lines to safety. Good old Homer. She wondered where he'd gone from there, and if he'd managed to survive. He'd always said if he lived through it, he was going to retire and do some of the things he'd always wanted to do all his life. She hoped he'd made it.

The sun caressed her face, and she basked in it, hoping its warmth would help thaw the cold dread that so often caught her in its grip when she thought back over the way she'd used herself, and been used. All the soft words of love with so many different men, that held no meaning, and the promises of intimacy that were never quite fulfilled. She flushed, remembering how many times she'd been forced to take just one step further, and how close she'd often come to sacrificing the one thing that had kept her from experiencing complete shame and degradation for what she'd been doing.

Sometimes, thinking back, she amazed herself at having been able to avoid what she'd been so afraid would someday become the inevitable. Maybe one reason she'd never given in was that she knew she'd never be able to live with herself if she had. Suddenly the whole thing seemed so absurd. She'd been willing to risk her life for the Union cause, and did, during all those years, but from the very beginning she'd vowed to herself that no matter what, and regardless of the importance of her mission, she'd never give herself completely to any man just to achieve her goal. She knew there were others who had, but to her the price wasn't worth it. When she gave herself totally to a man, it would be for love, not to seduce secrets from him. Ridiculous, perhaps, in light of what was being asked of her, but it was the one part of her life that still belonged to her. The government had no right to it, war or no war.

She frowned, shaking the cobwebs of remembrance from her mind. That was all behind her now. What lay ahead was what was important, and hiding here in the school-room wasn't going to stop the inevitable from happening. It was only prolonging the suspenseful agony that would stay with her until she faced Warren Granger again, and she pushed the glasses up higher on her nose, straightened the skirt on her dress, smoothed a hand across her sleeked-back hair, turned, and headed for the door.

It was noon when she finally came face to face with Warren again. She was just finishing lunch with Rhetta in the dining room, and they were still sitting at the table. Gar and Mrs. Brandt had already eaten and excused them-selves, and Gar was outside playing, while Mrs. Brandt had gone to check on something the twins were doing. Hearing a slight noise, Jeanine glanced toward the door-way, and her face suddenly paled.

Warren was standing in the arched doorway, staring at her, a peculiar look on his face. She had no idea how long he'd been standing there, but he was still in his clothes of the night before, and his hair was rumpled, although his eyes weren't quite as red. They hadn't heard him approach because he was in his stocking feet and carrying his boots, but as he spoke, Rhetta also looked his way.

"I didn't know we had guests," he said as he leaned sideways against the doorframe.

"It isn't guests, Warren," Rhetta corrected, her eyes mirroring her disapproval. "Miss Grayson arrived a day early."

"Oh, forgive me, dear sister," he blurted, feigning contrition as he straightened, then tiptoed gingerly into the room as if not wanting to jar his head. He dropped his boots beside one of the chairs, then sank onto it cautiously. "I realize I should be more discreet, arriving in this sordid condition, but you should have warned me."

"If you came home at a decent hour, we could have."

"What time was it?"

"Griff said about two. Don't you remember?"

"Hell no." He leaned on the table, rubbing his temples with both hands. "I don't remember anything that happened last night."

Rhetta sighed. "Thank God!"

"I suppose I was my usual obnoxious self?"

"You might say that." Rhetta glanced quickly at Jeanine, then back to her brother. "Only I suggest we just forget it for now, all right?" She leaned back and pulled the bell cord, and in seconds Crystal was at the kitchen door. "Bring Warren a cup of coffee, Crystal," she said. "Make it strong and black."

Crystal nodded, disappearing back into the kitchen.

"My, my, we are touchy today, aren't we?" Warren said insolently, then smirked as he glanced over at Jeanine. He was sitting at the head of the table where Jeanine assumed Griffin Heywood usually sat, and he began studying her intently. "My sister didn't introduce us properly, Miss Grayson," he finally said. "I'm Warren Granger, black sheep of the family."

"For God's sake, Warren!" Rhetta's voice was sharp. "Do you have to be so vulgar?"

Warren smirked, amused as Crystal came back in, set a cup in front of him, poured the coffee, then left again. He looked down at the cup. "Well, she might as well know if she's going to be part of the household," he answered, and lifted the cup, blew across the top, then glanced over at Jeanine again before taking a sip of the hot brew. "You're not afraid of black sheep, are you, Miss Grayson?" he asked, watching her closely.

"I'm pleased to meet you, Mr. Granger," Jeanine said, ignoring his remark and hoping she looked unpretentious enough to get by with her masquerade. Surely he'd have recognized her by now if he was going to, but except for the way he was staring at her, she'd seen no look of recognition in his eyes.

"See," he said, turning to Rhetta. "She's glad to meet me."

"You're disgusting!"

"You'll have to excuse my sister, Miss Grayson," he said, turning to Jeanine again. "But she's rather a snob."

"Really, Mr. Granger . . ." Jeanine flushed crimson as she felt Rhetta's cold eyes on her.

"Warren, either be decent or leave." Rhetta's jaw tightened angrily. "We can do without your sarcasm and nasty remarks."

"And without me too?" he answered, an edge to the usually pleasing tone of his voice. "Don't bet on it, dear sister." There was a touch of malice in the way he said it. "Without me here you'd have to take your spite out on Griff, and I can't imagine my dear brother-in-law putting up with it. Not even from you."

Rhetta's eyes blazed furiously. "That's enough, Warren!"

He looked like he was about to say more, then changed his mind and turned once more to Jeanine, his forehead creasing into a slight frown this time.

"Have we met before, Miss Grayson?" he suddenly said, surprising her. "There's something . . . you look vaguely familiar."

"Not . . . not that I know of," Jeanine answered timidly, realizing her voice sounded anything but convincing. Her hands were clammy, and her heart had begun to pound heavily. "I've never been west before."

"It's your eyes." He sighed, the sarcasm completely gone now from his voice, and there was a wistful look about his face. "They remind me of someone I knew once. Her eyes were the same color," he said softly. "It's remarkable."

Jeanine tried to stay calm. "You thought a great deal of her?"

"As much as one can in just three days," he answered, then straightened abruptly, as if pulling himself away from a daydream. "Afterward I learned what she really was," he went on, and a touch of bitterness crept into his voice.

Jeanine frowned. "I don't understand."

"Maybe I'll tell you about it someday," he said. "But for now, it's not important. It's just that . . ." He frowned momentarily, then cleared his throat. "The memory's painful, that's all."

"I'm sorry."

"It's not your fault." He smiled quickly. "You can't help having blue eyes, now, can you?"

"No sir." She wiped her mouth with her napkin, conscious of the fact that her face was still flushing deeply. "Now, if you'll excuse me, I promised myself I'd take a walk about and familiarize myself with things today, since Gar's lessons won't be starting until Monday." She stood up. "Mrs. Heywood?"

"Go right ahead."

Rhetta watched Warren tip a finger to his head in a farewell salute to her as he said, "Till we meet again, Miss Grayson." Then Jeanine felt both Rhetta's and Warren's eyes on her as she left the room.

"Where did Griff find her?" Warren asked once Jeanine was out of sight.

Rhetta glanced at her brother. "Mrs. Brandt found her. Seems she was recommended by a friend." Her eyes narrowed. "Forget it, Warren," she said abruptly.

Warren leaned back in his chair. "But she's got a damn good figure, and those eyes . . ."

"You'll leave the woman alone," she snapped. "Bad enough you carouse with those tramps in town."

"Don't worry," he assured her. "She's not my type anyway."

"See she stays not your type."

"Now, that sounds like a challenge."

"It's an order."

"Yes, dear sister."

"And will you quit calling me 'dear sister' in that insipid tone."

Warren grinned. "You do hate me, don't you?"

"That's not true." She inhaled sharply. "It's just that sometimes you can be so aggravating."

"And you're not?"

"That's beside the point."

"Why? Because you've got a reason?" His eyes hardened. "Believe me, dear sister, I have as much reason as you do to hate the world, so don't think you have a monopoly on life's disappointments because from where I sit, I'd say you pretty well have it made."

Rhetta glared at him. If he only knew. She sighed and stood up, afraid he'd see the hint of tears in her eyes. "Just remember what I said, Warren," she cautioned, her voice softening some toward her brother. "She came here to teach, not fight off your advances. Now I have some things to do before Griff gets back from town."

Warren watched her leave, then turned back toward the table, staring at the dirty plates and empty coffee cup in front of him. His head still ached, and there was a painful gnawing in his stomach, but he paid little attention to either of them. Instead, for some reason, he couldn't seem to erase the sight of the new governess's big blue eyes from his mind. They were such an unusual shade, and even the ugly wire-rimmed glasses covering them hadn't been able to hide the vibrant way they'd glistened when he looked into them.

He closed his eyes for a minute, trying to conjure up a mental picture of the woman she'd reminded him of. He'd spent only a few days with her, but how many times he'd seen posters of her, both before and after the world had learned what she really was.

Suddenly he opened his eyes again, frowning, as a tingling sensation began at the nape of his neck, traveling quickly down his spine, making him tremble. It couldn't be, yet the resemblance . . . Coincidence? The blond hair, blue eyes . . . But would she have changed that much? Maybe he was only imagining it. After all, it had been about two years ago, and he'd been with her such a short time. It could be only wishful thinking, but then again . . . why not? How easy for her to try to lose herself in obscurity out here where no one would even think of looking. The idea was fascinating. By God, he was going to find out. He'd have to take it slow, but he'd find out, and he smiled wickedly as he leaned back and pulled the bell cord. Suddenly he was famished.

4

Outside, Jeanine had been wandering about the ranch for the past hour, looking things over. Since it was Saturday, there were a few men about, but she'd avoided any contact with them, hoping to keep to her image of the shy, unassuming schoolteacher. Now she leaned against the split-rail fence that surrounded the pasture and gazed back across the lawn toward the house, apprehensive about going back inside. Her first encounter with Warren seemed to have gone well, but there was no use pushing her luck, and she hadn't seen him leave the house as yet. She hadn't seen Gar either. He seemed to have disappeared somewhere in the myriad of barns, stables, and carriage houses. She hoped he was all right, but then Mrs. Brandt had told her earlier that he took care of himself quite capably.

Seeing movement out of the corner of her eye, she turned toward the lane beyond the main barn and watched two riders leaving, heading toward the timberline that began where the pasture ended. They were kicking up dust that swirled haphazardly before settling again behind them, and she watched until they reached the end of the lane and disappeared among the trees. The afternoon was hot and the strong breeze that whipped at her hair did little to cool things, bringing with it the scent of roses mixed with the pungent odor of manure from the pastures and barns.

Suddenly she straightened, putting a hand over her eyes

71

to shade them from the sun as she saw Gar running toward her from the flower garden at the back of the house. He was waving frantically and calling her name.

"I've been looking all over for you," he gasped breathlessly as he reached her. "I want to show you Comanche."

"Comanche?"

"My horse." He was in front of her now, breathing heavily, excitement shining in his eyes. "Would you like to see him?"

"I didn't know you had a horse of your own. I'd love to see him."

"Good." He took her hand and began pulling her with him toward a building near the main barn. The building was belching smoke from a huge stone chimney that extended from its roof. "Pa gave him to me this summer," he prattled on as he hurried her along. "He even broke him for me. Before I got Comanche, I rode old Blossom, but she's so slow. I sure was happy the first time I saw Comanche, and he's been gelded already—that way he don't bother the mares."

She took a quick glance at him, watching the serious crease in his forehead. "You know about gelding?" she asked, surprised.

He was wearing a hat that shaded his face, but she saw the flush beneath the freckles on his nose. "Yes, ma'am," he answered. "A rancher has to know about things like that." He sounded so grown-up. "At first we were goin' to use Comanche for breedin', but it ain't good to use a breedin' horse for ridin', and Pa knew I wanted him real bad."

"So he changed his mind?"

"Yup." They stopped in front of the building that was belching smoke. It was open on one end, and Jeanine felt heat from the fire that was glowing on the hearth, the clang of metal against metal ringing in her ears. She had purposely avoided the building earlier; now Gar was pulling her inside, where a big burly redhead with a bushy mustache, bare to the waist, was sweating profusely as he wielded a hammer, putting a shoe on a sleek roan horse.

"I found her, Cory," Gar said anxiously as he stopped, waiting for the foreman to finish.

Cory swung the last blow, then ran his hand over the iron shoe to make sure everything was secure. He dropped the horse's hoof, stepped away from him, and straightened, grabbing a bandanna from his back pocket, mopping the sweat from his face. His brown eyes slowly sifted over Jeanine from head to toe; then he looked down at Gar, still holding the teacher's hand.

"I thought you weren't goin' to make it back 'fore I finished," he said, taking a deep breath, blowing upward a bit to cool off his face.

"Cory does the blacksmithin' for us, and Comanche throwed a shoe this morning," Gar explained, glancing up at Jeanine. "This here's Miss Grayson, Cory," he said, his eyes filled with admiration. "And this is our foreman and Pa's best friend, Cory McBride."

Jeanine was staring at the huge man, whose massive shoulders were bronzed, muscles rippling and bulging conspicuously. He was taller than Griffin Heywood, and much broader, with a warm smile, and his eyes were twinkling, amused as he drew them from the small boy beside her and looked directly at Jeanine.

"Mr. McBride?" Jeanine said.

Cory nodded. "I'd shake your hand, Miss Grayson," he said self-consciously as he wiped his hands with the bandanna, "but I'm afraid I'm a bit dirty."

"No need," she answered, then let go of Gar's hand and walked over as the roan gelding Cory'd been working on pranced around some and turned toward them, nuzzling Cory's arm with his nose. "And this is Comanche, right?" she said, reaching out, stroking the side of the horse's long sleek neck.

"Ain't he beautiful?" sighed Gar.

Cory grinned. "The boy already knows good horseflesh. Someday he's gonna make a hell of a good rancher."

"That's what I keep tellin' Pa, and I wish he'd take me with him on the drive," Gar said unhappily. "It ain't right, Cory. I'll be eight next year, and he ain't goin' till spring.''

Cory glanced at Miss Grayson, who was still stroking the horse, letting him sniff her hand. ''What about your schoolin'?'' he asked as he reached for his shirt, pulling it onto his sweaty body, tugging at it here and there to straighten it, then began buttoning it, before reaching for his leather vest. ''We sure couldn't take Miss Grayson on the drive with us, and you know dang well your pa ain't gonna let you lose all that schoolin' just to go on a cattle drive.''

Gar looked up at Jeanine rather hesitantly. ''But it still ain't fair.''

''Who said life was fair, young 'un?'' Cory went on. ''Seems to me I been cheated a number of times already along the way.'' He glanced at Jeanine and winked, then looked once more at Gar. ''Besides, why would you want to go on a dirty, noisy cattle drive when you can stay here and spend your days with a pretty little lady like Miss Grayson here?''

Jeanine could feel herself flushing self-consciously as Cory reached out and grabbed the reins on Comanche, then continued talking to the boy.

''Now, if you've a mind to have that ride today, go get your saddle and we'll mount up. Cinnamon don't seem to be around, so I guess I'll have to take you myself.'' He was leading the horse from the blacksmith shed and looked over at Jeanine as they stepped out into the afternoon sunshine. ''Do you ride, Miss Grayson?'' he asked as Gar disappeared in the direction of the barn.

She stared at him for a moment, not knowing whether he was inviting her along or just asking out of curiosity. ''Not as well as I should, I imagine,'' she answered truthfully. ''But then, I never owned a horse of my own, and being raised in the city . . .''

''You're more used to ridin' in a buggy than sittin' in a saddle, right?''

''That's about it.''

''Well, you're welcome to join the boy and me if you'd

like,'' Cory said. "I'm sure Gar'd be pleased, wouldn't you, young 'un?'' he asked as Gar reappeared from the harness room carrying a saddle that was almost as big as he was.

"What's that, Cory?'' he asked.

"I thought maybe it'd be nice if Miss Grayson came along with us.''

"Oh, would you?'' Gar begged. "If you ain't used to ridin' much, you could ride Blossom. She's a good old horse, really, and Cory could saddle her for you.''

Cory straightened the saddle blanket that had been on Comanche's back while he'd been replacing the horse's shoe, then took the saddle from Gar and swung it up, settling it in place, pulling the cinch tight. "I could have Blossom saddled in no time,'' he said, looking straight at Jeanine.

The thought was inviting, but it had been ages since she'd been on a horse, and she'd never been much of a rider. What to do?

"Please?'' Gar pleaded.

How could she resist such an ardent plea? "All right,'' she conceded. "But I'll have to go change.''

"I'll get Blossom ready while we're waiting,'' Cory said, and Jeanine smiled, nodding, then pushed the glasses a little higher on her nose and left hurriedly, heading for the house.

Her dark green riding skirt was tucked away in the armoire, along with her scuffed leather riding boots, and she found a cream-colored shirtwaist to wear with it. After fastening the row of tiny buttons up the front of the shirtwaist, she made sure her hair was slicked back, pushed the glasses up on her nose again, then went downstairs, heading through the kitchen toward the back door, Crystal's voice stopped her.

"I thought you said you was goin' ridin' with Cory and the boy,'' she said abruptly from where she sat at the kitchen table peeling potatoes.

Jeanine turned. "I am.''

"In that skirt?''

Jeanine looked down at her wool skirt. "Is there something wrong with it?"

"If I know Cory, and I do, there won't be no sidesaddle on old Blossom."

"But I can't wear pants!"

Crystal set her knife down, wiping her hands on her apron as she stood up. "I didn't think you would," she said. "Now, you wait here, I'll be right back."

Jeanine stood waiting patiently while Crystal disappeared up a set of stairs at the far end of the kitchen that led to the servants' bedrooms. She was back down in a few minutes, carrying a garment made of soft doeskin.

"You're about the size I was a number of years back," she said as she handed it to Jeanine, who stared at it curiously. "No need to go back to your room. You can change in the pantry where you took your bath this mornin'."

Jeanine held the garment up. It looked like a skirt, but was separated in the middle, making full pants so she'd be able to ride astride.

"I made it some years back," explained Crystal as she sat back down and began peeling the potatoes again. "Indian women wear leggings beneath their skirts, and I thought, why not just improve on it, since I learned to ride astride when I was with them."

Jeanine frowned self-consciously.

"Now, don't tell me Cinnamon didn't tell you all about what happened to me when I was a girl," Crystal went on matter-of-factly. "Three hours on a buckboard with that darky yesterday, and you probably know almost the whole history of everyone at Trail's End. Now"—she motioned toward the strange riding skirt—"put it on. I think it'll fit just fine."

"Thank you," Jeanine said, and moved awkwardly toward the door to the back room where she'd bathed earlier.

A few minutes later, she was joining the foreman and Gar near the main barn where they were waiting with the horses saddled. The riding pants felt a little strange, but she was pleased about having them on when she saw the saddle Cory McBride had put on the horse they called Blossom. Crystal was right. It wasn't a sidesaddle.

"Where's your hat?" Cory asked when she reached them, and Jeanine automatically stroked the pale gold hair on her head, making sure it was still secure in the bun at the nape of her neck.

"All I have are some frilly bonnets," she answered.

Cory turned to Gar, who was patiently waiting for permission to mount. "Run over to the bunkhouse, young 'un, and tell one of the men to give you that old hat the Kid's had hangin' beside his bunk collectin' dust. The one with the bullet hole in it."

Gar handed his horse's reins to Cory and scurried off toward a long, low building on the other side of the drive.

"A bullet hole?" Jeanine asked.

Cory smiled. "He caught it in town one night when he got too close to a couple of cowpokes with a grudge. Said every time he wore it, he ended up gettin' in trouble, but like most of us, it ain't natural to throw anythin' away that still has wear in it, so he hung it up, intendin' to use it again sometime. Never did, though, and it should fit, since the Kid ain't full-growed yet." He started to lead the horses after Gar, and she followed.

The hat fit fine, although Jeanine eyed the hole in it skeptically before putting it on; then the three of them mounted up and headed down the lane where she'd seen the two other riders disappear a short while before.

When they reached the far end of the pasture, she saw that the lane led on into the woods, and they followed it, letting the shade from the trees overhead cool them some. A short way into the woods, however, and they turned off the lane onto a well-worn trail, riding for about a mile before leaving the woods again, and cutting across a draw.

It seemed strange to have a horse beneath her again, and to be riding astride. The last time had been when she'd dressed in men's clothes and fled Montgomery, Alabama, with Homer at her side and a contingent of Confederate soldiers at her heels.

She watched as Gar, riding a little ahead of them,

manuevered around a clump of boulders; then she and
Cory followed, reining up a few minutes later as they rode
up to the edge of a small lake.

"Pretty, isn't it?" Cory said as he looked out across the
water.

Her eyes scanned the scenery. It was beautiful. Much
more so than she had imagined. Usually when she heard
men speak of Texas, she thought of sand, sagebrush, and
parched earth, things she'd seen in pictures, but so far
Trail's End was proving her wrong. True, it was a good
description of much of the rangeland out here, but sand-
wiched into the hills and valleys between stretches of
rocky, arid plains, were plush grasslands, their small lakes
and rivers fed by wayward mountain streams from farther
to the northwest. They were staring now at one of those
small lakes.

"This is where we have picnics," Gar said enthusiastically as he rode Comanche over next to Jeanine. He
pointed farther ahead, at the edge of the water, to where a
huge old hickory tree rested against a gigantic boulder.
"And that's Indian Rock," he explained. "It's got Indian
signs all over it. Pa said they used to have some kind of
ceremonies there a long time ago. That's where we always
spread the food out, under the old hickory tree."

"Well, if I'd known that, we'd have come out for a
picnic today," she said, hoping to please him. "Maybe we
can have one next Saturday."

"Oh, could we?"

"I don't see why not. Unless your father objects."

"He won't, will he, Cory?" the boy asked.

Cory eyed the youngster, his eyes warm with affection.
It had been obvious since Gar had first mentioned her
name to him earlier in the day that the boy was infatuated
with this young woman who'd come to Trail's End to be
his teacher. "Young 'un, I don't know of any reason your
pa could possibly find not to let you have a picnic next
Saturday. Unless maybe you don't do your schoolwork
durin' the week, that is."

"I wouldn't do that, Cory," Gar protested. "Pa said if I

don't learn how to read and write and do numbers, I'll never be able to take care of Trail's End when I grow up." He gazed around at the landscape, then patted Comanche on his neck. "And I don't ever intend to leave Trail's End, not even when I grow up, ever."

Jeanine saw the admiration and love in the boy's eyes, and she turned to the foreman. "Mr. Heywood wouldn't object to us coming out here for a picnic next week, would he?" she asked.

"He might have you bring Cinnamon along, since you're not too familiar with the territory, and he doesn't like Gar ridin' too far from the house by himself," he answered. "But he's pretty lenient with the boy. I doubt he'll say anything."

"Cinnamon told me the Indians keep pretty clear of Heywood land," she said, watching his reaction.

"He's right," Cory agreed. "They do, but we've been having some problems lately."

"Oh?" They reined their horses about, heading along the edge of the lake, following Gar, who had decided to move on. "What kind of trouble?" she asked.

Cory told her about the water-hole poisoning the day before, the shooting and payroll robbery last month, and a few other things that just didn't add up. "Griff keeps insisting it's just someone trying to keep us from makin' the drive next spring, but I think there's more to it."

She eyed him curiously. "Does he have any enemies?"

"What man doesn't?" Cory straightened, angling his hat somewhat against the sun. "But there's no need for you to worry. Only it might be good not to roam too far if you're out ridin' alone, and make sure, if the boy's with you, that you keep a good eye on him. I don't like the whole mess, and until we figure out what's really goin' on, I think we'd all better be careful."

"I'll remember," she said, and instinctively her eyes began to scan the trees and hills ahead for anything out of place as they spurred their horses into a loping canter, catching up with Gar.

A little over an hour later, they were heading back down

the lane toward the barns. Jeanine's rear end was sore, since she wasn't used to the saddle, but she was pleased they'd asked her to go along. She found Cory McBride an easy man to talk to, and through him, had discovered that both he and Griffin Heywood had been in the Confederate Army, only neither man had served east of the Mississippi River, easing somewhat the fears she had had earlier, when she thought perhaps Griffin Heywood had recognized her. But with Cory's revelation, the fear became even a more puzzling aspect. If Griffin Heywood hadn't been staring at her because he thought he'd recognized her, then why had he been staring? And she was still frowning, trying to find the answer, as they rode into the barn and unsaddled the horses.

That evening, much to Jeanine's surprise, there were no empty places at the end of the dinner table. Even Warren stayed home. A feat his sister thought quite remarkable, since it was Saturday night. Conversation was lively all during dinner, although Jeanine stayed out of it unless directly invited, hoping they'd continue thinking she was just what she'd claimed to be.

However, when dinner was over, they all retired to the parlor, where once more her fears of being unmasked began to surface, when Gar started telling his Uncle Warren about how wonderfully she could play the piano, and how well she could sing.

"I used to play piano and sing in the church back home," she confessed shyly as they all stared at her; then she continued to add more to the blatant lie. "My uncle did the preaching on Sunday, and he used to get so upset every time I learned one of those vulgar new songs, as he called them."

"Where was home?" Griff asked, and she glanced over at him, hoping she'd say the right thing.

This was one time it'd be hard to lie. She'd never been good at imitating the distinctive drawl of the South, even though she'd inadvertently picked up many of its idioms during the war years when she'd lived side by side with Southerners, but to try to keep it up for an indefinite period of time would have been far too trying, so she had done nothing to disguise her voice.

"It was in Ohio," she answered, being truthful for a change, because that's where most of her parents' relatives had lived, and she'd spent some time there.

"I knew she was a Yankee," Rhetta said arrogantly. "I just knew it."

"The war's over, Rhetta," Griff reminded her, but Rhetta's eyes narrowed.

"Only on paper, Griff. Can you imagine what the folks in Raintree are going to think when they find out we've got a Yankee working for us?"

"Who cares what they think?" He glanced at Jeanine, then back to Rhetta. "Besides, she doesn't sound much like a Yankee to me."

"That's because I'm from the southern part of Ohio, Mr. Heywood," Jeanine said, the second statement she'd made that was at least partially true. "And surprising as it may seem, it's just far enough south that we do talk somewhat differently than most Ohioans. And there were also many people from our little town who sympathized with the Confederate cause. In fact," and she lied again, uneasily, the flush on her face only adding to what seemed to be an appearance of timidity, "I did spend some time for a while with a maiden aunt in South Carolina just before the war broke out."

"That's the only time you were in the South?" Warren asked, joining the conversation.

Jeanine glanced at him curiously, but was saved from answering when Crystal stepped into the parlor, interrupting them.

"Excuse me, Mr. Griff, Mrs. Heywood," Crystal said. "But Mr. Vance has come callin'," and as she stepped aside, Jeanine watched the portly gentleman who'd ridden in with her on the stagecoach the day before, step into the room past Crystal, followed by a younger man, who was obviously his son. The resemblance between the two men was a subtle one, but it was there all the same, although the younger man was taller and leaner, with no beard, and piercing hazel eyes that seemed to change color as they took in everything with one sweeping glance. He was attractive in a dark, brooding way, his black hair deepening the weathered tan on his face, making his smile appear cynical, as he and his father greeted the Heywoods.

"Well, what brings you two all the way out here?" Griff asked as he reluctantly greeted them. "I know it's not a pleasure call."

Miles Vance, the older man, squared his shoulders, trying to make himself look taller as he shook hands with Griff. "On the contrary, Griff," he answered. "It's always a pleasure to see you and your family again."

"I'd believe that if I didn't know you so well, Miles," Griff answered. "Like I said, what brings you and Jarrod this far out of your way?" and Griff glanced quickly at the younger man behind Miles Vance, then back to Miles.

Miles released Griff's hand, surveyed everyone in the room, his eyes resting curiously for a minute on Jeanine; then he reached over, took a cigar from a box on a stand beside him near the door, bit the end off, and began to light up, as they all watched.

Jeanine could tell Miles Vance was enjoying himself, and she could also feel the tension in the room as Griff stared at him.

Miles exhaled a cloud of smoke, then relaxed, taking a deep breath. "I heard tell you had some trouble the other day, Griff," he said, fidgeting the cigar about nervously between his fingers.

Jeanine saw Griffin Heywood tense, his eyes hardening as Warren said, "Hey, there, he's been eavesdropping, Brother Griff. Or do you suppose he's got inside information?"

Griff's eyes held a warning as he glanced sharply at Warren, who was sitting on the piano bench holding Gar between his legs, hugging the boy. "No need to antagonize, Warren," he answered, pretending a calm he didn't feel; then he looked back at Miles. "Besides, I'm sure Miles doesn't know a thing about our difficulties, now, do you, Miles?" he asked.

Vance cleared his throat. "Only what the folks in town are sayin'," he cut in quickly. "They said somethin' about you losin' cattle. Seems to me you've been havin' more than your share of bad luck lately," he went on. "That's why I thought maybe I oughta come over."

"And make me another offer?" asked Griff.

"Well, why not? Stands to reason. You keep goin' like you're goin', and you won't have nothin' to bargain with before long."

"Trail's End's a long way from going under, Miles, and you know it," Griff challenged. "Besides, you're starting to push now, and I don't like being pushed. This is the third offer you've made me since I got back, and it doesn't sit any better with me than the other two did."

"I think he's tryin' to tell you somethin', Pa," Jarrod Vance said from where he stood directly at his father's elbow. "I think he's insinuatin' you know more about his trouble than you should."

Miles had stuck the cigar between his teeth; now he snatched it out quickly and wiped his mouth, staring at Griff. "Well, hell now, boy, you know that ain't so," he bellowed, and Jeanine would swear he looked genuinely hurt. "You know I wouldn't do nothin' to force you into no corner. I admit I'm no angel, and me and your pa went back a number of years with our differences, but you know I never pulled no dirt on him, and I wouldn't on you neither. I respect you runnin' Trail's End, the same as I did him."

Griff eyed him skeptically. "You're sure about that?"

Miles's jaw tightened. "Dead sure," he said stubbornly. "I've made no bones over the years about wishin' Trail's End was mine, and I'd take it off your hands tomorrow, if you'd let me, but I'd never try to force you out, no more'n I did your pa, boy, and that's a fact."

Jeanine wondered if Griff believed him.

"Then why do you always manage to show up right after we've had trouble, to make me another offer?"

"It's the timin', Griff," he answered. "Now, I didn't have nothin' to do with anything that's happened since you got back, you've gotta believe that, but in the same breath, I ain't so dumb that I can't try to take advantage of it. I'd be a fool not to try.''

Griff stared at him for a minute, then smiled wryly. ''I guess you would at that,'' he said. ''Especially since you'd give about anything short of your right arm to own the place.''

''Like I said,'' Miles went on. ''The offer's always open. Hell, just because I ain't plannin' to go in on this drive with you don't mean I'm not on your side. I'd just rather sell my steers for three dollars a head than take a chance on losin' all of them on the trail. How about it, Rhetta?'' Miles looked over to where Rhetta was standing next to her brother. ''Surely you don't think I'd have a hand in all this?''

Jeanine noticed Rhetta'd been watching Jarrod Vance ever since he and his father entered the room; now suddenly her eyes were drawn to the father, and she straightened, moving away from Warren to stand beside her husband.

''He's right, you know, Griff,'' she said, her voice softening huskily as she slid a hand through Griff's arm, locking elbows. ''If he'd wanted Trail's End that bad, why wait till now? He had a better opportunity while you were gone and your father was ill.''

Griff felt the pressure of Rhetta's arm through his, and instinctively put his left hand over where her hand was. Maybe Rhetta was right, and maybe not, but at the moment it might just be best not to push the issue too much. He frowned.

''All right, Miles, for right now I guess I'll have to concede that it seems out of place for you to suddenly try something after all this time. Especially since you know that if worse came to worst, I'd rather sell some of the land off a parcel at a time, and keep just a few hundred acres and the house, rather than lose everything.''

''And bust up Trail's End? You're crazy, Griff,'' Miles blustered. ''Your pa fought and almost died for this land, and you'd be willin' to cut it up in little pieces?''

"Don't worry, I won't have to," Griff said firmly. "If the winter doesn't get too bad, we should be able to drive enough cattle north to pull Trail's End out of debt and build her up even better'n what she was before the war." He straightened, pulling away from Rhetta, and walked toward the far end of the room. "Now, since you've more or less convinced me that your motives are honorable, would you care for a drink?" He took a decanter from the liquor cabinet and began to pour.

Miles and Jarrod Vance moved farther into the room, and Jeanine, who'd been standing at the other side of the room near the French doors, saw Miles stop when his eyes suddenly fell on her again.

"Say, she's the young lady who rode the stage in from Dallas with me yesterday, ain't she?" he asked, staring at her curiously.

Mrs. Brandt had been standing next to Jeanine, holding her breath earlier when the subject of Jeanine's past came up; now she took a step forward.

"This is Gar's teacher," she explained quickly, an arm at Jeanine's elbow, and Jeanine felt the slight pressure of the woman's thin fingers through the material of the blue cotton dress she'd put on when she'd returned from her ride with Gar and Cory. "Miss Grayson's going to be living at Trail's End."

"Well, well," Miles said as he extended his hand to take the glass of brandy Griff had poured for him. "You and your pa always were sticklers for book learnin', Griff." He took a sip of the brandy, then nodded toward Jeanine. "How do, young lady?"

"This is Mr. Miles Vance, and his son, Jarrod," Mrs. Brandt said, and Jeanine quickly pushed the glasses higher onto the bridge of her nose.

"Mr. Vance," she said, acknowledging his nod, then looked directly at his son. "Mr. Vance."

Jarrod's eyes swept over her appraisingly, and against her will she felt a sudden dislike for the younger man. He looked as if he were in his early thirties, his smile when he greeted her pleasant enough, and unlike his father, he extended his hand, shaking hers with an almost slow caress, but there was something . . .

"Miss Grayson, is it?" he remarked as he released her hand.

"Yes sir." Jeanine felt uncomfortable with all eyes on her. Not only because she was embarrassed by the intense way Jarrod Vance was studying her, as if he could see right through her clothes, but because she was forced to hold back her disgust and pretend shyness, when she'd like nothing better than to slap his face for what she knew he was thinking. It was there in his eyes, and how many times she'd seen that look over the years.

Griff handed Jarrod a glass, then began pouring himself a drink as Jarrod went on.

"You're from back east?" he asked.

"Does it matter where she's from, Jarrod?" Griff interrupted. "The point is, we needed a governess for Gar."

"Just curious," he answered, and Jeanine could feel his eyes trying to penetrate beneath her disguise as Rhetta spoke up.

"Which reminds me, Miss Grayson," Rhetta said. "It's close to Gar's bedtime. If you'd kindly take him up?" Rhetta reached out toward Gar, who looked like he was ready to protest, but instead gave his Uncle Warren a kiss, then left the comfort of Warren's arms and took his mother's hand, letting her usher him off toward Griff. "Now, say good night to your father," she ordered curtly, "then let Miss Grayson take you up and tuck you in."

Well, that's one way to get rid of me, Jeanine thought as she watched the look on Rhetta's face while Gar said good night to his father. Rhetta's head was high, her eyes avoiding her husband and son, instead resting on Jarrod Vance, who was no longer looking at Jeanine but was returning Rhetta's look intently. Was it imagination, or was Rhetta Heywood trying to send an unspoken message to Miles Vance's son? Interesting. Jeanine took a deep breath and looked away quickly, hoping neither had caught her watching them, as Gar came toward her; then the two of them left after excusing themselves.

"I don't like Mr. Vance," Gar confided to her as they made their way upstairs.

"Which one?" she asked.

"Neither of 'em, really."

"Any special reason?"

" 'Cause they're always sayin' nasty things about Uncle Warren."

"Oh . . ."

"Uncle Warren really ain't so bad," he went on as they reached the landing, then started down the hall toward his room. "It's just that he gets sick sometimes, and people don't understand, but Pa and me, we understand."

"I see," she said, opening the door to his room and stepping inside, lighting the lamp on the dresser. Sometimes the things Gar said really surprised her, and he had such a knowing look on his face, as if he really knew what life was all about. "Do the Vances live close by?" she asked as he headed for the tepee to put on his nightclothes.

"They're our closest neighbors toward town." He disappeared into the tepee, and his voice was muffled as he continued. "Old Mr. Vance and my grandpa never did get along too well, I guess. Seems like they was always feudin' about somethin'. I suppose it was 'cause our ranch is bigger than the Double V Bar."

"That's the name of the Vances' ranch?"

"Yes'm." He emerged in his nightshirt and once more dropped beside the bed to say his prayers, including her in them again as he had last night. When he was through, she tucked him in, but before she had a chance to blow out the lamp, he said, "Miss Grayson?"

"Yes, Gar?"

"Don't you think Uncle Warren's nice?" he asked.

She smiled awkwardly. "Why, yes, I suppose so, but I don't really know him too well yet."

"I think he likes you," he said sheepishly.

She blushed. "I think your uncle likes all the ladies."

"Oh, no, ma'am." He was serious, his forehead pinched into a scowl. "I saw him watching you." He snuggled farther into the covers. "Miss Grayson?" he asked again.

This time she sat on the edge of the bed. "What now?"

"Do you suppose, if he likes you, you could maybe get to like him too, and then maybe he'd quit gettin' sick all the time?" he asked. "Pa says he drinks and gets sick 'cause he don't have no purpose in life. Could you maybe be his purpose, do you think?"

She frowned. "Gar, I think it's nice of you to want your uncle to have a purpose in life," she answered hesitantly. "But what you're asking . . . it's impossible."

"Why? You could love him—I know you could if you tried."

"Gar . . ." She reached out and smoothed the covers beneath his chin. "There are some things we can't make ourselves do, and loving people is one of them. Either we do, or we don't, but we can't make it happen, as much as we might want to."

"Well, I'm gonna pray it happens, then," he said firmly. "Because Uncle Warren needs somebody."

"You're very observant for a little boy," she said, but he disagreed.

"No, ma'am, it's just that I like Uncle Warren, and when you like somebody, you just know things." He smiled. "You know what I mean?"

She stared at him a moment, then smiled back. "Yes, I guess I do," she answered, and leaned over, kissing his cheek. "Now, you'd better get to sleep, young man."

He turned over. "Good night," he said, and she blew out the lamp, then left the room.

When the door was closed behind her, she stood for a minute going over the conversation she'd just had with him. He was right. His uncle wasn't such a bad sort, and a pang of guilt made her wince. Ah well, there was no way she could undo the past, especially now, when she was so busy trying to ensure some sort of future for herself.

She started down the hall, then stopped suddenly when reaching the balcony where she could look down into the foyer. What on earth was she doing? She'd been headed back downstairs, and to go back down there now was just courting trouble. Hadn't she breathed a sigh of relief when the Vances had shown up just at the right time? If she went down there now, there was no guarantee that Warren wouldn't resume his subtle cross-examination of her, and if Griffin Heywood asked her to play the piano and sing . . .

Her hand was resting on the top rail of the balcony, and she let go, retracing her steps back down the hall until she reached her own room, and as she opened the door and stepped inside, she could hear the clock down the hall strike nine. She shut the door behind her, then leaned against it, sighing. It was still rather early in the evening to retire. What to do now? Although she knew there was no way she could take a chance on going back downstairs, she wasn't a bit sleepy.

She straightened uneasily, and stared toward the French doors to the balcony, open to the warm night. Why not? Who was to see her? She crossed the room quietly, leaving the lamp unlit, and stepped out onto the balcony, gazing down toward the open French doors to the parlor, straining her ears, as a gentle breeze wafted upward, carrying voices with it.

Now and then she could hear Rhetta Heywood's laughter, or Miles Vance's booming voice, and once Warren stepped over to the French doors, looked out, then disappeared again inside. After a few minutes the soft strains of music floated up from the room, and she realized Rhetta must be playing the piano. It was an uncomplicated little song Jeanine had known how to play since she was a child, but unfortunately, Rhetta wasn't playing it all that well. No wonder she was so eager to have Jeanine put Gar to bed. Ah well, General Sheridan had never told her life at Trail's End would be easy.

She listened for a while longer, letting the warm night soothe her, then went back inside, undressed in the dark, sat on the edge of the bed and took her hair down, brushing it the usual hundred strokes, then climbed beneath the covers, but it was a long time after the music and laughter stopped before she was finally able to drop off into a troubled sleep, her first full day at Trail's End over.

SECOND TIME
91

5

Sunday at the ranch was always the same. The family rose early, dressed in their finest, and were escorted to the small building in town that alternated as church, school, and meeting hall, arriving for the services at eleven o'clock. After the services, they ate a noon meal at the only restaurant in town, next to the Empire Hotel, visited with various friends in town, and returned to Trail's End in time for dinner at seven. Rarely was the routine changed.

The servants were welcome to go or stay, as they wished, the only requirement being that they return to the ranch in time to fix the evening meal. The cowhands, including Cory, alternated their weekends at the ranch, some staying out on the range with the cattle, while the rest had a little relaxation from the tedious work of roping, branding, and keeping the herds together.

The next day, Sunday morning, shortly after breakfast, Jeanine stood at the huge windows in the dining room, overlooking the front drive, and watched the buggy and riders disappearing down the drive. She had risen early, but declined the offer to join them, using the excuse that she wanted to go over the lessons for Gar's first day of schooling. In actuality, she thought Warren would be going, and had made up her mind to avoid being around him as much as possible. But to her dismay, he'd suddenly decided to stay home too, so now, after the buggy disappeared between the rows of stately sycamores that lined the drive, she hurried to the classroom, shut herself inside, and refused to come out, pretending there was just too much to do. She even told Crystal to bring her lunch to the classroom, so she wouldn't have to join Warren in the dining room.

She'd been working for a little over an hour when the first knock came. Straightening, she moved to the door and leaned against it.

"Yes?"

"Miss Grayson?"

There was no mistaking who it was. She opened the door a crack. "Yes, Mr. Granger?"

"Don't you think you're carrying this school business a little too far?" he said, hoping to talk her into coming out. "After all, today's Sunday. Not even teachers work on Sunday."

"I'm afraid this one does, sir," she answered firmly. "Please, I'm sorry, but there's so much to get ready for the first day."

"Not even one minute to spare out of a whole day?" he asked.

She sighed. "I'm sorry, Mr. Granger. Now, if you'll excuse me," and she closed the door without giving him another chance to protest, walked back to the desk, and stood beside it, waiting apprehensively to see if he'd give up. After a few seconds without another knock, she sat down again, relieved. There was no way she was going to give in to his pleas. In the first place, she could think of no logical reason why he had decided to take a sudden interest in her unless he'd become suspicious, and if he had, she wasn't about to let him try to confirm his suspicions. And in the second place, even if he wasn't suspicious, she wasn't about to give him a chance to become suspicious. There was too much at stake, and she wasn't that big a fool.

Two more times that morning he tried to get her to come out and join him. Once for a cold glass of lemonade, and again for a short walk and to relax a little. Both times she continued to say no, and she was relieved after lunch when Crystal came to take her dishes back to the kitchen, informing her that Warren had left a half-hour before, heading for town. He'd finally given up, at least for the moment.

Her first week as a teacher was a hectic one, simply because she didn't really know what she was doing, even though she'd gone over the material they were using carefully. But Gar was a good pupil, and Peggy and Beth were eager to learn, so that eventually everything began to run more smoothly. Her days were spent teaching and her nights with preparations for the next day, and by the end of the first week she began to realize that the task she had taken on was far more difficult than she thought it would be. It not only could be frustrating, but tedious at times, and there were days when she felt like she wasn't making any headway at all; then Gar or one of the twins would do something really rewarding, and she'd admonish herself for having wanted to give up. Besides, she was beginning to feel at home at Trail's End.

Warren was gone most of the time, helping Griff and the others out on the range, and when he did decide to come back to the ranch, she managed to keep her distance, although at times it was rather hard, because he could be quite persistent.

But Griffin Heywood was another matter completely. Although she had begun to feel more at ease on the ranch, as the days went by she was still uneasy around him. Especially when his eyes seemed to follow her so often, and caress her in such a strange way. He wasn't at home a lot, but still, whenever he came into a room, he seemed to dominate it, and there was no way she could ignore him. Not that she really wanted to. Common sense told her that ignoring him was the only way she was going to survive at Trail's End, but she had spent too many years listening to her common sense, and for the first time in a long time she began to rebel against it, telling herself that just once she was going to pretend it didn't exist. It was a dangerous game to play, and she knew the consequences could be devastating for her, but for some reason, she couldn't seem to help herself. Griffin Heywood was an unusual man, and her reaction to him was just as unusual, and no matter how hard she tried, she knew she'd never be able to pretend he didn't exist, so instead she tried to hide her feelings as best she could and hope for the best. After all, there was no place else for her to go. Trail's End was her last resort.

Her one consolation was that although Griffin Heywood's eyes said one thing, his actions said another, often to the point of being so reserved toward her that it seemed as if he resented her presence. And although he had been the one who had championed her on her arrival, as the days went by his reactions toward her became rather irritating, and Jeanine began to wonder if he had changed his mind about her being there. Nothing was said, however, so she assumed it was just his natural way. After all, after living under the same roof with the Heywoods for only a few days, she soon learned that things at Trail's End weren't all they seemed on the surface. There was an undercurrent of emotions she couldn't quite put her finger on. Something was wrong, but what?

It was early Friday evening, the end of her first week. Jeanine sat at her desk correcting papers that Gar and the twins had handed in that afternoon. She hadn't even thought of Warren all day, but now suddenly she was brought back to the reality of the situation she was in as Gar knocked, then came in, smiling warmly.

"Miss Grayson, I hope you don't mind," he said, "but I asked Crystal if she could fix us fried chicken and pie for the picnic tomorrow."

She stared at him, puzzled for a minute, then smiled uneasily. "Oh heavens, that's right," she said, remembering, but not wanting him to know she'd been so busy she'd forgotten about promising him the picnic. "I forgot tomorrow was Saturday. The week went so fast." She laid her hands on the papers, hoping she looked contrite enough. "I forgot to ask your father too."

"Don't worry, I asked him," he said, pleased with

himself. "And he said we could go and we could take Uncle Warren with us too, how's that?"

"Uncle Warren?"

"Uh-huh. He just got back with some of the men a few minutes ago. I hope you don't mind. I'd rather have him go with us than Cinnamon."

She stared at him, trying to think of something to say, an excuse not to go, anything. But there was no way she could get out of it. God help her, she thought as she stared at Gar, how was she going to keep Warren at arm's length for a whole afternoon?

To her surprise, when the next day arrived, things seemed to go quite well. Crystal packed a lovely lunch for them, and the day was warm and balmy. They rode out from the ranch shortly before noon, and arrived at Indian Rock just in time to eat, and as the day went by, the conversation stayed neutral, although there were moments when she caught Warren staring at her rather curiously. But he never once said anything to make her think he had any suspicions as to who she really was, and she began to feel a little less apprehensive.

It was late afternoon. They had finished eating some hours before, and now everything was packed back in the picnic basket, ready to go. She and Warren were sitting with the basket between them while they watched Gar hunting for frogs and snakes at the edge of the lake. He was only a few feet from them, and turned back, his eyes shining.

"Do you think maybe we could come again sometime, Miss Grayson?" he asked anxiously.

Jeanine smiled. "If you'd like."

"And could Uncle Warren come again too?"

She took a deep breath. So that was it. Gar was trying to play matchmaker. She glanced over at Warren, then back to Gar. "I'm sure your uncle has much more important things to do on his Saturday afternoons than spend them with us, Gar," she answered nervously, pushing the glasses back up on her nose, but Warren objected.

"Sounds like your teacher doesn't like my company, Gar."

"Nonsense." Jeanine flushed. "I don't mind really. It's just that . . . I thought you might have work to do."

"You'll soon learn, Miss Grayson, that Warren Granger doesn't do much of anything anytime except have fun," he confessed.

"Oh?"

"Shocked?"

"Not really." She straightened, watching as Gar stood up and joined them, poking gently at a frog in his hand. "But it does seem a waste." She reached out and took the frog from Gar, staring at the poor creature, which was already looking for a way to escape; then she looked at Warren. "Surely you're suited to something."

"Wine, women, and song," he answered flippantly.

"In other words, you're lazy."

"Lazy? Heavens no, Miss Grayson. And the name's Warren," he corrected her. "But I don't think you understand. I'm not lazy. I have an enormous amount of energy, but I dislike work immensely." His smile was twisted and cynical. "It's so much more fun to do the things one likes."

"Does Mr. Heywood agree with you?"

"Griff? Hell no." He took the frog from her and stood up, then went down to the lake and set it at the edge of the water before turning back to face her. "Griff tolerates me because of Rhetta, but then Griff's not an ordinary brother-in-law. That's why I don't mind helping with this drive he's set his mind on."

"Ah yes, that does require work, doesn't it?"

He laughed, and walked over, draping an arm about Gar's shoulders, his amber eyes crinkling mischievously. "Do you think I'll survive, Miss Grayson?"

He was teasing, and she knew it. "I think you'd better be careful, Mr. Granger." She stood up. "Work might start to agree with you."

"Never," he said, watching her brush grass from the riding skirt Crystal had given her. "That's one statement I can make without reservations. Work will never replace a rip-roaring Saturday night in town. Now''—he gave Gar a nudge toward where the horses were ground-reined, grazing—''go bring the horses, young 'un,'' he said, and reached over, grabbing the picnic basket. ''The sun's running low in the sky, and if I don't get you two back in time, your pa'll be sending a search party out for us.''

Jeanine felt a little sad as she let Warren help her mount, then watched as he and Gar both swung into the saddle, and she wondered: what would Warren have been like if she'd never entered his life back in Richmond? And all the way back she couldn't help the guilt feelings that kept gnawing at her, something she knew she was going to have to put up with for the rest of her stay at Trail's End, whether she liked it or not, and she heaved a sigh of relief as they rode into the barn. She felt sorry for Warren, but there was no way she could change the past. All she could do was try to blot it from her memory for a while and hope he'd never see through her masquerade.

After they'd dismounted, she and Gar took the picnic basket with them, left Warren in the barn unsaddling the horses, and headed for the house, running into Beth and Peggy just returning from a trip to town. Cinnamon had driven the buggy for them, and they'd had the usual four-man escort.

Jeanine watched the men on horseback heading for the barn where Warren was; then she and Gar joined the twins as they stepped down from the buggy, their arms full of packages.

''Here, let me help,'' she offered, shifting the picnic basket to her left hand.

Cinnamon clicked to the horses, flicking the reins, taking the buggy toward the carriage house as Beth handed Jeanine one of the packages she was carrying, almost dropping another before Gar caught it.

''What'd you buy?'' Gar asked, hefting the bundle he'd caught securely against his chest. ''It's heavy.''

Beth grinned. ''It's material.''

''Wait till you see what we got,'' Peggy added, eyeing

Jeanine from behind the stack of bundles she was balancing as they started toward the back porch. "We're gonna have the prettiest dresses at the dance."

Jeanine began walking beside them. "What dance?" she asked.

"That's right, you don't know." Peggy glanced over to her sister. "We forgot to tell her."

"Then we better do it now," Beth said, and as they finished making their way up the back steps and on into the kitchen, the twins explained to her about the Independence Day celebration on September 15. "We didn't have no celebration while the war was goin' on, so it oughta really be somethin' this year. And it's on a Friday night— that means the dance'll be on Saturday night and the doings'll take up the whole weekend."

Jeanine stared at the girls, frowning as she followed them into the kitchen. "But Independence Day's the Fourth of July," she corrected them hesitantly.

"Not that Independence Day," Peggy replied as she tossed her packages on the table. "We're talking about Texas's independence from Mexico."

"Oh . . . ." Jeanine handed Beth the package she'd carried in, then set the picnic basket on the counter near the sink. "Looks like the teacher needs a history lesson," she said sheepishly, and turned back to face them. "Do I get another chance?"

Both girls laughed, but it was Gar who spoke up as he handed Beth her bundle of material. "You can't blame Miss Grayson, Beth," he said, defending her. "She wouldn't be expected to know, bein' a Yankee and all."

Beth frowned. "Who says she's a Yankee?"

"She did."

Peggy was staring at Jeanine now too. "You are?"

Jeanine began to feel uncomfortable again, and nervously pushed the glasses up on her nose. "Well, not really," she answered, hoping they'd believe her. "I am from Ohio, but I tried to explain once before that we lived close to the southern border, and many of us sided with the South."

"See, Gar," Beth said. "I knew she wasn't no real Yankee. And I bet you spent a lot of time in the South too, didn't you, Miss Grayson?" she added. "I can tell by the way you talk."

"She used to visit an aunt in South Carolina," Warren said as he stepped through the kitchen door, joining them, his eyes directly on Jeanine. He had let the ranch hands who'd arrived back from escorting the twins to town finish taking care of the horses, then followed Jeanine and Gar into the house. Now he leaned against the doorframe. "At least that's what she told us last weekend. Am I right, Miss Grayson?" he asked.

Jeanine looked at him curiously. All afternoon he'd neither done nor said anything to make her think he suspected her in any way, but now, as her eyes caught his, there was an intensity in them that made her wonder.

"Yes, that's true," she answered.

"Then you're gonna have to come to the celebration," Beth said anxiously, and Jeanine drew her eyes from Warren's steady gaze, trying to concentrate on the twins again as Beth began opening one of her packages, her dark eyes flashing excitedly. "Everybody's gonna be there," Beth said. "It wouldn't seem right if you weren't. And just look at the material we bought. Open yours too," she told Peggy, and Peggy opened one of her packages, to reveal a bolt of shiny pink taffeta. "There's enough here that if you don't have a dress to wear, we could probably make you one."

Beth's material was blue taffeta, and she held it out with her hands to show Jeanine.

Jeanine walked to the table and reached out, touching the material both girls were holding out to her. "It's very pretty," she said, watching the afternoon sun streaking in at the window beside the table highlight it. "But I won't need a new dress. In the first place, I doubt if I'll even be going, and if I should, I already have a dress."

"Oh, I remember," Peggy said as she set her material back on the wrapping paper and took off her bonnet, smoothing her long dark hair back behind her shoulder.

Then she began opening some of the other packages they'd brought back with them, some things their mother had asked them to pick up for her in town. "You have that pretty red dress I hung up for you the day you came," she went on. "You can wear that."

"If I go."

"Why wouldn't you go?" asked Warren, who was still standing in the doorway.

Jeanine pushed the glasses back up on her nose again. "I might have too much to do," she answered. "Besides, Mr. and Mrs. Heywood may not approve. After all, I'm not a guest here."

"Nonsense." He straightened, hung his hat on a hook behind the door, and walked over to the table to stand beside her. "Why should they care what you do on weekends?" He saw the reluctance in her eyes. "In fact, I'm surprised they haven't mentioned it to you already. I guess it just slipped their minds. I'll have to bring it up tonight at the dinner table."

"No need for that," she protested. "I'm sure if they want me to go, they'll let me know."

But he did bring it up, much to Jeanine's discomfiture, and she was flushing profusely that evening as Griffin Heywood's eyes met hers across the dinner table.

"I'm sorry, Miss Grayson, I should have thought of it myself," Griff said, noticing her embarrassment. "I've been so busy with the roundup, it completely slipped my mind. Of course you're welcome to go. We'll be staying at Sheriff Higgens' home while we're in town, and Crystal and the girls usually stay with a friend, since it isn't wise to be traveling back and forth every day. If you'd like, I can see that reservations are made for you at the hotel for the weekend. I really see no reason why you can't go, since nobody much will be here at the ranch, except Mrs. Brandt and a few men who'll be looking after things."

"You aren't going?" Jeanine asked the housekeeper, who was sitting in her usual spot next to Rhetta.

"Too many memories, Miss Grayson," she answered curtly. "I'd rather stay here than take a chance on bringing them all back. Besides''—she glanced over at Griff, her eyes hardening, a little displeased—''someone has to look after the place.'' Jeanine knew by the tone of her voice there was no use pursuing the matter further, so instead she graciously accepted Griff's offer, and hoped she wasn't making a mistake, because for the rest of the meal she could feel Warren's eyes studying her, and wished she knew what he was thinking. She wasn't about to try to find out, however, and was pleased, after dinner, when he announced he was going into town.

The next day, she again stayed at the ranch while the Heywoods attended church, only this time she didn't have to worry about Warren. From what she learned during the talk at breakfast, he hadn't come home the night before, and it was Griff's speculation that they probably wouldn't see him again until late Sunday evening, a guess that proved to be right. However, by Monday morning he'd sobered up enough to ride out with Griff, Cory, and the rest of the hands, and Jeanine was relieved. She'd been so afraid he'd beg off and she'd end up having to keep out of his way all day again.

The rest of the week went well. She saw very little of Griff or Warren, since they were out on the range most of the time, and her days were spent in the classroom, while her evenings were spent preparing lessons for the next day and helping Crystal and the twins with their dresses.

The more time she spent with the cook and her daughters, the closer they became. Crystal had a great sense of humor and an uncanny insight about people, and the twins were a delight to have around, having inherited much of their mother's personality. By the end of the week, all three were calling her Jeanine and to her surprise she was actually beginning to look forward to the weekend in town.

At first she'd been apprehensive. After seeing the Confederate flag on the wall at the Empire Hotel the day she arrived, and learning from Mrs. Brandt and some of the remarks different members of the family had made, that sentiment in Raintree was still hostile regarding the outcome of the war, she had made up her mind not to go near the town unless it was an absolute necessity, just in case she might meet someone who had run into Jeannie Gray during the war years. But then she'd realized, if Warren hadn't recognized her, it was doubtful anyone else would either. So she'd begun to like the idea of having a few days she could really call her own, to do as she liked, because even though her time away from the schoolroom was her own here at the ranch, it seemed like she was forever preparing lessons or being called on for something, leaving little time for herself.

Even Rhetta seemed to be looking forward to a weekend away from the ranch, and besides helping her daughters with their dresses, Crystal, who was as adept with a needle as she was in the kitchen, was kept doubly busy altering a dress for Rhetta to wear to the dance, ripping out seams when Rhetta wasn't satisfied and restitching and refitting over and over again until she was about to chuck the whole thing.

"Why doesn't she just do it herself if she doesn't like what you're doing?" Jeanine asked Crystal one evening when they were sitting in the kitchen talking while Crystal sewed the same seam back together for the third time.

Crystal laughed. "Rhetta Heywood sew a dress?" She eyed Jeanine skeptically. "That'd be like asking the Queen of England to do dishes."

"Then why didn't she simply buy a new one?"

"Money," Crystal said, and knotted the thread, then bit off the end, surveying her handiwork. "Griff wouldn't let her." She set the work down, relieved, hoping this was the last time she'd have to change it. "Things haven't been going any too well around here financially," she informed Jeanine. "Griff's had to dole out the money carefully. That means no frills and furbelows for anybody, including Rhetta. She don't like it, naturally, but there isn't much she can do. There's the hands to pay, the ranch to run, and now Gar's schoolin'. That's why this cattle drive is so important. If Griff don't make it to Abilene with the herd, he might have to break up Trail's End.

Sellin' part of it would get the debts paid, all right, but it'd probably break his heart too.''

Jeanine was surprised. ''But Peggy and Beth got new dresses.''

''With their own money. They've been savin' up for months just so's they'd have enough. Besides, I think they've both grown two inches the past year and filled out in places that don't fit too well in the party dresses they wore before the war, so they needed 'em. But Rhetta's got enough clothes upstairs from the buyin' sprees she went on before the war to last another year or two without worryin'. That's her whole trouble, she got spoiled, buyin' anythin' she wanted and never worryin' about where the money came from, but the war's left a lot of folks with problems, and Trail's End's no exception.''

''I guess I can see then why she resents my being here,'' Jeanine said.

''Money ain't the reason she resents you,'' Crystal replied. ''Rhetta was dead set on sendin' Gar back east to school. She loves the boy in her own way, I guess, but she ain't much for motherin', and that would've gotten him out of her hair.'' She shrugged. ''Oh well, I shouldn't be gossipin' about the missus, I guess, but it just upsets me every time I think of it. That boy's such a darlin'. Which reminds me, Beth and Peggy said to ask you if you'd spend some time with them while we're in town over the weekend. They'd like to show you around.''

''I'd love to,'' Jeanine said, so they made plans while Crystal worked on the girls' dresses for the rest of the evening, and that night when Jeanine settled under the covers, for the first time since her arrival, the familiar feel of them and the soft intimacy in the room almost made her feel at home.

Shortly after dawn on Friday morning, September 15, Jeanine sat in one of the carriages as they started down the drive, and she glanced back at the house, watching Mrs. Brandt standing alone on the front steps watching them leave. How terribly lonely she looked, and what a strange woman she was, quiet and efficient, running the household remarkably well in spite of Rhetta Heywood's spoiled demands and unnecesssary interruptions. And it was quite obvious that Mrs. Brandt did run the household. That, Jeanine could tell even after only the short time she had been at the ranch. Mrs. Brandt wasn't friendly like Crystal and the twins, and seemed stern and remote at times, yet Jeanine felt a strange sort of kinship with the woman, especially since the first day of her arrival, when she'd discovered that Mrs. Brandt, and only Mrs. Brandt, seemed to know the identity of her benefactor.

Jeanine drew her eyes from the housekeeper and leaned over the side of the buggy so she could see up ahead. Cory, Spider, and the Kid were on horseback leading the procession, while Griff drove the first carriage, Rhetta and Gar by his side, and Griff was still wearing a pair of buckskins. She'd seen him in little else since her arrival, although today the buckskin jacket he wore over his shirt and vest was beaded and trimmed with fringe. It was an incongruous contrast to Rhetta's fancy blue watered-silk suit, flowered hat, and ruffled parasol, and sitting between them, Gar was a small replica of his father, even to the way his hat was pulled down at an angle to protect his eyes from the early-morning sun.

The carriage she, Crystal, and the twins were in was being driven by Warren, and behind them Cinnamon was ambling along at a slow pace with the buckboard and all their luggage. At the tail end of the strange porcession were Dustin and Luke, on horseback, riding rear guard.

The sun was already up, with the day threatening to be warmer than usual, as Jeanine settled back again against the carriage seat, ready for the tedious ride into town. A little after ten o'clock that morning the entourage from Trail's End finally rode into Raintree, joining a myriad of other wagons and carriages already lining the streets. The day Jeanine arrived, the town had been quiet, few people about. Now it was teeming with people, many of them waving and calling to the Heywoods as they passed by.

Jeanine gazed about at the red-white-and-blue banners

hanging on the buildings, and buntings of the Lone Star state displayed in all the windows. They not only made the air festive but also seemed to make the weather-beaten buildings in the small town look newer and less drab. Even the platform in the middle of town where a small band was rehearsing had been built especially for the celebration, and as they rode by the bandstand, headed for the hotel, the strange sounds of the musicians tuning their instruments, along with small boys running in and out among the crowds of people, throwing firecrackers, spooked the horses so that Griff and Warren had to fight to keep them in line.

Cory, still on horseback, yelled, trying to chase the kids away, clearing a path for them, and a few minutes later Griff and Warren pulled the carriages up in front of the Empire Hotel. Griff climbed down and came back to the buggy Jeanine was in, reaching a hand up to help her.

"If you'll step down, Miss Grayson, we'll just make sure Mr. Ed has your room ready," he said, addressing her.

She took his hand, letting him help her; then he walked back to the buckboard, where Cinnamon handed him down the suitcase she'd brought. As he carried it past the other carriage, heading toward the door of the hotel, he told Warren to go on ahead and take Crystal and the girls to Nellie Watchek's, then he joined Jeanine and they went on into the lobby, while Rhetta and Gar waited.

"How's everything, Barney?" he asked Mr. Ed as he set Jeanine's suitcase down in front of the desk.

Barney Ed glanced at Jeanine, noting the blush on her cheeks and the way the end of her nose was red from sunburn where the brim of her flowered straw hat didn't quite cover it, and he remembered the day she'd arrived in Raintree. Rumor had it that she was a Yankee. He'd wondered about that ever since, but being diplomatic, he wasn't about to bring it up. Not today anyway, and he looked back again to Griffin Heywood.

"Everythin's fine, Griff," he answered congenially.

"You have Miss Grayson's room ready?"

"Shore do. We got your message just in time." He turned toward the curtains behind him. "Jasper . . . Jasper!" He turned back to Griff. "That boy's sure hard to keep track of today, always sneakin' off with his friends. Jasper!"

Jasper's head poked through the opening in the curtains, freckles glistening beneath the sweat on his face, and he was panting vigorously. "I hadda carry Mr. Ogilvy's big bass drum all the way from his buckboard to the bandstand," he gasped, out of breath. "Earned a whole two-cent piece for it, though."

"How about another two-cent piece?" asked Griff. "All you have to do is carry Miss Grayson's suitcase to her room."

"Great!" Jasper's face beamed. "Wish there was more holidays." He made his way around from behind the desk. "I could do right well with at least one holiday a week."

"How about Sunday?" asked Jeanine.

"Around here? Shucks, ma'am," he retorted disgustedly, "Sunday's a holy day, not a holiday. I don't make hardly nothin' on Sundays."

"Well, carry her bag up, son, and you'll get your other two-cent piece," Barney said. "It's room ten, and open the door for her." He gave Jasper the key. "Then get back down here, there's still work to do."

Griff handed the boy a two-cent piece and Jasper stuffed it in his pocket, then picked her suitcase up and began struggling with it, heading toward the stairs.

Griff looked down at Jeanine, who was watching Jasper. The glasses on her nose slipped down a bit and she pushed them back up nervously, a gesture he'd watched her do a lot; then she drew her eyes from the young boy and looked up at him. Their eyes suddenly met, and for a moment neither said a word. Griff was looking at her in that strange unnerving way again, and she wondered, was she reading something in his eyes that really wasn't there, or did he look at all women the way he was looking at her? God! She wished she knew, because at the moment she was being swept by emotions she was unable to ignore, and it was frightening.

"If there's anything you need, just ask Barney," he finally said, breaking the silence that hung between them. "He'll give you a hand. My family and I'll be a short way down the road, at the edge of town. The sheriff's house is within walking distance, but we'll be using a buggy. If you'd like, after you're settled we could pick you up . . . after all, you don't know anyone in town."

"That won't be necessary," she answered hesitantly. The thought of watching him and his wife enjoying each other's company all afternoon wasn't her idea of having fun. "I think I'd rather just mosey around and get acquainted on my own," she said. "That is, if you don't mind."

"Not at all. But be careful," he warned her. "Some of the men can get pretty rowdy."

"Don't worry, I can take care of myself."

"But I do worry," he said abruptly, and his eyes darkened uncomfortably. "I'd hate for there to be any trouble . . ."

"There won't be, please . . ." Her flush deepened. "But I thank you for caring."

"Not at all." He straightened, his eyes boring into hers, and she felt herself tremble. "I'd better go," he suddenly said, his voice deepening. "Remember, if you need anything, just tell Barney or his son."

She nodded.

"Good day," he said curtly, looking beyond her, outside to where Rhetta and Gar were waiting for him in the buggy, and he almost sounded angry with her.

"Good day, Mr. Heywood." She watched him leave, stepping off the hotel step, sunlight catching his hair, turning it to burnished gold seconds before he donned his hat again; then, as he climbed in beside Rhetta and drove away, she turned to Barney Ed. "You said ten, sir?" she asked.

"Yes, ma'am."

She nodded a quick thank-you, then went upstairs, passing Jasper on his way back down already. She got the key from him, but when she reached the room, he had left it unlocked for her. It was a nice room at the front of the hotel, with a door opening onto the upstairs balcony that ran the length of the porch roof. She set her hat on the bed and opened her suitcases to see if there was anything that wasn't rumpled that might be cooler than what she had on, but her dresses were so wrinkled and messed up. Only one thing to do, and she grabbed the whole lot, carrying them all down to the lobby, arranging with Mr. Ed to have someone press them, with the promise she'd have them back before noon; then she returned to her room, locked the door behind her, and leaned back against it.

Not only was the ride in from Trail's End hot and tiring, but the hotel room was like a furnace, with little air stirring, even though the window was open, and she could feel her camisole sticking to her beneath the jacket of her green velvet suit. She straightened and unbuttoned the jacket, slipping it off, hanging it over the back of a chair; then she began fanning some air into the camisole as she walked over to the window, pulling an edge of the curtain aside to look out, staying partially hidden behind it.

The town looked so different from the day she'd arrived. People were all over the place, and she glanced up the street, watching as a group of about fifteen riders rode into view, making their way down the dusty main street, until they reached one of the two saloons in town. Then she watched them dismount, tie up at the hitch rail, and disappear into the Golden Cage. She frowned, having recognized Miles and Jarrod Vance among the riders. They were evidently the crew from the Vance ranch, the Double V Bar. Crystal told her it was named that for its brand with two V's side by side and a single bar through them. She had added a little more, too, to Gar's comments about the Vances the day after their visit to Trail's End, and Jeanine, remembering her conversation with Cory McBride the day she'd ridden with him and Gar to Indian Rock, wondered if Miles Vance had been telling the truth that evening.

According to Crystal, the Double V Bar not only hired

saddle tramps, but Miles Vance had been known to stretch honesty to the limit in some of his business dealings.

"I never did like the man," she'd said one evening when she and Jeanine were working on the twins' dresses, and Jeanine had to admit that she too had taken a dislike not only to Miles but also especially to his son. Jarrod made her feel uneasy in a frightening way and she couldn't figure out why, because she'd also discovered by talking to Crystal that Jarrod had managed to avoid being in the army, so she had no worries there. Still, he made her nervous.

She released the curtain and turned, walking to the dresser, where she straightened her hair and cleaned her glasses, using some water from the white pitcher on top of it. She wished she could just chuck the glasses out; however, with Warren around it was impossible. Satisfied that they were clean enough, she set them on the dresser and walked to the bed. It'd be at least another half-hour, maybe more, before her clothes were pressed and brought to her room, just enough time for a short rest. Stretching out on the bed, she sighed. Her back had been sore and stiff from the long ride and the bed felt good.

The band outside on the platform quit tuning their instruments and struck up a vigorous rendition of "Dixie," which first brought a frown to Jeanine's forehead, then a slow smile to her lips. What other song would they play under the circumstances? she thought, and figured she'd probably hear it a lot more before the weekend was over. She closed her eyes, beginning to relax, when suddenly there was a knock on the door.

She opened her eyes slowly and lay there for a couple seconds, then heard the knock again. This time she got up and slipped her glasses on, then put on her jacket, buttoning it up as she crossed the room. Opening the door hesitantly, she expected to find someone bringing back her dresses. Instead, startled, she stared hard at Warren, who was staring back at her, grinning outrageously.

"Surprise," he said. "I decided it wasn't right for you

to wander around town alone, so I'm going to be your escort."

"But . . ."

"No buts," he said, his amber eyes sifting over her appreciatively. "Just grab your hat and come along. I've reserved a table next door at the restaurant and the food's getting cold."

"You don't understand." She was at a loss. "My clothes are due back from being pressed. I can't leave."

"Oh hell, don't let that bother you. Barney'll bring them up." He was refusing to listen to her excuses. "Now, do as you're told," he ordered. "I've got the whole day planned. Lunch next door, the races, and I hear there's a medicine show at the edge of town that should be more exciting than some of the political speeches."

"But . . ."

He brushed past her and snatched her straw hat from the dresser, holding it out to her. "Here, please . . ." he begged, suddenly looking contrite. "I didn't mean to startle you, but when Griff said you were going to be wandering about alone, I thought it'd be a good idea. Believe me, it's not very enjoyable trying to have fun all by yourself."

She finally found her voice. "Mr. Granger . . . Warren, I don't know . . . I'm Gar's teacher, what will people say?"

"If that's what's worrying you, forget it," he said, hoping to reassure her. "The fact is, they'll probably think I've lost my mind." A smile twitched the corners of his mouth as his eyes swept over her severe hairdo, then rested on her wire-rim glasses. "I'm afraid you're a far cry from the usual young ladies I've escorted about town."

She flushed as a pang of guilt seized her. Maybe she should go. After all, if she hadn't put laudanum in his wine, then copied the plans he'd been carrying, he wouldn't have lost his commission and started drinking. So since it was her fault the folks in Raintree thought of him as something less than respectable, maybe she should be the one to help try to change that image. And if he hadn't recognized her when they'd gone on that picnic . . .

"You win," she finally said halfheartedly, taking the hat from him and fastening it atop her head. And before she had a chance to change her mind, he'd grabbed the key to her room off the dresser, shoved her reticule in her hands, locked the door behind them, and ushered her down to the lobby, where he stopped by the desk just long enough to leave the key with Barney Ed so he could take her dresses up when they arrived, instructing him to hang them in the armoire. But as Jeanine let Warren escort her out the door, she glanced back to the hotel lobby, where the Confederate flag still dominated the far wall, and she began to wonder if she was really doing the right thing.

6

Even though Warren's arrival had been a complete surprise, in a way, she was glad. The thought of spending the day alone hadn't been too intriguing, although she hadn't necessarily wanted to spend it with him.

After lunch at the restaurant, they strolled around town, and Warren kept introducing her to everyone they met, while pointing out the various shops and businesses along the way. Everything was closed except the restaurant where they'd eaten, and the saloons. Even the door to the *Beacon Journal*, the only newspaper in town, was locked when Warren tried it, and he seemed disappointed.

"Is something wrong?" she asked when he frowned.

"No." He shook his head, hoping to appear casual. "It's just that I was hoping you could meet the editor." He released the doorknob and turned back to her. "He's quite a fellow."

"Maybe we'll run into him somewhere."

"Hmm . . . perhaps, maybe." He glanced about; then his frown suddenly faded and he smiled again. "Who knows. Oh well, I'm sure you'll get to meet him before the weekend's over. In fact, I'm going to make certain you do," and his smile broadened as he took her arm, directing her away from the building so they could cross the street, heading toward where a crowd had gathered to watch some young boys run a footrace.

Sometimes during the afternoon, when Jeanine looked at Warren, she had the worst time remembering that she was no longer in Richmond. He was gay, charming, and attentive, his carefree manner just as she remembered it, and it was as if the years had rolled back, only they hadn't, and she kept having to tell herself this was 1865, not 1863, and she was in Texas, not Richmond. Having to keep her guard up all day like that was not only nerve-racking, but took its toll on her so that she was really relieved when the festivities finally began to subside and she could talk Warren into taking her back to the hotel.

It was late, and she was exhausted as she leaned back against the wall in the hallway, waiting for him to unlock the door to her room for her with the key they'd retrieved from the desk clerk downstairs. He swung the door open, and she put her hand out for the key.

"You mean I'm not going to be invited in for a nightcap?" he asked.

She eyed him curiously. "You know there's no liquor in my room." He dropped the key reluctantly into her hand, and she smiled wearily as she suddenly realized that he hadn't taken a drink all day. "Besides," she said as she stepped past him, "it's late. I've had a lovely day, but I am tired."

"Tomorrow?" he asked, his voice lowering intimately.

She turned back, facing him. "You must not have paid much attention to the twins on the way in this morning," she reminded him. "I promised to spend Saturday with them, remember?"

He looked disappointed, but not for long. "Then I'll just have to be satisfied with escorting you to the dance tomorrow night," he stated boldly, and his eyes bored into hers. "I'll come for you about seven."

"But . . . you never . . ."

"Did I really have to, Jeannie?" he suddenly asked, emphasizing the name "Jeannie" as he took a step toward her, and Jeanine inhaled, startled, her stomach beginning to tighten from fear. "The resemblance is too striking," he went on insistently, as she held her breath. "When I'm with you it's like being with her."

"What do you . . . ?"

"Don't pretend," he demanded huskily as he studied her. "The hair's fixed differently, yes, and the glasses, but the name's almost the same, and your eyes . . . the smile." He reached out, pulling her into his arms.

"Please," she pleaded desperately, trying to hold him away, her hands hard against his chest. "Don't spoil it, Warren. I'm not Jeannie whoever she is . . . I'm Jeanine, Jeanine Grayson . . . I can't be your Jeannie, please. You're making a mistake."

He tensed, still holding her as he searched her face. "So many times today it was as if I was back in Richmond . . . as if we . . ."

"Warren, please . . ." she gasped breathlessly.

His eyes narrowed momentarily, his jaw tightening, then slowly his grip on her loosened. "I'll pick you up at seven," he suddenly whispered, his voice breaking. "Good night, Miss Grayson." He turned abruptly, without saying another word, and disappeared down the hall.

She stared after him for a long time, trying to get over the impact his sudden accusation had had on her; then finally she came to her senses and shut the door, realizing she was close to tears. Why? Why did she have to run into Warren? Why couldn't he have lived somewhere other than Raintree, Texas? And she thought he hadn't been suspicious. What a fool she'd been to think she could get away with it. She should have known better.

She walked to the dresser, picked up a match and lit the lamp, then replaced the chimney, watching the flames lick at the wick while she slowly removed her bonnet. After setting the hat on the dresser, she smoothed her flaxen hair back with both hands, then sighed, heading for the balcony to open the door to let in some air. The room was stifling and the breeze felt good, so she stepped outside for a minute, breathing deeply, trying to ignore the remembrance of Warren's eyes as they begged her to admit who she really was. Moving to the railing, she stared down into the street below, now much quieter at this late hour, and she tried to calm the knot of fear that had been twisting inside her since the moment he'd called her Jeannie.

Suddenly she squinted, eyes adjusting to the dark as a man stepped from the shelter of a building a couple doors down from the hotel and began crossing the street. His walk, the way he held his head. There was no mistaking who it was. She'd seen that long familiar stride enough lately to know. When he reached the other side, Warren hesitated for a minute, undecided, as if fighting a battle with himself, then suddenly straightened stubbornly, and she watched him walk through the swinging doors of the Golden Cage Saloon.

The next day was sunny. Jeanine had slept fitfully, and although she'd been refreshed when the day started, wearing the pink dress she'd worn the first evening she'd been at Trail's End, her long wait for the twins had been nerve-racking, especially after her parting conversation with Warren the night before. By the time the twins arrived to escort her to Nellie Watchek's, where they were to have lunch before joining the day's festivities, she already felt worn out and bedraggled.

Nellie, a dressmaker, was Crystal's best friend. Widowed some years before, she'd raised a daughter, Carrie, now the same age as the twins, and a son, Thad, a few years older. Thad was a tall, brawny lad and it was obvious when they reached Nellie's and Jeanine was introduced to him that he was smitten with Beth, who seemed to return his feelings openly. In fact, all during the meal they flirted subtly with each other, adding to the general air of gaiety that seemed to hover over the dinner table. Because of last night, however, Jeanine had a hard time entering into the casual banter. But she did try to enjoy herself, and hoped they'd interpret her quieter-than-usual manner as being part of the subdued personality she'd adopted since arriving at Trail's End, and once they all finally left Nellie's, joining the crowds, the rest of the day was almost a repeat of the day before. Only this time she was with Crystal and the twins, who at the moment weren't paying too much attention to her as they visited with the Kid and some of the other hands from the ranch.

It was late in the afternoon and they were near the edge of town waiting for the horse races to start. Jeanine sighed, then glanced about. She had spotted Griff with Rhetta and Gar when they'd first arrived, and now she saw him again, only this time he was astride a beautiful black stallion she'd seen at the ranch earlier in the week, and men were clustered about him, wagering on the next race. His hat was pulled down to shade his eyes, and he seemed to be searching the crowd. For Rhetta, she presumed, but suddenly his eyes found hers and he froze, staring at her intently. She felt a warmth flood through her clear to her toes as she stared back at him, and for a long time neither of them moved; then slowly he drew his eyes away, once more looking over the heads of the people.

She could feel the warmth in her face, knowing it had to be flushed, and glanced quickly toward the others, hoping they hadn't noticed. They hadn't, being totally engrossed in trying to find enough money among all of them to bet on the race. They had been having elimination races all day, and now the six best horses, which included Griff and his black stallion, were getting ready for the final race to claim the fifty-dollar purse.

Jeanine avoided looking his way again, and turned from the twins, hoping perhaps to see Gar, letting her eyes wander to where some carriages were pulled to one side, making room for the race. Gar was there, all right, sitting in one of the carriages with Cinnamon beside him, his eyes intent on his father. Only as she caught sight of Gar, she also caught sight of something else, and for a moment she frowned, puzzled, her thoughts racing in disbelief.

Quite a distance behind the carriage Gar was in was some sort of warehouse or barn. It was near a cluster of trees, a little away from the crowds who were standing with their backs to it, and as she watched Gar, she could see movement near the open door of the building. Ordinarily she wouldn't have paid much attention to the couple who were sneaking furtively into the old building, but she had instantly recognized the hat the woman was wearing as the one Rhetta had worn when she'd left for church the Sunday before. The one she'd been wearing when Jeanine had first caught sight of the Heywoods when they'd arrived at the races earlier. It was an unusual bonnet with bright orange and yellow flowers nestled amid russet bows that matched the color of the dress she'd been wearing, and Jeanine remembered thinking how pretty the hat looked on Rhetta, and feeling a little disappointed because she knew the colors would look terrible on her with her pale hair. She stared at the door of the barn now, unable to take her eyes from it, wishing she could have spotted them earlier, in time to see who was with Rhetta. Her eyes stayed glued to the doorway and she kept on staring, trying to will her brain to remember more closely the details of what she'd just seen. Then, a few minutes later, she inhaled sharply. A man's figure was emerging from the shadows inside the building, and now, suddenly, as she watched, she had her answer. Jarrod Vance was standing in the shadowed doorway, and as Jeanine continued to watch him intently, he hurriedly surveyed the crowds, evidently missing seeing her, then stepped quickly away from the door, heading for the bulk of the crowd where the horses were lining up.

After he left, Jeanine kept her eyes on the doorway of the old building, again waiting, and sure enough, a minute or so later, her eyes confirmed what she had seen just a short time before, as Rhetta Heywood also emerged from the building. Her face looked flushed as she finished straightening her bonnet; then, while Jeanine watched, staring curiously, Rhetta moved stealthily away from the doorway, melting into the crowd for a few mments before joining Gar and Cinnamon in the carriage.

Jeanine frowned uneasily. Now, what was that all about? She continued to watch as Rhetta sat down beside Gar; then she followed Rhetta's gaze as Rhetta looked off to where the race was about to start, and the frown on Jeanine's face deepened even more. She had thought Rhetta would be watching her husband, but she wasn't. Her eyes were fixed steadily on Jarrod Vance, who was now mounted on a prancing sorrel. Jeanine studied Rhetta, who was unaware she was being watched. Mrs. Heywood continued to stare at Jarrod Vance for a few moments longer while he nudged his horse forward, falling in with the other horses at the starting line; then Rhetta drew her eyes from him, letting them settle on her husband, who was already in line right next to Jarrod.

Griff was still looking over the crowd, and Jeanine saw Rhetta catch his attention, smiling, her hand raised in a good-luck gesture as if she'd been in the carriage all the time, waiting for him to look her way. Griff tilted his head, acknowledging her gesture, and surprisingly, Jeanine saw him smile back, a rather crooked smile, but one of the few smiles she'd seen on his face since her arrival at Trail's End, except when he was playing with Gar.

Now Jeanine was really puzzled. Out at the ranch there seemed to be a tenseness and restless agitation most of the time in the Heywoods' relationship, but here in town, for some reason they seemed different. She hadn't seen too much of them since their arrival yesterday, but when she had run into them, she noticed that Rhetta was making none of her usual sarcastic insinuations, nor was she as sharp and critical of the people around her. On the contrary, she was warm toward everyone, especially her husband. Hanging on his arm devotedly, yet avoiding overplaying her role, so that she appeared no different from any other loving wife and mother. Jeanine thought perhaps it was because the ranch was so isolated, making it easy for people to get on each other's nerves, and being in town afforded them the change of pace needed to mellow the everyday irritations that often cropped up in a marriage. But now, after witnessing what looked like a clandestine meeting between Rhetta and Jarrod, she wasn't so sure.

She took a closer look at Jarrod as he waited for the starting gun. He called something to Griff next to him, then laughed arrogantly. However, whatever it was didn't seem to have much effect on Griff, who only laughed back, taunting Jarrod the same way he'd been taunted, his horse skittishly pawing the dirt.

This particular race was always held every year there'd been a celebration, but it wasn't really the money that attracted everyone, making it one of the most important events of the holiday. It was the prestige of having the fastest horse in the territory, and Griff's stallion looked in excellent shape. He pawed and pawed restlessly as they waited for the signal to start, and Jeanine watched Griff pull his hat down a little tighter on his head, then settle more comfortably in the saddle.

Suddenly the gun went off and the black stallion shot forward as if hit viciously on the rump, the other horses taking off with him, and for a few seconds all the horses seemed to stay neck and neck, each trying to pass the other. Then slowly Griff felt a surge of strength beneath him, which felt good, and the stallion he was riding began to pull away from the others. Within seconds he was almost two full lengths ahead of them. Griff bent low, urging his mount on, yet still not giving him his head, holding back just enough until the right moment; then he glanced back quickly for a bare second, in time to see Jarrod also begin to draw away from the others, and suddenly, before Griff realized it, the two horses were side by side, both men vying for the lead.

Jarrod was huddling low too, almost lying against the neck of his sorrel, trying to get more speed from the animal, but it didn't seem to be doing any good. He couldn't get past Griff. Dust flew in his eyes, and he could feel the grit of it in his teeth; still, he lowered his head even more.

They had reached the halfway point already, and now both men straightened, but just long enough to rein their horses to the left in a ninety-degree turn, almost brushing against a pole that had been put in the ground indicating the end of the run. Then once more they hunched low in the saddle, pounding down the stretch of dusty road toward the finish line.

Griff could feel excitement throbbing through him. He

knew Jarrod's sorrel was fast, and beating him was going to be a real challenge. His jaw tightened stubbornly as he caught a glimpse of Jarrod out of the corner of his eye, then watched the sorrel pass him, leading now by a little more than a head.

"Not yet, boy," Griff whispered breathlessly to the big stallion he was riding, his hands tightening hard on the reins. "Not just yet." He glanced ahead to the finish line, still some distance away. Then suddenly, when they were about fifty feet from the finish line, "Now!" he shouted, giving the stallion his head, and with almost supernatural strength the sleek horse laid his ears back, stretched his neck, increasing the length of his stride, and with the roar of the crowd ringing in his ears, Griff felt a sense of elation as horse and rider became like one, driving past Jarrod and his sorrel in one last spectacular lunge, leaving the other rider to catch their dust.

"I told you!" yelled the Kid, his words almost lost in the pandemonium that followed, as he spun around to face Peggy, who'd been jumping up and down beside him. Unable to contain himself any longer, he took her into his arms, gave her a quick kiss, then began whirling her around excitedly, only to accidentally brush against Jeanine, throwing her off balance.

"I'm sorry, Jeanine," Peggy apologized quickly, embarrassed as she and the Kid stopped twirling and made a grab for Jeanine, while Jeanine fought to stay on her feet. She managed it somehow, and automatically reached up, holding her glasses in place.

"Please . . . I'm all right," she assured them, then began straightening her clothes, and by the time they were through fussing over the incident, Griff had already slowed his horse and was accepting everyone's congratulations, while Jarrod, who had also slowed his horse, then drawn him to a halt, still sat in the saddle staring hard at Griff, an unusually intense look in his hazel eyes.

Jeanine made sure her straw bonnet was still on straight, then looked up just in time to see Jarrod glance off toward the Heywoods' carriage, where Gar was beaming with pride, hands clasped in front of him, his face red from excitement. But it wasn't Gar Jarrod was staring at, it was the boy's mother, and for a brief moment Jeanine caught what looked like a sneering smile on Rhetta's face. Then suddenly Rhetta once more turned her attention toward her husband, who was trying unsuccessfully to ride his horse through the crowd toward the carriage. Again Jeanine had an overwhelming feeling that something strange was going on. She was brought quickly back to the moment, however, by Crystal.

"I knew that horse was a winner the day Griff broke him," Crystal said proudly, and nudged Jeanine lightly with her elbow. "Ain't he somethin'?"

Jeanine glanced back toward horse and rider, but her eyes settled only on the rider, although no one seemed to notice. "He certainly is," she agreed, then felt her ears tingle explosively as Griff, still maneuvering his horse slowly through the crowd, glanced toward them, catching her staring at him again, and a lazy smile tilted the corners of his mouth. Not again! she thought as she felt her face start to flush. Why does just a look from him do this to me? She'd blushed more the past two weeks at Trail's End than she'd ever blushed before in her life, and it was an uncomfortable feeling. One she could easily do without. She took a deep breath and forced herself to look at his horse instead, then turned as Beth grabbed her hand, urging her to follow the rest of them as they headed toward where the men had been betting so they could collect the money they'd won.

Since no one could seem to remember who contributed how much to the wager, they decided to spend all their winnings, which wasn't much, on food. And although Jeanine wasn't really all that hungry, she gladly let them drag her off toward where some of the townspeople were having a steer roast. Away from the worst of the crowd, and most of all away from any further contact with Griffin Heywood.

It was close to five-thirty when she finally stood in the doorway of the hotel waving good-bye to Crystal, Nellie, and the two young couples as they crossed the dusty main street heading back toward Nellie's, where they'd change for the dance. She'd discovered that Thad was taking Beth, and the Kid was escorting Peggy, and she watched both couples now as they waved back, laughing and teasing each other, and quite suddenly she felt a pang of regret.

She'd never had the chance to experience the thrill of a first love and enjoy the carefree relationship with boys that Crystal's girls and some of the other young people about town had. Her life had been the theater from the time she was first able to walk and talk. It wasn't only that her parents were both show people and never stayed in one place long enough for her to get acquainted with young men, but also there were few young people on the stage, since respectable people often frowned on actors and actresses. And after her parents' untimely death when she was barely in her teens, she'd been too busy keeping food in her mouth and trying to stay out of the clutches of all the do-gooders who continually tried to send her off to some orphanage or other, supposedly for her own good, to worry about boys. Thank God her theatrical training, and the fact that she'd developed early in life, had made it possible for her to pretend she was older than she was, and by the time she was sixteen no one seemed to care anymore that she was on her own. But she had missed part of growing up, and now, watching the young couples together made her feel a little sad.

She turned slowly and tried to make her way inconspicuously through the crowded lobby, glancing at the clock on the wall behind the clerk's desk as she passed. She had not quite an hour and a half to rest a little and change clothes before Warren was due. That is, if he hadn't changed his mind. She hadn't talked to him all day, although she had seen him off and on as she and the others made their way about town, and one thing had been bothering her. Every time she had seen him he'd had a drink in his hand, and she suddenly felt uneasy, wondering if he was going to be sober enough even to go.

After reaching her room and opening the balcony door to let some air in, she took her glasses off, set them on the dresser, then slipped out of her pink dress, sat down on the edge of the bed, took off her shoes and began rubbing her feet. Between all the walking yesterday and today she could only hope they'd hold up for the dance. Thank God she had a change of shoes. Sometimes it helped. She reached down, set her dusty walking shoes aside, then went to the dresser, poured some water into the basin, and began to wash, her thoughts still centered on Warren and what tonight would bring.

The cool water was invigorating, refreshing her somewhat, but it still couldn't quell the turmoil inside her. She finished washing, put on her red ball gown and a pair of kid slippers that were a little more comfortable on her feet, then stood before the mirror that hung over the dresser. Her hair was a mess and would have to be redone. She loosened the chignon, let it fall, then began to brush it vigorously.

The brush had barely touched her hair for the third stroke when she was brought up short by a knock. She stared hesitantly at the door. It was too early to be Warren. She couldn't have taken that long to dress.

Walking over, she leaned close. "Yes?" There was no answer. She pressed her ear against it, listening warily. "Who's there?"

This time a hushed voice came from the other side, barely audible. "Jeanine, it's Homer. Homer Beacon."

Her mouth fell and she straightened, staring at the closed door for a long hard second, unable to believe she'd heard right.

"Jeanine, let me in," he pleaded. "Please?"

She blinked, realizing the enormity of what was happening, then turned the key in the door and opened it a crack.

"Homer?" she asked, peeking out; then she swung the door open wide and Homer Beacon strode into the room, letting her close the door quickly behind him.

"I don't believe it," she cried, trying to keep her voice down as she stared wide-eyed at the secret agent who'd once worked with her as her manager. "This is insane. Where'd you come from?" she asked shakily.

His hat was in his hand and he was frowning as he faced her, his huge gray eyes intense. "I live here," he answered.

"You live here?"

He rubbed the back of a hand over the muttonchops at his jawline, a habit he'd acquired over the years. "You've seen the *Beacon Journal*?" he asked.

Her knees weakened and she leaned back against the door for support. "Oh, my God!"

"Are you all right?"

She nodded hesitantly. "Yes . . . I . . . I should have known." She swallowed hard, and straightened, quickly composing herself. "So that's why he wanted me to meet you. He was hoping to prove his suspicions."

"I kept avoiding you all day yesterday," he offered quickly. "And today too. I wanted to see you alone first because I was afraid if you suddenly bumped into me you'd give yourself away."

"I would have, too," she agreed, then studied him more closely. He'd changed little from the last time she'd seen him. But really, it hadn't been that long ago. Not even a year. "I had no idea you were out here," she said, her voice growing steadily stronger as the shock of seeing him again began to wear off. Her eyes warmed, and she stepped toward him, holding out her arms. "Oh, it's good to see you again," she said, finding herself engulfed in a firm hug.

He breathed deeply, holding her close, knowing instinctively from the moment he'd seen her riding into town the day before in one of the Heywood carriages, trying to look as unattractive and unpretentious as possible, that something was wrong.

"It hasn't been going well, has it?" he asked.

His arms eased from about her and she pulled away, looking up at him. "Does it ever for someone like me?" She tensed. "Lord knows I've tried, but theaters need customers, and putting my name on the billing wouldn't have been practical, at least in the North. And I didn't dare show my face in the South. There are too many people who don't forget. That's why the glasses and all. Only I guess it hasn't fooled Warren.'' She frowned. ''But how have you gotten away with it?'' she suddenly asked. ''He has to know who you are, and he hasn't tried to hang you from the nearest tree. I thought with sentiment in the town what it is . . .''

''I managed to convince him I knew nothing about your spying activities, at least not until the night you were found out. I told him I was strictly your manager, and only your manager, and that I was as shocked as everyone else to discover what you'd been doing. I told him that when I heard the soldiers were looking for you, I was afraid they'd think I was in on it with you, so I disappeared rather than take a chance on no one believing me.''

''He accepted it?''

''It took some convincing.'' His gray eyes studied her curiously. ''But tell me, what are you doing way out here? I thought maybe you'd have headed for Europe or found yourself someone and settled down to raise a family by now.''

She drew away from him and began slowly brushing her hair again. ''I'm Garfield Heywood's governess.''

''I know that,'' he said. ''I found that out yesterday. But why here?''

''It's as good a place as any—at least I thought it was until I ran into Warren.''

''But Raintree . . . what made you pick Raintree?''

''Me? I didn't pick it, Sheridan did,'' and she remembered the argument with him that day in his office. ''Coming here was his idea, not mine,'' she explained.

Homer frowned, and Jeanine liked the familiarity of seeing that distinctive frown of his again after all these months. It looked like he might have lost a little more hair on top, but she'd never let him know. He was already self-conscious enough about the bald spot slowly working its way back from his forehead. Bad enough he'd always hated being shorter than most men, and now losing his hair too. But at the moment his gray eyes were deepening with uncertainty.

"What is it?" she asked, instinctively feeling something was wrong.

He continued to stare for a few seconds, then shrugged, trying to be nonchalant. "It's probably nothing," he answered. "But then again . . . Did the general say he knew the Heywoods?" he asked.

"From what I gathered the day I arrived, he only knows their housekeeper, Mrs. Brandt." She walked over to the dresser, set the hairbrush down, and started twisting her hair back into its chignon. "Why do you ask?"

"No special reason, except that the Heywoods have been having trouble lately."

"So I've heard."

"And you're sure Sheridan didn't send you out here with the idea of maybe trying to discover what was going on?"

She glanced sideways at him in the mirror. "You don't think . . . Does he know you're out here?" she asked.

"Not that I know of. I left the service the end of May and I've only been here since July."

She fastened the chignon down tightly, then turned to face him. "Coincidence?"

"Has to be."

"I don't know . . ." She stared at him, her eyes suddenly sparking. "Homer?"

"Forget it," he said quickly, knowing all too well what she was thinking. "I've been doing fine on my own."

"You've been investigating?"

"I run a newspaper, Jeanine. It's my job."

"Learn anything?"

"Not much, except that the trouble started when Griff came back and took over the running of Trail's End."

"But you have no idea why or who?"

He shook his head. "Nope, unless someone's trying to stop the cattle drive he's planning."

"Cory McBride thinks someone's trying to kill Griffin Heywood."

"That's possible too, I suppose, but who?"

She hesitated. "Jarrod Vance?"

"What makes you say that?"

"Something I saw today." She told him about what she assumed was a clandestine meeting between Jarrod and Rhetta earlier at the races. "What do you think?" she asked when she'd finished.

"Hmm . . . it's peculiar, all right, but . . ." He watched closely as she picked the wire-rim glasses up and put them on. Strange how she was still a fascinating woman even with the glasses and the severe hairdo. It wasn't so much that she was beautiful, but her eyes were always so alive, and she had a sensuous way of smiling that made men all too aware of the passion they suspected was hidden beneath that smile. He'd have recognized her anywhere. He thought over what she'd just told him. "You sure it was Rhetta Heywood?" he asked.

"Absolutely."

He rubbed his chin. "I've never heard a breath of scandal about either her or Griff since I've been here," he said, rather surprised. "Fact is, from what everyone says, she even behaved herself while he was off fighting, and everyone talks about them as if they're the ideal couple." He looked thoughtful. "Now, Jarrod is another matter. I guess he went to Mexico when the war broke out, and came back about a year ago. Never was in the army on either side. Bought his way out, from what most folks say. Used the excuse that raising horses and steers for the army was more important than getting himself killed on the front lines."

"And his women?"

"The usual, as far as I know. Hadn't thought much about it until now, but I don't think I've ever really paid much attention." He was skeptical. "But Rhetta Heywood . . . I don't know . . . Besides"—he tried to convince himself too while he was at it—"if anything's been going on, wouldn't someone have discovered it by now?"

"It's a big country, Homer."

"But a small town."

"I won't argue that point." She slicked her hair back,

making sure it was staying in place. "You are going to let me help, aren't you?" she suddenly asked.

"You already have a job."

"So do you."

"Be reasonable, Jeanine," he argued. "How will you have time to teach young Gar and help me too? It just wouldn't work."

"All I have to do is keep my eyes open," she answered, taking a ruby necklace and earrings from the dresser, putting them on, then making sure the necklace was straight in front. "That shouldn't be too hard."

"You could get hurt."

"How? Besides"—she turned, her eyes pleading—"you said yourself that General Sheridan might have sent me here on purpose."

"It was only a thought."

"One I liked." She moved over to him and reached up, toying with the lapel on his suit jacket. "Please, Homer. For old times' sake. Let me try to help," she pleaded.

He hesitated, yet knew he'd give in. He'd lost a wife and daughter years ago, and Jeanine had seemed almost like a daughter to him from the first day they'd met, and he was reluctant to deny her anything. "Oh, all right," he conceded. "But only if you promise not to go looking for trouble. Keep your eyes open for anything unusual, but don't get in anyone's way. One thing for sure, the hired help at Trail's End are a close mouthed lot, so maybe I can learn something with you on the inside. Only remember, if Heywood's foreman thinks whoever it is is trying to kill Heywood, they could try to get rid of you too, so watch yourself."

She smiled impishly. "You know, I think I'm going to enjoy this." Her eyes sparkled behind the glasses. "I'm afraid being a teacher isn't quite as exciting as I thought it'd be."

Homer had a strange feeling he should have insisted she stay out of it, but knowing Jeanine as well as he did, he knew she'd stick her nose in anyway. Besides, there was something about the way her eyes shone that intrigued him, and he knew she was actually going to enjoy the challenge.

"But don't forget that the Heywoods hired you to teach," he cautioned.

She shook her head. "I won't. It's just that I guess once you go through something like we did, life without the intrigue and that little edge of danger to it doesn't seem too terribly exciting."

"Now, don't get carried away, Jeanine," he warned her again. "We were lucky back in Montgomery."

She nodded, then smoothed the lapel of his suit coat. "Which reminds me, Warren's due any minute. He can't find you here."

"I know." He covered her hand with his. "And don't worry, when we meet at the dance, I'll swear I never met you before in my life."

"You think he'll believe you?"

"Not really. But there isn't much he can do about it, is there?"

"It seems like a dirty trick to play on him, I know," she said softly. "But there are still too many people who remember what Jeannie Gray did, and would be willing to honor the price on her head, and I don't intend to give anyone the opportunity to collect."

"They won't." He kissed her cheek, then released her hands and they headed for the door. "Now, I'd better get out of here before I ruin everything."

He reached for the doorknob, but she stopped him. "No, I'd better do that. Only Homer, I never thought. If I learn anything, how do I get in touch with you?"

"Unless it can't wait, just keep it," he said quickly. "I'll get in touch with you." She nodded, then opened the door, and gingerly peeked out, letting him know the hallway was empty. He looked at her one more time. "Take care, Jeanine," he said hurriedly, then stepped into the hall, shut the door behind him, set the black hat he'd been carrying firmly on his head, straightened decisively, and started toward the stairs, while Jeanine stood back in the hotel room staring hard at the closed door, still a little bewildered over this new turn of events.

7

Warren was ten minutes late and she could tell he'd
been drinking. He was still fairly sober, so she assumed
what he'd consumed so far was getting some chance to
wear off before he downed more, or he'd have passed out
long ago, but he wasn't as carefree and gay as he'd been
the day before. His eyes were bloodshot and he didn't
seem too steady on his feet, but his words weren't slurred,
although he talked somewhat slower.

She wished she didn't have to go with him, but couldn't
think of a good excuse not to, and knowing Warren, he
probably wouldn't have accepted one anyway, so she'd
have to manage. She stood with the door open, watching
as he stared at her, transfixed.

"Well, are you just going to stand there gaping?" she
asked.

He walked in, then turned, still staring intently.

She glanced down at her ball gown, then back to Warren. "Is anything wrong? My dress on backward or something?" She tried to be nonchalant, but her insides felt like
jelly.

"Hell, don't mind me," he said flippantly. "I've been
trying to drown my sorrow all day, and just when I think I've
got it made, I see you again and all of a sudden I'm sober."

"You are?"

"Well . . ." He smiled sheepishly. "Almost."

She took a white embroidered silk shawl from the bed, wrapping it about her shoulders. "Shall we go?" she asked. No use procrastinating. It wasn't going to change anything.

He opened the door, gesturing graciously. "After you, dear lady," and she was still eyeing him warily as they left the hotel.

The dance was in full swing when they finally reached Sheriff Higgens' place. He and his neighbors had cleaned out his barn, the largest so close to town, and a platform was set up at one end for the band, which consisted of violin, guitar, mandolin, and a piano they'd lugged out from one of the saloons. Warren helped her down from the buggy as best he was able, since he wasn't coordinating too well, and she prayed no one would pay much attention as they stepped inside.

Everyone seemed to be enjoying the dance. She held tightly to Warren's arm and managed to maneuver him toward an empty corner, where she hoped they'd be inconspicuous; then, still holding his arm, she surveyed the room. It was a little hard to see the dance floor with so many people standing about, but she spotted Beth dancing by with Thad Watchek, followed a few minutes later by Peggy and the Kid. Funny she should suddenly wonder what the Kid's real name might be, but then he didn't seem to mind being called the Kid, so it didn't really matter. She still couldn't help wondering, though. It did seem rather unusual.

A few seconds later she caught sight of Crystal smiling up into Cory McBride's face as they danced by, and she smiled to herself. Crystal's face was revealing far more than Jeanine suspected Crystal wanted it to, and Jeanine suddenly realized why Crystal was so content working at Trail's End.

The music was inviting, but she wasn't about to let Warren make a fool of himself on the dance floor. At least not until he sobered up a little more, so she declined his offer to join in the lively two-step, but gave in a short while later for a slow waltz, and the first person they

passed as they set out on the dance floor was Griffin
Heywood, dancing with a plump woman in her mid-forties,
who, Warren had pointed out to her the day before, was
the sheriff's wife. Griff had left Rhetta by the punch bowl
deep in conversation with some of the other ladies from
town, and now he nodded slightly as he went by. Once
more Jeanine fought to keep from turning red, which she
knew was her usual color when he was around.

As the evening wore on, things became even more and
more unsettling. Warren hadn't taken a drink so far since
their arrival, and she hoped he was sobering up, but it was
going to take longer than she thought and every time he
looked at her his eyes seemed to narrow curiously, as if he
was holding back, waiting for something. But what? Homer? No doubt, and she was thankful he hadn't made an
appearance as yet. They danced only the slow dances, but
she didn't mind really. Occasionally one of the other men
would ask her to dance, and Warren, although giving his
permission, would stare disgustedly, never taking his eyes
from her until the dance ended.

No matter whom she danced with, however, it wasn't
only Warren's eyes she felt watching her, it was Griffin
Heywood's. And more than once she felt intimidated by
his presence.

He'd relinquished his buckskins tonight for more formal
attire, and was wearing a black suit with a gray satin vest
and a white shirt with a slim black cravat knotted into a
bow at the throat. It did little to change the effect he
always had on her. To make matters worse, Warren was
dressed almost identically, as were a number of the other
men, but on them the clothes just didn't seem the same,
and she was very much aware of Griff's presence, especially when she'd accidentally catch sight of him staring at
her.

Damn the man anyway, she'd thought more than once
as she gazed about the big barn, trying to avoid his searching eyes.

It was just past nine-thirty when she caught sight of
Homer standing near the open barn door. He'd slipped

inside unnoticed, and now when their eyes met, he glanced away quickly, saying something to a man standing beside him. Jeanine hoped Warren hadn't noticed, but it was wishful thinking.

"Aha, there's the fella I've been wanting you to meet," Warren suddenly said, his eyes steadfast on Homer, and Jeanine said a silent prayer. "Hey, Homer!" Warren called out as he dragged her off the dance floor, then grabbed her elbow, ushering her toward Homer.

Homer glanced over abruptly, watching the couple bearing down on him.

"I've got someone here I think you know," Warren offered a little too loudly as they reached Homer, and he made her stop directly in front of Homer, who leaned back slightly as if taking a good look.

"Well, Homer?" Warren asked, a satisfied look on his face.

Homer continued staring at Jeanine for a few seconds, showing no sign of recognition; then he looked back at Warren. "Well, what?"

"Don't you recognize her?" Warren asked, beginning to frown.

Homer looked at her again, then back to Warren. "Am I supposed to?" he asked.

"Dammit, Homer. Don't do this to me," Warren said, his face turning crimson. "You know very well who it is. It's Jeannie, Homer . . . Jeannie!"

Homer shook his head, pretending ignorance. "I don't know what you're talking about, Warren," he answered, trying to keep his voice calm.

"You have to," Warren interrupted belligerently. "Don't pretend with me, Homer, it won't do you any good, I know better. Her name isn't Jeanine, is it, Homer? It's Jeannie and you know it."

"I know nothing of the sort," Homer answered, and reached out, hoping to persuade Warren to stop, but Warren slapped Homer's hand aside before it touched his arm.

"Dammit, Homer. It's her, it has to be," Warren cried,

his amber eyes ablaze. "Tell me it's Jeannie, Homer, please," he begged.

Homer took another look at Jeanine, knowing how much she hated to hurt Warren like this, yet knowing it had to be. They called it survival. "If you mean the Jeannie I'm thinking of, Warren, no." He shook his head. "You've been drinking. You're all mixed up. She doesn't even look like Jeannie . . . surely you of all people should see that."

People were beginning to gather around now, and Homer tried again to calm him down.

"You're creating a scene, Warren," he said solicitously. "Now, why don't you just forget it and go back to your dancing?"

Warren straightened, about to release another verbal attack, when Cory suddenly shoved his way through the crowd, interrupting him.

"Hey, Warren," he said, ignoring the people standing around. "You promised me a dance with the teacher, remember?" and Warren, taken by surprise, stuttered hesitantly for a few seconds, then watched, frowning, as Cory, without waiting for a reply, caught Jeanine by the arm and ushered her off toward the dancers, whirling her back to the dance floor as the music continued.

Jeanine glanced up at Cory curiously as they began dancing. "Thank you for rescuing me," she said softly.

"Don't thank me, thank Griff," he replied. "It was all his idea." He glanced over to where Warren had joined some men who were passing around a bottle. "I wish he wouldn't drink like that." Cory went on frowning, and his big red mustache twitched as he looked back at her. "What the hell was he talking about back there, anyway?"

She shook her head. "I don't know . . . I wish I did."

"Whatever it was, he was really riled." He saw the pained look in her eyes. "Sorry, I didn't mean to make you uncomfortable," he said. "Just forget it for now, and enjoy yourself," and he began humming to the music, his voice deep and mellow.

When the music finally stopped, they joined Crystal and some of the others near the refreshment table. Jeanine was still upset, but trying not to show it. She'd lost sight of Warren shortly before the dance ended, but had become aware of Rhetta and Griff Heywood standing only a few feet away talking to friends, and Homer was off in a corner by himself, trying to look inconspicuous. She stood out the next two dances, sipping on a glass of punch Crystal had handed her before dancing off with Cory, then moved farther away from the refreshment table, once more catching sight of Warren. He was nursing the same liquor bottle, only he was all by himself now, and her stomach tightened into knots as she saw him down one drink after another, eventually leaving only a few dregs in the bottom of the bottle.

She didn't like it, but there was nothing she could do. Unable to watch any longer, she looked away, watching the dancers, again hoping maybe he'd pass out before causing any more trouble.

Suddenly she felt someone beside her, and inhaled, holding her breath. "Put down the glass, you're coming with me," Warren ordered, and grabbed her arm hard, just above the elbow, his fingers digging into her skin.

She tried to pull away, but he was holding too tightly, hurting her. Not wanting to create any more of a scene, she set the glass down and let him usher her awkwardly across the room toward where Homer was standing. Not again! she thought disgustedly, and tried once more to pull away, but more vigorously this time, the smell of his whiskey breath turning her stomach. But he still wouldn't stop or let go. He held onto her like a leech, until they were once more face to face with Homer. Her heart sank.

"Now, Homer," Warren demanded, and his voice cut the air like a knife as Homer stared at him hard, "look at her, look close. Homer, who does she look like?" he went on stubbornly. "Forget the glasses and dowdy hair. It's her, it has to be. Dammit, it's Jeannie, Homer, and you know it is," he yelled. "No one could look so much like Jeannie and not be her!"

Everyone was staring now, but he didn't seem to care and his voice rose even louder. "Goddammit, Homer.

What the hell's wrong with you? You know damn well I'm right!'' he bellowed recklessly. "Tell them, tell everyone who she is, Homer. Tell everyone who she really is!'' Jeanine's face paled; Homer's turned red with frustration.

The music stopped abruptly, and suddenly Griff was beside Jeanine.

"Come on, Warren, that's enough," Griff ordered, but Warren was furious.

"Enough, hell!'' he yelled, his eyes still on Homer, lips white with rage. "This son of a bitch knows what I'm talking about! He knows her, I tell you, and dammit, I'm gonna beat the truth out of him!''

Warren lunged toward Homer, and Jeanine screamed, but Griff was too quick. His hand snaked out, chopping downward, catching Warren sharply on the nape of the neck, and with a frantic moan Warren flailed the air for a second, trying to stay conscious, then suddenly sprawled on the floor at Homer's feet, out cold.

Griff was breathing heavily as he stared down at Warren for a long hard minute, then he motioned for Cory and Luke, who'd followed him over.

"Haul him into the house and dump him on the bed,'' he said, straightening his clothes. "He'll have to sleep it off,'' and he tugged at the end of his coat sleeves, then smoothed a stray strand of hair from his forehead, watching closely as they picked Warren off the floor and headed out the door with him, trying not to be too rough.

Jeanine wanted to melt into the floor, but instead she trembled and looked up at Homer, tears in her eyes. She'd never dreamed Warren would go this far.

Griff turned to her, ignoring the crowd. "Are you all right?'' he asked.

She nodded, one hand clutching her throat nervously. "I . . . I think so.'' Her voice faltered. "If you don't mind, though, I think I'd better leave.'' She started for the door, then remembered her shawl and headed toward the chair where she'd left it.

"Here, let me,'' Griff said, and he reached the shawl

before she did, snatching it from the chair, holding it out for her to put on.

Jeanine stared at him for a moment, then turned her back to him, letting him put the shawl across her shoulders. Her lips were trembling, but it wasn't because of Warren, not all of it. Warren's outburst had upset her, but she'd taken a lot over the years. It was the violence behind it that bothered her. That, coupled with Griff's intervention. She could feel everyone's eyes on her.

"I'll take you back to the hotel," Griff said. "It's too far for you to walk alone this time of night."

She glanced back over her shoulder. "There's no need."

His eyes darkened stubbornly. "I said I'll take you." He turned to Homer. "Tell Rhetta I'll be back shortly," he said, and took Jeanine's arm, ushering her through the whispering crowd, unaware that Rhetta didn't have to be told, she'd heard every word.

"All right, everybody!" Homer hollered as Jeanine and Griff headed out the door. "Fun's over, let's dance," and as the music started up again, everyone slowly started to go back to the dance floor. Everyone except Rhetta Heywood, that is. Instead, she moved slowly to the door of the barn and leaned against the side of it, watching her husband and her son's teacher walk off into the darkness.

"I'll hitch the buggy," Griff offered as they left the barn, but Jeanine stopped him.

"No, please. I'd rather walk, if you don't mind." She leaned her head back and gazed up at the night sky. The stars looked so close you could almost touch them and the air smelled fresh and sweet. "Please, I need to calm down."

He watched her for a minute, then took her arm. "It'll probably do us both good, come on," and they started walking down the drive toward the main road.

His hand dropped from her arm. "I saw you at the races," he said, trying to make conversation. "How did you like Che-ak?"

She glanced over, watching the moonlight turn his hair

to burnished gold. How tall and well built he was, and he walked with such ease, even in his heeled boots. "If you mean the horse you rode today, he's beautiful," she answered.

"And headstrong." He cleared his throat and looked over, watching the reflection from the moon light up her eyes while it flirted with their shadows. He frowned. "Speaking of being headstrong," he said, "I have to apologize for Warren."

"No need, really," she answered. "He was drunk. He probably won't even remember it."

"On the contrary. He had just enough to make him mean, but not enough to make him forget."

"Oh?"

"Maybe I'd better tell you something about Warren, and you might understand," he began, and while they walked back toward town, he proceeded to tell her a story he thought she didn't know, but one she was all too familiar with. To her surprise, Warren had confided everything to Griff. Jeanine had been proud to serve the Union cause during the war, but too often had detested some of the methods she'd been forced to resort to, and now, as she listened to Griffin Heywood recounting how Warren had met the notorious Jeannie Gray and naively let her steal the contents of the dispatches he'd been carrying, causing him to lose his commission, she suddenly felt cheap and dirty. If only there'd been another way, but there hadn't.

"The strange part, Miss Grayson," Griff said, finishing the tale as he unlocked the door to her hotel room, then handed her the key, "is that Warren thinks you look a great deal like her, and I guess I can see where he's right." He suddenly reached out, tilting her chin up, his blue eyes probing hers. "I saw her perform once at a theater in St. Louis about a year before the war started," he confessed, surprising her completely. "I know it was a long time ago, but she was a young woman hard to forget. I know. I sat through two of her performances. If I wasn't a married man, I'd have gone backstage and invited her to dinner. Almost did, too, then thought better of it. My life was complicated enough without asking for trouble." He hesitated, then went on, his voice lowering intimately. "Warren keeps telling me she has the bluest eyes this side of heaven, Miss Grayson, but unfortunately I never got close enough to see for myself."

"And did he also say she hid them behind glasses because she's almost blind without them?" she asked softly, all too aware of the touch of his fingers on her chin. She'd finally managed to quit flushing when he looked at her; now, instead, she trembled slightly, but he didn't seem to notice.

The corner of his mouth twitched but he didn't smile; instead a frown knit his brows together, deepening his eyes to a stormy blue. What was it about the woman that seemed to stir him so? Her lips were soft and sensuous, but it wasn't just that. It was everything about her, and yet he couldn't explain why. He fought against the warm sensations that were quickening his pulse and making his heart pound erratically. They were the same strange feelings that had compelled him to go back a second night to see Jeannie Gray perform. It couldn't be possible—the whole idea was insane. Jeanine Grayson was quiet, unpretentious, even timid at times, her manner too shy and reserved to ever have been on the stage, and yet . . .

"I'd better get back," he said, his hand dropping from her chin. "I hope you're not still too upset."

"I'll be all right," she answered. "The night air was refreshing, and the story about Mr. Granger quite revealing. I guess I can understand his frustration, but . . ."

"He'll get over it, I'm sure. The important thing is that you're all right now."

"I'm fine," she replied softly. "Thank you again for walking back with me. It helped."

"My pleasure." He watched the door close behind her, then stood staring at it for a long time before finally leaving.

Inside the room, Jeanine walked slowly toward the balcony, removing her shawl on the way, tossing it haphazardly onto the bed. The room was dark, but instead of lighting the lamp, she unlocked the door to the balcony and stepped outside. What a strange day it had been. First seeing Rhetta Heywood with Jarrod Vance, then Homer's sudden appearance, and now Griffin Heywood's new revelation. No wonder he'd been staring at her. She'd never dreamed he'd seen her in St. Louis. That was so long ago. She could faintly hear music, and cocked her head to one side, listening for a second, then walked to the railing, staring off in the direction of the sheriff's barn. The dance was still going strong.

She looked down at the street again. The town was deserted, even the saloon quiet, the street empty except for one man. Griffin Heywood's catlike walk had become as familiar to her over the past two weeks as Warren's was, and she watched him now, making his way along the boardwalk, staying close to the building. He was strolling along slowly, hands in his pockets, his tall frame silhouetted in the moonlight.

Suddenly, as he started past a narrow alley, she gasped, startled, and stared in disbelief as two men jumped from the shadows, grappled with him just long enough to get a good hold, then wrestled him into the alley and out of sight. It happened so quickly that at first she just stood there dumbfounded, staring. Then, as the full impact of what was happening hit her, she whirled about, lifting her skirts so she wouldn't trip, ran back through her room, into the hall, down the stairs, across the empty lobby, and on out the front door onto the boardwalk.

No one else was around, only she didn't even take time to look, but kept right on running as fast as she could to where she'd seen the men attack Griff. She was panting hard by the time she reached the alley, and stopped abruptly, suddenly realizing the danger she could be in. Instinctively she pressed up against the nearest building and inched her way closer. Now she could hear an occasional curse, a few grunts, and the unmistakable splat of knuckles against flesh, then more cursing.

Taking a deep breath, she inched along the edge of the

building and slipped into the alley. This end was deep in shadows, but the other end was flooded with moonlight, and she could see everything clearly. There were two men with Griff. One behind him, struggling to get back to his feet, the other in front of him, on his way to his knees, and Griff was still hunched over from the blow he'd just landed in the man's stomach. She saw Griff stand motionless for a brief second, watching as the man in front of him hit the ground; then he straightened quickly, ready to take on the other man again, but he was too late.

Jeanine screamed, calling his name, hoping to warn him just as the butt of the man's gun came down on the back of his head, buckling his knees, only Griff didn't go down.

As Jeanine tore from the shadows, running toward him, still yelling, the man who'd hit Griff, disgusted because Griff hadn't fallen, and realizing the woman running toward them screaming might not be alone, shoved Griff hard, plastering him against the building, then grabbed his partner by the arm, pulling and dragging him to his feet, and the two of them disappeared quickly out the other end of the alley.

Griff was still leaning back against the building, rubbing the top of his head with both hands, when Jeanine got to him, and without thinking, she reached up, searching, her fingers lightly caressing the moist cut on his head, feeling the lump beginning to swell beneath it.

"My God, you're hurt," she gasped breathlessly.

He winced. "It's nothing."

"You're bleeding."

"Just broke the skin a little. That's all. No need to worry." His fingers covered hers and he lifted her hands from his head, lowering them to his chest, where he cradled them tightly in his while she stared up at him.

"They could have killed you."

"Which is what they were hoping to do, I presume."

"Why?"

"Who knows?" He blinked, closing his eyes, warding off the pain of the blow some, then opened his eyes again. The shock was finally wearing off and he straightened a little, but still held her hands, looking down into her face. "But what the hell are you doing here?" he asked, surprised. "I left you back at the hotel."

"I was on the balcony watching when they jumped you."

He studied her face for a minute, then smiled, relaxing back against the building, and his voice when he spoke was hushed, softly teasing. "Do you always stand on balconies late at night?"

She could feel her face growing hot. "When I have a lot on my mind, yes." She tried to pull her hands from his, but his fingers tightened.

"Where are you going?"

"I . . . I have to get back."

"To an empty hotel room? Nonsense." His voice was husky, full of warmth. "I haven't thanked you yet for scaring them away."

He was so close, and he was looking at her again in that strange sensual way he had that made her feel uncomfortable.

"There's no need for thanks," she whispered hesitantly, frightened by what she knew she shouldn't be feeling.

He still held her hands close against his chest, then suddenly raised the left one, deliberately opening it, and pressed his lips caressingly against her palm. Jeanine shivered, a flood of warmth shooting through her from head to toe. Her hand felt like it was on fire, and her knees weakened.

As his lips brushed lightly against her palm, his eyes searched hers relentlessly, wallowing in the passionate yearnings he saw mirrored in their depths. He drew her closer against him, and she suddenly realized his other hand was at her waist now, and she didn't even know when he'd put it there. Her right hand was resting against the front of his suit coat and he drew his lips from the middle of her other hand, then lowered it until they were both side by side again, resting on his chest. Inhaling deeply, he let the intoxicating warmth of her nearness run rampant through him, then reached up, gently lifting the glasses from off her nose, holding them away from her face.

"My God, they're so blue . . ." he murmured softly. "Your eyes are so blue . . ."

She trembled. "You . . . you don't know what you're saying," she protested. "They must have hit you too hard."

"I know exactly what I'm saying," he answered, and the timbre of his voice brought a flood of new feelings to her. "If only . . ."

Her hand was shaking as she reached up and took the glasses from him, setting them back in place again.

"Please," she whispered, "I have to go. You musn't . . ."

His arm left her waist, but instead of releasing her, he took her face in both his hands and gazed at her hungrily. His mouth was so close that his breath caressed her lips and she felt the stirrings that had begun in her loins slowly beginning to build until she wanted to cry out, and suddenly, as his eyes devoured hers, something strangely exciting passed between them that she couldn't explain. She wanted to crawl inside him and lose herself in his body, anything to nurture and keep alive the painfully sweet sensations that were taking hold of her. It felt wildly wonderful. She'd never felt like this before in her life. It was delightful yet terrifying all at the same time, and she never wanted it to end, yet knew it had to.

"You can't go," he murmured breathlessly, his mouth barely touching hers. "Not yet."

"I must!" Her breath was raspy, uneven, and she could hardly breathe. "Please . . . let me go."

"I'll go with you."

His lips touched hers ever so lightly, but it was just enough to shake her back to her senses.

"No, God no!" she suddenly gasped. She shouldn't be here, they shouldn't . . . If he walked her to her room . . . It was madness. She pulled as far from him as she could, wrenching her face from his hands. "I'll go alone . . . please," she begged.

He started to reach for her, his hands aching to hold her again. "Jeanine!"

Her eyes were wide, her breathing unsteady, as she shook her head. "I can't!" she cried.

He frowned, straightening, the sudden realization of what was happening to him like a dash of cold water in the face. "Then go." She hesitated momentarily. "Dammit . . . go!" he groaned helplessly, fighting the urge to keep her here, and as she moved hesitantly back into the shadows at the far end of the alley, he rubbed the back of his hand against his lips, trying to wipe away the remembrance of his lips brushing against hers.

Jeanine's steps faltered, and it was as if she was in a daze as she made her way along the boardwalk, back to the hotel. She reached the door to the lobby and stopped for a second, staring back toward the alley where she'd left Griff, and her heart turned over inside her. His tall muscular frame was leaning up against the building now while he watched her intently.

Griff saw her disappear into the hotel, then sighed, his emotions warring inside him. Reaching up, he touched the cut on his head lightly, remembering the way her fingers had felt. Dammit anyway. What was the matter with him? Why had he let her get to him? Ever since that first night at Trail's End when he'd looked into her eyes and realized there was something about her that he'd never come up against before, he'd tried to avoid her as much as possible. It had been hard because she always seemed to be about, but he'd managed somehow. Now this. He should have let someone else bring her back to the hotel. Why hadn't he?

He straightened and glanced up at the balcony that fronted the hotel, squinting, trying to see if maybe she was standing there again, but she wasn't, at least not where he could see her. He was a damn fool and he knew it. There was no room in his life for another woman, and never would be. He'd made that decision a long time ago and it was time he started remembering it again.

Shaking his head as if trying to clear it, he slowly turned, one eye on the shadows around him to make sure he wasn't going to be jumped again, his thoughts trying to make some sense out of his insane actions tonight, and he was still cursing his stupidity as he slowly headed back toward the sheriff's barn.

The next morning, Jeanine sent word with Jasper, inquiring as to when Crystal and the twins would be leaving to go back to Trail's End. She knew they'd leave earlier than Griff and Rhetta, and she was certain Warren wouldn't be riding with them. A message came back to be ready by eleven, Cory would pick up her and her suitcases at the hotel, they'd all eat lunch at Nellie Watchek's, then Cory'd be driving them home. An arrangement she was quite thankful for, and they arrived back at Trail's End about four o'clock Sunday afternoon.

When they were all settled in again, Jeanine offered to help Crystal with dinner while the twins unpacked the suitcases, but Crystal refused her help, and in a way Jeanine was glad. Their conversation had been strained during most of the ride back, because of questions and remarks over last night's unfortunate incident, and she'd been afraid that Crystal might bring the subject up again and start asking too many questions if the girls weren't around. So she was grateful to be able to shut herself off in the classroom and try getting things ready for the next day's schoolwork without having to try to think up answers to questions she didn't want to hear.

The Heywoods arrived home about half an hour before dinnertime, and without Warren, which didn't surprise Mrs. Brandt in the least. She merely assumed he'd been on another of his binges. However, as they all sat about the table that evening, Jeanine couldn't help but feel the tension that seemed to permeate the room.

Only Gar was in a gay mood, knowing nothing about the incident at the dance, and still excited about his grand weekend, volunteering all sorts of information about what Mrs. Brandt had missed, babbling on incessantly as all boys will about the horse races, the medicine show, the band concert, until finally Rhetta couldn't stand any more.

"For heaven's sake, Gar, will you shut up!" she suddenly yelled, interrupting him, her dark eyes flashing angrily. "If I hear one more 'you should have seen,' " she said, "I think I'll scream!"

Gar inhaled sharply, and stopped abruptly in the middle of his sentence as all eyes centered on him. He stared at his mother, startled. Then, as tears gathered at the corners of his eyes, he hung his head, the smile that had wreathed his face and made his eyes sparkle only moments before, gone.

"Good Lord, Rhetta," Griff said angrily, knowing the boy was humiliated. "Let him have his fun. Just because our weekend was a fiasco doesn't mean he has to suffer for it."

"I can't stand his constant prattling," she snapped irritably, staring furiously at her son. "All he's done since we got home is rattle on and on."

"So he enjoyed himself."

"Well, let him talk about it when I'm not around. I don't want to be reminded."

"May . . . may I please be excused?" Gar murmured timidly as he looked over at his father, and Jeanine knew he was trying hard to hold back the tears.

"Go ahead, son." Griff nodded, and Jeanine's heart went out to the boy.

"I'll go with him," she said quickly, as Gar stood up, and she saw the relief in the boy's eyes as he looked at her. "I promised to read to him after dinner," she lied, winking at Gar furtively, and Griff, seeing the wink, but not wanting to call his wife's attention to it, watched as Jeanine stood up and left the room with Gar in tow.

Rhetta's eyes were smoldering as they settled on Griff and watched his eyes follow Jeanine and Gar from the room.

"I knew that woman meant trouble the first time I laid eyes on her," she said spitefully, and Griff turned to her curiously.

He frowned. "Because she's nice to Gar?"

"Because of last night."

"Now, don't go blaming last night on Jeanine," he said, defending her.

"Oh . . . now it's 'Jeanine,' " she said sarcastically. "How nice."

Griff's stomach tightened warily. Now he'd put his foot in it. "What am I supposed to call her?" he asked. "It's her name."

"What's wrong with 'Miss Grayson'?"

"Be reasonable, Rhetta. You all call her Jeanine, including Gar."

"I hadn't noticed."

"Well, I have. Besides, quit changing the subject. You know damn well last night was Warren's doing."

Rhetta wiped her mouth, then put the napkin beside her plate. "Did it ever occur to you that he might have had a good reason?"

"He was drunk."

"Not that drunk. You heard him." She leaned toward Griff, frowning. "What if she is that woman . . . that Jeannie Gray?"

"Don't be absurd."

"I'm not being absurd. We know nothing about her." She glanced over to Mrs. Brandt, who'd been quietly listening to their tirade and who'd been quickly briefed by Griff, shortly before dinner, about Warren's conduct at the dance. "After all, Mrs. Brandt never did say who recommended her."

Mrs. Brandt's eyes narrowed and she glanced over to Griff. "A friend," she said, and looked back to Rhetta.

"What friend?"

"Does it matter?" Griff asked, defending the housekeeper this time. "The important thing is that she's an excellent teacher and Gar likes her. Can she help it if your brother's an irresponsible lovesick fool?"

"I knew you'd blame it on him."

"Who am I supposed to blame it on?"

"She led him on, Griff, and you know it," she cried angrily.

"Led him on? She's hardly the type to lead any man on."

"Oh no? You are naive. She's been making eyes at him ever since she arrived."

"The hell she has." His eyes darkened. "Warren's trouble is he's never gotten over Jeannie Gray and he sees her in every blond woman he meets."

"Well, what if she is Jeannie Gray?" she retorted angrily. "How do we know? We've never seen the woman. It's not impossible, you know."

"But unlikely." He'd never mentioned to Rhetta the fact that he'd seen Jeannie Gray on the stage years ago. For some reason he'd just never been able to confide in her. "Besides," he said as he went on trying to resolve the problem, "even if she was Jeannie Gray, why should it matter? The war's been over for months."

"Warren's war will never be over." Her fists clenched. "That woman scarred him for life, Griff, and you know it," she said. "If Jeanine Grayson is really Jeannie Gray . . ."

"Homer Beacon said she isn't, and he should know. Now, why would he lie?"

"Then you're still going to let her stay?"

"I never intended anything else."

Her face flushed and she glared at him. "You'll rue the day," she said bitterly, and stood up. "Mark my words, Griffin Heywood. Someday you'll be sorry you ever set eyes on that woman," and she pushed her chair back angrily and left.

Mrs. Brandt looked unhappy. "I'm sorry, Griff."

"Forget it," he said, leaning back in his chair. "It isn't your fault any more than it's mine. How were we to know she'd look so much like Warren's nemesis?"

"You don't suppose . . ." She was hesitant. "By some quirk of fate . . . she couldn't be the same woman, could she?"

"I wish I knew," he said, staring off into space, remembering the look in her eyes last night. "I don't know."

He looked at her curiously. "Phil Sheridan would know better than to do something like that to us, wouldn't he?"

"He didn't know about Warren, Griff. And if she was trying to disappear . . ."

"But here . . . ?"

"Do you want me to write to him?"

He thought for a minute, then shook his head. "Let it be for now," he said, and leaned forward, picking his glass up from the table, finishing the last of the wine in it, then stood up. "If I change my mind, I'll let you know."

"As you say," she said, and a worried look filled her eyes as she watched him leave the room.

Jeanine sat on the patio and read to Gar until bedtime, finally managing to ease some of the heartache the scolding had brought him; then, after tucking him into bed, she went to the classroom, using her preparations for the next day as an excuse to stay out of everyone's way. It had been bad enough facing Griffin Heywood again when they'd sat down at the dinner table. Tonight she certainly didn't want to bump into him in one of the halls, with no one else about.

After making sure everything was set for morning, she shut the last book, blew out the lamp, plunging the room into darkness, and left the desk, sauntering over to the window at the back of the room, where she could look out over the patio. She didn't want to leave the room. It had become a refuge for her the past few weeks. Whenever she wanted to be alone, avoiding the rest of the family, she'd slip off to the schoolroom with the excuse that she had lessons to get ready or papers to grade, and nobody bothered her. She was safe here, alone.

The moon was just coming up over the trees, and she folded her arms, remembering the moon last night, and once more a flood of desire melted through her.

Suddenly, as she stared off beyond the patio into the flower garden, a movement caught the corner of her eyes, and she turned toward the French doors to the parlor just in time to see Rhetta slip furtively through them, then lift the skirt of her pale lavender dress and start making her way through the myriad of flowers toward the shadows behind the stables and carriage house. Jeanine squinted, trying to see better in the darkness, wondering what she was up to, then held her breath in surprise as a man stepped briefly from the shadows behind the carriage house, just long enough to grasp Rhetta's hands. Then the two of them melted into the dark shadows, where it was impossible to see anything anymore. She wondered: Jarrod Vance? Or was she perhaps having an affair with one of the ranch hands? Could it be?

She was staring out the window, trying hard to sort it all out in her mind, when the door behind her opened, and she turned, startled.

At first Griff didn't see her standing at the back of the room, but the movement as she turned caught his eye and he stepped inside, closing the door firmly behind him, letting the moon coming in the window behind her serve as their only light.

"I was wondering where you were hiding," he said, adjusting his eyes to the darkness as he walked toward her. He was wearing his buckskins again, and they made his presence even more overpowering.

"I wasn't hiding," she lied softly.

"Weren't you?"

"No."

"I wouldn't blame you if you were." He hesitated, staring down at her, forcing his feelings to stay with the train of thought that had brought him to her. "I came to thank you," he said quickly, trying to keep his perspective.

She frowned, puzzled. "For what?"

"For not telling anyone what happened."

"Oh?"

"I mean about the men jumping me." This time he was embarrassed and uncomfortable because he too knew there was a great deal more than the attack not to tell anyone about last night. "I'd rather no one knew about those men," he went on. "It'd only worry everyone unnecessarily." He took a deep breath. "I also want to apologize."

He sensed her discomfort, but had to go on. "I shouldn't have done what I did last night," he said, his voice lowering intimately. "It was a terrible position to put you in. I don't know what came over me. I had no right . . . Can you forgive me."

Her eyes fell before his steady gaze, and she blushed profusely. "There's nothing to forgive," she mumbled softly.

"Isn't there?" He reached out, his hand beneath her chin, forcing her to look up at him. "Why do you always make me feel like this?" he suddenly asked.

She could hardly breathe. "Like what?"

"Like a tongue-tied schoolboy one minute"—his voice deepened sensuously—"and like taking you to bed the next?"

He hadn't planned to say what he'd just said, and frustrated anger surged inside him, tightening his jaw.

"What is there about you . . . who are you, really?" he asked harshly, and she held her breath momentarily, wishing he hadn't asked.

"Does it really matter?" she answered.

His voice softened again. "Yes . . . it matters to me," he said.

Her heart suddenly leapt to her eyes and she was breathless. "Then who do you think I am?" she asked.

He stared at her, devouring her, his closeness making her head spin. Everything she'd fought against was happening; she could feel it deep inside. The thrill at his touch, the way she melted all over when he was near, the ecstatic leap of her heart every time he spoke to her or walked into a room where she was. She shouldn't have stayed, because as she gazed blatantly into his eyes, she knew she was falling hopelessly in love with him.

For a moment she thought he was going to kiss her, and her lips trembled; but he just stared at her as if searching for an answer to her question, yet not wanting to give it then.

"Damn you and your blue eyes, woman!" he finally blurted, and dropped his hand from her chin. Straightening abruptly, and still looking into her eyes, he stared at her hard for a brief second longer, as if fighting a battle within himself; then he turned and left the room, slamming the door behind him.

She stared at the closed door, her face pale, hands shaking, then turned back toward the window again, looking off in the direction of the stables and the dark shadows where the moonlight couldn't reach. Somewhere out there Griffin Heywood's wife was having a clandestine meeting with another man, yet Jeanine was the one who felt guilty, because she knew now, with a certainty, that she was in love with the woman's husband, and even the knowledge of Rhetta's assumed betrayal couldn't erase the guilt she felt.

During the war, when married men made passes at her, she'd never let it bother her because there was a war going on and it was her job. The men had meant nothing to her. She'd flirted, cajoled, played up to them, done everything except sleep with them, just to learn the secrets they carried, never thinking of her part in their infidelity to their wives, and now suddenly she wondered how many marriages might have suffered because of her actions, and the thought was frightening.

She raised her eyes to the heavens, staring up at the stars, a lump in her throat. "Forgive me, God," she whispered softly, and vowed that it wouldn't happen again. Not if she could help it. It was too late to leave Trail's End, she'd come to stay, but somehow she'd try to avoid Griffin Heywood. If Rhetta Heywood lost her husband, it would be her own doing, not because of something Jeanine did, and she glanced over toward the shadows at the back of the stable, aware only of a slight blur of movement in the darkness that showed someone was still there; then she turned quickly from the window and left the room, heading upstairs to bed. The long weekend that had once promised so much was finally over, and for so many reasons now she wished it had never come.

8

The next two days were hard for Jeanine to get through, but she managed with the lessons somehow. Peggy and Beth were shaping up beautifully as students and were both able to help Gar a great deal with his own work. And in the evenings, when class was over, Jeanine went out of her way to help the twins learn some of the manners and graces they'd have learned had they gone to a boarding school, as well as helping them lose some of the crude manner of speech they'd been used to.

Rhetta still resented her presence, however, and did little to hide it whenever Griff wasn't around. She was nasty and sarcastic, treating Jeanine more like a servant than her son's teacher, and Jeanine, keeping true to the image she'd brought with her of the timid, unpretentious schoolteacher, let her get away with it, even though she hoped and prayed someday she'd be able to get even. Evidently Griff never suspected anything, for when he was there, Rhetta was all sweetness and light, and Jeanine would have given anything to be able to tell him the truth about his precious wife.

Warren was a problem too. He didn't come home until Monday evening, and then it was with the help of friends. And he didn't sober fully until Tuesday afternoon, at which time he proceeded to apologize to Jeanine for getting drunk and passing out. Not only didn't he remember the fight or confronting Homer, but he never mentioned a word about being suspicious of her true identity, but she knew the suspicion was still there. It was in his eyes every time he looked at her, and she made it a point to avoid him as much as possible, the same as she was doing with Griff.

Keep your nose to the grindstone, she kept telling herself. That way you'll keep out of trouble, and she submerged herself in her work, spending more and more time in the classroom and with the twins.

The days went on uneventfully. Then one Wednesday afternoon some weeks later, she had a surprise. When the Kid came back from town with the mail, there was a letter in it for Jeanine. A letter that had been mailed in Raintree. The Kid teased her about it, as did Crystal, and although Jeanine recognized the handwriting and knew who'd sent it, she played dumb, telling them it was probably a note from Nellie Watchek about a dress she'd promised to make for her when she had the time.

In reality, she slipped off to the schoolroom and read the letter she knew was from Homer. He sent instructions for her to meet him at Indian Rock, a place he was sure she'd have heard of by now, and the time was Friday, right after her classes and before dinner. There was no way she could let him know for sure she'd be there without tipping her hand, so she destroyed the note and waited nervously for Friday, hoping nothing would happen to make it impossible for her to go.

By the time Friday rolled around, she was like a coiled spring, tense with wondering what he might have discovered. And after releasing Gar and the twins for the afternoon, she ran up to her room, put on the riding skirt that Crystal had given her, tightened the chignon at the nape of her neck, grabbed the Kid's old hat from the foot of the armoire where she'd thrown it the last time she'd worn it, and headed for the stables, tucking the green shirtwaist she was wearing into the waistband of her skirt.

The Kid was the only one around and she was glad. At that she was going to have to do some explaining, because she'd ridden very little since her arrival. There'd been the day of the picnic with Warren and Gar, and a couple of times with Gar and Cinnamon, but never alone.

"Sorry, Miss Grayson," the Kid said when she asked him to saddle Blossom for her, "but I can't do it."

"Why not?"

"Because Mr. Heywood said not to let you ride alone."

"I'm only going for a short ride," she argued. "What's it going to hurt? I'm not going to steal the horse."

His face flushed. "I know that . . . but my orders—"

"Then I'll do it myself."

"You can't."

"Look," she pleaded, "I only want to ride as far as Indian Rock. I know the way. I've been there with Cinnamon and Gar, and I feel restless and all out of sorts. If I don't get away from here just for a little while, I think I'll go crazy. Please?" she pleaded. "Blossom's an old horse, I won't get hurt." She straightened stubbornly. "And I mean it. I can saddle him myself if I have to."

He hem-hawed around a few minutes longer, then finally gave in. "All right," he conceded. "But mind you, I shouldn't be doin' this."

He went to the corral, threw a rope on Blossom, brought her out, saddled her, then handed the reins to Jeanine.

"But remember, only to Indian Rock," he said firmly, and Jeanine smiled warmly, her blue eyes sparkling behind the wire-rim glasses, making his disregard of orders seem a little more palatable.

"I promise," she assured him, and she turned the horse toward the lane that led to the woods and Indian Rock, nudging the old mare in the ribs, putting her into an easy canter.

The afternoon was sultry, the air dry, and the sun hotter than she'd thought, so it was a relief when she finally rode off the lane onto the path that led through the woods and into the shade. But before going any farther along the trail, she reined Blossom into some bushes where she was screened from the house, and watched just to make sure the Kid wasn't following. When she was certain no one was behind her, she pulled back onto the trail again and took off at a gallop, hoping she wouldn't be late.

Indian Rock was deserted when she arrived, so she dismounted quickly, fastened Blossom's reins to a nearby bush so the mare wouldn't stray, and sat down on a dead log to wait.

She didn't have to wait long. It was only a few minutes later when Homer rode into view, coming upon her from the far end of the lake, having cut across Trail's End property where he'd have the least chance of being seen.

"Hi, pigeon," he greeted as he got down, tethering his horse next to hers. "Glad you got the letter."

"I thought maybe I'd missed you," she said. "I was later than usual, had to change my clothes, and then the Kid wasn't going to saddle a horse for me."

Homer rubbed his seat and stretched, moving his legs stiffly up and down. "I've gotta quit sittin' at that desk so much," he said, wincing. "I've been in the saddle all day and am I sore."

She smiled slightly, watching him limp toward the log where she'd been sitting waiting. "Why've you been riding so much?" she asked as he sat down, sighing, and he glanced up at her, his eyes intense.

"Sit down, I'll explain."

She sat beside him, pulling the hat low on her forehead, shading her face from the sun, since the shade from the hickory tree didn't spread quite to the log.

"Go on," she said. "I'm listening."

"I'd better start at the beginning." He settled a little more comfortably beside her on the log. "You asked me to find out what I could about Rhetta Heywood." He looked pleased. "I had no idea what I was getting into."

"Oh?"

"To start with, Rhetta was rather wild when she was younger, and it seems her first great love was Jarrod Vance. Of course, you have to remember, she was young then, maybe sixteen, seventeen. They were pretty thick until Garfield Heywood came home from college back east."

"Gar . . . ? You mean Griff's younger brother?"

"Young Gar's namesake, right. Seems he and Rhetta were a steady twosome right up to the night he was murdered."

"Murdered?" Jeanine scowled. "Crystal said he was dead, but she never mentioned anything about murder."

"Maybe because they never found out who did it. He was shot in the chest at close range, but the official verdict was death by person or persons unknown."

Her scowl deepened. "Then when did Griff . . . ?"

"Marry her?" He laughed cynically. "That's the catch, pigeon," he said. "He married her barely a month later." He eyed her warily. "Seems strange, don't it? Especially since I've learned that he hardly knew she existed until after his brother was out of the picture. Now, there's some folks think maybe Griff wasn't all that innocent and might have been seeing her behind his brother's back, and fought over her with Garfield, but I think I'd rather chalk that up to jealousy on the part of the tellers, more'n anything else, especially since Griffin Heywood had an airtight alibi the night of the murder. General opinion is that he tried to console her, and the two just happened to fall in love."

"You agree?"

"I don't know." He shook his head, puzzled, then shrugged. "Seems likely, I suppose, but then there's folks who say Griff tried to break Rhetta and his brother's liaison up a number of times while they were going together because he didn't think she was good enough for his brother, called her a gold digger, and voiced his opinion about her reputation more than once to people, and publicly too. Seems strange he'd change his mind like that so soon after his brother's death."

"Then why?"

"Could be he killed his brother, but not over Rhetta, leastways not in a fit of jealousy. I wouldn't put it past Rhetta to blackmail him into marrying her if she knew about it. After all, she'd still have the Heywood money regardless of which Heywood she married."

Jeanine stared off toward the lake, her thoughts trying to

catch up with her reasoning. "I can't believe Griff'd kill his brother," she said, shaking her head. "It just doesn't fit. Besides, you said he had an alibi."

"Well, there's gotta be a reason why he married her somewhere, honey."

"Maybe he did fall in love with her."

"I suppose . . ." He didn't look any too convinced. "He could have, I guess. Crystal and Mrs. Brandt were around then, maybe they know some of what went on. If you could just get them to talk. If anybody knows anything about the Heywoods' private life, it'd be one of them, or even the foreman, McBride. He's closer to Griff than his brother was. One thing I'll say for the Heywood crew, though, they don't gossip. Nobody in town knows anything about what goes on at Trail's End."

"And you expect me to loosen their tongues?"

"You can try. Maybe you can work on Warren."

"Warren? Have you forgotten the dance?"

"I hear tell he didn't even remember anything about it except that he passed out."

"But he's still suspicious." Her eyes hardened. "Besides" —she reached down and picked up a stick, toying with it absentmindedly—"I promised myself I wasn't going to play with people's emotions anymore. It's a deadly game, Homer, and one of these times I'm liable to be the one to get hurt."

He eyed her curiously. "Are you in love with Griffin Heywood?" he suddenly asked, then knew he'd guessed right by the look on her face.

There were tears in Jeanine's eyes. He always could see right through her. "What else did you find out?" she asked, changing the subject, and he sighed. She really didn't have to answer his question. He already knew the answer.

"I thought you might like to know," he said, going along with her. "There are six men who've been hanging around town off and on the past few months, and I've discovered that every one of them works for the Vances. Not on the regular payroll, mind you. I don't think old man Vance knows about them. I'm not sure, we'll have to find out. But that's where I've been all day, watching them. This morning I followed two of them out to an old mine on the Vance property that's been abandoned for years. I stayed long enough to learn that all six of them are staying there. And just before I left, Jarrod Vance showed up. He looked like he was the one who was giving all the orders, too."

"What kind of men are they?"

"Riffraff. Men who wouldn't care what they did for a dollar."

"You think they might be the ones trying to kill Griff?"

"It's possible."

"What about Miles?"

"Who knows?" He shook his head. "All I know is that I'd sure as hell like to find out what they're up to. Doesn't look like they're doing much of anything but lying around most of the time, and nobody pays good money to anybody just so they can lie around." He straightened, wincing a little from his sore muscles, the muttonchops on his cheeks twitching nervously. "Now, what about you? What have you learned?" he asked.

She told him about the men attacking Griff the night of the dance, but left out her intimate scene with him afterward. That, Homer didn't have to know about. "He doesn't want anyone to know," she went on. "And there's something else. The next evening when we got back to Trail's End, Rhetta met a man at the end of the flower garden, and they disappeared behind the stables. It had to have been prearranged."

"You think it was Jarrod?"

"That I don't know, but he's the only one I could think of. I doubt she'd be meeting any of the ranch hands, but I can't be certain. Not with Rhetta Heywood. But if it was Jarrod, they were probably making plans the day before when I saw them at the races."

Homer frowned. He didn't like the way things were shaping up. "I've checked out Heywood the best I could, Jeanine," he said thoughtfully. "The man has no enemies.

At least none that I think would want him out of the way bad enough to murder him."

"What about the drive he's planning?"

"I hardly think that'd be a reason. Most folks don't even think it'll ever come off. Nobody's ever done it before, and chances are nobody will."

"He's certainly determined."

"But that's no reason to kill him. Chances are the drive'll fall apart on its own without help from the outside."

"And if it doesn't?"

"It's too farfetched, Jeanine." He stood up and began moving his stiff muscles, hoping to get all the kinks out.

"Well, someone's trying to kill him," she insisted irritably. "And if it's not because of a personal grudge, it could be because of Rhetta, although if it's Jarrod, it seems strange he never tried it before. He's had years."

"Maybe he hoped Griff wouldn't come back from the war."

"That's possible."

"Anyway, he's been in Mexico for quite a few years." Homer looked pensive. "Besides, I heard tell old Zebediah Heywood hated his son's wife, and the family lawyer, John Scott, told me Rhetta would never have gotten a thing from the ranch if anything had happened to Griff while Zeb was still alive. His will had left Mrs. Brandt to handle Gar's inheritance in case Griff didn't survive the war. Since Zeb's death, Griff hasn't bothered to make a will yet."

"What does that have to do with it?"

"Simple, my dear," he answered. "If anything happens to him now before a will is made out, Rhetta Heywood would have everything her way. Jarrod could have Griff's wife and the ranch too."

"And Gar?"

"That's the nice part. As his guardian she'd control his part of the inheritance too until he came of age, and I'll bet he'd be lucky to see a cent of it by that time." He stood looking down at her. "I guess Rhetta loves her son, from what I hear, but I also learned that she loves money too. Maybe even more. Who knows?''

''Then I think we'd better find out what's going on, and fast.''

He nodded. ''But how?''

''I wish I knew.''

He thought for a minute, taking off his hat, wiping the sweat from his balding pate before putting the hat back on. ''Maybe we can smoke someone out,'' he said hopefully.

''You have an idea?''

''Think you can talk Griff into making a will?'' he asked, surprising her.

''Me?''

''Yes, you.''

''How will that help? He'd just leave everything to Rhetta.''

''That's where you're wrong. It seems that old Zeb's will left everything to Griffin Heywood, all right, but only on one condition, and that is that sometime during the first year after Zebediah's death, Griff has to set up a new will naming Master Garfield Heywood his sole heir, with Mrs. Brandt in charge of administering the estate for him if he's not of age yet when something happens to Griff. In case the will isn't made out during that time, then as soon as the year is up, Griffin Heywood would lose the ranch and Gar would become sole heir, with Mrs. Brandt and/or Griff administering the estate as his guardian. If anything happened to both of them, the lawyer, John Scott, would administer the estate for the boy until he's of age, leaving Rhetta with nothing.''

''Hmmm . . . he really must have hated her,'' Jeanine said. ''But why give Griff a year to set up a will?''

''There was a war going on, Jeanine, remember? It takes time for news to catch up with people, and Zeb had no idea it was going to end when it did. The will stipulated that if Griff was killed in the war, the second part of the will regarding the boy and Mrs. Brandt would become effective. However, Zeb left no instructions as to who would inherit if Griff came back from the war, then got

himself killed during the year before having a will made
out. The word 'war' is the key to this whole thing, I'm
sure. It's an oversight on Zeb's part, but a legal matter that
can work to Rhetta Heywood's advantage."

"Why hasn't he made a will, then?"

"Any number of reasons, I guess. The lawyer was on a
trip north somewhere when Griff got back, and Griff's
been so busy with the ranch. Besides, his main interest is
that Gar inherit everything someday, and he probably figures if he just lets the year lapse, the boy will inherit
anyway. I don't even know if he's aware of the consequences of not having a will. Either that or maybe he
doesn't care if Rhetta inherits a share of the ranch."

"If that's so, then we're right back where we started."

"Not necessarily. Even if he's in love with Rhetta, he
can't leave the place to her—his father's will is specific
about that—and I'm sure he doesn't love her so much he'd
purposely let somebody kill him before he had a chance to
make out a will, just so she could have it all. He's not
stupid. I think maybe he just doesn't think his life's in
danger and hasn't thought much about it." He reached out
and she took his hand, letting him pull her to her feet.
"But he does care for the boy, and maybe a bug in the
right ear might start things rolling," he went on. "It's up
to you, pigeon. Think maybe you can manage it?"

She brushed off her riding skirt and glanced up at him.
"I'll try," she answered halfheartedly. "But I doubt I'll
accomplish much."

"You don't want to see Griff in a pine box, do you?"
he asked.

She looked pensive. "Naturally not, but I have a hard
enough time talking to him as it is. How am I going to
bring up the subject of a will?"

"You'll think of something." He stretched, then put his
arm about her shoulder and they began strolling back
toward the horses. "I'll send word again if I learn anything more," he went on. "In the meantime, don't forget
to see if you can find out if Crystal or Mrs. Brandt knew
what went on when Griff's brother was killed."

"And if I learn anything, how do I reach you?"

"You can't." He squeezed her shoulder. "Not without taking a chance on someone discovering we really do know each other, so just wait until you hear from me."

"I'd better get back before they send someone looking for me," she said, and he helped her onto her horse. "Take care, Homer, please," she cautioned him, and he smiled, patting her hand.

"You too," he said, and she leaned down, kissed him on the cheek, then spurred her horse into a gallop, heading for Trail's End. Seconds later, he too mounted, then rode off in the opposite direction.

That evening at dinner, Griff's chair was empty again, as it often had been since he'd decided to make the cattle drive north.

"I can't imagine what keeps him out there so long," Rhetta said when Gar complained because his father wasn't home yet. "I'm sure, though, dear, that it must be important," she tried to assure him. "Especially since he knows how much you miss him."

Jeanine listened to their conversation, wondering if he was really staying away because he was so busy or if he was staying away because of her. Or maybe he was avoiding his wife. After all, Rhetta wasn't the easiest person to live with, and lately she'd been more sarcastic than ever, and especially with Griff. It was only logical he'd want to steer clear of her sharp tongue, although he didn't seem to let it bother him all that much. In fact, he often snapped back at her, and the fight would be on, making Jeanine wonder what their love life could possibly be like. Explosive? Indifferent? Or maybe it had become a habit after all these years. Who knew? But then, it wasn't really her business, or rather it shouldn't be. Still, she couldn't help wondering.

Griff usually arrived home about half an hour after they finished eating, and ate in the kitchen, with Gar and Crystal's pleasant chatter for company. Jeanine didn't blame him. Tonight, however, he didn't even show up then. Gar's bedtime came and went, and still he wasn't home.

Not surprisingly, Rhetta seemed more irritated than worried, as Jeanine unexpectedly discovered shortly after putting Gar to bed. She hadn't meant to eavesdrop, but had been on the patio reading and was about to come in, when she saw Rhetta and Mrs. Brandt in the parlor.

"I certainly don't know what's getting into Griff lately," Rhetta was telling the housekeeper. "It seems like he's getting more and more irresponsible, especially where Gar's concerned."

The housekeeper was irritated. "You mean because he didn't get home to play checkers with him tonight?" she asked.

"No. Because he promised he would. He shouldn't make promises he knows he won't keep."

"You know he's been busy."

"That's no reason to break a promise."

"I'm sure it wasn't done intentionally," Mrs. Brandt answered. "But he has so much on his mind."

Rhetta watched Mrs. Brandt rearranging some flowers in a vase on one of the stands. "You amaze me, Mrs. Brandt, really you do," she said sarcastically. "I do believe, no matter what Griff did, you'd find an excuse for him, wouldn't you?"

"An excuse?" The older woman quickly thrust a beautiful rose into place in the vase, then glanced over at Rhetta. "I don't have to make up excuses for him, Rhetta," she said. "But if that's how you want to look at it, it's up to you, only Griff's like my own son, and I don't like to see you nagging at him. I think he deserves a little happiness."

"Are you insinuating he's not happy?"

"He's your husband, my dear," she snapped, watching Rhetta fume. "You should know."

Rhetta glared at the housekeeper, her dark eyes narrowing. For a second it looked like she was going to offer a rebuttal, then thought better of it, and lifting her nose in the air, spun on her heel, used one hand to keep the full skirt of her crimson silk from swinging too high, and stalked out of the room.

Jeanine saw Mrs. Brandt shake her head in dismay as she watched Rhetta leave; then the housekeeper sighed and turned back to the vase, making one last adjustment on the flowers before she too left the parlor.

Jeanine had watched the byplay between the two women with interest. Neither of them had seen her near the French doors and she was glad, because it wasn't often she was able to glean such astute knowledge about Mrs. Brandt's feelings. The woman was not only untalkative when Jeanine was around, except about the day's business, but also offered little insight into her personal feelings, whether it had to do with Gar, the house, or anything else connected with Trail's End, and so far her attitude toward Jeanine had been unusually distant.

Afraid Rhetta or Mrs. Brandt might decide to come back into the parlor, and not feeling like talking to either of them, Jeanine changed her mind about going in, and turned, heading back along the patio and flower garden to the French doors that opened into the library. She wasn't tired tonight really, maybe because of the excitement of her meeting with Homer that afternoon. Whatever it was, she felt little like shutting herself away in her room, so decided to stay downstairs after all. There was a lamp lit in the library on the stand behind the sofa, and she turned it higher, then lit another beside the chair where she'd decided to sit. After turning the wick up so she could see better, she found a book to read, then sat down, pulled a footstool over to prop her feet on, and tried to relax. She was wearing a midnight-blue cotton dress with a high neck edged in ruffles, with tight sleeves to her wrists, and she spread the skirt out across her legs, leaning back. Her position wasn't any too ladylike, but then no one was around, so she didn't much care.

It was a little over an hour later when she blinked, suddenly coming back to reality as Crystal came in to lock up for the night.

"Heavens, I thought you was in bed," Crystal said as she stared at Jeanine. "It's close to ten-thirty."

Jeanine realized she'd been doing more daydreaming than reading, and she straightened abruptly in the chair, dropped her feet from the footstool, and tried to look a little more dignified. "Then Mr. Heywood's home?" she asked.

Crystal shook her head. "Not a sign of him yet," she said, and started toward the French doors, then changed her mind. "I left the kitchen door unlocked for him." She looked directly at Jeanine. "Are you planning to stay up some?"

Jeanine nodded. "Yes, I guess . . . for a while. I thought I'd read a little more."

"Good." Crystal motioned with her head toward the French doors. "Then would you mind makin' sure the doors are locked before goin' up? I was gonna lock 'em myself, but it could get stuffy in here for you."

"Don't worry, I'll see to them," Jeanine assured her, and waved halfheartedly in response to Crystal's warm "Good night" as she left the room.

Once Crystal was gone, Jeanine stared at the open French doors for a minute, then sighed, relaxing again, and propped her feet up on the footstool, where they'd been before, once more settling back with the book. Only, again, as before, her thoughts wandered far from the words she was absentmindedly reading. Slowly she let the book fall to her bosom and gazed off into space, not really looking at anything, just staring, then reached up lazily, took off the glasses, and laid them on the stand beside her.

What a relief. For some reason, maybe because of the sultry heat earlier in the afternoon, the bridge of her nose was sore and tender, and it felt good to get the glasses off, if even for a few minutes. She rubbed her eyes, then sighed and relaxed into the chair again, once more trying to read. How long she stayed like that, she had no idea. It must have been fifteen, twenty minutes or even more, it was hard to keep track, but now her eyes were drooping again, the words on the pages blurring, and once more the book dropped to her breast.

Suddenly she heard a man clear his throat and bolted upright, almost dropping the book on the floor. Her eyes widened in disbelief as she glanced quickly toward the open French doors, where Griffin Heywood was standing, leaning against the doorframe, holding his left hand on his right arm just above the elbow. Dried blood covered his left hand and his right shirt sleeve, and fresh blood was starting to seep between his fingers. His boots were dusty, there was dirt all over his buckskin pants and vest, and he looked dog-tired, as if he'd walked for miles.

"Well, don't just sit there gawking, woman, come here," he ordered quickly, ignoring the fact that he'd frightened her, and she slid from the chair, forgetting all about her glasses on the stand, stumbled momentarily over the footstool before catching her footing again, then hurried across the room.

"You're bleeding!" she gasped, staring at the blood oozing between his fingers.

"I know." He was almost too calm. "Come on," he said, and motioned outside with his head.

Her first impulse was to refuse, but something in his eyes, the intensity behind their hard gaze, thwarted any protest she might have made. Even so, she was still reluctant and moved hesitantly at first, following him out to the patio, through the flower garden, and to the back of the house; then they made their way across the small expanse of lawn between the back porch and the carriage house, where he headed for the barn. But instead of going into the main part of the barn, he stopped in front of the door to the harness room and waited for her to open it for them. It was pitch dark inside, and after they'd entered, he gently kicked the door shut behind them.

"There's a lamp to your left hanging on a peg about three steps from where you're standing," he said, his voice barely a whisper in the darkness. "Can you reach it?"

She stepped over and reached up. "I've got it."

"Good. Now, there's a small table to your right, about a step. Set the lamp down."

He waited.

"It's down."

"You'll have to get the matches," he instructed her. "They're in my shirt pocket and I don't dare let go of my arm because I don't have the faintest idea how bad I've been hit. All I know is that it started bleeding again, and this is the only way I can keep it from bleeding all over the place."

He was vaguely visible in the darkness, and she moved over until she was directly in front of him.

"They're in my left front pocket," he offered.

She hesitated for a moment, unable to control a slight trembling inside at the thought of being so near him, and he sensed her reluctance.

"You're not going to back out on me now, are you?" he asked huskily. "I need your help."

She bit her lip nervously, then reached up and began fumbling at the front of his shirt, her fingers searching for the pocket. If he only knew how hard it was for her to touch him. She could feel his muscles flexing beneath her fingertips, the sensation profoundly disturbing, and she was so close that his breath was warm against her forehead, the masculine smell of him affecting her like an intoxicating wine.

Griff held his breath as her fingers probed in the dark, hunting for the matches. The top of her head brushed lightly against his nose, bringing with it the familiar fragrance he'd begun to associate only with this strange woman, and he began to wonder what brand of perfume she wore. Suddenly he wished he'd left her relaxing in the library and roused someone from out at the bunkhouse instead. He didn't need this. He was in enough trouble as it was, although he had to admit he was enjoying the way his body was responding to her nearness. That was the whole damn trouble, though, and had been ever since he'd first met her. He had no right to react this way, with her or any other woman. There was no way, however, that he could deny what she was doing to him, and he tried to keep her from pressing too close, hoping he wouldn't give himself away.

He heard her quick intake of breath as her fingers discovered the edge of the pocket, then began to delve into it, hunting for the matches. The tips of her fingers touched the matches once, lost them, then came up with them again, and she breathed deeply, relieved.

"I have them," she whispered.

"Good girl." His voice was barely audible and he tried to pull his emotions back to a semblance of order, this time sounding somewhat more commanding. "Light the lamp," he said. "Then, under the table there's a washbasin the boys use for soaking leather. Set it on the table."

She was both reluctant and glad to move away from him. Reluctant to lose the quiet intimacy his nearness had brought to her, but glad she was able to retreat from a situation she knew all too well could easily get out of hand, because although he'd tried to keep her from knowing what she was doing to him, she had inadvertently brushed a little too close, and knew he was feeling the same tortured agony she was feeling.

When the lamp was finally lit and the room no longer in darkness, she at least felt a little more secure.

He walked over to a large trunk in the corner. "Come here," he ordered briskly. The trunk was covered with a layer of dust and dirt. "There's a bottle of whiskey in the bottom," he went on when she reached him. "It's under a bunch of leather straps. Get it."

She opened the trunk, rummaging around inside until she found the bottle, raising it high in the air. "Got it." She smiled, looking up at him, and for the first time in days he smiled back at her, that same unnerving smile that always made her feel so warm inside.

"I'm afraid Spider's going to light into Luke when he finds it missing," he said.

She stood up, rather surprised. "I thought you didn't allow the men to drink when they're working."

"I don't, so they've been hiding a bottle in there for years, thinking they're getting away with something. It's usually only a little nip they steal occasionally, so it doesn't really hurt anything.'' He started walking back toward the table, and she followed. ''I'll sure as hell hate to disillusion them, though, by letting them know I knew it was there,'' he said. ''But if they raise too much fuss about it being gone, I might have to.''

There'd been a small glass inverted over the top of the bottle, and Jeanine set it on the table, uncorked the bottle, then lifted the bottle to pour.

''Hey, don't waste it,'' he said, sliding his free hand over the top of the glass, while still keeping his other hand pressed to the wound. ''That's the only disinfectant we have.''

''But it's going to hurt.''

''I've had worse. Here, I'll show you.'' His voice deepened. ''Unbutton my shirt.''

She stared at him but didn't move.

''I said unbutton my shirt,'' he insisted, and his eyes bored directly into hers.

She reached up slowly, gingerly unbuttoning his shirt, and he moved his arm just enough so she could pull it open, exposing his chest. Her eyes narrowed, bewildered at the sight of two deep, ugly scars etched across the soft, curling hairs on his chest.

''It's an old Indian custom,'' he explained briefly. ''I was suspended and whirled from a medicine pole by ropes through my flesh, and compared to that, this feels like a sliver.''

She shuddered. Even in the dim light from the lamp, she could see that the scars were deeply embedded. Without thinking, she reached out and touched one of them, making him tremble as she ran her finger along it gently, wishing she could wipe both of them away.

''Now help me off with the shirt,'' he said, abruptly bringing them both back to reality, and she drew her hand back quickly so he could let go of his right arm just long enough for her to help him pull the shirt sleeve off his left arm. But when she tried to pull his arm out of the right sleeve, she discovered that the blood had dried, sticking the material to his wound, and he winced.

"Rip it above the wound," he said, taking a knife from the sheath at his gunbelt. "Use this."

She slit the material and cut away the sleeve above the wound, then watched as he took the shirt off the rest of the way, then pulled an old chair over, sat on it, and held his elbow down in the basin she'd set on the table.

"It's all yours," he said, glancing up at her expectantly.

"What makes you think I know what to do?" she asked.

"Schoolteachers always know what to do," he said, half-smiling.

She tried to ignore his teasing remark, and picked up the whiskey bottle, beginning to work on his arm. Her fingers moved deftly as she poured on small amounts of whiskey, let it soak into the material, then began loosening it and prying it from the wound. All the while she could feel his eyes on her, taking in every detail as he studied her, and it was making it almost impossible for her to keep her hands steady.

Griff watched the rapid rise and fall of her breasts beneath the dark blue material of her dress as she leaned close, and he knew her breathing was unnaturally fast. Her jawline would first tighten, then relax, her full lips moving easily with the movements of her hands, sometimes curving provocatively, with her tongue barely visible, and he wondered what those lips would feel like beneath his. She was such a strangely sensual woman, and the thought of making love to her sent a thrill running through him that almost made him sigh aloud.

Damn! She had no right to do this to him, he kept reminding himself. He'd promised himself when he'd married Rhetta . . . Damn her anyway! Yet he couldn't keep his eyes from her face. And her hair . . . it was like pale gold in the flickering lamplight.

"How'd it happen?" she finally asked, interrupting his thoughts.

"I was bushwhacked," he said, trying to be nonchalant as she continued working on his arm.

"Your horse?"

"Shot out from under me. That's why I had to walk. Left my saddle back there too."

"Any idea who?"

"Not the slightest. It was too dark."

She began stripping the cloth off slowly, hoping not to disturb the wound too much. "This should be done in the house with soap and water," she said as a piece of the material let loose, and she pried it off with her fingers.

"You're doing fine," he answered, and looked down at the open wound on his arm. "You can check, but I'm sure the bullet went straight through."

He was right, and she began to sponge off both places with the whiskey. "You're lucky." She patted gently at the wound with a piece of what was left of his shirt. "It could have been worse if it had hit the bone. As it is, you'll probably just be sore awhile." She stopped what she was doing. "It's going to have to be bandaged, you know."

He glanced up at her. "I'm well aware of that." His eyes moved to the skirt of her dress. "Are you wearing a petticoat?"

Her face reddened. "What does that have to do with your arm?"

"Well, are you?"

"Yes, but—"

"We need bandages. It'll do better than nothing."

"My petticoat?"

"Don't worry, I'll buy you a new one." He straightened, his elbow still in the basin with the whiskey, red now with his blood. "Look, I don't want anyone else to know about this," he explained quickly. "I'll just tell everyone my horse broke his leg and I had to shoot him. I can pick up my saddle and jacket tomorrow. But for tonight you can get this thing bandaged for me, and no one'll know the difference. You see, someone thinks I'm lying out there on the range somewhere dead, and when I show up tomorrow in town, alive, they're going to be in for a big surprise.''

"You think whoever it is will give themselves away?''

"It's possible.'' He took a deep breath. "Now, about that petticoat . . .''

The flush on her face deepened as she picked up the knife from where she'd set it on the table, then turned her back, reaching up under her dress. She ripped off a piece of her petticoat and turned, facing him again, then tore the material into strips, folding a strip of it into a thick pad and putting it over the worst of the wound, before beginning to wind the rest of the bandage around it.

He watched her closely again, wondering what it was about her that was so different tonight. Her hair wasn't as tight to her head as it usually was, with a few soft ringlets floating about her ears and at the side, but it wasn't just that. Suddenly he tensed, then hoped she hadn't noticed. The glasses! She wasn't wearing her glasses and she was no more blind without them than he was. He was about to mention the fact, then changed his mind when she spoke.

"There, I'm through,'' she said, surveying her handiwork.

He looked it over, pleased that no blood seemed to be seeping through the bandage. "Good,'' he said. "Now you can get me a clean shirt. I don't dare get it myself. Crystal or Mrs. Brandt might be wandering about.''

She stared at him curiously as he went on.

"They're in the second drawer down in the large bureau in my bedroom. I think there should be a light blue one right on top.'' He stopped suddenly, frowning. "What's the matter?'' he asked as she continued to look puzzled.

"But . . . Mrs. Heywood,'' she managed to stammer hesitantly. "What about your wife?''

"What about her?''

"Won't I wake her?''

"Wake her?'' He searched her face for a minute, then suddenly realized what she was talking about, and his face showed surprise. "Oh, I thought you knew,'' he answered softly. "My wife and I don't share the same bedroom,

Miss Grayson.'' He saw the flush on her cheeks deepen to a bright crimson.

"I . . . I didn't know," she blurted hurriedly, more aware now than ever of her folly in being here.

"Well, now you do," he said quickly, then went on. "Go to your room first," he said, hoping to ease their situation to some extent, "to the balcony, then across to the French doors of my room. They're probably open, but if not, use my knife and slip it under the latch. It should give easily, and Crystal's probably left the lamp on the dresser burning low, so you should be able to see. She usually has it lit for me when I'm running late." He picked the knife up from the table, holding it out for her. "The bureau's on the far wall near the bed. Think you can do it?"

She took the knife from him, and their eyes met briefly. "I think so," she whispered softly, then quickly turned away, and without saying another word, afraid she'd make a worse fool of herself, moved to the door and slipped quietly outside, breathing a sigh of relief.

The moon was high as she made her way across the drive, then through the gardens to the library, and once more entered it through the French doors, but all the while her thoughts were running rampant.

In all the weeks she'd been at the ranch, she'd never suspected they didn't sleep together, and no one had ever let on. Now, as she thought it over, she'd never seen Rhetta going in or out of the master bedroom. But where? There were only four bedrooms in the wing where she slept. Hers, Gar's, Warren's, and a guest room opposite Gar's. It had to be in the other wing, where Mrs. Brandt's room was. She'd assumed all the other bedrooms in that wing of the house were for the servants, then remembered that she'd thought the first bedroom on the right was another guest room. It was probably Rhetta's.

She stopped abruptly just inside the doors to the library, trying to control the pounding of her heart. She mustn't be foolish now. Just because they slept in separate bedrooms didn't mean a thing. Lots of people slept in separate bedrooms. There was no reason to jump to any wrong conclusions. She straightened, forcing her mind back to the task she had to do, then started to cross the room, when her eyes fell on the stand next to the chair where she'd been sitting.

My God! She stopped, hands flying to her face, and her heart sank. Her glasses! All that while she'd been out there in the harness room with him without her glasses on. A sickening feeling gripped her as she slowly moved to the stand and picked them up, staring at them in disbelief. Damn! What must he be thinking? She sighed. Or had he even noticed? He hadn't said anything. Oh, Lord! Saying a quick prayer that he hadn't realized what she'd done, she put them back on, adjusting them onto the bridge of her nose, and inhaled stubbornly. Well, all she could do was hope, and she finished crossing the library, heading for the hall that led to the foyer and the stairs.

She managed to reach her bedroom without seeing anyone, and moved out onto the balcony without having to light the lamp, then went across the balcony to the master bedroom. He'd been right. The doors were open and the lamp on the dresser was turned low; it was the first time she'd ever been in his room, and she took a second to gaze about. It was more like a sitting room, with a fireplace and chairs at one end, the bed on the north wall, and it was definitely a masculine room. She moved to the bureau, finding the blue shirt right where he said it would be, then left, going back downstairs the way she'd come.

She'd been gone only a short time, but it had been long enough for Griff to clean and empty the basin, put away the empty whiskey bottle, throw out his bloody shirt, and he was standing waiting for her.

She opened the door to the harness room and quickly darted inside.

"Did you see anyone?" he asked as she leaned back against the door trying to catch her breath.

She shook her head. "No, no one."

"Good."

She held the shirt and knife out to him. "Here."

He slid the knife back into its sheath, then put the shirt on, buttoning it up, tucking it into the top of his buckskin pants. She watched intently, remembering what it had been like when she'd searched for the matches, and the intimacy between them as she'd cleaned and dressed his wound, and she wondered if he had been as aware of her as she had been of him.

After making certain his clothes were straight, he made one more check to be sure everything was the way it had been when they'd come in, then put his hand about the chimney of the lamp and blew, plunging them into total darkness again.

Jeanine held her breath. She could hear him walking toward her, and instinctively moved to one side, away from in front of the door.

"We'd better go now," he whispered from only a few inches away, and she pressed hard against the wall behind her.

The door opened inward and he moved sideways, directly in front of her, holding the door open barely a crack, just enough to let a stream of moonlight in.

"I'll wait until I see the light in the library go out before going in," he whispered. "In case anyone's up and about. You go first when I give the signal." He looked down at her. The pale shaft of moonlight streaming in through the crack in the door was on her face now, and he inhaled sharply. She looked so lovely, all soft and ethereal, and he was so close.

Jeanine stood motionless, poised, waiting for him to tell her to leave, yet all too aware that she didn't want to go. Then suddenly his body brushed hers in the darkness, their eyes met and held, and it was as if the whole world stood still while they were lost in each other. Then slowly she felt his arm circle her waist.

Her lips parted and she caught her breath to protest, but he drew her even closer, and she could feel her heart pounding in her ears.

"Jeanine!" he sighed, his voice low and vibrant. He spoke only her name, but it was enough to make her tremble inside. "You don't need these," he went on huskily, and reached up, removing her glasses. "You never did," and he folded them deftly, then shoved them into his shirt pocket.

She started to speak, but the words were muffled against his mouth as his lips came down on hers, soft and yielding at first, then more demanding. He held her close, his hunger for her growing as he kissed her, and all the longing of the past few weeks broke inside Jeanine, awakening long-dead feelings. Feelings denied herself for too many years. She melted against him, letting his lips possess hers completely, letting his hands mold her to him, running up and down her back desperately as they kindled the fires of passion in both of them that had lain dormant for all too long.

His lips left her mouth briefly, and he murmured her name over and over again, letting his lips brush her neck, his breath hot against her flesh. Then, groaning helplessly from deep inside, his mouth captured hers once more, and Jeanine wanted to cry out from the sweet pain that coursed through her.

Griff was all too aware of her body yielding beneath his hands, her lips like soft hot velvet, and he felt himself hardening. He shuddered deep in his loins. My God! He'd never felt like this before in his life with any other woman.

Suddenly he stopped kissing her, and buried his face between her neck and shoulder, once more breathing the sweet fragrance that seemed to surround her, and he pulled her even tighter into his arms. At that moment he wanted her more than he'd ever wanted any other woman before, yet knew it was sheer folly. Somehow he had to get himself under control again. If not for his own sake, then for hers.

"Oh Lord, Jeanine," he moaned against her ear. "I'm sorry, forgive me."

Her hands were on the back of his neck, her fingers softly caressing, her lips brushing his skin just above his shirt collar, warming him clear through, and she felt as if she'd explode inside.

"Forgive you? Oh, Griff, what's there to forgive?"

Her voice was sweet to his senses, soft, inviting, and he knew if he didn't do something and do it quickly, everything would be lost. Without warning, he reached up, grabbed her arms, roughly prying them from about his neck, then thrust her from him.

Jeanine tried to cry out, but nothing came as he turned his back on her and walked away, losing himself in the darkness of the harness room, while she stood motionless, the pain of his sudden rejection instantly plunging her into depths of despair. Her hands were shaking and tears rose to her eyes. She wanted to die. Her lips were trembling as she finally found her voice. "Griff . . . ?"

"Go in the house, Jeanine," he commanded huskily, not daring to even look her way. "Please, just go in."

"But . . . what did I do wrong?"

"Nothing . . . just go!"

She could hardly believe what she was hearing, and clutched her arms about herself where his arms had held her only moments ago. Her whole body was still so alive, so full of longing, and her voice was barely a whisper.

"Then why?"

"Dammit, go!" he yelled across the darkness that separated them, and there was no way she could see that his eyes were pressed tight while he fought the natural instincts of his body. All she knew was that he didn't want her. Griff stiffened, waiting, then cursed silently to himself. Dammit, why didn't she go? He'd take her right here and now if she didn't leave, and he knew it. You could fight a thing just so long.

Thankfully, yet guiltily, he finally heard a soft cry from behind him, more like the cry of a wounded animal, and when he turned, it was just in time to see her slip through the partially open door. Quickly he moved toward it, opening it a little farther, and watched, his heart heavy with longing, as her lone figure moved across the drive.

Jeanine ran blindly toward the house, eyes flooded with tears, unaware that while Griff watched her unhappily from the harness room, another pair of eyes was also watching her from behind a curtain in one of the upstairs bedroom windows.

Rhetta Heywood stood motionless behind the curtain in her room and watched Jeanine disappear into the house, then turned her eyes once more to the harness room, and a few minutes later her eyes narrowed as she watched her husband emerge from the same doorway and make his way toward the back kitchen door. As she watched them, engrossed, her fists clenched, face whitening with rage, and she swore under her breath, eyes sparking dangerously. Then, a few minutes later, her mouth set with determination, she finally left the window and slipped back in between the cool sheets of her big empty bed.

9

Jeanine closed the door to her room and leaned back against it, letting the tears fall freely. She should have listened to her common sense the day she arrived, and never stayed. Now it was too late. She took a deep breath, straightened, and stared across the room toward the open French doors. Well, standing here feeling sorry for herself wasn't going to help.

She lit the lamp on the dresser, then began to undress, wiping the tears from her eyes, determined that she wasn't going to let what happened ruin things for her here. After laying her underthings on the chair near the window, hanging her dark blue dress back up in the armoire, and slipping on a pink lace-trimmed nightgown, she reached up to unfasten her hair and froze. My God! She'd done it again, but this time the glasses were in Griff's shirt pocket, and she'd left him standing alone out in the harness room. How on earth was she going to get them back?

She touched the bridge of her nose where the glasses usually rested, then shrugged. There was nothing more she could do tonight, that's for sure. She'd have to get them tomorrow somehow. She finished unfastening her hair, letting it fall down onto her shoulders, took the brush from the dresser, and blew out the lamp, then sat on the edge of the bed in the dark, toying with the hairbrush nervously, her body still trembling.

It was going to be so hard to forget, and she wondered if she'd really ever be able to. She remembered so clearly the way his arms had held her, and the strength of his mouth against hers. If only the hunger inside her could have been fulfilled.

She reached up absentmindedly and tossed the long flaxen hair from her shoulders to her back in disgust, cursing General Sheridan for sending her here. Of all the men she'd known, why did she have to pick Griffin Heywood to fall in love with anyway? Why couldn't she have picked a man who didn't already belong to someone else? And that was another thing. Just because Rhetta didn't share the same room with Griff was no proof whatever that they didn't share the same bed occasionally.

She sighed and finally began brushing her hair, letting her thoughts wander while tears once more collected in her eyes.

Then, after a few minutes, she suddenly straightened, alert, the brush dropping from her hair. Glancing toward the balcony from where she'd heard a slight noise only moments before, she caught sight of a lone figure silhouetted in the moonlight, and there was no mistaking who it was. She took a deep breath, starting to get up.

"No, don't come near me, please," Griff said roughly when he saw her stirring. "Just stay there, Jeanine, and don't move," he pleaded softly. "Because if you were close enough to me again so I could take you in my arms, I might never let go this time, and we'd both be sorry."

He hesitated, but only momentarily, then stepped into the room and walked over, setting something on the dresser. "Your glasses," he explained, his voice husky with emotion. "I figured you'd want them for morning."

She found her voice, only it was shaky. "Thank you," she whispered.

He'd been hoping she wouldn't answer, and yet welcomed the sound of her voice in the quiet room. Straightening slowly, he turned from the dresser, hoping he could force his eyes to ignore her, but it was impossible. The moonlight that had made her only a vague shadow just moments before was now bathing her all over with its misty glow, turning traitor once more to Griff's feelings. How could he possibly ignore someone who looked so lovely?

Her hair was falling loose about her shoulders, her thin pink nightgown barely concealing the fullness of her breasts where it hung low in front, and her face, sprinkled with the tears she'd been trying to conceal, was devoid of all illusions. This was the woman he'd seen beneath the glasses, behind the facade of unpretentiousness she'd let the rest of the world see, and his eyes fell on her hungrily, drinking in the sight. She was like something unreal, and he was drawn to her as if he had no will of his own.

Without realizing how he'd gotten there, he suddenly found himself standing before her, and with only a slight hesitation, he reached down, took the brush from her hand, and tossed it aside on the nightstand, then leaned down, gently lowering her onto the bed, his own body stretching out beside her. He was partially on his stomach, gazing into her eyes, and there was no need for words between them. Slowly, reverently, he lowered his head, first kissing away her tears, his tongue lightly claiming them, leaving her cheeks burning where it had touched, then his lips caressed her mouth lightly, and she felt a wild elation seize her.

"I didn't mean to make you cry," he whispered softly, his lips against hers. "Oh God, Jeanine, I didn't mean to make you cry."

She reached up, her fingertips smoothing his hairline. "I know," she murmured, and he trembled. "I guess I cry too easily."

"No." His hand molded itself to her cheek and he drew back, unable to take his eyes from hers. "You have every right," he went on softly. "Only I wish I could take the tears away, but I can't, and that's what hurts." He leaned down and kissed her again, more deeply this time. "You know what's happened, don't you?" he said, his voice low, hushed, his mouth close to hers.

She searched his face.

"I've fallen in love with you, Jeanine," he went on. "And I can't seem to help myself."

"No, you can't," she cried softly. "I won't let you."

"It's too late." He kissed her again, this time devouring her lips fervently, as his yearning for her began to overwhelm his reason. His hand moved from her face to her breast, easing beneath the filmy cloth of her nightgown, and as she parted her lips, letting him taste the promise of what was to come, his hands began to coax to the surface the passion she'd been hiding.

She moaned ecstatically, twisting and turning eagerly beneath his hands, accepting his caresses, until suddenly, as he raised his head and leaned back, sitting up at the edge of the bed, his hands fumbling at the buttons on his shirt, a spark of sanity tore its way into her heart, and she let out a soft cry.

"No!" she begged, reaching out, grabbing his hands to keep them from finishing their task. "I can't, Griff. It's no good," she gasped breathlessly. "It's not right. I can't."

He stared at her, feeling the strength of her hands keeping him from unbuttoning his shirt the rest of the way, and a sickening feeling tore through him. He wanted her so badly it hurt, yet . . .

His eyes searched hers. It'd be so easy to make her change her mind. There was love in her eyes, and surrender so close to the surface, but he couldn't ignore her plea. She'd become so very special to him. A bright light in a life of regret. If he forced her to give in to her emotions now, when her conscience cried so hard against it, she'd only become another reason for regretting.

Slowly his hands turned beneath hers and he clasped her fingers, covering them, holding her hands close against the heat of his body, where his shirt was only half-buttoned.

"You're right," he whispered, his voice raw with emotion. "Damn, I know you're right, but how do I tell myself to stop feeling?"

"You have to . . . we both have to," she pleaded. "I can't give myself to you, Griff. I just can't," she went on.

"Rhetta would always be in the way . . . I could never live with that."

He held both her hands in one of his, and reached out with the other hand, touching her face, his fingers wiping away a tear that had formed at the corner of her eye.

"If only . . ." he began. Then his hand cupped her face, his eyes darkening with a mixture of anger and defeat. Anger at himself for letting this happen after all these years, and defeat at the knowledge that there was no way he could change the way things were. "You drive a hard bargain, Miss Grayson, ma'am," he said softly. "One I'm not sure I can keep."

"It's one you'll have to keep," she answered softly. "Because I won't play the whore."

"You think I'd ask that?"

"Not in so many words, no, but that's just what I'd be as your mistress, and I'll have no part of it."

He released both her hands and stood buttoning his shirt as he walked over and stared out the open window on the wall next to the French doors. His body was aching from want of her, and his heart felt as if it was trying to survive a whirlwind.

Breathing deeply, he tried to still the violent emotions racing through him, but it wasn't all that easy.

"All right, you win," he finally said after a few soul-searching moments. "I'll promise to try to keep my distance, but I won't give you any guarantees. I can't."

He turned, facing her, wishing he could die to ease the torment. She was sitting on the edge of the bed again, only she had pulled the brocade bedspread up around her like a shawl, no doubt hoping to discourage him. It did little good.

"I'm sorry, Griff," she said tearfully. "I wish—"

"I know," he interrupted curtly, then took a deep breath, straightened stubbornly, and forced himself to turn from her, walking toward the French doors. When he reached them, he turned once more, staring back to where she huddled on the edge of the bed, the moonlight still playing in her hair. Oh, how badly he wanted her, needed her, but there was no way.

"Good night, Jeanine," he murmured huskily, and without waiting for an answer from her, he turned, stepping onto the balcony, and melted into the dark shadows outside.

Jeanine stared after him for a long time, the tears falling unchecked down her cheeks. Then slowly, as if in a trance, she drew her feet from the floor, curled up on the bed, buried her face in the pillow, hugging it close to her, and cried herself to sleep, wishing she'd never come to Trail's End.

The next day was impossible for Jeanine. In the first place, her eyes were red and puffed from crying most of the night, and she had a hard time trying to make up excuses for them. And to top it off, there was no way she could avoid running into Griff. It was Saturday, with no classes, and it was the first Saturday he hung around the house all day. He didn't seem too worried about retrieving his saddle and jacket from the night before, either, but busied himself working on ledgers and entertaining Gar, and just knowing he was in the house made her nervous. He too seemed to be exceptionally edgy, and more than once she heard him snap at Rhetta with little provocation on Rhetta's part, and there were also moments when he was even short-tempered with Crystal and Mrs. Brandt. When Jeanine was in the room he was even worse.

She wished she could run and hide, but it was impossible. She couldn't run from herself or him, and every time their eyes met, it was like a shock running through her clear to her toes, and if he was forced to speak to her, his voice cut through her like a two-edged sword, bitter yet sweet. She fought to stay calm in his presence, but wasn't succeeding too well, which was quite evident at the lunch table when she passed a dish his way and his hand happened to touch hers. She almost dropped the dish, catching herself just in time. But he knew, and she knew he knew as his eyes studied her blatantly, the naked desire in them all too evident, and she flushed profusely, self-consciously looking around to see if anyone else was watching. No one was. Mrs. Brandt was talking about something with Rhetta, and Warren and Gar were laughing over a tale Warren had just finished telling the boy.

For Jeanine, however, the moment was shattering, and it was all she could do to fight back the tears, and for the rest of the meal she was in misery. Even that evening at the dinner table, her food seemed to stick in her throat, and she wished she could crawl under the table.

It was later that evening, shortly after dinner, when Jeanine finally happened to remember what Homer had said about the will. And after remembering, she thought back over the past evening, more constructively this time, trying not to think of the part that hurt so badly, but only the first part of the evening, when Griff had appeared at the library door wounded. It was all too evident now that Homer was right. Someone wanted Griff dead, and wanted him dead now, when there was no will to be contested. But there was no way she could bring the subject of a will up with Griff. She'd have to think of something.

Later that evening as she sat in the classroom pretending to go over some papers, using it as an excuse to be away from the others, she suddenly thought of a way that might work, and a few minutes later she'd joined Mrs. Brandt in the library.

As usual on Saturday evenings, the housekeeper was at the desk going over household accounts and paid little attention when Jeanine wandered in. She only nodded, greeting Jeanine briskly. Jeanine mumbled a quick hello and moved to one of the shelves, hunted for and found a book, then sat in the big armchair where she'd sat the night before, pretending to read.

Her back was to Mrs. Brandt and she'd glance back furtively now and then, hoping to be able to pick a good time to interrupt her, only Mrs. Brandt kept right on, busily working.

Time went on and Jeanine continued to stall; then finally, as she turned again, once more glancing at Mrs. Brandt, she saw the housekeeper set her pen down and

lean back in her chair, relaxing a bit. Well, it was now or
never, and it might be the only chance she'd get.

Jeanine set her book down and stood up, walking over
to the straight-backed chair that was set to one side of the
desk.

"Mrs. Brandt, may we talk?" she asked, surprising the
older woman, and Mrs. Brandt straightened, frowning,
then motioned for her to sit down.

"What is it?" she asked.

Jeanine lowered herself onto the chair, folding her hands
demurely in the lap of her dark green cotton dress. As
usual she felt uncomfortable under the housekeeper's scrutiny. "I hope you don't mind," she began, "but I've been
rather worried."

"Worried?"

"Yes, about the trouble here at Trail's End," she explained. "Every time I ask about it, though, no one seems
to want to tell me anything, and just changes the subject."

Mrs. Brandt closed the ledger on the desk in front of
her, then folded her hands firmly on top of it as she stared
at Jeanine. "Who told you we were having trouble?" she
asked, her mouth tightening.

Jeanine shrugged self-consciously. "Oh, everyone.
Warren, Mrs. Heywood, the people in town. I've heard
remarks here and there."

Mrs. Brandt's eyes were steady on Jeanine. She had
liked this young woman from the moment she'd met her.
She seemed young, wholesome, and quite intelligent, and
most of all Gar liked her. It wasn't until she'd seen Griff's
eyes sifting over Jeanine possessively, and seen the strength
of character that lay beneath the soft, deceptive facade
Jeanine presented to the world, that she'd begun to have
reservations about hiring her. She was certain now that
there was more to Jeanine Grayson than what showed on
the surface, that she wasn't the innocent young schoolteacher she'd thought her to be at first, but a woman
who'd seen more of life than most women dared. Still, she
couldn't seem to help liking her in spite of all the misgivings.

"Just what does the fact that we might be having trouble have to do with you?" she asked curiously.

Jeanine fidgeted a little. "Well, I am part of Trail's End now, and if anything happened to the ranch or Mr. Heywood, I'd be out of a job, wouldn't I?"

"What makes you think something might happen to Mr. Heywood?"

Jeanine flushed. She couldn't tell Mrs. Brandt about last night, yet had to tell her something. "Crystal and Cory are both worried," she answered, hoping she could get her point across. "I've heard them mention it a number of times. And since I am a part of the household, I think I have a right to know what's going on. If payrolls have been robbed and men killed . . . I'd hate to think my life might be in danger too."

"It isn't."

"But how can you be sure? And what's going on?"

Mrs. Brandt took a deep breath. "I wish I knew, Jeanine," she answered seriously, and her eyes dropped to her hands as she unclenched them, then stood up. She walked to the side window and glanced out, as if watching some faraway scene. "All we know is that ever since Mr. Heywood came back from the war, we've been having one problem right after another. He thinks someone's trying to stop the cattle drive he's planning for next spring. Let's face it"—she turned back to Jeanine—"if it's successful, we've won a battle, not only for Trail's End but also for the rest of the ranchers in Texas. If not, then Miles Vance has an idea he can waltz right in here and take over."

"Then you think that's all it is . . . someone trying to stop the cattle drive?"

"What else would it be?"

Jeanine shrugged. "I don't know. I thought maybe . . ."

"Well, what is it? Don't just hem and haw," Mrs. Brandt said abruptly. "If you have any idea, if you've seen anything we haven't seen . . ."

"Not really," Jeanine said, stalling for more time. How was she ever going to bring up the matter of the will? Well, maybe she could pretend to just blunder into it.

"But I do remember Crystal telling me that Mr. Heywood was supposed to have been carrying the payroll that was robbed, and that the man carrying it was killed, so I guess I was just thinking that something might happen to Mr. Heywood with all that's going on, and if it did, it might affect my staying here. But then"—she tried to look a little less sure of herself—"I guess there wouldn't be any need for me to worry, really, would there? I mean, Mr. Heywood probably has a will, and even if something happened to him, Mrs. Heywood would no doubt keep me on here to teach Gar." She sighed. "At least I'm hoping she would. But then"—she glanced furtively at Mrs. Brandt—"she might decide to send the boy back east. What do you think?" she asked.

Mrs. Brandt had been listening closer to Jeanine than she'd planned, and now suddenly she was brought up short. "What was that you just said?" she asked abruptly.

"I was wondering what you thought."

"No . . . not that," she replied. "I mean about a will."

"A will?"

"Yes. You said Mr. Heywood probably has a will. What did you mean? What do you know about a will?"

Jeanine frowned. "I . . . I don't know anything," she stammered, pretending innocence. "I just assumed that he has one."

Mrs. Brandt's eyes hardened. "I only wish he did," she said, and came back to the desk. She opened the ledger again, then straightened, turning once more to Jeanine. "He never made one before going into the army because his father was still alive, and he hasn't taken time since he's returned," she informed her almost absentmindedly.

"Then if anything happened to him . . . ?"

Mrs. Brandt gazed off toward the fireplace, a faraway look in her eyes. If anything happened to him, she thought to herself, that bitch would control everything and Gar would end up the loser. If anything happened to him . . . ? Good Lord, was it possible? Could Crystal and Cory be right? But it didn't make sense. Still . . .

"Mrs. Brandt," Jeanine said rather timidly, "is anything wrong?"

"Wrong?" She drew her eyes from the fireplace and once more looked at Jeanine. "No, my dear, nothing's wrong," she answered as if distracted for a moment, then pulled herself together again and took a deep breath. She sat down at the desk again and picked up the pen. "Now, if you don't mind, I do have work to finish, and . . . Oh yes," she went on in her usual brisk manner, "don't worry yourself over Trail's End. I'm sure the answer behind everything is the roundup and drive next spring. There's nothing for you to fret over. Mr. Heywood will handle it. Now, if you don't mind, I really must go over the household accounts."

Jeanine knew there was no use saying anything more. She could only hope it had been enough to set the housekeeper to thinking.

"Not at all," she said. "I'm sorry, I didn't mean to bother you," and she excused herself, went to the chair where she'd been sitting earlier, picked up the book she'd been pretending to read and put it back on the shelf, then quietly left the library as Mrs. Brandt once more began concentrating on the ledger in front of her.

Jeanine stood just outside the library door for a minute, contemplating where to go. She didn't want to go to the parlor. Griff was in the parlor playing checkers with Gar while Rhetta sat on the sofa embroidering. And she didn't want to go to the kitchen because she knew Crystal and the twins hadn't really believed the story she'd told them about why she'd looked so miserable this morning, and she didn't feel like answering any more questions. She could go back to the schoolroom, but there was nothing to do there really except sit at the desk and stare at the walls. About the only other alternative was to go to her room. Peggy and Beth had been teaching her how to knit, and she could prop herself up in bed and work on the scarf she had started, until she got tired enough to sleep.

After weighing her final option against the few other alternatives she had, she decided her bedroom and the knitting sounded like the best idea, but just as she reached the foot of the stairs, she ran into Griff and Gar. She'd completely forgotten that it was close to Gar's bedtime, and now she stared at the two of them apprehensively.

"Oh, there you are," Gar said warmly as he smiled at her. "We were wondering where you were, weren't we, Pa?" he said, looking up quickly at his father, and Griff nodded reluctantly.

"Yes, son, we were." His eyes met Jeanine's, and as usual, his heart quickened anxiously. She was wearing a deep green dress, and looked lovely tonight, but then she always looked lovely, and he remembered the way she'd looked last night with her hair flowing onto her shoulders. He cursed silently to himself. God! How was he going to forget? It was maddening. He hadn't wanted this. Not at all.

"I was doing some reading," she said. "But Mrs. Brandt's trying to work and I'm afraid I was disturbing her."

"She's in the library?" Griff asked, his voice a little harsher than he'd intended it to be.

Jeanine felt a sharp pain shoot through her chest. "Yes," she murmured, wishing he wasn't so angry with her, yet knowing it couldn't be helped.

He glanced down at Gar. "Would you mind too much if Miss Grayson took you up tonight, son?" he asked. "I have to see Mrs. Brandt about something important."

Gar squeezed his father's hand. "It's all right, Pa," he said. "We have all day tomorrow."

Griff glanced at Jeanine. "Do you mind?"

"Not at all."

He leaned down, kissed Gar and gave him a big hug, then watched the two of them ascend the stairs before turning and heading for the library.

Mrs. Brandt was still sitting at the desk and had just closed the ledger when Griff walked in.

She glanced at him sharply. "Oh, good, I was just going to start looking for you," she said, "There's something we have to discuss."

"First I'll have my say," he said, eyes glistening dangerously.

"Oh?"

"I want you to write to Phil Sheridan."

Her eyes hardened, and she stared at him, puzzled. "You want that now?"

"More than ever."

"But why?"

"I have to know for sure, that's all," he answered.

She leaned back, eyeing him curiously. "Why don't you ask her yourself, Griff?"

"Will you write to him or shall I?"

She shook her head. "All right, I'll write," she conceded. "But it won't change your feelings for her either way, and you know it."

"I don't have any feelings for her!" he stated angrily, and stalked over to the French doors, where he stood with his back to her, staring out.

Mrs. Brandt's eyes narrowed as she saw the stubborn set of his shoulders, and knew she'd guessed right.

"I'm not blind, Griff," she said anxiously. "Nor is Rhetta."

He whirled on her. "She means nothing to me!"

"If you say so." She watched him closely.

"And I'm not sending her away just to please Rhetta, either," he retorted.

"Then you'll regret it." She stood up, leaning forward on the desk. "She'll ruin your life, Griff. If she hasn't already," she said boldly. "If you didn't already have a wife, it wouldn't matter, but you can't keep her under the same roof with you. It isn't fair to you or her, and you don't dare get a divorce. You know that. The scandal would ruin everything." She tensed. "Send her away, Griff, please," she pleaded.

"I can't."

"You'll have to." She walked around the desk to face him squarely. "Let me tell you something, Griff," she said, determined to make him listen. "You probably should have been told years ago, but that's beside the point. The important thing is that I'm telling you now. When I married Jessup Brandt, it was to leave an unhappy home, not for love, although we got along well, and he was good to me. When we settled here, your father and Jess became close friends, and when Jess was killed saving Zeb's life, your parents took me in. I was grateful for that, Griff, more than you can ever imagine, but to this day, I know I should never have come."

Her usually stern face softened slightly, the lines of age and sorrow etched indelibly on it, now overshadowed by a warmth in her eyes that was rarely seen.

"Griff, I'd been attracted to your father even while Jess was alive, and I never should have entered this house," she went on. "It was only a short time later that I realized I was hopelessly in love with Zeb, and unfortunately, he eventually fell in love with me too. Zeb was like you, Griff, strong and virile. You do him proud. I had no hopes, though, of ever becoming his wife, because your father, although married to a woman who despised him, was afraid to get a divorce. I know you learned about your mother long ago, Griff, otherwise I couldn't tell you this, although I know you've probably guessed as much."

He stared at her intently. "But why didn't you and Father . . . after Mother's death?"

"Why?" She wrung her hands, then rubbed her arms nervously. The air had a nip in it. "For the same reasons you won't get a divorce," she answered. "Your mother's scandalous behavior was bad enough for your father to try to live down. If people had learned about us, your father was afraid they'd only say your mother had reasons for her infidelity. That the love we had for one another drove her to other men's arms, and Zeb couldn't bear that." She paused a moment, the memories almost too painful to bear. "I loved your father all those years, Griff, yet shared nothing with him as his wife. I should have left, and sometimes I hated him for not sending me away, because look what I am now, a bitter old woman." She reached out and grabbed his forearm. "You can't bring scandal on the Heywood name now, Griff, please," she pleaded.

"For your father's sake, and his memory, you can't let anyone learn the truth about Garfield and the rest of it, and if you tried to divorce Rhetta, she'd tell the whole world why you married her, and you know it. But you can't do what you're doing to that young woman, either. Send her away, please, Griff. Forget her. Put her out of your life. You owe Rhetta that much."

"I owe her nothing."

"Your brother, then!" Her hand moved higher on his arm and she gripped it tighter. "Please, Griff, you owe it to your brother and Gar!"

Suddenly she realized there was something bulky beneath his shirt sleeve. Her eyes caught his. "What's this?" she asked abruptly.

He glanced down to her hand on his arm. "It's nothing, really . . ."

She grabbed his wrist, her fingers tightening. "Griff, show me!"

He sighed, eyeing her sheepishly, then unbuttoned the sleeve, rolled it up, and showed her the bandage.

"Last night?" she asked.

"Someone took a shot at me."

She frowned, the pieces suddenly fitting together. "And Jeanine knows about it?"

"How did you know?"

She nodded knowingly. "That's why," she said, then realized Griff had no idea what she was talking about. "Jeanine was in here earlier and hinted that you might be in danger, and she was talking about a will," she explained quickly. "I think maybe she was trying to warn me without coming right out and saying something."

"I made her promise not to tell."

"Why?"

"Because someone doesn't expect me to show up in town tomorrow, and when I do, they're in for a big surprise." He rolled his sleeve back down, fastening the buttons. "But what's this about a will?"

"It just happened to come up in our conversation."

"She knew about it?"

"Oh no. I'm sure not, but you should get that will made, Griff," she went on insistently. "You know the stipulations in your father's will, and if anything did happen to you now, without a new will being made Rhetta'd bleed this place dry before Gar got old enough to fight her." She was emphatic. "And I'll write to Phil Sheridan too, if that's what you want."

He stared at her hard for a minute as if contemplating, then straightened deliberately. "Never mind," he said bitterly, feeling defeated. "I don't really care anymore who or what the hell she really is," and he turned, stalking from the room, Mrs. Brandt's eyes following him, and she wished again, as she had so many times over the years, that he could have been her son.

Upstairs, Jeanine tucked Gar in, then leaned over and kissed his forehead. "Tomorrow's Sunday, so get a good night's sleep, young man," she said.

He stared at her as she straightened again, then gave his covers an extra little pat here and there.

"Miss Grayson?" he said as she turned to blow out the lamp on the dresser. "May I ask you somethin'?"

She gazed down into his hazel eyes. He was such a delightful boy. Mischievous at times, but always trying to please. "What's that?" she asked.

He patted the edge of the bed. "Could you sit down here?"

She smiled at him, then sat down, waiting patiently.

His face crinkled into a frown and he seemed rather embarrassed for a minute, then began to talk. "You're . . . you're not going to leave us, are you, Miss Grayson?" he asked suddenly, and she was taken quite by surprise.

"Leave you?" This time it was her turn to frown. "What made you ask that?"

"Mama said she was going to ask Pa to have you leave," he answered innocently. "Of course, Uncle Warren told her not to and they had a big argument about it because he told her he has reasons for wantin' you here, only it ain't none of her business."

"Your uncle said that?"

"Uh-huh . . . but I know what his reason is. It's 'cause he likes you, I know. So you see, I told you you could be his purpose."

"Oh, Gar," she said fondly, and reached out, touching his cheek, hating to have to disappoint him, but knowing she couldn't let him go on thinking his attempt at match-making would work. "I only wish I could be your uncle's purpose in life," she said. "But you see, I don't love him, and I don't think I ever could. I'm sorry."

"Are you already somebody else's purpose?" he asked.

She shook her head. "No."

"Then I'm gonna pray you change your mind," he said stubbornly. "Because Uncle Warren really needs some-body."

"If you wish," she answered reluctantly, not wanting to shatter his dreams completely, knowing he was a sensitive boy. "But for now, I think you'd better get that sleep so you'll be bright and fresh in the morning. And I won't leave Trail's End unless I absolutely have to. In fact, I'll consult with you first on the matter if it ever comes up. How's that?"

He nodded. "I'd like that," he said quickly, and turned over, settling down comfortably. "Good night, Miss Grayson."

"Good night, Gar," she whispered softly, then blew out the lamp and left the room. Once in the hall, she stood for a minute staring toward where the faint light from the lamp on the stand outside the master bedroom illuminated the balcony, her thoughts going over the boy's conversation.

Out of the mouths of babes . . . hmmm . . . So Rhetta Heywood was trying to get rid of her. Why? Jealousy? Maybe. Even though she was obviously having an affair with someone else, and Jeanine was sure that someone else was Jarrod, that didn't mean she wouldn't still try to hang onto her husband. But then there was no way Rhetta could know about last night, so why would she be jealous? It was more than likely that she just didn't like her, and wanted to keep her away from Warren. What a mess.

Ah well, she couldn't change what already was, all she could do was try to make the best of it, and as she walked down the hall, entering her own bedroom, prepared for a lonely evening of trying to master the intricacies of knitting, she prayed with all her might that somewhere, somehow, there was an answer for all that was happening.

10

It was late the next evening, Sunday, at dinner that Jeanine learned her conversation with Mrs. Brandt had been worthwhile. The Heywoods had gone into town in the morning and returned for dinner as usual, and they were almost through with the meal when Warren strolled in. He'd left for town early Saturday night and was just returning home, only this time he wasn't drunk, although he had been drinking. Jeanine could always tell when he'd been drinking, even a small amount. Not only were his eyes bloodshot, but he was always argumentative and sarcastic with the people around him, as if he enjoyed hurting them.

"Well, well, cozy little party we have here," he said flippantly as he entered the dining room, pulled a chair up, sat down, and pulled the bell cord, asking Crystal to bring him a plate.

"It's about time," Rhetta said, eyeing him disgustedly as she fingered her napkin. She hated his drinking. "And where were you today anyway?" she asked. "I didn't see you in town."

"Oh, but I saw you, dear sister," he answered slyly. "Don't worry, I saw you."

Her face reddened. "Now, what is that supposed to mean?"

"Wouldn't you like to know." He smiled sheepishly.

"And I saw Brother Griff too." His smile twisted wickedly as he began filling the plate Crystal brought him. "Visiting your lawyer, Griff?" he asked casually.

"I stopped by John's place, yes," Griff answered. "But I'm afraid he's out of town. The will's going to have to wait again, I guess."

"The will?" Warren laughed cynically. "You mean you finally remembered you're supposed to make one?" He glanced at Rhetta. "How does that stick in your craw, dear sister?" he asked.

Rhetta's eyes narrowed. "Shut up, Warren!"

"What's the matter, Rhet," he said, watching his sister closely. "Don't you like being reminded that you'll never be mistress here?"

Her chin tilted up defiantly. "I never expected to be," she answered haughtily. "After all, I didn't marry the ranch, Warren, contrary to your nasty opinion. I married Griff. I could care less who owns or runs Trail's End."

"My word, spoken like a devoted wife. Bravo, my dear, bravo!" he chided. "You deserve an award for that performance."

"For heaven's sake, Warren," Griff cut in irritably. "There's no reason to be so sarcastic. Besides, I'm sure Miss Grayson isn't interested in listening to your petty little remarks."

"Aha!" Warren turned to Jeanine, who'd been trying to be as inconspicuous as possible. "Speaking of Miss Grayson," he said, and began searching his pockets, "that little boy at the hotel, what's his name . . . Jasper, he gave me a letter to give to her," and he pulled an envelope from his pocket, turning it over so she could see the back. "If you'll notice carefully," he went on, waving it in front of them dramatically, "the seal hasn't been tampered with, and the contents are still intact. That was one of the conditions of delivery. The other being to hand it to you personally, mamselle," and he handed it to Jeanine with a flourish.

She took it gingerly and stared at it. Her name was written on the outside, but the handwriting wasn't Homer's. She frowned, continuing to stare at it, making no attempt to open it, while she wondered who could have sent it.

"My goodness, the lady gets a letter from a mysterious admirer and acts like it's a death sentence," Warren quipped.

Jeanine blushed. "What makes you think it's from an admirer?" she asked.

"Well, I don't think you're in love with me, darlin'," he answered, smiling. "So there must be someone else," and Griff, who'd been watching Jeanine's reaction, saw her face fade from scarlet to a sickening white.

"I think you've said enough for one evening, Warren," he said quickly. "Now, either keep your mouth shut or leave."

Warren glared at Griff for a full second, as if he wanted to say something more, then glanced down at his plate, thinking better of the idea. But a smirk still played around the corners of his mouth as he began concentrating on his food.

"Well, if you'll excuse me," Jeanine said uncomfortably, and she stood up, then turned to Gar beside her, who'd been having a hard time following the adults' conversation while he ate his dessert. "When you're finished, Gar, come to the library," she said, "and I'll read you that story I promised." Then she looked over toward Warren. "Since Mr. Granger thinks my letter's from an admirer, then it's probably best I read it in private," and without giving anyone a chance to comment further, she pushed back her chair, turned, and left the room.

Gar swallowed the piece of pie he'd been chewing, then reached over and tugged at his father's sleeve.

"Yes, son?" Griff asked.

The boy's eyes saddened. "Pa, Miss Grayson's admirer won't take her away from us, will he?" he asked innocently. "I wouldn't want that."

Griff glanced quickly at Rhetta. Her eyes were smoldering angrily as she waited for his answer, and he could think of nothing else to say except, "No, I'm sure he won't, son. At least not for a while." He patted the boy's head affectionately, wondering himself whom the letter could be from.

Jeanine could hardly wait to read the letter. Only it turned out not to be a letter, but a short note stating that if she wanted incriminating information regarding the trouble at Trail's End, she was to be at Indian Rock Monday afternoon at five o'clock. It was signed simply "A friend."

She had no idea who'd sent it. A friend of Homer's? But then, no one knew she knew Homer. Unless there was someone else in town besides Homer and Warren who'd known her before. It was a possibility, if only a vague one. She frowned as she sat at the schoolroom desk reading it over again to herself, studying it carefully. Then again, maybe Warren wrote it himself so he could get her off somewhere alone. She shrugged, sighing. Well, she'd have to chance it. Trap or no trap, she'd never know if she didn't go, so tucking the letter into the side pocket of her skirt, she headed for the library to keep her promise to Gar.

Jeanine thought Monday afternoon would never come. Griff left the ranch early in the morning with Cory and some of the men to check on the water holes and ride out onto the range to see how things were going; then they were going to head into town on business later in the day.

Griff was doing a good job of concealing his wounded arm, and Jeanine noticed he was favoring it very little as she stood at the back door watching him and the men ride out. She'd purposely stalled coming down for breakfast, waiting until she saw them all out by the barn, so she could avoid running into him. She liked Crystal's pleasant chatter in the mornings but could do without Griff's presence to remind her of the hopeless situation she was in.

The day went as usual for Jeanine, although her anxiety made her nervous. Then shortly after classes were over, she once more found herself down at the stables dressed for riding, wearing the same clothes she'd worn on Saturday, right down to the Kid's old hat with the hole in it. The Kid wasn't around this time, though. He'd gone with

Griff and Cory. This time Spider was the one she had to convince about knowing what she was doing.

And he did give her a problem at first; however, once he knew she'd saddle a horse for herself if she had to, he was a trifle more obliging.

"You're sure now that you know the way?" he asked again as he turned the horse over to her.

"I told you I did," she insisted. "Now, please, don't worry. I'll be all right, and I won't be gone long either. I'm only taking a ride to Indian Rock, and it isn't all that far. And yes, I know it'll be getting dark soon," she added quickly, anticipating his next remark.

Spider shook his head, muttering something about stubborn women, then smirked as Jeanine swung into the saddle. She may look like a timid little lady, he thought to himself, but danged if she don't have a bit of piss and vinegar in her, and he was still smiling inwardly to himself as he watched her heading old Blossom down the lane toward the woods on what she told him was just a casual ride so she could relax.

She reached Indian Rock about half an hour earlier than the specified time and climbed down, tethering her horse where it had been before when she'd met Homer. No one else was in sight yet, so she walked to the edge of the lake and stared in for a while, then went back near her horse again and sat on the log she and Homer had used, letting the events of the past weekend filter through her thoughts, trying to find a reasonable solution for her dilemma.

Suddenly a twig snapped behind her, and she started to turn, when a rough male voice cut her off, and she froze.

"Don't move one more muscle," the voice said, and she heard the distinct click of a gun's hammer being cocked. "There's a gun pointin' right at your head, little lady," he went on, "and I ain't squeamish 'bout killin' women. Now, you just sit tight!"

She wasn't about to move. Whoever it was certainly wasn't bluffing, and she figured he must have been hiding behind a thick outcropping of bushes just beyond the rock in order to sneak up on her as quietly as he had.

"Now, stand up nice and easy with your hands away from your sides," the voice ordered.

This was ridiculous, insane! What did he want with her? If she could only catch him off guard she'd at least have a chance, but it was impossible, because as she heard him move up directly behind her, she also realized he was being joined by more men. She could hear the rhythmic clomp of horses' hooves, squeaking leather, and furtive mumbling.

She stood up as ordered, arms held out, then almost protested, but changed her mind as her hat was knocked off, her glasses snatched from her nose, a blindfold slipped over her eyes, and a gag tied across her mouth. This done, the same voice ordered her to turn around and walk.

Now for sure she knew there were at least two of them, because the hands pushing her were too close to belong to the voice giving her the order.

"Here's your horse. Git up!" the voice said, and she fumbled about, trying to reach the reins. They wouldn't let her, however, and instead she was boosted from behind, and set firmly in the saddle.

"Hands in front," the gruff voice went on, and she held her wrists together reluctantly while someone wound a rope around them and secured them to the saddle horn. Her heart was racing and she tried to scream, but with the gag on it sounded ridiculous, like an animal whimpering.

"Shut up!" the voice said, and she quit trying to protest, not sure what the man might do if she didn't.

The note had been a trap, all right. But who? Why? Warren was stubborn and could be vindictive, but he'd never resort to something like this.

She could hear movement and scuffling about her; then suddenly the horse beneath her began to move forward, and her world became a living nightmare. She had no idea where they were going, and being blindfolded as well as gagged, there was no way she could even watch for any landmarks. All she could do was listen for something, anything that might help, while the fear of what lay ahead held her on the edge of terror.

She'd been in bad predicaments before, but never anything like this. Slowly, as time went on, she realized the only way she was going to get through this was to stay calm and not panic, and that meant using her head. She began to remember what Homer had said about the men on Vance's payroll, and listened more intently, trying to count the voices. There were at least six, maybe more, and she tried to keep track of them as best she could.

At first they didn't talk too much, but the longer they rode, the more they began to say to each other, throwing gibes back and forth occasionally, and talking about incidents some of them had shared in the past, sometimes laughing over them. Maybe they were taking her to that place Homer had told her about on the Vance property, she began to think as they rode along. It was the only thing she could think of really, yet this whole thing just didn't make sense.

Then suddenly a new fear began to grip her, and she tensed as she realized that a few of them were seasoning their conversation with vulgar remarks and talking about what they could do with her, given the chance. She cringed, terrified at the thought, and prayed that their ideas would stay nothing more than just talk.

Time passed and still they kept moving. Her wrists were blistered and chafed from the rough rope, and she was stiff and sore from so long in the saddle. At first she had felt the late-afternoon sun on her face, and its warmth had felt good, helping to still some of the fear inside her. But as the hours rolled by, the sun descended, and the fear she'd been managing to keep under control during the past few hours once more began to take hold of her.

It was cooler at night now since it was late fall, and without a jacket she began to chill badly. Her kidnappers didn't seem to notice, however, and tears welled up in her eyes beneath the blindfold. She didn't even have the Kid's hat anymore. They'd tossed it aside on the ground back at Indian Rock, along with her glasses. She was tired, cold, humiliated, and hurting all over from being so long in the saddle, yet the only time they stopped was once, so she could relieve herself. Even then she wished in a way they hadn't taken the time, because it was a degrading experience for her, since the man with the gruff voice accompanied her. Her hands were freed momentarily for the task, but the blindfold and gag stayed in place, and then she was once more put on her horse and secured to the saddle horn. Her one consolation was that it was dark, and she hoped the others had been unable to see her while they took care of their own needs.

Now, as she wondered how much longer they were going to keep riding, she pressed her arms closer to her body for warmth, but it did little good and she inhaled sharply, the musty scent from the rag tied over her mouth almost making her sick. If she could only sleep, but that too was impossible.

As the night wore on, the cold seemed to penetrate every bone in her body, and she grew so tired and weary that she kept nodding, almost falling from the horse. Then she'd vaguely remember that her wrists were tied to the saddle horn and jerk her head up again, straightening, only to undergo another mile or more of torturous riding.

It wasn't until what seemed like hours later, when she finally felt the sun beginning to slowly warm her head and face again, that she realized morning had come. The men had quit talking as much during the night, and so far no one had bothered to mention anything about it being daylight. But there was no mistaking the feel of the warmer morning breeze against her face as the temperature began to rise and the sun started beating down on her bare forehead.

Leaning back and shifting her weight in the saddle the best she could, she suddenly hesitated as one of the men broke the silence and she heard Jarrod's name mentioned, only to hear an abrupt, ''Shut up!'' follow it, from the gruff voice. Again there was silence as they moved along, the only sound that of the horses' hooves against the dry dusty ground.

She guessed from where the sun seemed to be hitting her the hottest that it was perhaps close to noon when her horse was finally pulled to a halt, and she felt someone untying the rope from her saddle horn, and seconds later, her wrists still fastened together in front of her, she was dragged from the saddle. Her legs started to give out when her feet hit the ground, and she suddenly felt strong hands grasping her shoulders, helping to hold her up.

"You suppose maybe we oughta give her some water?" someone asked, and she heard the creaking of leather and spurs jingling, figuring the rest of them were dismounting too.

"Won't hurt, I suppose," the voice said from close to her ear, and Jeanine's legs were trembling as she felt someone else fumble at the gag that was covering her mouth.

Moments later the gag fell free, and she tried to move her mouth, slowly at first, getting the circulation back in her jaw muscles. Her jaws were stiff and sore, and felt as ridiculously weak as her legs had at first, but after a few seconds they began to feel normal again, and now she felt a flask shoved roughly against her lips. As the water trickled onto her dry tongue and into her mouth, she never thought anything could taste so sweet, and even though her wrists were still tied together, she tried to help whoever was giving her the water, lifting her hands, trying to tilt the flask higher. The water was cool, only it hurt to swallow at first; still she relished every drop.

"Hey, go easy with it," the voice cautioned from close to her ear again. "That's gotta do you all the rest of the way back, you know."

"Hell, Burke," the man who was obviously holding the flask said. "She ain't had nothin' since we grabbed her. It's a wonder she ain't passed out on us already."

"It's your water," the voice answered, and now Jeanine felt the flask being drawn from her mouth, water dripping sloppily onto her chin, and she dragged her arm across her chin, wiping it clumsily.

She swallowed hard and tried to force more strength into her wobbly legs. "Why are you doing this . . . why did you kidnap me?" she managed to mumble as whoever had been helping her stand up began shoving her toward some unknown destination.

It had to be the voice, because he answered her gruffly while she stumbled along.

"You don't have to know why, lady," he said. "All you gotta know is to do what you're told."

"But . . . this is insane," she protested. "Where are you taking me . . . what are you going to do . . . where are we?"

"You hear that, boys?" the voice called sharply as Jeanine's forward progress was stopped by a slender tree. "The pretty little thing wants to know where we are." She felt the man fumbling with the ropes at her wrists again, and sighed, realizing he was tying her to the tree trunk. Then she felt a hand on her back and tensed, holding her breath. It began to move sensuously to the base of her spine, then back up again, stroking lightly between her shoulder blades. "Well, let's see now," the voice went on as the hand continued massaging her back. "We're someplace between Trail's End and the Comanche, wouldn't you say, boys?" and he was answered by a few straggly affirmatives from the others.

She straightened, exhaling apprehensively as the hand on her back stealthily moved to the nape of her neck. Her first instinct was to kick at him, but common sense told her the gesture would be futile. Now, don't get scared, she kept telling herself. But she was already so scared she was trembling inside.

"What are you going to do with me?" she asked again, her voice unsteady.

The man's hand dropped from the nape of her neck to her buttocks, and Jeanine held her breath, cringing, as he gave her buttocks a quick firm grasp before letting go.

"I know what I'd like to do with you," the voice said. "Only there ain't no time."

"Why ain't there?" one of the others piped in. "We should get somethin' for losin' a night's sleep."

" 'Cause I said there ain't." The voice was firm.

"It wouldn't take long, Burke." It was the other man again.

"I said no. It's near high noon, and Cheroot said the war parties usually head out early. That means one might be reachin' the pass right about now. So if you don't hightail it outta here right away, you're gonna miss 'em, and this whole thing'll get botched up."

"But why me?" It was the same man again.

" 'Cause you know the language, that's why."

"But . . . a war party . . ."

"Hell, you're a half-breed, ain'tcha? That oughta count for somethin'."

Jeanine heard the other man grumble something unintelligible, but the voice went on.

"Tell 'em you're a friend of Cheroot's, then tell 'em we got a guest we'd like 'em to take off our hands. See if you can get one of 'em to come back with you."

She heard the man make a couple more attempts at protesting, then give up and ride out. Everything was quiet for a few minutes while the rider's hoofbeats faded in the distance. Then a different voice cut the silence.

"We still got time while he's gone, Burke," the new voice urged expectantly.

Jeanine was still wearing the blindfold, yet she could sense that the man with the gruff voice was still close enough to her to touch her, and she waited, dreading what might happen next. However, his answer surprised her.

"Time? How long you think he's gonna take?" he asked. "An hour? He'll be back in less than half that time, and I ain't gonna get caught with my pants down, and neither is nobody else. Besides, they ain't gonna want somebody who's half-dead, and by the time you boys got through with her, that's just what she'd be. Now, get your minds on somethin' else and forget it."

"But, Burke—"

"Shut up!"

Again there was silence, and now Jeanine suddenly felt her body relax and she slid down the trunk of the tree until she reached the ground. It was hard and gravelly, but at least she could lean against the tree trunk, and she listened intently to the sound of boots crunching, thanking God as she realized the man they called Burke was joining the others a few feet away. Inhaling deeply, she relaxed, relieved, and everything grew quiet again while they waited.

About twenty minutes must have gone by when she heard the voice grunt, there was a scuffling of boots again, and she tensed.

"Hot damn!" the voice said anxiously. "He made it back, and there's one of 'em with him."

She heard boots grating on the ground again as someone, and she assumed it was the voice, walked in the direction toward where she could also hear horses approaching; then all she could distinguish was a lot of mumbling. A few minutes later the boots came back, in her direction this time, and someone began untying her, then grabbed her arm and pulled her to her feet, dragging her toward where she'd heard the approaching horses. They still hadn't removed the blindfold, and she stumbled a number of times over the uneven ground before finally being jerked to a stop and told to stand up straight by the voice, who also added, "Sorry, lady, but this is where we part company," and she was suddenly shoved forward again; then she heard the boots moving back in the direction they'd just come from, leaving her standing alone.

Her hands were still tied in front of her, and she knew she'd been in the shade before, because now she could feel the hot sun on her face again. Straightening stubbornly, not knowing what to expect, she took a deep breath, then felt the hair at the nape of her neck rise. A clear sweet odor assailed her nostrils and she breathed in deeply again, just to make sure. There was no mistake. At first she hadn't recognized it, but then, as the familiar scent surrounded her, she suddenly realized what it was.

Gar had told her that his father said the Comanche used spicewood to cover themselves and their belongings with, and he had let her smell a piece of it that he kept in his drawer as a sachet. The scent was a strong one, not easily forgotten, and that's what she was smelling now. There

was only one logical reason for her to be smelling spicewood, and she bit her lip nervously as she heard the creak
of leather behind her, then the sound of hoofbeats, and
knew the men who'd brought her here were riding off.

She held her breath, waiting, listening as the pounding
hoofbeats faded in the distance. She wanted to pull the
blindfold from her eyes, but was afraid to. Sweat broke
out on her forehead, and she could hardly swallow as she
waited for something to happen. Whatever it was, it couldn't
be any worse than what she'd already been through. At
least she hoped it wouldn't be. Determined to keep from
panicking, she held her head up courageously as she stood
waiting in the hot sun.

Once the sound of hoofbeats was gone, everything became so quiet Jeanine would have sworn she was alone. A
bird twittered somewhere nearby and she heard the faint
rustle of a breeze stirring the leaves on the tree she'd been
tied to. Other than that the dark world around her was
silent.

Then suddenly she heard a grunting sound, and the
unmistakable scrunching of sandy dirt and gravel. Once
more she tensed, then felt the blindfold being loosened. It
dropped from her eyes and she stood motionless, then tried
to open them, slowly at first because the sun was blinding
and she'd had the blindfold on for so long. At first she
couldn't see anything; then, as she blinked her eyes and
they began to adjust, she felt a sickening dread come over
her as she found herself staring up into a pair of dark sloe
eyes that stared back at her curiously.

She had never been this close to an Indian before. A few
had wandered into Raintree occasionally but she had seen
them only from a distance. This Indian was barely a foot
from her, his steely eyes watching her from a painted face
that looked grotesque. He was naked from the waist up,
and his chest had the same scars on it she'd seen on Griff's
chest, only they were almost hidden under a number of
huge medallions that reached almost to his waist. Blue-
black hair, plaited with colorful strips of cloth and feathers, hung past his shoulders, and he wore leggings

ornamented on the sides with tufts of feathers and more medallions. He was an impressive yet frightening sight, his powerfully built muscular body bronzed and toughened from the sun.

The hair at the nape of her neck prickled as he continued to stare down at her for another few minutes; then he reached out curiously and touched a strand of her long blond hair as if the sight of it was something new to him. Her breathing was light and shallow while she waited to see what he would do.

After a few minutes more of inquisitive scrutiny, he suddenly straightened proudly, took a deep breath, grabbed her arm roughly and dragged her over to where the men had left Blossom tied to a cottonwood tree, and without further ceremony lifted her up as if she were weightless, depositing her in the saddle. Then he grabbed her horse's reins and headed toward his own horse that was standing ground-reined waiting for him. Reaching down, he snatched his horse's reins from the ground, leapt easily onto its back, and still without having said one word to Jeanine, dug his horse in the ribs and took off with Blossom and Jeanine in tow, heading away from the grove of cottonwoods into the hills to the northwest.

It was half an hour after dinnertime, and dark already, when Griff strolled into the kitchen at Trail's End after leaving Cory out in the barn to put away his horse for him. He carried a package under his arm and was whistling, but stopped abruptly, frowning as he caught sight of Crystal. Her face was pale and she looked upset.

"What's the matter with you?" he asked, realizing she seemed relieved to see him.

"I thought you'd never get home." She wrung her hands together. "We can't find her nowhere, Griff," she said. "She just ain't around."

"Who isn't?"

She swallowed hard. "Miss Grayson, Jeanine . . . she's gone!"

"Gone?" His own face paled. "Where?"

"That's just it. We don't know."

At that moment Mrs. Brandt came in. "Thank God," she said. "I thought I heard you out here."

"What's all this about Jeanine being gone?" he asked, making no attempt to cover for using her first name.

Mrs. Brandt shook her head. "It's nothing, I hope. But Gar's crying so. She didn't show up for dinner, and Rhetta said she was probably resting in her room. But she's not there, and she's not in the classroom. We've searched the whole house and can't find her."

"Have you looked outside . . . the barns, stables?"

"Not thoroughly."

He tossed the package he was carrying onto the table, then headed back outside, onto the small back porch, calling for Cory, who showed up a few seconds later at the barn door.

"Tell the men I want a search made," he yelled roughly. "Miss Grayson's missing. I want her found!"

"My, my," Rhetta said sarcastically from behind him. "Such a fuss over one little old governess."

Griff whirled, eyes narrowing as he caught sight of Rhetta standing in the doorway between the kitchen and dining room watching him.

She sauntered the rest of the way into the kitchen. "No doubt she had a rendezvous with her gentleman friend from town," she went on. "You know, dear, the one in the letter she got on Saturday. She's probably enjoying herself at our expense. I wouldn't put it past her."

"Did it ever occur to you that she might be hurt?" he asked.

"Hurt?" She laughed. "From what I've seen of Miss Grayson, she can well take care of herself. Besides, how could she possibly get hurt, and why should you care if she did?"

"I care because she's another human being, but then that doesn't mean anything to you, does it?" He glared at her. "You know, sometimes I wonder if you even have the capability of caring for another human being besides yourself. Do you?"

"I don't care about her, I can tell you that," she answered, her lips tightening angrily. "I don't care whether she's hurt, dead, or what. I've had enough of Miss Jeanine Grayson, and I just don't care!"

"Well, I do!" He stared at her hard for a moment, then turned without saying another word and left, heading for the barn.

Rhetta watched him go, her eyes blazing. "You'll be sorry," she muttered softly. "You'll see, Griffin Heywood. You'll be sorry you ever laid eyes on that woman," and she turned abruptly, going back into the dining room, letting the door swing back hard in her wake.

Crystal watched Mrs. Brandt as the older woman's eyes followed Rhetta from the room. Even though Rhetta had half-whispered the words, as quiet as the kitchen was, both women had heard her, and Crystal wondered what Mrs. Brandt must be thinking. Although neither woman had mentioned it, both knew Griff's feelings for Jeanine were anything but platonic and Crystal was certain now that Rhetta had also come to the same conclusion. She was about to ask Mrs. Brandt if she had any idea what Rhetta was mumbling about, when Cory bounded up the back steps and stuck his head in the door.

"We're headin' for Indian Rock, Crystal," he said hurriedly. "Spider said he saddled a horse for her late this afternoon, and she headed that way."

Crystal stepped out onto the porch, with Mrs. Brandt standing in the doorway behind her, while Cory joined Griff and the men out by the barn, and the two women stood watching solemnly as they rode off, their torches lighting the darkness as they moved in a long line down the back lane toward the woods.

"If Jeanine's out there, they'll find her," Mrs. Brandt said, remembering the determined look on Griff's face when he left the kitchen.

Crystal nodded. "I hope you're right."

But two hours later, the men rode back in, tired and empty-handed.

"I want you to pack me a bedroll, Crystal," Griff

ordered curtly as he entered the kitchen, slamming the door behind him.

Crystal had seen the men ride in and had been waiting apprehensively. "You didn't find her!"

"No, but I think I know where she is."

He started toward the door to the dining room, when she stopped him. "Griff?" she asked, pointing toward the table. "What am I supposed to do with that?"

He stopped for a second, staring at the package he'd tossed there earlier, and a bittersweet pain filled his chest. He shivered, his eyes softening. "It's a petticoat, Crystal," he said, his voice strained. "Take good care of it for me until I get back, will you?" and he turned abruptly without giving her an explanation for his strange request and left her standing in the kitchen, puzzled, as he went on up to his bedroom and began changing into a full set of buckskins.

A faint knock on the door interrupted him as he slipped on his fringed shirt, and when he opened the door, Gar was standing there, his face streaked with tears.

"Crystal said you didn't find her, Pa," he said timidly. "Was she right?"

Griff stooped down, resting his hands on Gar's shoulders. "That's right, son, I didn't," he answered softly. "But I will."

"You know where she is?"

"I think so."

"Then you'll bring her back?"

"If I can." He pulled the boy to him, hugging him hard. "Believe me, Gar," he tried to reassure him, "if there's any way possible, I'll bring her back."

Gar pushed himself away so he could look into his father's eyes. Both their eyes were filled with worry, and Gar's were filled with tears. "You like her too, Pa, don't you?" he asked innocently.

"Yes, Gar, I like her," he replied.

Gar sniffed. "I knew you did," he went on. "I only wish Mama did. She said she hopes you never find her. That's not right for her to say that, is it, Pa?" he asked.

Griff touched Gar's cheek, brushing a tear from it, then kissed him. "Your mother's just a little confused, son," he said, trying to make amends for Rhetta's cruel remarks. "I'm sure she doesn't really mean it," and he gave him another hug, wishing Rhetta hadn't said anything to the boy. Then he released him, straightening abruptly, telling him not to worry and to go back to his room. After the boy had gone, he slipped back inside the bedroom and finished putting on his buckskins.

His moccasins made no noise as he hurriedly left the bedroom and descended the stairs, but as he walked across the foyer, heading toward the dining room, Rhetta spotted him and called from the parlor.

"Griff?"

He stopped, retracing the last few steps, and stood in the doorway.

She frowned. "Where are you going?"

He stared, studying her. He had to admit she was really, truly beautiful with her dark hair soft and shining, the dusty-rose dress she wore tonight revealing her ripe, graceful body. She was woman enough for any man with her sensuously seductive mouth and dark eyes. Too bad he knew the true woman behind the deceptively perfect facade she showed to the people in Raintree. This was the woman he'd married, the woman he'd promised to love till death do us part, and there was a bitter taste in his mouth.

Her eyes narrowed, sparking dangerously when he didn't answer.

"You're going after her, aren't you?" she asked, and her voice trembled slightly.

"What do you expect me to do, pretend she doesn't exist?" His eyes darkened. "You'd like to see the Indians get their hands on her for what you think she did to Warren, wouldn't you?" he accused.

"No!" Her jaw clenched stubbornly. "Not for what she did to Warren," she shot back. "But for what she's doing to you."

"Me?"

"I'm not blind, Griff, I know what's going on," she

said bitterly. "She comes out here pretending she's so innocent, wearing those dowdy old clothes. She's that spy, and you know she is. She's really Jeannie Gray," she went on. "She's ruined Warren's life, and now she's ruining mine."

"Yours? You ruined your own life years ago, Rhetta, when you seduced my brother," he answered stubbornly. "Don't go blaming her."

"You'll never forget that, will you?" she cried. "You'll never forget or forgive."

"How can I when I'm reminded of it every time I look at Gar?"

Rhetta moved gracefully across the floor until she stood in front of him, her dark eyes lustrous and eager, mouth sensuously alive. "Don't do this to us, Griff," she pleaded softly. "Please . . . we could have such a good life together . . . it'd work out, I know it would." Her mouth raised to his. "Why don't you accept it . . . I'm your wife, Griff, your wife . . . please, I want to be treated like a wife."

His face darkened as he stared at her, knowing she'd try every trick she knew to stir him, just like always. Just like she'd been doing every chance she had since he'd come home. But it wasn't going to work.

"You'd like that, wouldn't you?" he said angrily, and reached out, sinking his hands into her fancy hairdo, twisting her hair violently, making her wince. "You'd like me to give in just once, wouldn't you, Rhetta?" he said. "You'd like me to carry you to bed and sink myself into your lecherous body, wouldn't you, but I won't. Never, do you understand? No matter how hungry I am for a woman, I'll never touch you, so you might as well give it up. I told you years ago, you can have my name, use my money, and I'll pretend to the world to be your loving husband, but you'll never have me. I'll do as I damn well please," and he flung her head from his hand, knocking her off balance.

Her face was livid as she caught herself against the piano, her mouth twitching nervously, and her anger rose to a fever pitch. "Griff! You can't go after her!" she cried hysterically. "You can't!"

"I have to," he snapped back. "I know what the Comanche do to white women, Rhetta, and by God, since I brought her here, I'm the one to go after her."

"You'd risk your neck for her?"

"You forget, I used to live with them. They know me, and if I go alone, there's a chance—"

"Please, Griff, no," she begged. "What will people say? What will they think? If you go after her, the pretense'll be over and everyone'll know our marriage has been a farce. Please, Griff, you can't go after that woman! You can't, Griff."

"Can't I?" he yelled, flinging the words back to her. "Well, just watch me, madam!" and he stalked off, leaving her staring after him, her face ashen.

She leaned against the piano, breathing heavily, her hands shaking. He was going after her, and he'd probably find her too, and everyone would hear about it and start talking. Not that they weren't talking already. They'd been talking ever since the night of the dance when he'd walked Jeanine back to the hotel. God, how she hated that woman! And Griff, pretending Jeanine meant nothing to him. She'd seen the look in his eyes even before the night she'd watched them from her window, and now, with Jeanine around, he wouldn't have to take his routine trips to Dallas.

Her fists clenched. Right in her house . . . right under her nose. Well, she wasn't going to let it happen. He'd not keep a mistress in her house, she wouldn't stand for it. And it was her house, no matter how much Mrs. Brandt tried to run things her way. She straightened, trying to pull herself together, fussing at her hair, smoothing her dress once more, going over everything that had happened.

Griff was heading for Comanche territory; that meant something had gone wrong. They weren't supposed to have turned her over to the Comanches. She'd told Jarrod to have them get rid of her, not turn her over to the Indians. She wanted Jeanine dead, not alive somewhere.

Couldn't anyone ever do anything they were told? If Griff brought the schoolteacher back now, everything would be lost, because once she told Sheriff Higgens about Burke and the others, they'd lead him right to her and Jarrod. They had to do something. Somehow Jarrod had to stop Griff from bringing Jeanine back, but first she had to get to Jarrod.

Not tonight, though. She couldn't leave the house tonight. Besides, there would be time in the morning. It'd take Griff at least a full day to reach the Comanche.

She straightened, determined, and headed toward the stairs. Yes, tomorrow I'll find Jarrod, she thought, and he'll make things right again. He has to. A few minutes later, as she stood at her bedroom window watching Griff's vague shadow down near the barn, riding away on Che-ak, she wondered how long it would be before the whole mess was over, and she sighed unhappily.

11

The night was dark, the moon not up yet, and the air brisk as Griff picked up the trail again about a mile from Indian Rock. Crystal had made sure he'd eaten first and he was almost too full, but it was probably for the best because he hadn't brought any food with him.

It was going to be harder tracking them at night, since he couldn't stay in the saddle and was forced to use a torch, but the ground was soft enough that the hoofprints were easy to follow, and what made it even better was that Jeanine was riding Blossom. Blossom was the horse Gar had always ridden before Griff had given him Comanche, and Griff had put a nick in each of the mare's front shoes, so that if Gar ever wandered off and got lost, he'd be easy to follow. Now those nicks were coming in handy, leaving a clear imprint among the other hoofprints.

They had at least a five-hour start on him, and tracking was slower, but he only ran into trouble once, when they crossed a stream and came out of the water a quarter of a mile farther down, and he lost time finding the trail again in the dark.

They were weaving a roundabout pattern, but definitely heading toward the Comanche. At first he'd thought of leaving their trail and breaking off toward where he knew Chief Horse Back would be camping this time of year and try his luck at getting him to help, but there was always

the chance that they'd circle back away from Indian territory again and he'd lose them altogether. If that happened,
he'd never forgive himself, so he'd made up his mind to
keep tracking them, no matter what, and as the night wore
on, although the going was tedious and exasperatingly
slow at times, he still kept moving.

It wasn't until early the next morning, as the first few
streaks of dawn began to filter in among the trees, that
Griff finally put out the torch he'd been using and tossed it
aside, then mounted Che-ak for the first time since he'd
started tracking them. He'd been traveling relentlessly all
night, the patience and stamina drilled into him years ago
while he lived with the Indians the only thing keeping him
on his feet, and he had to admit it felt good now to relax,
letting the big black stallion carry him.

He became even more dogged than ever in his pursuit
now that it was daylight, and the only time he stopped all
day was when nature forced him to, then he'd move
steadily on again.

Finally, shortly before nightfall, their trail led him to a
small grove of cottonwood trees, and he reined Che-ak to a
halt. Still sitting in the saddle, he surveyed the place
closely. They had stopped here, he was sure of it, and
after a few minutes he dismounted and began quickly
skirting the area, reading sign. He was right. Not only had
they stopped, but they'd turned Jeanine over to an Indian,
and it took him only a few minutes to pick up the trail of
Jeanine and her new captor, with Blossom's nicked shoes
standing out prominently next to the Indian's unshod horse.

He moved even faster now because he knew that once
inside the Indian camp it'd be a matter of only hours
before Jeanine would be claimed as a slave, and although
the Comanches moral laws regarding their own women were
strict, there were no laws governing slaves. Often they
were passed and sold from one brave to another, as Crystal
had been, and he couldn't let that happen to Jeanine.

He shuddered, determined that she wouldn't end up
beneath a Comanche, and with the little daylight left to

him, as the sun began sinking low in the west, he urged
Che-ak even faster, his eyes intent on the tracks he was
following. He'd reach her, he had to, or die trying.

It was early evening and not quite dark yet when the
Comanche brave, with Jeanine in tow, rode out of the
scrub trees and moved down a worn trail toward the valley
below. The Indian camp was on the banks of a small river
and was larger than what Jeanine thought it would be, the
brilliant sunset embellishing it with a golden-red glow,
making it seem almost unreal. But it was real, all right,
too real.

She'd been almost two days without sleep already, and
her eyes felt heavy, her body aching with fatigue as she
clung to Blossom's saddlehorn as hard as she could to
keep from falling off. They were making their way down a
steep incline that left them exposed to anyone who might
be watching, and she didn't want to fall now. Her hair was
straggling about her face, making it hard to see, and her
clothes were ripped, dirty, and streaked with sweat, but by
now she didn't much care what she looked like. Her only
concern was trying not to give in to the fear that could
mean the difference between life and death for her.

She and the Indian had met up with what she assumed
was a war party earlier in the afternoon, shortly after
riding away from where her abductors turned her over to
him, and for a while, as her new captor conversed with an
Indian who was obviously their leader, she sat in the
saddle staring at the painted warriors surrounding her.
Then, after a few harried minutes, she sighed, relieved,
when her captor reined his horse away, leaving the others
behind, and took her with him, heading once more into the
hills to the north. She'd been afraid they were going to kill
her right then and there, and thanked God they hadn't,
because even though she felt miserable, she didn't want to
die, because as long as there was breath in her body, there
was still a chance she could somehow get out of this mess.
If not today, then tomorrow. She was determined to sur-

vive, if for no other reason than to get revenge on whoever had done this to her.

She hadn't so much as spoken a word to the Indian during their long ride here, or even tried, for that matter, because she was certain he wouldn't understand. Nor had she shed a tear since she'd been turned over to him. All the while they were riding, she kept trying to remember some of the things Griff had told her about the Comanche that first night she'd arrived at Trail's End, and one thing he'd emphasized more than anything else was that the Indians admired bravery. Maybe that's why she couldn't cry: she kept remembering his words and was trying her best to live up to them, hoping things would be easier for her if she did.

Still, as they rode closer to the camp, nearing the tepees where people were beginning to gather to stare at them, she once more became sick with fear.

Hostile faces stared up at her, unsmiling and unfriendly, and she swallowed hard. They were still astride, and her knuckles were white as they gripped the saddle horn. Then finally the Indian stopped their horses in front of one of the large tepees not too far from the edge of the river. He dismounted and walked back to Blossom, dragging her from the saddle, while everyone watched, and she wished she could just cut loose and scream. Yet knew she didn't dare.

Her wrists were all bloody, and her hands so numb he'd had to pry them from the saddle horn, but it was her legs that almost betrayed her. She'd been in the saddle for so long that when he set her on her feet, her knees started to buckle, and it was only by sheer effort, and fear of what might happen if she collapsed, that she had the strength to stand. She could feel her legs shaking beneath her, but wasn't about to give in, and as the Indian grabbed her arm and whirled her around, shoving her ahead of him toward the tepee, she clenched her jaw stubbornly, trying not to look afraid.

There was an Indian woman standing next to the entrance of the tepee where they were headed, and her eyes sifted over Jeanine curiously as the Comanche brave pushed Jeanine forward, past her, then motioned for Jeanine to go inside. She hesitated for a second, then ducked, entering the strange dwelling, where she stood for a second looking around.

The only light inside the tent came from a sunken fire in the center of the dirt floor, and it was producing a foul-smelling smoke that turned Jeanine's stomach. Besides being rank and horrid-smelling, it burned her eyes, and she wished she could turn and leave, but knew the idea was hopeless, as she was prodded once more from behind, pushed roughly to the other side of the tepee, then shoved down onto an old buffalo robe. She hit the ground hard, and lay with her head against the shaggy fur, holding her breath, with her face toward the outside wall, waiting for what was to come next, but nothing more happened. No one touched her or said anything, and she suddenly realized she couldn't hear another sound in the tent.

She lay quietly for a few seconds more; then, when still nothing happened, she slowly turned her head and was surprised to discover she was completely alone. She hadn't heard him leave, but the Comanche was gone. She wanted to cry from relief, but instead mustered up the little energy she had left, and with her hands still tied, managed to draw herself into a sitting position, resting her head forward on her knees, and swallowed hard, wondering: What now?

For a long time she sat there as if in a stupor, too tired to move around and explore the place to see if there was anything she could use to cut her hands free, yet too frightened to close her eyes in sleep. She must have waited for some ten or fifteen minutes, then suddenly tensed as a shadow fell across the opening of the tepee and the woman who'd been standing outside earlier came in, carrying a large bowl. It was filled with some kind of soup, and she knelt down, offering it to Jeanine, who stared at it helplessly, then held up her hands to show the woman they were still tied.

The woman nodded knowingly, and set the bowl down,

then reached to a sheath at her waist and drew out a knife. While she cut the bonds on Jeanine's wrists, for the first time since the woman came into the tent Jeanine finally got a good look at her face as her head turned toward the light from the entrance, and the shock was unnerving.

The woman would have been quite pretty if not for her nose. It was horribly disfigured, the skin peeled back, with the cartilage exposed, and Jeanine shuddered, remembering Griff telling her that the disfigurement was the Comanche's punishment for adultery. In spite of her own predicament, Jeanine felt sorry for her.

When Jeanine's hands were finally free, the woman massaged them, oblivious of the blood that smeared her own hands, and it wasn't until she was sure Jeanine could move her fingers freely again that she stopped, slipped the knife back in its sheath again, and handed Jeanine the bowl.

The soup was hot against Jeanine's parched, swollen lips, and she could hardly swallow. She sipped at it carefully at first, until it cooled some, then finally managed to get it all down, after choking a few times, making her eyes water. The Indian woman was watching her closely all the time, and although Jeanine was grateful for the soup, the woman's presence made her nervous, so that she self-consciously dribbled some down her chin as she finished the last of it. She wiped her chin off with the back of her hand, then handed the bowl back to the woman and huddled against the side of the tepee again wondering what to expect next.

To her surprise, the woman stared at her curiously for a few minutes longer; then, as if making a quick decision, she quietly stood up and left, without retying Jeanine's hands.

Jeanine stared down at her wrists, the blood already scabbing where the flesh was raw. But then, why would they have to tie her hands together anyway? Where would she go? There was no way she could leave without being seen.

Suddenly it all seemed so hopeless, and a strange feeling of lethargy began to flow through her. She tried to shake her head clear, but it didn't seem to help and for some reason she was having a hard time focusing her eyes. As she stared at her hands, they began to blur, and her head began spinning sickeningly. Then, unable to stay awake any longer, and not wanting to, she sighed a deep sigh, slipped slowly down until her head rested on the smelly old buffalo robe, and within minutes fell into an exhausted sleep.

Nothing awakened her that night. Not the Indian man and woman coming in to sleep, nor the dog that sniffed around her face and went out again. Even when morning came, she kept right on sleeping while the woman fixed her husband's breakfast and the two of them left the tepee to begin the day's routine.

It wasn't until the sun cleared the trees and the noise in the Indian village picked up in volume that she finally began to stir. Slowly at first, as if waking from the dead. Her eyes opened first, and with their hesitant perusal of her surroundings, the reality of where she was, and everything that had happened, once more came back to her, and this time tears did well up in her eyes.

She didn't want to cry, but the strength that had nurtured her the day before just didn't seem to be there, and she sniffed, trying to wipe away the tears. Slowly, agonizingly, she began to move, and managed to push herself into a sitting position. She was sore all over, from the pounding in her head to her stinking feet, sweaty and cold in her worn riding boots, and every movement was an effort at first. Then, as her muscles once more became used to the activity, the movements didn't seem quite as painful.

She glanced about the empty tent, unaware that she hadn't been alone all night, the uncertainty of what might lie ahead of her making her want to scream. But she wasn't going to scream. She'd let the tears fall here, when she was alone, where they couldn't see, but she'd never let them know how afraid she was. Her tear-filled eyes settled on the patch of sunlight streaming in at the opening of her tepee, and suddenly she began to wonder what was happening back at Trail's End. Would they miss her? Surely someone would wonder what happened, or maybe they wouldn't even care.

She bit her lip. No, that wasn't right. Griff would care, she was certain, and Gar, but it wouldn't do any good. Rhetta would never let Griff do anything about it, and really that was as it should be, wasn't it? After all, Rhetta had seen him first. He belonged to her . . . it was foolish to even think of him, even now.

She still had no idea why she'd been kidnapped, and couldn't even guess at a reason, unless maybe she and Homer had been right, and Rhetta and Jarrod were the ones trying to kill Griff. They might have been getting too close to the truth. If so, then there was no reason for her even to hope Griff would come to her rescue; he was probably dead by now. It was the only possible reason anyone would have for trying to get her out of the way where she couldn't interfere.

She pulled the pants legs of her buckskin riding skirt up and began massaging her leg muscles, trying to ignore the soreness in her back and thighs, then moved onto her knees and crawled awkwardly toward the entrance flap, peeking out. Everything looked as normal as she might expect it to, remembering Griff's description of what a Comanche village was like. The woman who'd brought the soup to her was sitting only a few feet from the entrance, her back to it, and there were a number of people milling about, while some hides were stretched on drying racks just a short distance beyond where the woman was sitting. And as she watched, a group of children ran by, shouting and laughing, with a bunch of yapping dogs nipping at their heels. Nothing unusual seemed to be going on.

Her knees were sore from the rough floor of the tepee, and after a few minutes she ducked back away from the opening and crawled back again to the buffalo robe, where she curled up, hugging her legs to her chest, leaning her chin on her knees, and waited for something to happen, but nothing did. Time went by, and still no one came. It was as if they'd just forgotten all about her. The dogs were still barking, people talking, and the normal camp sounds went on around her, but no one came to check on her or bring her food, and she became apprehensive. If they'd just get whatever they were planning for her over with. The waiting was nerve-wracking; the suspense of not knowing what to expect next almost as cruel as what they might be planning to do with her.

Hours went by in which she imagined a number of horrible ways to die, as well as imagining all sorts of frightening fates that might be awaiting her. Then, it must have been noon or a little after when she realized the whole camp seemed to be noisier than usual. Before, she had heard only the sounds of everyday activity; now suddenly, besides the shouting and yelling going on, some drums had started a rhythmic cadence that was throbbing intensely, as the wind carried it through the village, vibrating against the walls of the tent, and she felt a chill run through her.

She straightened apprehensively, wondering what it was all about, yet afraid to go near the tent flap to peek out, for fear she'd be seen. The commotion went on and on for some time, and still she waited, huddled back against the side of the tepee, hoping no one would come for her, yet knowing deep down inside that her hope was only wishful thinking. A few minutes later, she was proved right when she heard someone talking to the Indian woman who'd been sitting outside guarding her, and her heart sank. They were only strange guttural sounds to Jeanine, and she couldn't understand any of it, but a few seconds later the woman came into the tent, stared at her curiously for a moment, then motioned toward the opening she'd just come through.

Jeanine stared back at her. The woman obviously wanted her to leave, but she was afraid to move, afraid of what was waiting for her out there. Instead she huddled closer against the tent wall.

Undaunted, the woman set her mouth stubbornly and bore down on Jeanine with determination. Then with a strength Jeanine was surprised to see in a woman, even an Indian woman, she leaned over, grabbed Jeanine by the arm, pulled her to her feet, and began pushing her toward the opening, leaving no way for Jeanine to protest. The woman was taller and heavier than she was, and all Jeanine could do was try her best to stay on her feet. She ducked her head and reluctantly stumbled through the opening; then, once outside, the woman released her, and Jeanine stopped abruptly, straightening as she adjusted her eyes to the light and gazed about curiously. She'd swear it looked like everyone in the camp was assembled, and they were all standing motionless, staring at her in such a strange way that it made her hair stand on end.

Suddenly she felt a gentle nudge from behind and whirled around. It was the same Indian woman again, only this time she was smiling a broad smile, nodding her head and motioning for Jeanine to keep going, nudging her gently and pointing on ahead past Jeanine. Jeanine frowned and didn't move, but once more the woman was stubborn. Her smile never wavered, seeming permanently fixed across her face, and she kept pointing first to Jeanine, then off toward the crowd.

Well, Jeanine thought, her heart pounding erratically, if that's what she wants. Maybe I'll finally find out what they have planned for me. Hesitantly, her feet reluctantly accepting the orders she was giving them, Jeanine began to do what the woman wanted, and moved forward, toward the myriad of faces watching her. She moved slowly, not knowing what to expect, her heart in her throat; then, curiously, as she drew closer to the crowd, they began to move back, opening up a path for her. She stopped to watch them, her frown deepening, but the woman behind her was insistent, and kept shoving at her, so she started moving again, still walking hesitantly, wondering why everyone was staring at her so. She checked the buttons on her dirty shirtwaist. Miraculously, they were all still intact and fastened; then she reached up, running a hand through her hair. It had fallen from its chignon shortly after her capture, and hung loose and straggly onto her shoulders, strands of it flipping into her face occasionally as a breeze that was blowing caught at it, teasing it.

Other than that, she imagined she looked like any other half-dead captive, so why the curious looks and strange behavior?

Then, as she slowly took her eyes from the staring faces surrounding her and looked up ahead to where the path they were opening for her led, she froze, unable to believe what she was seeing, and gooseflesh rose on her skin, once more bringing tears to her eyes.

At the end of that long line of dark faces stood Griffin Heywood . . . or was it Griff? She gulped back the tears, blinking her eyes just to make sure, but it wasn't a mistake. It was Griff!

He was wearing fancy beaded buckskins, right down to the moccasins, and beside him was an Indian wearing the biggest headdress Jeanine had ever seen. The Indian's face was broad and weather-beaten, a scowl furrowing his forehead above a wide nose and piercing eyes. Several necklaces with huge medallions hung on his chest, and large bracelets adorned his wrists, but it was the man himself who commanded her attention. He stood proud and stern, and she knew he must be an important chief. Yet, there was Griff standing beside him, apparently unharmed.

She stood quietly, staring, her mind trying to comprehend: How?

Again she felt herself being pushed from behind, and she moved closer, but cautiously this time, until she was only a few feet from Griff and the Indian. She wanted to run to Griff and hang onto him, never letting go, but knew she didn't dare. His eyes were as intense as the Indian chief's as he stared at her.

Suddenly the chief held up his hand, motioning for her not to come any closer, and she stopped, still staring at both of them curiously, aware that with her hair so bedraggled and her clothes such a mess, she must look atrocious.

The old Indian chief pointed at her, moving his hand slightly to get her attention, then spoke. His English wasn't very good, but by listening carefully, she managed to understand him.

"Tosi Nuit . . . your man?" he asked, gesturing from her to Griff, then back to her again.

Jeanine glanced at Griff. What should she do? What should she say? She saw Griff nod slightly, and frowned. Did he want her to answer yes? Oh Lord! Again Griff nodded, so slightly it was barely noticeable, and this time she looked directly into his eyes. Suddenly she knew.

"Yes," she answered softly, her voice trembling with emotion.

The old Indian smiled broadly, then said something to Griff in what she assumed was Comanche, and they conversed for a few minutes while she waited. When they finally finished talking, Griff walked over to her, put his arm around her, and started ushering her away from the crowd, toward the riverbank and a small cluster of trees, where he stopped next to a large cottonwood, letting her lean back against it.

"Sit down," he suggested, his eyes intent on her. "You look terrible."

"Well, what a nice compliment," she muttered wearily, and sank unceremoniously to the ground.

He sat down beside her and reached out, tilting her face toward his. "That's not what I meant, and you know it," he said.

She flushed under the dirt. "How?" she asked, motioning toward the Indian with the huge headdress, who was still watching them, although he was too far away to hear them.

"You mean how did I get here?"

She nodded, leaning back more comfortably against the tree.

"When we discovered you were gone, and it was obvious where they were taking you, I had no choice," he explained. "I met Chief Horse Back late yesterday afternoon on his way back from a raid. Since he said this camp was the only one close by, I figured you'd be brought here, so I came in with him. At his invitation, of course."

He was sitting close to her and leaned over, taking her hand in his, wincing at the scabs on her wrist that covered where raw flesh had been only last night. "I'm sorry you were treated like this," he apologized.

Jeanine quivered at his touch. It was over and done, and now all she wanted to do was forget it if she could. At least until she was able to get even. She gazed into his eyes and a warm glow spread through her. She had never dreamed she'd be so happy to see anyone in her whole life.

"It'll heal," she replied, embarrassed by his concern. Then, "Griff, will we get out of this?" she asked.

"We should." He paused, twining his fingers possessively around hers. "I had to tell Chief Horse Back you were my woman, Jeanine," he said softly. "It was the only way I could possibly get you out of here, so you're going to have to play along with it." He saw the hesitant look on her face. "If I'd told him you were my son's teacher, he'd have only said get another teacher. He'd never have let me leave with you," he explained quickly. "I told him we were planning to get married, when a disgruntled suitor took you away against your will, and when you refused to marry him, he vowed that if he couldn't have you, I wouldn't either. That's why Chief Horse Back asked you what he did a few minutes ago."

"They believed you?"

"I think so." He shook his head worriedly. "I'm not sure. As well as I know these people, sometimes it's still hard to tell just what they're thinking."

"Then we can leave?" she asked.

He squeezed her hand. "Not exactly. I'm afraid it's not quite that easy."

"But you said . . ."

He faced her squarely, uncertain how she was going to accept what he had to say.

"Jeanine, he wants us to get married before we leave," he explained hurriedly. "In fact, he won't let me leave camp until I've made you my wife. I think he's testing me to see if I'm telling the truth."

"But that's impossible." Her blue eyes widened as she stared at him. "You're already married!"

"Shhh . . ." He put a finger to her lips. "Not so loud," he admonished. "He'll hear you. Besides, this would be an Indian ceremony."

She removed his finger from her mouth, continuing to object. "But the law might recognize their marriage ceremonies. You can't be married to both of us."

He stared at her, angry at himself for having fallen in love with her, and angry at her because he didn't want to love her and wished she hadn't come along to complicate his life, but she had, and now, for the first time in his life, he threw all caution to the wind.

"To hell with the law!" he said viciously, his eyes boring into hers. "If marrying you is the only way to get you out of here, then we're getting married, do you understand?"

She stood up, still protesting, trying to keep her voice low so the Indians wouldn't hear. "You're crazy, Griff," she said as he followed her to her feet. "I can't marry you, Comanche or otherwise."

"Don't get stubborn."

"I'm not!"

"Then what do you call it?"

Her eyes sparked, and she tossed her head, turning away from him. "You don't have to save me," she said angrily. "No one told you to come after me. Besides, what does it matter anyway what happens to me?"

He grabbed her shoulders, forcing her to face him. "Jeanine, be sensible," he pleaded anxiously as he searched her face. "You have no idea what they'll do to you."

"I don't care!"

"Well, I do, damn it!" He looked disgusted. "Don't you want to live? What's the matter with you, anyway?"

"Don't you know?" she asked, straightening, as she stared into his stormy eyes. She was trying to keep from shouting. "Don't you really know?" He stared back at her, his eyes hardening as he realized fully what he was asking her to do, yet knowing there was no alternative.

She sighed, her voice barely a whisper. "You already have a wife, Griff," she went on hopelessly. "What about Rhetta? What if this Indian chief suddenly remembers Rhetta?"

"He won't."

"How can you be sure?"

"This is the first I've seen him since before the war, and he had no idea then that I was married. I'm afraid I've never bragged much about my wife." He saw the uncertainty in her eyes. "He's heard rumors, Jeanine, that's all, but I assured him they were just that, rumors, and I think he believed me, or wants to." He shook his head. "But if you don't go along with me, he'll know I was lying, and neither of us will get out of here alive. Can't you understand that?"

"But . . . I thought you said they made white women slaves?"

"They do, usually, but now, since I've shown up . . . Jeanine, I lied to Chief Horse Back. If he finds out, we won't have a chance in hell."

"Oh, great. You're a big help, you are." Tears welled up in her eyes. "Why didn't you just leave things as they were? Why'd you have to come after me?"

"You know why, damn it," he answered. "Now, look." He pulled her into his arms, holding her close. "You're going to marry me in a Comanche ceremony whether you like it or not, do you understand?" he ordered her. "So you might as well start pretending you like the idea, because you're going to have to be convincing." His voice lowered fervently. "Now, kiss me, dammit, and look like you're enjoying it," and before she could even try to answer, his mouth quickly covered hers, moving savagely against her lips.

She started to fight him at first. Then suddenly, as she realized it was useless to struggle, she froze, stiffening in his arms, hoping he'd release her. Only he didn't. Instead, he kept right on kissing her, and the kiss deepened, gentling to a searing caress until Jeanine knew she was lost. All her good intentions slowly began to vanish, and with a groan she melted against him, her arms moving slowly up to encircle his neck, and she kissed him back.

Griff felt her surrender, and his mouth softened instinctively, as a thrill of hope spread through him. He kept on kissing her, his lips sipping at hers lovingly, all thoughts of Chief Horse Back, who was standing only a few feet away, completely forgotten. He'd been wanting to do this for days. Just to feel her mouth beneath his again. . . .

After a few passionate moments of forgetting why he was kissing her, but only that the sensation was like tasting a bit of heaven, he drew his mouth reluctantly from hers, pulling his head back to gaze down at her.

"That's better," he whispered huskily, his voice vibrating through her.

She was still trembling from the force of her own passion in returning his kiss, and her breathing was short, erratic. "It's the only way?" she asked unsteadily.

"The only way." His arms were still around her, and her hands caressed his neck, then moved to his shoulders.

"When?" she asked.

"There'll be a feast in our honor tonight, and tomorrow morning before we leave, there'll be a ceremony." He hated lying to her about the ceremony, but she was reluctant enough about the whole thing already. If she knew the truth, he knew she'd refuse, but once under way . . . He couldn't take chances. They had to get out of there alive. "You'll spend the night in the chief's tent," he continued explaining as he looked down at her. In spite of the tangled hair and dirt-smudged face, she still had the power to stir him. He sighed. "The women will be coming soon, and they'll take you to clean up, then give you clean buckskins to wear, so just do as you're told, and try to follow their sign language. I think you'll get the idea, and remember, try to look happy. Your life depends on it."

She shut her eyes. "I'm scared, Griff."

He bent down, kissing her longingly, and she trembled. "Just remember to keep looking like a woman in love," he said. "And don't look surprised when I kiss you. They're going to expect it. Comanche are a suspicious lot.

If they knew I was lying about who you really are, they'd have both our necks.''

She frowned. "I'm sorry about before," she apolo gized. "Thank you for coming.''

His eyes darkened, and it was hard for her to tell what he was thinking. "When you love someone, you don't have much choice," he said simply, and as their eyes met, she felt the strength of that love crying out to her.

He kissed her once more, then released her and took her hand, leading her docilely back toward where Chief Horse Back waited.

The rest of the day went just as he said it would. The first thing the women did was help her bathe in the river, then give her a vapor bath. Griff had told her that the Comanche were famous for their steam bathing, and she had to admit that her sore muscles responded gratefully to its warmth, then afterward with her filthy hair washed to a glowing, golden sheen, she finally slipped into the long buckskin shirt and leggings, with the beaded moccasins replacing her sweaty riding boots, and felt almost normal again.

The feast began shortly before sundown, with the men, including Griff, seated in a circle, smoking a pipe, while the medicine man made his medicine, translating dreams, and predicting all good fortune for the village. Then the drums began again, and the men joined the rhythm, their chanting echoing through the valley as they began to perform their ritual dances, faces and bodies streaked with paint.

At first Jeanine sat with the women, watching, and although she tried not to show it, the warriors frightened her. Most of them wore buckskins shirts, breechclouts, and leggings trimmed with bright feathers, since the weather was getting cooler. But a few were still bare from the waist up and the look on their faces was wild, untamed, their eyes watching her suspiciously while they kept time to the drums.

The women seemed friendly enough, she supposed, yet she noticed the unusual interest they seemed to take in her blond hair. It was falling into soft curls on her shoulders, and every once in a while one of them would move toward her and touch it, then giggle and move away, talking and laughing. She wasn't sure whether they were making fun of it or admiring it. And that was another thing. The women seemed to giggle a great deal, glancing over at her surreptitiously, as if they were sharing some sort of secret.

Later in the evening, when she was sitting next to Griff, eating, she mentioned it to him.

"They think my choice of a bride is hilarious," he said, his eyes drifting to her shapely figure, hidden beneath the buckskins. "They say you're not built for work, and your hair's like straw. To them you look funny."

"And to you?" she asked softly, her blue eyes staring into his.

"To me you're built perfectly for what I'd like to do," he teased, watching her blush, and he reached out, running his finger from her lips to where her breasts divided, which brought another round of giggles from the Indian woman, making Jeanine's blush deepen even more.

The food was sumptuous, but Jeanine didn't feel like eating. Everything was so strange to her, and she was still trying to shake the memory of having been kidnapped, and the humiliating way she'd been treated. Her stomach was tied in knots, and she ate sparingly of rabbit, venison, buffalo, and a variety of fish baked on hot coals and served with cornbread and cakes made from pecan flour. For dessert there were dried plums cooked to a pulpy mush and served over hot walnut meal and topped with thick honey. She had to admit it was good, but her queasy stomach could take only so much.

Some of the men and women continued dancing, while the others ate. Then they changed places, and when the main part of the meal was over, the festivities still went on, as both men and women continued to entertain their honored guests. Then suddenly, as the moon reached a point in the sky that seemed to have some significance to him, Chief Horse Back stood up, raised his hands in a silent gesture, and the festivities finally came to an end.

"Now, just do as you're told," Griff told her quickly as he ushered her over to stand in front of the old Indian.

He said something to the chief in Comanche, and the Indian looked stern for a moment; then Griff said something else, and he grinned broadly.

"You come," Chief Horse Back said in English, as he motioned toward her; then he addressed his wives in Comanche.

The chief had six wives and a number of children, but tonight he'd sleep in the tent of his first wife, whose children had already left their father's tepee. So the others watched with Griff as Chief Horse Back, his wife, and Jeanine walked off to the chief's tent. Chief Horse Back reached out and pulled back the flap. This tepee was much larger than any of the others, and was decorated with an antelope head to signify that it was a chief's tent. He motioned for Jeanine to enter.

She glanced back hesitantly to where Griff stood watching, then ducked down, entering the tepee, followed closely by Chief Horse Back and his wife.

The tent was also far more elaborate inside than the one where she'd spent last evening, with a large sunken fire in the center, and polished cedarwood poles holding it up. Colorful blankets and thick hides were scattered about, and in the very back of the tent, one large bed of blankets and furs was laid out. The chief pointed to it.

"You sleep," he said, again in English.

Jeanine walked over and stood looking down at the bedding. The chief's wife had followed her over, and now she pulled back the top covers, then smilingly pointed inside and poked at Jeanine's clothes, making motions as if she were undressing. She kept this up until finally Jeanine realized what she was trying to tell her, and Jeanine blushed profusely. She wasn't about to undress in front of the woman and her husband. If she undressed at all it would only be after climbing under the covers.

The chief said something to his wife, and Jeanine assumed he called her to him, because after once more insisting she remove her clothes, the woman joined her husband, and they both moved across to the other side of the tent. Jeanine watched him take off his huge headdress and lay it aside; then she quickly turned her back so she wouldn't be able to see any more, as she realized he too was going to undress for bed. Without any more hesitating, she kicked off her moccasins and knelt down, climbing into the bedding.

Once under the furry blankets, she decided she'd better do as the chief's wife had instructed, and wriggled from the buckskins, stacking them in a neat pile where the woman had indicated in her sign language; then she pulled the covers up to her chin and glanced surreptitiously to the other side of the tent. The chief and his wife were huddled together in their own bedding now, so she breathed a sigh, turned over and tried to sleep, wondering what the ceremony would be like in the morning, and thanking God that for tonight she could at least try to forget some of the torturous pain she'd endured on her long ride.

Time went on, and the fire burned low, but Jeanine just couldn't seem to relax. In the first place, the chief and his wife were still stirring. She tried to keep from looking their way, but every once in a while she'd hear the woman giggle and the chief mumble something. Then too, a couple of times she heard strange noises near the entrance flap. When this happened, the chief raised up, glancing toward the entrance, and the noise stopped.

Finally, exhausted, unable to keep her eyes open any longer, and glad that tomorrow would also bring her freedom from the terrible nightmare she'd been through, she fell asleep. She had no idea how long she'd slept, but suddenly she stirred, and her eyes abruptly popped open. She was wide-awake, but why?

The tent was dark, the fire only smoldering embers, and she lay quietly, listening. The chief and his wife were snoring and wheezing at the other side of the tent, but she could also hear someone else breathing, and whoever it was, was so close to her, she could reach out and touch him. The strong scent of spicewood filled her nostrils and she held her breath, unable to move.

"Who's there?" she whispered breathlessly.

"Shhh . . . it's me," Griff answered, pulling back the top of the blanket, and before she could protest, he slid in beside her, his body pressed against hers.

"You're naked!" she gasped, startled to feel his bare skin against hers, and his hand covered her mouth quickly, before she could scream or protest any further.

He was gentle but firm with her. "This is it, Jeanine," he whispered huskily as he leaned close to her ear. "I didn't dare tell you before, but this is the marriage ceremony . . . not tomorrow, now. I made it to your bed without being caught, and I'll spend the night, and in the morning you'll be my wife."

She mumbled against his hand, her body twisting, trying to get away from the shock of his warm flesh against hers.

"Please, no," he whispered anxiously. "Forgive me for not telling you, but I knew you'd never say yes."

Suddenly Chief Horse Back raised up. "Tosi Nuit?" he called loudly, and Griff felt Jeanine tense, then quit struggling.

Her skin was soft and warm against him, and as Chief Horse Back called his name loudly again, he felt her body relax a little.

Jeanine listened while Griff answered the Indian, and they exchanged a few words in Comanche; then she reached up, trembling, and took his hand from her mouth.

"What did he say?" she asked.

He gazed down at her, the faint light from the almost dead fire casting shadows across her face so that her eyes shone a golden green.

"He told us not to be too noisy, and wished us happiness." He stroked the hair from her face, and she trembled.

"Oh God, Griff," she cried, her eyes misty. "I can't stay here with you like this!"

His hand dropped to her shoulder, traveling possessively to the middle of her back, kneading her soft skin. "Would it really be so terrible?" he asked, and bent down, his lips brushing her ear, sending shivers clear through her. "Let me make love to you, Jeanine," he whispered, kissing her neck lightly.

Tears flooded her eyes. Oh God, she loved him so much, yet she was so torn inside, so afraid.

He kissed her temple, tasting the salty tears that clung there. "You're crying." He was surprised, and raised up, once more looking down into her face. "What is it?"

"It's foolish, I know . . ." Her voice was trembling. "But I've heard women say it hurts so terribly the first time."

He wiped the tears away with his fingers. "I won't hurt you, Jeanine," he whispered softly, then ran his hand gently down her jawline, and kissed the trail his fingers had left. "I could never hurt you, you know that. Let me love you, please," he begged fervently.

She wanted to relax with him, yet her eyes darkened fearfully.

"Are you afraid of me, Jeanine?" he asked, searching their blue depths.

She stared up at him, her heart beating wildly, still conscious of his warm body half-covering hers. "I . . . I don't know . . ." She bit her lip. "Oh, Griff, I don't want to be."

His hand moved from her face to her breast, his fingers barely touching the nipple, and he caressed it tenderly. "Does this frighten you?" he asked.

His hand felt good, and she took a deep breath, feeling a quickening deep down inside, and her voice was breathless as she answered, "No."

Griff knew he had to go easy. His head came down, his tongue tracing the path his fingers had made, and the quickening inside Jeanine became a surging fire that ripped through her like a whirlwind, beating tumultuously in rhythm with her heart, then twisting deep, settling frantically in her loins.

She grabbed his hair, trying to still the wonderful sensations that were forging their way through every nerve in her body. Yet at the same time, she basked in the warmth they brought with them. She was still afraid, yes, but eager to banish those fears, and she moaned ecstatically, letting his caresses soothe her.

His lips moved to her mouth. "I can't stay here and not touch you, Jeanine," Griff pleaded fervently, his own body on fire. "There's no way I can. Let me prove to you that it won't hurt, that what you're feeling now is only the beginning."

By now she was light-headed and dizzy, her body aching for something she couldn't name, a pleasure she was certain was there for the taking. Still . . . What was she to do? Oh, sweet Jesus! She could hardly breathe.

"We can't, Griff," she gasped brokenly. "Oh God, Griff, what of Rhetta? What of your wife?" she cried helplessly, but he was beyond caring.

"To hell with Rhetta," he groaned passionately, and his lips captured hers, drinking in the love he knew she'd gladly give once all barriers between them were gone. And as his lips sapped the strength of resistance from her, Jeanine knew there was only one way to still the ache inside her. Surrender.

Griff took his time with her, his mouth possessing hers eagerly, yet gently, while his hands continued to arouse her, erasing all her fears, until, by the time he moved above and entered her, she clung to him desperately, letting him take her completely, and arching to meet him in a moment of ecstasy that carried them both beyond caring about anything except the moment.

When the first sweet thrill of their union was over, she lay beneath him, warm and trembling, her body more alive than it had ever been before in her whole life, and she could feel him buried deep inside her. For the first time in her life Jeanine was selfish, thinking only of what she felt, never wanting it to stop, and when, only a short time later, he began to move again, she moved with him, her body still glowing, her mind still in a heaven all its own, and as the kiss they shared deepened, they both knew this was a night they were never to forget. A night filled with love so intense that neither of them cared to see the dawn.

12

It was still early, the sun barely over the horizon as Rhetta stood in the kitchen of the dilapidated old house adjacent to the abandoned copper mine on the Vance property and stared across the cluttered table at Jarrod. Griff had been gone since last night, and by now her nerves were really on edge.

"How could you be so stupid," she yelled angrily as she faced him. "I said I wanted her dead . . . we agreed."

"How was I to know Burke and his men would turn her over to the Indians?" he shot back, and his eyes hardened. "Besides, we said it had to be done so we wouldn't be involved. They didn't know he used to live with the damn Comanche, so they probably figured it was a perfect solution."

"You should have told them."

"I didn't think it mattered. If I'd known what they were planning, I'd have told them, but they never even let on . . ." His eyes flashed dangerously. "I just told them to get rid of her."

"Well, at least it's not too late to do something about it." Her lips pursed nervously. "I just hope when you send them back this time that you make it clear just what they're to do."

"Don't worry, they'll have their orders. And I'll handle Griff and the schoolteacher myself this time."

"How?"

"I'll think of something."

She straightened, glancing about the messy room. Clothes were strewn around any old place, and dirty dishes still lay in the sink.

"How long do you think it'll take them to get back?" she asked.

He shrugged. "Who knows? It all depends on where they might have contacted the Indians. If they happened to run into a war party in the hills, they could be back anytime between midnight and tomorrow morning. If they made it all the way to one of the camps, they may not be back until sometime tomorrow night."

"In the meantime, we just bite our nails and hope, I suppose. Is that it?"

His eyes sifted over her appreciatively, and suddenly he began to hunger for the body he knew was concealed beneath the deep purple satin dress she had on. "We don't have to bite our nails," he said recklessly, and came around to her side of the table. "There are other ways we could spend the time." He reached out and drew her into his arms. "I missed you," he whispered.

She gazed up at him, trying as she always did to tell herself some love was better than none at all. "You just saw me in town Sunday."

"With all those people around?" He reached up, caressing her cheek. "It's hell not being able to touch you," he said huskily. "Since Griff came home I've made love to you so few times I can count them on one hand." He cupped her face in his hand. "A man needs more than that."

"You have the women in town."

"Those sluts? I told you before, I won't go near them." He glanced up at the silly little hat she wore, all decorated with flowers and feathers, the satin ribbons matching her dress. How beautifully the violet hues brought out the deep coffee color of her hair and eyes. And her lips. His eyes moved to her mouth, watching the corners tilt provocatively. "You're what I want . . . all I want, Rhet," he said. "You know it's always been you . . . and now . . ."

He bent down and his lips touched hers, lightly at first; then he drew her even closer, and the kiss deepened. As usual, Rhetta kissed him back, although her heart wasn't really in it. Only the physical pleasure he brought her mattered to her anymore, and there were times when even that didn't seem important.

Strange, she thought as his lips played about her mouth, trying to coax an answering response from her, when she'd married Griff, she'd never expected to fall in love with him. How miserably fate had dealt with her! If only the war hadn't come along. She'd been so certain the years would mellow him, and that, given enough time, she could break through the wall he'd set between them. But now, after being gone so long, any headway she had gained during those first few years of their marriage had been lost. Since his return, he was more determined than ever in his resolve never to touch her. And now Jeanine Grayson had to come along, making matters worse. Thank God Jarrod didn't know the real reason she'd talked him into getting rid of Gar's teacher. If he had, he never would have gone along with it, and he'd have been furious. But she couldn't tell him she was jealous. He'd never understand. Sometimes she didn't even understand herself, because while she seethed inside with jealousy over Griff's obvious feelings for Jeanine, she also knew there was no possible way she could change things, and that Griff was going to be lost to her forever. If only . . .

She felt Jarrod pull her closer against him; then he drew his mouth from hers and she opened her eyes, gazing helplessly into his. Jarrod's hazel eyes were glazed with passion, his face flushed, and she felt him tremble.

"I won't let you go, Rhet, I can't," he murmured breathlessly. "It's been too long," and conceding to herself the need to fill the void Griff's denial of her had caused, Rhetta let him lead her from the messy kitchen to what had once been the parlor but now housed a dusty bare floor, tattered window curtains, a dresser that was falling apart, and a double bed, the grimy sheets on it in careless disarray.

"Not here!" she protested reluctantly, but Jarrod's fingers were tight about her wrist.

"Here!" he answered, and she raised her hand to wrench her wrist from his grasp, then saw the look in his eyes.

Jarrod wasn't about to let go, and she knew it. At least not until he knew he'd be able to have his way with her. His eyes narrowed, anticipating what lay ahead. "We have the whole place, not a soul to bother us."

"But here? It's so dirty. Not here, please, Jarrod," She pleaded. "I can't stand the filth."

"Come on, Rhet, this is cleaner than the dirt floor of the line shack, and better than the ground, like last time." He reached up, cupping her head in his hand again, his thumb rubbing along her jawline, almost hurting her. "Don't start having second thoughts, sweetheart," he whispered softly. "We're in this together, you and I, and there's no way we can change things now. You belong to me now, sweeting, and don't you forget it. That means both body and soul, and right now I intend to claim the first one." He kissed her, his mouth savoring hers as if he were tasting a heady wine. "Now, don't be foolish," he went on against her lips. "You know what I can do for you . . . what it's like with us, Rhet . . . you know you always give in, that you've never been sorry yet," and as he kissed her again, letting his lips trail from her mouth to her neck, Rhetta knew he was right.

In spite of the worn gray sheets that smelled of sour sweat, and the musty odor that seemed to permeate everything in the room, all was forgotten as she let him undress her slowly and warm every part of her, caressing and teasing until they both lay naked, twisting and turning on the bed in the throes of a passion that seemed to consume them both.

Jarrod had been the first for Rhetta years ago, and the way things were going, he'd no doubt be the last, and she'd never know what Griff's arms might have held. All she could do was imagine, and that's what she did now.

Would it have been the same, or better? As Jarrod brought life back to her body, awakening her once more to the depths of what he was feeling, arousing desires in her she'd thought she'd had to trade for respectability, Rhetta reluctantly let go of the dreams she'd nurtured for so long and gave herself up to him and to the wild, untamed emotions that too often made her fight the world and all those around her because they could rarely be fulfilled.

She gasped, and sighed, and eagerly accepted him, oblivious of the shabbiness around her, eyes filled to overflowing with surrender, and as he too lost himself in loving her, they both knew that life and love had made them what they were, and there was no going back to what they might have been. A bond had forged between them years ago. A bond they couldn't break, and Rhetta seemed to sense that nothing short of death would ever end it. As Jarrod trembled, then lay still against her, his body covering hers, she knew only too well that somehow this had been her destiny from the very start, yet wished somehow she could have changed it and Griff wouldn't have to die.

She listened to Jarrod's unsteady breathing, then moved slightly, making him aware once more that she was there.

"For heaven's sake, Jarrod, don't smother me," she whispered breathlessly. "It's bad enough I let myself be brought to this."

He raised himself and stared down into her face, flushed and pink from exertion. A thin film of sweat dampened her skin, and her dark eyes were quickly losing their languid expression. "Don't fool yourself, sweetheart," he answered cynically. "You know damn well you enjoyed every second." She stared up at him, her eyes darkening. Enjoyed? Yes, I guess I did, she thought unwillingly, or I'd never let him have his way like this. But oh God, why couldn't it be Griff instead? Why? Why? Why?

"You've made your point," she said miserably. "Now what?"

He kissed her, then slipped from the bed, picked her clothes up from the floor, shaking the dust from them, then threw them at her on the bed. "Now I think I'll go have a talk with Homer Beacon," he said as he reached for his own clothes, then watched her finish dressing.

She settled the fancy hat back on her head after readjusting the clasps that were holding her hair in place. "Why go see him now?" she asked curiously.

"Because when he finds out about the teacher disappearing, he might just take a notion to tell somebody about Burke and his men, and I don't need Sheriff Higgens nosing around here."

Jarrod grabbed the edge of the dirty sheet they'd made love on and flipped it back over the foot of the bed so the telltale spots on it would dry, promising himself that before using the bed again he'd have to bring a clean sheet from the ranch; then he followed Rhetta, who'd already traced a dusty path back to the kitchen.

Rhetta cringed uncomfortably as she glanced about the filthy kitchen, feeling as dirty as the place looked, and promising herself a long luxurious bath when she got back to Trail's End. "What if the men come back while you're gone?" she asked.

He shook his head. "They won't, but just in case, I'll leave a note telling them to stay put." He came up behind her, put his arms around her, and kissed her neck just below the ear, then sighed. "Now, run along home, sweetheart," he urged. "Everything's going to work out fine, you'll see." He kissed her again, his hands caressing her waist, remembering what it was like to feel her naked flesh. "We'll be together soon for keeps, don't worry," he whispered softly. "And we'll have Trail's End too. Just a little longer. I'll send word as soon as they're brought here—then you'll know it's only a matter of time."

She took a deep breath, once more regretting what had to be. If only Jarrod hadn't come back to Raintree and discovered the truth. But then, life wasn't built on ifs, it was built on reality, and he had come back. Now there was nothing she could do but accept things as they were. Her jaw tightened stubbornly and she stepped away from Jarrod's hands, then turned to face him.

"I want them dead this time, with no mistakes, Jarrod,"

she said. "I'm weary of this whole mess, but since it has to be, then get it over with."

"Don't worry, I will," he said. "I'll find a way. And I'll send word when it's done." He straightened, adjusting the gunbelt on his hips, then stepped over, taking her arm to escort her from the house. "Come on, now, there's nothing more to do until the men return. Go home, pretend you're still angry because Griff's gone, put on a good show. Then, when he doesn't return, remember to play the grieving widow."

They walked out onto the porch and stood for a minute, scanning the surrounding hills. Just a few more days, she thought as she watched the sunlight warm the earth, filtering into the trees that clung precariously to the hillside beyond the abandoned mine entrance. Just a few wretched days and she'd no longer have to kowtow to Mrs. Brandt's sharp tongue or climb into an empty bed at night or play wife to a man who hated her. Only a little longer, and she'd be mistress of Trail's End.

Anger at Griff for rejecting her helped take the edge of pain from the thought of never seeing him again, and she turned once more to Jarrod.

"Remember, no mistakes this time, Jarrod," she said bitterly. "We can't afford any. It's up to you."

He smiled, then reached out and took her hand, helping her down the rickety porch steps and into the buggy, still tied to the hitching post out front. "Like I said before, Rhet," he told her as he handed her the reins, "I've been waiting for years to claim what's rightfully mine, and I don't intend to lose you again."

He gave her a quick kiss, then stepped back and watched as she maneuvered the buggy away from the house, and a smile continued to tilt the corners of his mouth as he thought of what it would be like to know he'd taken not only Heywood's wife from him but also his ranch.

He'd been ready to kill the day she'd married Griffin Heywood, and had even pleaded with her not to go through with it, but Rhetta had been determined. She'd been young then and the Heywood money had been more important to her than anything else, but with Garfield Heywood dead he thought for certain she'd change her mind. However, she hadn't, and for years he'd brooded over losing her. Now all that would be over. He'd finally have what he wanted.

He straightened as he watched the buggy disappear in the distance, leaving only a cloud of dust behind; then, as the sounds around him stilled, making him a little wary of the quiet, he shrugged off the ominous feeling that was beginning to grip him and headed for his horse, ground-reined only a few feet away. Once in the saddle, he reined the horse in the opposite direction from where the buggy had disappeared, and headed for Raintree and the newspaper office. Because first, before he could do anything else, he had to have a talk with Homer Beacon.

Sunlight streamed in through the tent flap as Jeanine stirred in Griff's arms, pulling the blanket up over her bare shoulder. She opened her eyes to find him staring at her intently, his own eyes warm with desire. Snuggling closer, she felt the warmth of his body against hers, his hard sinuous muscles pressing close.

"It's time to leave," he murmured reluctantly.

She clung to him, and he kissed her desperately, awakening desire in both of them all over again.

"I wish we had the time," he whispered, his lips against hers; then he drew his head back a little. "But we'd better go while we can. The chief's been known to change his mind." He kissed her again, quickly this time, yet just as passionately, then slipped from the covers and found the bundle of clothes where he'd placed them when he entered the tent last night.

"I'll wait outside," he said after putting them on. "Hurry," and he straightened, the power of his masculinity seeming to fill the tent as he stopped for a brief moment to gaze into her eyes; then he left, ducking under the flap.

The bed was still warm where he'd lain, and it smelled of spicewood. Jeanine felt it with her hand, then shut her eyes as tears began to surface. What now? she thought. Oh

God! How much she loved him. She rolled onto her stomach, her head on her arm, and let the tears fall; then, deciding that feeling sorry for herself wasn't helping matters any, she quickly wiped the tears from her eyes, promising herself she wasn't going to cry again.

Chief Horse Back and his wife had already left the tent, so she crawled from the covers and slipped into her clothes. The air chilled her, and she trembled. Whatever was ahead, it wasn't going to change just because she wished it to. Life didn't work that way. At least it didn't seem to for her. So after putting the buckskins on, she tied her hair back with a strip of rawhide so it wouldn't fly in her face while she was riding, pulled on her moccasins, and left the tent.

They ate a quick breakfast, with the chief and his wife for company, packed up enough food for a couple of days, and within an hour after sunup were riding out of the camp, heading back toward Trail's End, with Chief Horse Back's blessing to take with them.

By noon the sun was high and the air had warmed considerably. Griff knew the land well, and they made good time, yet all the while they were riding, neither of them mentioned the night before. It was there between them, haunting them, and every time their eyes met, Jeanine could feel the tension building inside her, yet they talked about everything except their predicament. They talked of the landscape, speculated as to why she'd been kidnapped. But not one word was spoken about the love they'd shared last night.

Jeanine knew what they'd done was wrong, but had been unable to say no, and it had seemed so natural when it happened. But now, in the light of day, reality had set in and brought with it shame and guilt. She glanced over at Griff now, astride his black stallion Che-ak as they made their way across an open stretch of ground, then urged their mounts up a small incline.

His hair caught the sun, turning it to gold as he held his head erect, watching and listening, his blue eyes intent on the trail ahead. Last night he'd made her forget everything but their need for each other, and this morning, waking in his arms . . . But now, since leaving the Indian village, he seemed so aloof and preoccupied, and she wondered, did he have regrets? Was he too feeling the guilt she felt or was it just that his mind was intent on getting them safely back? If she only knew.

She hadn't dreamed it would be like this, but she just couldn't forget that he was a married man, and it was torture for her, wondering what was going to happen when they returned to the ranch. The pain of realizing she'd probably spend the rest of her time at Trail's End jealously watching Rhetta sharing Griff's life, knowing there was no way she could change what was happening, yet loving him in spite of it, hurt terribly, and her heart constricted painfully as she watched him riding ahead of her on the trail. How very much she loved him, yet was it worth the guilt and hurt that were tearing her apart?

By evening they'd traveled a long way and were well out of what was considered Comanche territory, but Griff was still overly cautious. He'd picked an isolated place to spend the night, in a small grove of trees next to a gently flowing brook that splashed and bubbled, frothing over a shallow bed of rocks. And as soon as he had a fire built, he dressed a rabbit he'd shot earlier in the day and skewered it on a spit above the flames so it could cook slowly. Now the aroma filled the cool night air, making Jeanine's mouth water as she took the bedroll from off Blossom, where she'd carried it behind the saddle, and walked over, opening it, spreading it on the ground, then strolled over to the fire.

Griff watched her closely without her realizing it, as he gave the spit a turn, then secured it back in place again and stood up.

"What's the matter?" he finally asked, as he saw the vacant look in her eyes. All day as they rode along, he'd felt her withdrawing from everything around her, including him, and since they'd made camp, her silence had been all too noticeable.

Jeanine had been standing quietly, staring into the fire,

her thoughts miles away, on Gar, and Rhetta and last
night, and a thousand other things. She glanced at him, the
faraway look still in her eyes. Night shadows were already
falling and it was getting so dark it was hard to see his
face, the trees and woods surrounding them already deep
in shadows.

She sighed. "I wish I knew," she answered hesitantly,
then let her eyes be drawn once more to the crackling
flames of the fire, and she turned her back to him, staring
at it.

Griff walked over and put his arms around her waist to
draw her to him, leaning down, nuzzling her neck and
kissing her behind the ear, but she drew away, wrenching
free, and then turned to him, her face flushed.

"No, Griff, stop!" she cried, her voice breaking on an
angry sob. "Not again, not tonight! Please! I let you love
me last night because our lives were at stake, but not now,
not again. I told you before, I won't be your mistress,
ever, so please, let me be, and go back to your wife,
where you belong!"

Griff frowned, startled and surprised by her sudden
anger; then he laughed cynically as he looked down into
her face. "You're not too observant, are you, my lovely
little schoolteacher?" he said, his eyes searching hers.
"Telling me to go back to my wife. Jeanine . . ." The
laughter left his eyes, and he grew serious. "I've never
loved my wife, and I've never slept with her in all the years
we've been married, either."

"Don't lie!"

"I'm not lying."

"You're an expert at making love."

His mouth tightened. "I didn't say I'd never had a
woman. I said I'd never made love to Rhetta." His voice
softened again as he pleaded with her. "Jeanine, do you
honestly think any other woman has ever been given the
same love I gave to you last night?" he asked gently.
"Never."

She stared at him, puzzled, struggling to make sense of

what he was trying to tell her. "What did you just say?" she asked hesitantly.

He sighed, hoping this time she'd believe him. "I said I've never made love to any other woman the way I made love to you last night," he answered slowly. "I've never wanted to, Jeanine."

"No, not that," she said. "The other . . . about Rhetta."

"Rhetta?" He eyed her curiously. "I said I've never touched her."

"But Gar . . .?"

"Gar?" He winced, suddenly realizing what she was getting at, and his eyes deepened to a stormy blue, his rugged jawline tensing as if it were made of stone. "Ah yes, Gar. Let me tell you about Gar, Jeanine," he said roughly. "Let me tell you about *my* son."

She listened quietly, not moving a muscle, her eyes studying his face.

"I had a brother once," he began quietly. "Did you know I had a brother, Garfield?"

She nodded.

"You no doubt heard, then, that he was murdered, right?"

She nodded again.

"Good. But what you don't know is that the day after his murder, Rhetta came and told me she was carrying his baby." He glanced down toward the fire, staring into it as if remembering. "You didn't know my father, Jeanine," he went on as he looked back up at her. "He was a stern man who hated scandal and avoided it at all costs, and for a number of years he'd had problems with his heart. When Gar was killed, he had a heart attack, and knowing that the shock of learning about Rhetta might be too much for him on top of everything else, I tried to spare him. At first Rhetta wanted only money, but then, as we talked, she suddenly came up with an alternative. A fabulous idea, as she put it. That is, if I was willing. . . ." He looked at her helplessly. "What else could I do?" He paused and looked away for a moment, then looked back at her again and went on. "Father died without ever learning the truth,

Jeanine," he said quietly, "and the only people who do know are the ones closest to me, Mrs. Brandt, Cory, Crystal, and my lawyer, John Scott, now you. They helped me keep the truth from my father, Jeanine. You see, Gar's not mine, as everyone thinks. He's my brother's son."

She searched his face, wanting so badly to believe him, yet it all seemed so absurd. "But the two of you . . . everyone speaks so highly of your marriage . . ."

"You mean the farce we've lived all these years? It hasn't been that hard to fool folks around here, really, especially since they seem to want so hard to believe what they think they see." He stepped closer and took her by the shoulders, his fingers tightening. "Rhetta and I have a simple arrangement," he said carefully. "I pretend to be the dutiful husband, she the loving wife, and being gone the past four years just made things all the easier. You see, I'd decided a long time ago that I was going to stay clear of any other women, so I'd never have to worry about falling in love." He frowned, his voice deepening emotionally. "And then you came along." His hand moved up, caressing her face. "I kept fighting it, telling myself it wasn't true . . . yet knowing the whole time it was." His eyes hardened. "Dammit, Jeanine, I don't want to love you. It complicates everything—my life . . . Gar's . . ."

"Don't love me, then," she said bitterly, but he shook his head.

"It's too late for that." His eyes deepened to a brilliant blue, and he pulled her to him, holding her close.

"I meant it when I said I wouldn't be your mistress, Griff," she said, but his eyes bored into hers, sending shivers down her spine, making her tremble.

"You're sure about that?" he replied huskily, and she groaned.

"I guess I'm not really sure of anything anymore," she murmured breathlessly, and pushed her hands against his chest, trying unsuccessfully to pull away. "All I know is that I should have run from here that first day."

He half-smiled. "And where would you have gone, Jeannie Gray?"

Her eyes narrowed shrewdly. "How long have you known for sure?"

"I suspected it that first night when Warren knocked your glasses off in the hall. You looked so scared, and it was just enough to set me wondering. Then that night in the harness room, when you dressed my arm." He tilted her face up so he could look into her eyes. He never dreamed a woman's eyes could stir him so, and he trembled deep inside, his tanned face eager. "You know, I think I fell in love with you way back in St. Louis, that first time I ever saw you, long before there ever was a war, Miss Jeannie Gray," he said tenderly. "And the war has nothing to do with us either, please believe me." His hands caressed her as he spoke. "What has to do with us is wanting you so badly I ache inside, Jeanine," he whispered huskily. "It means looking into your eyes and feeling it clear to my toes, and knowing your lips are like sweet wine to intoxicate my senses. It has nothing to do with a war that's over. I don't care what you were then, only what you are now, and damn it, Jeanine, I want what you are!"

His mouth covered hers hungrily, and at first she started to resist; then, as his kiss flowed through her, over her, inside her, she melted against him, surrendering to his pleas, and for a few brief moments they forgot that someone had made an attempt on Griff's life and had tried to get rid of Jeanine.

Suddenly they both froze as they heard a gun being cocked, and a voice broke the stillness.

"That's good. Great! Stay right where you are and don't move a muscle," the voice said, and Jeanine's heart sank to her feet as Griff raised his head, reluctantly ending their embrace.

The voice was the same one that had brought Jeanine out here the night she was kidnapped. The same ugly voice that had forced her to endure those horrible humiliating hours of captivity. Only this time the man stepped out of the shadows, and as they both turned toward him, for the first time Jeanine could see his face.

He was wearing a rumpled brown shirt, black vest, hat, and pants, with a dirty red bandanna around his neck, and his ruddy lined face had a deep scar down the left cheek. Steely gray eyes reflecting the orange flames from the firelight glared at them, and Jeanine felt Griff's muscles tense as five other men joined the man with the scar, stepping deftly out of the shadows, and they all stood watching, two of them with their guns drawn.

"You can move apart now," the man with the scar said. "Slowly."

Griff didn't move, but held her tight, afraid to let go.

"I said move," the man said again. "Or the lady gets it first!"

Griff's arms slackened, and Jeanine stepped away, watching the taut expression on his face. Don't try, please don't try to jump them, Griff, they'll kill you, she pleaded silently, and hoped he could read the message in her eyes, because she knew he was like a coiled spring, ready to move any second. His eyes met hers, and for a brief moment she wasn't quite sure what he was going to do; then he glanced toward the man with the scar, evidently realizing the odds were against him, and Jeanine exhaled, relieved, as he held his ground.

"Cozy little setup ya got here," the man with the scar said as he looked at the rabbit cooking over the fire, then glanced off to where their bedrolls were spread out, then back to Jeanine and Griff again. "Looks like the boss was right, don't it?"

"And who's the boss?" asked Griff.

The man sneered. "Don't worry, you'll find out." He looked at the others. "No use lettin' the food go to waste, boys," he said. "Might's well eat before we leave." Then he motioned toward Jeanine and Griff. "Tie 'em up first, though," he ordered arrogantly. "I don't want 'em tryin' to think they can sneak off on us while we're takin' care of things." He leaned over, pulling a leg off the rabbit, juggling it in his fingers and blowing on it, then bit off a big chunk, maneuvering it about in his mouth until it cooled enough to swallow.

"Hold out your hands," one of the men said as he unfastened a length of rope from his belt, but Griff stepped in front of Jeanine.

"You can't put ropes on her again," he protested. "Her wrists are all scabbed up now. You do that and they'll bleed again."

"So?"

The man with the scar strolled over, still munching on the rabbit leg. "Don't worry, she ain't gonna break, Mr. Heywood," he said. "The boss said to fetch you both, but he didn't say we hadda be nice, now, did he?" He scowled. "You know, you oughta be damn glad we're short of time again, 'cause the boys was disappointed before, and they might just be real anxious to have a little fun with her."

Griff cursed under his breath as the man with the rope grabbed his wrists and quickly wrapped the rope around them so he couldn't try to use his fists. "Damn you," he blurted furiously. "I'd like to wring your neck."

The man with the scar took a step backward, the grin still playing about his mouth. "I bet you would." He laughed sadistically; then his eyes hardened as he glanced at his men. "Now, finish tying them up," he said, and sauntered back toward the fire while they still held guns on Jeanine and Griff, and finished securing their wrists.

After taking Griff's guns and his hunting knife from him, they led them both over to their horses, boosted them up, and tied them to the saddle horns, leaving their horses tethered securely to a nearby tree so they couldn't ride off. They then proceeded to clear out the area while finishing off the rabbit.

"Make sure you don't leave nothin' behind," the man with the scar said as he headed for the fire with a cup of water so he could put it out and scatter the ashes, covering them with dirt. "The boss said nobody's to know they headed back this way." When the place was finally cleared, without a trace of anyone having been there except for the horses' hoofprints on the soft ground, all six men joined Jeanine and Griff on horseback, and they headed away from the creek and the clearing, moving off into the woods, which were pitch dark now, and this time there was no need for blindfolds.

They'd been riding about four or five hours when Griff began to realize the surroundings were vaguely familiar.

"Well," he said as they topped the crest of a hill and started down the other side, making their way between some cedar trees. "If it isn't the Vance property . . . and I'll bet we're headed for the old copper mine, right?" he said. "I always did think Vance had a hand in this."

The man with the scar was riding beside Jeanine, and he stopped, pulling his pinto back, reining in alongside Griff. "So now you know," he said sarcastically. "But it ain't gonna do you no good, fella, 'cause you ain't ever gonna leave this place alive, you'll see," and he laughed, spurring his pinto viciously, passing everyone, taking the lead, bringing the procession down the hill to stop in front of an old ramshackle house.

A mine shaft was about a hundred yards from the house, and a small shack close to it with another larger barn some distance away. The place was nestled neatly in a small valley with a natural screen of hills on all sides. The man with the scar dismounted, giving orders to the others to bring the prisoners in, and Jeanine and Griff were dragged from their horses, shoved up the steps onto the porch, and pushed inside the old house.

The main room seemed to be the kitchen, but someone had ripped bunks from the bunkhouse out back and fastened them onto the far wall, where they looked out of place. A table stood in the center of the room, and besides being cluttered with dirty dishes and debris, it also held a lamp that the man with the scar lit, and when he turned it up, Griff and Jeanine gazed about, looking the place over more carefully. It had been well lived in, that was for sure, and its occupants were anything but tidy housekeepers, the bare floors gritty with dirt.

The room smelled of beer and stale food and there was a musty smell that seemed to cling to their nostrils, making them wrinkle their noses in disgust as they glanced at each other. To the right of them as they were shoved through the kitchen they could see through an open door to what they both presumed was the parlor, but which now seemed to have nothing in it except a bed and a lot of dust and dirt.

The man with the scar kept on pushing them toward another door at the back of the room, and as he swung it open, they could see in the flickering light from the lamp on the table that it had been unused for some time. After being forced inside, they were made to lie on the floor, their hands untied, then tied again, this time behind their backs, and their feet were fastened together too, so they wouldn't be able to walk, or even stand up.

The room was cold, dark, and dirty, devoid of any furniture except for a small table to the right of the door, and the back window was broken, letting in the cool night air. Griff guessed the room must have been a bedroom at one time, and after the men left, closing the door behind them, he tried to adjust his eyes to the darkness.

"Are you all right?" he asked Jeanine, who'd been left lying a few feet away from him.

She managed to push herself up, and leaned wearily against the wall behind her. "I . . . I think so," she answered hesitantly. "But my wrists are bleeding again, and with my arms pulled back like this, they're already starting to get sore."

Griff swore as he moved in the general direction of her voice, rolling and sliding across the floor until their bodies touched; then he wriggled into a sitting position and propped himself up against the wall beside her.

"We'll never get out of this alive, will we, Griff?" she said hopelessly, and laid her head against his shoulder.

He leaned down, kissing her forehead. "I just hope they don't get any funny ideas about you," he said. "Because I don't know if I'd be able to keep my head and stay put if they tried anything, and I sure as hell wouldn't be very much use to you dead."

"Oh, Griff, you don't think they would, do you?" she asked fearfully. "If they raped me I think I'd die!"

"Shhh . . . I'm sorry, I shouldn't have mentioned it."

He was upset with himself for frightening her even more. "It's just that it's been on my mind ever since that man threw it in my face before, when we were back at the campsite, and now that we're here . . ." He paused. "I don't mean to frighten you," he went on softly. "But we have no idea what to expect, and sometimes it's best to try to think of what we might do, just in case."

She snuggled closer to him, as much for warmth as reassurance. "Oh God, I love you, Griff," she whispered softly.

He took a deep breath. "Kiss me, Jeanine." His voice was rough and unsteady. "Kiss me now and don't even think about what might be . . . please," and she tilted her head up until his mouth found hers in the dark.

The kiss was long, soothing, yet passionately alive, warming them both, and when it was over she nestled her head back again on his shoulder and they sat quietly, listening to the conversation in the next room, taking in every word.

"When's Vance gonna get here?" they heard one of the men asking through the closed door.

"He should be here any minute now," answered the man with the scar. "So you can just forget any ideas you got about havin' fun with the little lady back there, you hear?" They heard him snort irritably. "I know you're mad 'cause I said no before. Well, once in a while I don't mind, but I don't want him walkin' in here to find you screwin' around."

"That's the trouble with you, Burke," the man said, disappointment in his voice, belying his words. "You always think I don't have nothin' on my mind but what's between a woman's legs. I ain't like you, you know." He tried to vindicate himself. "That wasn't what I was thinkin' of anyway."

"Wasn't it?" The man called Burke laughed. "You coulda fooled me, Red," and Griff knew the man they'd called Burke was right. The other man—it had to be the one with red hair—had been eyeing Jeanine greedily all along the trail, and now Griff felt Jeanine cringe, moving even closer against him as the conversation continued.

"How about the Heywood dame, is she comin' too?" someone asked.

Griff stiffened, suddenly alert.

"Who knows?" answered Burke. "We ain't got Heywood in there for nothin'."

"But why the lady, Burke?"

"Ain't you the dummy," Burke answered again. "You seen them kissin' when we come up on 'em. There ain't no woman gonna stand for a husband carryin' on like that."

"But if she's tryin' to kill him anyways, what's the difference?"

"Jesus! How should I know?" Burke snapped. "Why don'tcha ask Jarrod. He's the one told us to get rid of her. Besides, women's funny when it comes to husbands. Even if they hate their old man, they don't like no other females hornin' in on their territory. Does somethin' to their pride, I guess."

They listened to the talk for a long while, trying to distinguish one voice from another and put names to the voices. They knew now that the man with the scar was called Burke, the one with the exceptionally deep voice and red hair was Red. The others were still nameless as yet, but Jeanine would soon put a name to each voice and they were names she'd never forget, just like she'd never forget their voices.

She had felt Griff tense at the mention of Rhetta's name, and now she heard his voice, stunned and disbelieving. "I was so sure it was just someone trying to stop the cattle drive," he muttered tonelessly. "I should have guessed." He leaned his cheek against her forehead. "But why? I promised her that as long as there was no other woman I'd keep right on pretending, for Gar's sake."

"Then I came along?"

"No, it wasn't just your coming." He frowned. "It started before that, and that's what I don't understand. Unless she's just tired of pretending anymore, but couldn't face leaving Trail's End, and figured that by killing me before I made out a will, she'd inherit along with Gar.'' He paused a minute. ''But that doesn't make sense either, because even if I made a will leaving everything to Gar, she'd still get to stay at the ranch. Why would she want me dead?''

''I'm afraid, Griff,'' Jeanine said hesitantly, and he straightened some, moving into a more comfortable position so she could lean on him a little better.

''Shhh, don't worry, we'll get out of here,'' he said. ''I've got an idea.'' Then he cocked his ear. ''Wait.'' He listened closely, and Jeanine strained her ears. ''Horses,'' he said as he inhaled sharply. ''Maybe we'll finally find out what this is all about.''

They heard someone ride up out front, and the sound of boots on the front porch. Then the kitchen door opened, and the voices in the kitchen grew silent, waiting. Finally . . .

''Howdy, Jarrod,'' Burke said.

Jarrod's voice was sharp, edgy as he answered. ''Where are they?''

Someone must have pointed, because the next thing Griff and Jeanine heard was spurred boots scuffling hurriedly across the floor toward the room they were in, and when the door opened, they both blinked, trying to adjust their eyes to the light.

Jarrod was alone, holding a kerosene lamp up to light his way, and as he stepped into the room, shutting the door behind him, he stood so the light fell across their faces and stared at them for a long hard minute.

''Well, well,'' he finally said after putting the lamp down on the stand beside the door. His hands settled on his hips and he looked down at them cynically. ''I've waited a long time for this.''

Griff's face was like granite as he stared back at Jarrod. ''I figured as much,'' he said knowingly.

''To hell you did.'' Jarrod laughed. ''You thought someone was trying to stop your stupid cattle drive or that my father was trying to force you out, and you know it, Griff.

Why, you'd still be guessing if it wasn't for the little lady here,'' and he motioned with his head toward Jeanine.

"What does Rhetta have to do with it?" Griff asked as he watched the excited gleam in Jarrod's hazel eyes.

"You mean you haven't figured it all out yet?" he asked, sneering. "Hell, I thought you were smarter than that, Griff."

"She can't be in love with you."

"Why not?"

"She loves herself too much."

Jarrod looked smug. "That's only your opinion." He straightened arrogantly. "But I'll let you in on the secret, Griff," he went on, hefting his gunbelt to rest more comfortably on his hips, spurs jingling as his legs spread into a forceful stance. "I want Rhetta, and I want Trail's End, and with you dead I'll have both."

"And Rhetta's willing?"

"Let's just say she understands."

Griff studied him curiously. Jarrod was really enjoying himself at their expense, and he actually looked pleased as he tipped his hat back on his head of dark wavy hair, then hooked his thumb into a pocket at the front of the brown leather vest he was wearing, trying to look confident. But it was easy to tell he'd been riding hard. His brown pants were covered with dust, and the red striped shirt he wore was clinging to his sweaty torso. To add to that, he smelled of horse and saddle and looked like he needed a bath as well as a shave. Usually he wasn't so lax in his appearance, and Griff wondered if maybe he wasn't quite as sure of things as he pretended to be. Either that or else he was so sure of himself that he figured he didn't have to worry about what anyone thought anymore. Whatever it was, Jarrod seemed different, but in a rather frightening way.

"Whose idea was it to take Jeanine?" Griff asked, feeling uneasy under the man's steady gaze, but needing to know all the answers.

"You mean Jeannie Gray, here?" he asked, then chuckled deep in his throat, his brooding eyes sifting over her insolently. "Well, I'll tell you now. That was sort of a joint venture," he said curtly. "At first Rhetta was just put out because you didn't send the little lady here packing, and then, when Warren let on who he thought she really was, that really upset her. She kept begging me to get rid of her right then and there. But it wasn't until your precious schoolteacher here and that fella from the newspaper started sticking their noses into things that didn't concern them that I decided to go along with her suggestion."

"You mean Homer?" Jeanine asked, addressing Jarrod for the first time.

His eyes narrowed. "That's right, little lady, Homer Beacon, of the *Beacon Journal*. I knew he'd been asking a lot of questions, and then one day one of my men spotted him watching this place. When Beacon left, Red followed, and he went straight to Indian Rock, where you were waiting." He looked at Griff. "Now, that don't sound like coincidence to me, Griff, does it to you?" he asked. "Especially since, according to Warren, Homer Beacon knew Jeannie Gray."

"Homer was my manager during the war," Jeanine explained, knowing her masquerade was over.

"Oh, I know that," Jarrod answered flippantly. "But he was an agent too, wasn't he?"

"Where is he?" Jeanine asked, suddenly frightened by the look in his eyes.

"Funny you should ask." Jarrod's mouth twisted sardonically. "Let's see, now. Seems he had an unfortunate accident . . . if I remember right," he said. "Fell off a ladder in the newspaper office when he was getting some paper down off a shelf, and broke his neck. Too bad, too. He was a damn good newspaperman. They buried him Tuesday afternoon."

"You killed him!" she cried tearfully.

"Did I say that?" He gestured toward Griff. "Now, look, did I tell her I killed Beacon?" he asked, pretending innocence.

"You didn't have to," she answered heatedly. "Homer'd never slip and fall from a ladder."

"Your opinion, Miss Grayson," he cut in. "The sheriff thought otherwise."

Griff was furious. "You're pretty sure of yourself, aren't you, Jarrod?" he said.

Jarrod laughed again. "Why shouldn't I be?" His eyes suddenly hardened. "You don't have a prayer of getting out of here alive, Griff, and you know it," he taunted. "You see, the last anyone heard, you were on your way to the Comanche to rescue the schoolteacher here. Even your foreman and everyone else out at the ranch'll swear to that. A shame neither of you got back alive, isn't it?"

"It won't work," Griff warned him. "We were guests of Chief Horse Back, and he personally guaranteed our safety."

"Come on, now, Griff," he taunted. "You know damn well nobody's going to take a chance on going back into Indian territory just to find out if the two of you have been killed or not. No, as far as the world's concerned, they'll think the Indians took care of you." He looked pensive for a moment. "You know, I don't know whether to have your horses disappear with you or maybe let someone conveniently find them out near Indian territory with blood all over the saddles." He rubbed his chin thoughtfully. "After all, that black stallion of yours is really a beauty, Griff. It'd be a shame to get rid of a horse like that."

Griff glowered at him, his blue eyes stormy as Jarrod went on.

"And if we did that, we could even see to it that some of your clothes were found ripped and bloody. Wouldn't that be the thing." He paused for a second and frowned, then went on. "But then again, it may not be too good an idea to keep your horses around. Somebody might spot the boys trying to get rid of them. No, maybe it's best they disappear too." He smiled again, sneering. "Yeah, that's best. Oh, and I'm sure glad you didn't take time to make out that will leaving everything to Gar, Griff," he continued in the same light banter, as if he were just having a friendly talk. "Now, with you dead, Rhetta and the boy'll both share, and I don't think folks'll condemn me if I should happen to start consoling your widow, now, will they?''

"And Gar?" asked Griff.

"What about him?"

"Where does he stand in all this? If you hurt him . . ."

"I wouldn't think of it," Jarrod answered, and in the flickering lamplight he reminded Jeanine of the devil himself. He laughed wickedly. "After all, Griff," he said, looking full into Griff's face, so he wouldn't miss his reaction to what he was going to say, "a smart man doesn't go around killing his own flesh and blood, now, does he?''

"What the hell are you talking about?" Griff asked, his voice sharp, unyielding as he stared at Jarrod, trying to grasp his intent, and hoping he was wrong. His eyes were like ice as he inhaled sharply.

Jarrod smirked; then his eyes grew cold as steel. "Since Rhetta isn't here, guess I'll have to tell you the whole thing myself, won't I?" he offered, pleased that he was going to finally be able to get it out in the open. "It's time you knew anyway. You see, Gar isn't your brother's son, Griff," he confessed boldly. "He's my son," and his eyes narrowed shrewdly at the disbelieving look on Griff's face. "Shock you?" he asked, raising his eyebrows. "It shouldn't really. I loved Rhetta for a long time before your brother came along. But she had a crazy notion she could get him to marry her so she could become a Heywood. She didn't love him, mind you, and never would have, but then, she never loved me either, still doesn't. Like you said, there's only two things Rhetta loves, herself and money. I'm not even sure she really loves the boy, but he is mine."

"You're lying!" Griff yelled vehemently, but Jarrod was too sure of himself.

"Facts are facts, Griff," he said, enjoying what he was doing to the man he considered his enemy. "You can believe it or not. It's up to you. But have you taken a good look at your son lately, Griff? I have. Does he remind you of your brother? Of a Heywood? Or tell me, does he maybe have a strong resemblance to me, right down to the color of his eyes? Too bad you can't ask Rhetta, isn't it? But then, she'd only tell you the same thing.''

Griff was livid, yet tried to compose himself, letting the full truth sink in. ''You blackmailed Rhetta into helping you, didn't you?'' he said, his teeth clenched.

Jarrod grinned, then suddenly sobered, his eyes blazing. ''My father always wanted Trail's End and never got it,'' he answered viciously. ''Well, he was a coward, Griff, but I'm not. I will get it, and when I do, I'll be the richest man in Texas someday instead of always taking second best to the Heywoods!''

''You're insane!''

''No, just smart.''

''Smart?'' Griff's eyes darkened as he challenged him. ''I'd say you're pretty dumb,'' he taunted back. ''Because when I'm dead, you won't have any more hold over Rhetta, but she'll have one over you, for killing us, and then you'll be doing her bidding.''

Jarrod leaned forward, looking straight into Griff's eyes, and he smiled triumphantly. ''That's where you're wrong, Griff,'' he said, and saw Griff frown. Jarrod's mouth twisted arrogantly. ''Who the hell do you think killed your brother?'' he asked sardonically.

Neither Griff nor Jeanine was able to answer as they both stared at Jarrod, stunned by his question.

''I knew that'd get you,'' Jarrod said, and chuckled to himself. ''I knew you didn't know.'' He stopped snickering, and his voice deepened. ''She wanted him to marry her, and when he refused, she told him she'd tell everyone the baby she was expecting was his if he didn't. Now, no man's gonna put up with somethin' like that, Griff, especially when he knows damn well the kid ain't his 'cause he never touched her. That was one thing I'll say about your brother, Griff. Garfield thought too much of women to take advantage of them, even Rhetta, although she sure as hell tried to get him to change his mind many a time. Without being too obvious about it of course. But it didn't work, so she tried the next best thing. Only he didn't fall in line with her little plan, and you know what kind of a temper your wife's got. Why, when he laughed at her for suggesting something so ridiculous, she just up and shot him with her pa's old gun she used to carry in her hand-bag. Then she made her way back home, keepin' off the main roads so nobody'd see her, threw the gun she'd used down the well, climbed into bed, and when Warren came back from town that night, late as usual, she told him she'd been too sick to go out with Garfield when he came callin' earlier in the evening, and he'd gone on without her. Since nobody'd seen them together that night, nobody questioned her story. The next day they found your broth-er's body about a half-mile from town with a bullet in him.''

"You've known this all along?" Griff asked incredulously.

"Hell no." Jarrod eyed them both curiously. "Like you, I didn't know anything about it at all, not until last year when I came home from Mexico and happened to get a good look at Gar. He's the spittin' image of me at his age, and when I cornered Rhetta about it, the whole thing just happened to come out. No sir, Griff." He sighed, pleased with himself. "There's just no way she's ever gonna hold anything over my head, 'cause as far as I know, the gun she used that night is still at the bottom of that well. Now, the property may belong to somebody else, but they're still usin' that same well and I bet I could put my hands on that gun anytime I want, if I cared to go fishin' for it."

Griff was at a loss. He'd never suspected, nor had anyone else, and the sudden realization of all he'd put up with from Rhetta over the years, and all the time . . .

"What a stupid fool I've been," he groaned furiously, and leaned his head back against the wall, eyes shut. "What a damn, dumb, stupid fool!"

"You had no way of knowing, Griff," Jeanine said as she watched the agony on his face. "It was a natural mistake anyone could have made."

After a few seconds he opened his eyes and looked directly into hers, and she could see the sorrow, pain, and frustration mirrored there. All these years he'd loved

Gar, thinking the boy was his brother's son, raising him as his own, and he'd let Rhetta share his name, if not his bed, pretending to the world away from Trail's End that he loved her, and all along, she was the one who'd killed his brother. Jeanine sensed the hatred building up in Griff, and trembled, a little frightened by the intense look in his eyes as she stared back at him. How he must hate Rhetta.

"Now that you do know, it won't do you any good, though, Griff," Jarrod said, interrupting their short exchange of words, and they both looked up at him as he continued gloating. "Because you see, I've decided what I'm going to do with the two of you." He was quite pleased with himself again. "First, I'm going to take some of the men with me and ride back to the Double V Bar to get some dynamite. That should take the rest of the night, I suppose, but when I get back in the morning, you, the schoolteacher here, and your horses are gonna be taken into the old mine, we'll blast her shut, and no one'll ever know you're there. It's the best idea I've had yet. I should have thought of it before." He hesitated, then sighed. "Now," he said quite jovially, "since I may not get a chance to in the morning before you meet your maker, Griff, let me thank you for taking such good care of my son." He stared at them both for a second as if thinking. "You know, it's too bad really," he said thoughtfully. "You two do make such a nice couple." He stared for a minute longer, then straightened, adjusting the hat on his head before reaching over and picking the kerosene lamp up from the stand. "Well, I'd better be on my way," he went on, quite pleased with himself. "If I intend to get back here by morning, I'm really going to have to ride. It's late already," and he took a deep breath, then raised a finger to his hat, saluting them contemptuously. "*Adiós, amigos,*" he said curtly. "I'll be back about dawn." He walked out, pulling the door firmly shut behind him.

They both watched the door shut, but neither spoke as they listened to Jarrod in the next room, giving orders to the men. All but two would go back to the Double V Bar with him, and the two left behind would make sure their prisoners stayed put. Then when Jarrod and the rest of them returned in the morning, they'd seal Jeanine and Griff in the mine, making sure to blast both entrances shut, and no one would ever see the two of them again. The plot was foolproof, except for one thing.

After listening to Jarrod and the men leave, making sure everything was quiet and the two men left in the next room weren't going to come check on them right away, Griff leaned close to Jeanine's ear. "Move around so your back's to me," he whispered softly. "Then sit perfectly still and try not to wince or cry out if I should happen to hurt you. I think I can loosen your ropes so we can get out of here."

She was a little surprised at first, but her heart began to pound hopefully as she moved into position, then felt his fingers begin to pick at the ropes.

"This'll take all night, won't it?" she asked, her voice barely audible. "Your fingers must be almost numb, and they've had us tied so tight."

He leaned back as close to her as he could to whisper, "I've been in worse situations."

They listened cautiously to the sounds in the other room while he worked methodically on the ropes, trying as best he could to loosen them. His fingers were long and sinewy, but the ropes were tight and it was a slow process. Jeanine's wrists started bleeding again, and he swore softly to himself, wanting to stop, let her try to loosen the ropes on his wrists instead, but she urged him on, whispering encouragement, because she was certain she'd never be able to loosen his, especially with her hands almost numb. His fingers were stronger, and she knew it was the quickest way.

She bit her lip against the pain as other scabs broke open on her wrists, but still she wouldn't let him quit, and finally, after some fifteen or twenty minutes, she felt the rope slacken, then sighed, relieved as it let loose altogether.

It took only a few minutes more for her to finish slipping the rest of the rope from around her wrists, then untie the knotted rope fastening his wrists, and afterward they both sat in the darkness and untied their own feet, trying to be as quiet as possible. Then, just as they finished taking the last of the ropes from their ankles, one of the men in the next room started playing a guitar. Griff smiled ironically. They were in luck. It was just what they needed. The music would drown out any noises they might make, and since the place was old, the floors would no doubt squeak. Very carefully, so as not to be heard, he helped Jeanine to her feet, and they began to creep cautiously toward the window, both glad they were still wearing moccasins. Even so, the old boards groaned under their weight and they were forced to stop a few times just to listen. When the music didn't stop, however, they'd move again, slowly and quietly, sometimes on tiptoe, until finally, after what seemed like an eternity, they stood looking out through the hole in the broken pane of glass, trying to decide what to do next.

The window swung out instead of up and down like most windows, and Griff grimaced as he reached up to open it. Suddenly the guitar playing stopped and they both froze, holding their breath. However, after only a few harrowing seconds, it started up again and they both sighed, relieved, and once more Griff took hold of the window to open it. Although it creaked some at the hinges, this time the guitar playing didn't stop, and he swung the window wide.

Once it was finally open, Griff began to get a little more confident. The rusty hinges hadn't been as noisy as he'd thought they'd be, and now he lifted Jeanine up, set her firmly on the sill, then had her swing her legs over.

"Is it far down, can you see?" he asked, his lips pressed close, whispering in her ear.

She bent forward and looked out for a second, then leaned back against him again, whispering back, "It's not too far, about four or five feet."

He squeezed her hand, then scooted her sideways and climbed up beside her, still whispering. "I'll go first." He braced himself. "Count three to yourself, then follow," and he dropped to the ground, then stepped aside, waiting for her.

Within seconds she was beside him and his hand found hers in the dark. "Come on," he said anxiously. "We won't be able to get to the horses, and besides, if we did, they'd hear us for sure. We'll have to try to make it on foot."

They continued to hold hands as they moved stealthily away from the house.

"It's a long walk, I know," he told her. "But we've got the night on our side, and I know a few shortcuts." He squeezed her hand, then sounded more assured. "Let's just pray that they won't discover we're gone until morning," and after stopping for a minute so he could take their bearings, they started walking again, moving farther and farther away from the house, quickening their pace as they reached the base of the hills surrounding the place, then headed uphill, moving cross-country, in the direction of Trail's End.

13

Jeanine and Griff had been walking for hours, and now it was almost dawn. Although she was tired and hungry, she stayed right behind him as he motioned for her to follow him up the side of a steep cliff that looked like it was almost perpendicular.

At first, clinging precariously to the foot- and handholds he showed her, she was certain she'd never make it. But with encouragement from him, and a helping hand when she neared the ledge he was on, she managed.

The ledge was halfway up, with honeysuckle, wild grapes, and a number of other straggly vines making a backdrop behind them, and Jeanine was surprised when, after reaching the narrow ledge, she saw Griff scoop up a handful of the tangled vines and lift them carefully, showing her an opening that the vines had been concealing. It was only a small overhang but was just big enough for two people to hide in comfortably, and she crawled inside, quickly sitting down, then watched him follow.

"We'll rest here all day," he said as he settled down beside her, letting the natural screen of vines fall back into place over the opening. "It's too hard to travel in the daylight without being seen, and Jarrod's men'll be searching once they've discovered we're gone."

She leaned her head back against the cool earthen wall behind them, trying to ignore the bugs, beatles, and spiders that were scurrying for cover from their intrusion, and she was thankful to be wearing buckskins in case the insects decided to fight for what they thought was theirs. She brushed a spiderweb from the front of her hair, then leaned forward and peered through tiny openings in the vines. Sitting here, up so high, they had a good view in all directions, so no one could approach without being seen.

"I'm glad you decided we should stop," she said wearily. "I'm not only tired, but starved. I know there's nothing to eat, but at least maybe I can get a little rest. I'm just not used to this sort of thing."

He'd been watching her intently, and now he reached down, rummaging around inside a small leather pouch that had been hanging from his gunbelt. "Who said there's nothing to eat?" he replied, pleased with himself. "Compliments of Chief Horse Back," and he pulled his hand out, offering her a piece of jerky.

"How is it they didn't take that too?" she asked as she took it from him, then leaned back again.

He bit a chunk off a piece he'd kept for himself and wallowed it to the side of his mouth, stuffing it in his cheek so he could answer. "Carelessness. They were only interested in taking weapons, and probably thought we wouldn't be able to use it anyway." He placed a hand over the empty sheath on his gunbelt. "I sure wish they hadn't taken my hunting knife, though. I made it myself years ago when I was living with the Comanche, and I've had it for so long I feel naked without it."

"Maybe when this is all over you'll be able to get it back."

"I hope so," he answered, then bit off another piece of the dried beef, and it was quiet for a while, only an occasional word passing between them while they chewed on their jerky, relishing every bit. When they were finally through, he gestured to her, straightening back as best he could, and patted his lap. "Come on, now, lay your head down awhile and sleep," he suggested. "You could use the rest."

"And you?"

"Don't worry, I can sleep sitting up. I'm used to it, but you're not, and we've got a long way to go tonight after it gets dark."

She curled up beside him, with her head in his lap and his hand covered her shoulder.

"They really meant to kill us, didn't they?" she asked as she settled down, relaxing.

He stroked a strand of her pale hair back from her face where it was caught in the dampness on her sweaty forehead. "Not a very pleasant thought, is it?"

"I'm sorry about everything, Griff." She turned onto her back, with her knees drawn up and bent so she'd fit in the small space.

"You mean Rhetta and Gar?"

"Especially Gar. I know how you love him, and I can just imagine what went through your head when Jarrod said all those things to you back there." She reached out and he took her hand, holding it tight.

"I have one hell of a mixed-up life, don't I?" he said bitterly.

Her fingers tightened, and she drew his hand down to her mouth, kissing the back of it, her eyes warm with love. "You aren't going to let what Jarrod said change your feelings for Gar, are you?" she asked.

His jaw set firmly. "Never," he answered quickly. "Don't worry, Jeanine, that boy's still my son as far as I'm concerned, regardless of what Jarrod says. I raised him and there's no one going to take him away from me. Only I'm going to try to keep from telling him the truth about Jarrod, and about his mother, until I think he's old enough to handle it. Especially since he's never had any love for the Vances. I think it'd break his heart right now if he learned his mother had killed the man he was named after. I just hope I can persuade Rhetta and Jarrod to go along with me, because if they don't, that boy's going to have a rough time."

"How are you going to convince them?" she asked, frowning.

"I've been going over it in my mind ever since we left

last night," he answered. "And so far I haven't been able to decide what to do." He sighed. "I guess I might as well resign myself to the fact that I may have to let them go, to keep their mouths shut . . . I don't know. All I know is that this time things are going to be different." His eyes darkened. "This time it'll be my way, or else."

"Or else what?"

"I haven't thought that far ahead, either." He squeezed her hand. "But don't worry, I'll think of something."

She closed her eyes, content not only to be close to him but also to know that he wasn't going to let his anger and resentment carry over into his feelings for Gar. Somehow she sensed he'd feel that way.

"What happens when we get back to the ranch?" she asked after another few minutes.

He shook his head. "I wish I knew." He was thoughtful again for a second or two; then, "One thing for sure," he said, inhaling angrily. "Tonight's the last night Rhetta's going to spend at Trail's End, if I can help it." His voice softened suddenly, and he looked down into her face, smudged and dirty, yet still lovely to him. "Now keep those beautiful blue eyes of yours shut and get some sleep," he ordered. "You're going to need it," and he settled his head back against the dirt wall behind him, closed his own eyes, his hand still holding hers, and they slept.

Jarrod and the rest of his men sat astride their horses just beyond the open gate at the Double V Bar and watched Red disappearing all by himself in the direction of Trail's End, leaving a cloud of dust behind him as he faded into the night. Red was carrying a note from Jarrod to Rhetta, confirming the capture of Griff and Jeanine and telling her how he was planning to get rid of them in the mine. Then, after delivering the message, Red was to meet them all back at the old house.

Jarrod straightened in the saddle and looked about cautiously. It'd be at least another hour or more before dawn, but already lights were starting to go in the bunkhouse, and he wanted to be gone before the men really began stirring, so they wouldn't get wind of what he was up to. He'd managed to sneak the explosives without anyone knowing, and all he'd need now would be for his father to catch him packing dynamite on his horse. Besides, his father had no idea these men worked for him, and he'd mentioned to Jarrod one time about seeing them lazing around town, wondering who they were, what they were up to, and where they'd come from.

As soon as Red was out of sight, Jarrod motioned to the men, and they all reined their horses away from the gate, heading down the dusty road in the opposite direction; then, after a short distance, they moved off it onto an old trail that was a shortcut. They were riding slower now, however, than when they'd ridden in, respecting the power of the explosives they were carrying, and it was going to take them longer to get back than he'd planned.

It had been daylight for well over an hour when they finally reined up in front of the weather-beaten old house, and Jarrod, sitting rigidly in the saddle, stared hard at the two men standing on the porch steps waiting for them.

The men's eyes were downcast, their faces glum, and right away he knew there'd been trouble.

"What's wrong?" he asked hesitantly as he slid from the saddle, spurs jingling when he hit the ground, but neither man answered. Instead, they glanced at each other sheepishly for a second, then glared at him.

Suddenly the color drained from Jarrod's face as he realized what must have happened.

"You stupid idiots!" he yelled frantically, and lunged toward them, shoving them aside, knocking them off the steps as he cleared a path and ran inside.

The other men quickly dismounted, then followed after Jarrod, mumbling curiously among themselves as they made their way through the house, and by the time they reached the back room where Jeanine and Griff had been held captive, Jarrod was on the verge of hysteria.

"You assholes!" he shrieked furiously as he faced the two men who were supposed to have been guarding the prisoners. He'd scooped the discarded ropes up from the dusty floor, and now he shoved them in their faces. "You son-of-a-bitchin' idiots. I told you to watch them!"

"We did!" they answered.

"When?" His face was livid. "When they were climbing out the window? Jesus Christ!" He threw the rope back on the floor, then clenched his fists, and for a minute the men didn't know if he was going to swing at them or reach for his gun, and all eyes were alert, waiting, but he only stared at them, nostrils flaring, eyes ablaze.

Finally, unable to keep from venting his anger on something, he kicked at the ropes lying in the dust beneath the broken window, disturbing the telltale tracks Jeanine and Griff had made.

Carelessness, stupidity! They should have checked once in a while, and he should have kept the two of them separated. But they'd been tied so tight. If they ever got back to Trail's End now . . .

His eyes settled on the two men again, hard, intense. "Their horses?" he asked quickly.

The two men glanced at each other again for a brief second, then back to Jarrod.

"They're still out front where they were when you rode up," one of them answered. "Didn't you notice?"

"All I saw was your ugly faces," Jarrod snapped, and his eyes narrowed. "That means they're on foot wearing moccasins, and it's gonna be hell tracking them." He hefted the gunbelt more securely onto his hips. "Well, the damage's been done already," he added, his voice strained. "So let's see if we can keep it from ruining everything. If we can get to them before they run into anyone, we've still got a chance. If not, we're in trouble. Real trouble. Now, come on," and he left the room hurriedly, with all the men close at his heels.

They tried to pick up a trail beneath the window, but there was none. The grass was dried and brown, the dirt hard from lack of rain, and they were unable to tell whether a blade of grass was broken simply because it had dried out too much or been stepped on. So they just started searching, first on foot, then on horseback, trying to guess which direction they might take and why, hoping to second-guess them, and trying to keep from panicking.

"Dammit! He thinks like an Indian," Jarrod said as they reconnoitered some hours later at a prearranged spot after ending up empty-handed.

It was late afternoon and they'd been over every possible area they could think of between the mine and Trail's End a half-dozen times or more, even filtering out toward the open range and in toward town, but still they'd found nothing. Jarrod still hadn't shaved, and looked worse than ever. His eyes were bloodshot from lack of sleep and there was a strange anxiety in them as he sat his horse and surveyed the men around him.

Red had arrived back at the mine just as they were starting their search, and now Jarrod motioned toward him reluctantly, knowing what he had to do, but hating it.

"Come here, Red," he said wearily, and Burke moved his horse away, letting Red ride in close.

"Give me your pencil and paper again," he ordered the man, and Red reached into a small bag hanging from his saddle horn, coming out with pencil and paper. He handed them to Jarrod, who, using his leather pants leg for support, concentrated carefully as he wrote something down. Then, when he was finished, he folded the paper and handed it back to Red along with the pencil.

"Take this and ride back to Trail's End again," he told him firmly. "And do just as I tell you, with no mistakes, do you get that?"

Red glanced at the two men who were supposed to have been guarding the man and woman. "Yes, sir," he answered, sneering.

"Good." Fear lay in the depths of Jarrod's eyes, but he masked it well. "Once you reach Trail's End, make sure you don't give this note to anyone except Rhetta Heywood. Do you understand?"

"Yes sir."

"I don't care if they say she's sleeping or what. You tell

them that you're to give it directly to her and no one else. Is that clear?"

"Yes sir."

"Good. Now, remember, I want no mistakes this time . . ."

"Wasn't me let 'em get away," Red countered.

Jarrod's eyes snapped. "Well, see that note doesn't get away. We'll keep right on searching, just in case we might get lucky, but either way, we'll meet you back at the mine just before dark."

The man nodded, they split up again, and once more Red headed toward Trail's End, only this time the news he had for Rhetta wasn't what she was expecting.

It was late afternoon, close to dinnertime. Rhetta had been pacing the parlor for what seemed like hours now, the skirt of her silk lavender dress swishing loudly with each step, and she sighed as she turned once more toward the fireplace. Her dark eyes were alert, face worried, and she fidgeted nervously as she tucked one of the dark curls back into place over her ear and fixed it so it wouldn't come loose again. How much longer was it going to take? Her eyes grew misty.

She hadn't really wanted to go along with the killings, at least not Griff's. She didn't care what happened to Jeanine Grayson. After all, who could blame her for wanting the woman dead? But it was hard to live under the same roof with a man like Griffin Heywood and not fall in love with him, at least a little. And if it hadn't been for Jarrod's interference, she still might have had a chance with Griff, given enough time, because for the first few years of their marriage he'd been fairly decent to her. In spite of everything, there were moments when she was sure he'd eventually give in. Then the war came along.

She stopped in front of the fireplace and stared at herself in the fancy mirror that hung over it. If only . . . It wasn't that she wasn't pretty. She tilted her chin up and examined her face. What more could he have wanted? What did that snip of a schoolteacher have that she didn't have? Her lips trembled and tears gathered at the corners of her eyes.

She bit her lip. She knew very well what was wrong. He'd been forced into the situation, that was what was wrong. He hadn't wanted her right from the start, and suddenly she flushed, remembering their wedding night and the brutal way he'd rejected her. She'd worn her most revealing nightgown, fixed her hair just so, and hoped with all her heart that maybe he wasn't as hardheaded and stubborn as his brother had been. She should have known better, and her cheeks grew hot as the words he'd thrown at her that night rang in her ears again, from out of the past, haunting her.

"You can share my name, spend my money, and enjoy all the privileges of being a Heywood," he'd said bitterly as he reached for his coat. "But, by God, Rhetta, there's one thing you'll never have—me! Do you understand? I'll never soil my hands with you." He'd stalked out, slamming the door behind him. When he'd finally returned to their suite of rooms at the hotel later that evening, he'd slept on the sofa, and in all the years of their marriage, she'd been unable to break down his iron defenses, although she'd never given up trying. Even when he'd come back from the war.

Damn him! she thought angrily. He'd rather make routine trips to Dallas when he got the urge, and spend his time with whores, than give in to her. Her fist clenched. Just once! If she could have broken his defenses down just once, she'd have even been willing to get rid of Jarrod somehow. After all, it wasn't really all that hard to kill a man if you just didn't think too much about it. She'd gotten away with it before, and could have again.

She thought back to the night she'd killed Griff's brother. It had been so easy to pull the trigger. That part of it wasn't hard, really, if you were mad enough. It was the look on Garfield's face when he realized what was happening that had been hard for her to take at the time. But even that wasn't really so bad. It didn't have to bother a person, if the person didn't let it. Not really. You just pushed it aside and didn't think about it.

She straightened confidently. When Jarrod first learned the truth about her, she almost did get rid of him, then thought better of it, fortunately. First, she wanted to see if Griff would come back from the war, and if he'd changed any. Well, he did come back, but he hadn't changed. Sometimes he acted as if her sarcasm and sharp tongue were a penance he had to accept because of his brother's sins. Well, he wouldn't have to put up with her anymore, and now she was glad she hadn't gotten rid of Jarrod. Marriage to him would be better than what she'd been through the past eight years as a Heywood. It had to be, because at least Jarrod was in love with her.

Turning from the mirror, she walked over to the French doors and stared out into the garden, wringing her hands restlessly. If the time would only go faster. It seemed like she'd been waiting for word from Jarrod forever. What was taking so long?

She shut her eyes, and for a brief moment Griff's face stared back at her, questioning, accusing, and a sharp pain shot through her. Love was such a strange thing. It was there even when a person didn't want it to be. She kept telling herself that it had to be, that there was no other way. But wishing it didn't have to be didn't make the doing any easier to accept.

If you had only loved me, Griff, it might have been different, she murmured softly to herself. But now, with Jarrod knowing, and since Jeanine Grayson came along . . . Anger, jealousy, and frustration suddenly began to flow through her as she remembered standing in her bedroom window and watching the two of them leave the harness room that evening after their clandestine meeting.

Her eyes flew open, then narrowed viciously. They'd pay for humiliating her like this, and suddenly the thought of evening the score with both Griff and Jeanine overshadowed any tender feelings she had for him, making the thought of what was happening to them all the sweeter.

Revenge had a way of rejuvenating the soul. Let them die! Let them die together! she cried silently. I hate them both!

Her fists were still clenched, and her nails dug into her palms as she tightened them; then she turned slowly, cocking an ear to listen as the faint striking of the clock in the upstairs hall floated down through the quiet house, bringing her thoughts back to what lay ahead. Mistress of Trail's End, that's what she'd be. The clock had struck six. She relaxed a little, her breathing erratic, as a feeling of power swept through her. It was over by now. It had to be. All she needed was the confirmation.

She lifted her head haughtily, more elated than she'd felt for a long time. Soon, now, soon . . .

"Excuse me," Mrs. Brandt said, interrupting her daydreaming, and Rhetta whirled around, startled.

She hadn't heard the woman approach, and disliked surprises. "Well?" she asked irritably, trying to keep her voice steady.

"There's a man at the door asking for you," Mrs. Brandt answered, trying to ignore Rhetta's mood. "Says it's important he talk to you right away. It's the same man who was here early this morning."

"Good," Rhetta said with more assurance this time. "Thank you, Mrs. Brandt, you're excused now."

She watched the housekeeper leave, heading back through the foyer and on upstairs. How she despised the woman. And that was one of the first things she was going to do when she took over, get rid of Mrs. Brandt. She primped her hair, making sure it was still in place, smoothed her hands over the waistline of her dress, then walked to the front door, where Red was waiting.

She didn't like Red, nor any of the other men Jarrod had hired, but right now she was more than glad to see him as he handed her a slip of paper.

"I have orders to give this only to you, just like the other message," he said roughly, and she stared at the note in his hands.

This was it! The confirmation she'd been waiting for. Her fingers trembled as she hurriedly opened it, anxious to read the words that would tell her she was finally a widow. But instead, as she read it, the triumphant look on her face began to fade, suddenly being replaced by a look of shock so utterly horrifying that her eyes filled with tears and her face paled.

It couldn't be! It just couldn't! Her hands were shaking, her movements slow and deliberate, as if she was in a daze. She stared at the paper for a long time, not wanting to believe the words, but unable to erase them from before her eyes; then she glanced up at Red, her head moving slowly from side to side.

"It isn't true. It can't be!" she exclaimed, her voice breaking.

"I'm afraid it is, ma'am," Red answered, and Rhetta gazed down again at the note in her hand, then reluctantly raised a hand, gesturing toward him, dismissing him absentmindedly.

"You can go now," she murmured softly, and opened the door, still staring at the paper.

"Will there be an answer?" he asked.

"No . . . no answer," she said quietly.

"Yes, ma'am." Red nodded, put his hat back on his head, and left, letting her shut the door behind him. Once it was shut, she leaned back against it and closed her eyes, fighting for control.

God, no! Nothing was left! Griff and Jeanine were on their way back to the ranch, and all the planning had been for nothing. She crumpled the note in her fist until her knuckles were white. She wanted to scream, but knew screaming would only make matters worse.

Jarrod had written to meet him at the old abandoned copper mine before dark, and to bring Gar with her. The note had also said that he'd told Griff the truth about everything, and he had underlined the word "everything." Why? Why hadn't he just let Griff go on wondering? If she tried to stay now, with Griff knowing she'd killed his brother, she'd end up at the end of a rope for sure. She could strangle Jarrod, the fool!

Panic seized her, and she straightened. My God! What

if Griff got here before she was able to leave for the mine? She had to get away, not only from Trail's End but also Raintree. Jarrod would help. He had to. After all, now that he knew the truth about Garfield's murder, he was as guilty as she was. Besides, he'd killed Jake Harper, helped kill the man carrying the payroll, and killed Homer Beacon. Neither of them could afford to stay.

If she could just get to Jarrod in time, he'd know where to go. This time she really did have to count on him, and she straightened, starting for the stairs, almost bumping into Mrs. Brandt, who was on her way back down.

"Is it news about Griff?" Mrs. Brandt asked expectantly, and for a moment Rhetta's eyes had a vacant look in them as she stared at the housekeeper.

"Oh . . . no . . . no, Mrs. Brandt," she finally blurted, coming to her senses. "I . . . It's nothing, really. Only I do have to go out." She tried to pull herself together, forcing the anger, tears, and frustration to stay hidden from the nosy old woman. Her shoulders stiffened haughtily. "Will you ask Crystal to have Cinnamon hitch the buggy and bring it out front?" she said, her voice a little unsteady in spite of her efforts at self-control. "I'll drive myself today, and I think I'll take Gar with me. He's hardly been out of that schoolroom since Griff left."

Mrs. Brandt frowned. "You intend to ride alone?"

"I'm just going for a breath of fresh air, like I did the other day. I was perfectly safe and nothing happened." She regained some of her lost courage. "If I stay in this house one more minute, I'll go crazy, and I'm sure it'll do Gar good too." She glowered at Mrs. Brandt. "Now, will you please do as I ask, while I go get the boy?"

Mrs. Brandt didn't like it, but turned to leave. It was so unlike Rhetta to drive her own buggy, and taking Gar with her . . . ? But then, Rhetta had been acting strangely ever since Miss Grayson's disappearance. This was the second time since Griff left that she'd gone driving alone. She was up to something, but what? If only she didn't have to manage things at the house, she'd follow her. Suddenly a thought struck her, and as she headed toward the kitchen to find Crystal, Mrs. Brandt wondered where Cory McBride might be.

Rhetta watched Mrs. Brandt leave, then headed toward the schoolroom to get Gar. Since Griff had left he'd spent almost all his time there working on lessons.

"I want her to be proud of me when she comes back," he'd said one afternoon, and Rhetta was furious to think that a dowdy, unattractive schoolteacher like Jeanine Grayson could not only lure Griff into a sordid affair but also slowly steal her son's affections from her. How she despised her, and now . . .

She took a deep breath and opened the door to the schoolroom, then stepped inside, closing the door deftly behind her. Gar was sitting at the table he used for a desk, his hands supporting his chin, with both elbows propped in front of the book that lay open before him. He'd been reading, but when his mother walked in, his arms dropped and he raised his head.

"Is Pa back?" he asked anxiously.

Rhetta's jaw tightened. "No, your father's not back." She walked over and looked down at the book he'd been reading. "Must you always be doing schoolwork?" she asked, trying to keep her voice from betraying the fear that was gripping her insides.

"I like to."

"Well, how would you like to go for a short ride instead?"

"Now?" He didn't sound too enthusiastic.

"I've already asked for the buggy to be hitched," she said irritably. "You haven't been outside for a ride or to play since your father left. The ride'll do you good."

"Do I have to?"

"Yes, you have to." She watched his eyes darken angrily, just the way Jarrod's always did when he was forced to do something he resented doing.

"All right," he answered halfheartedly, and as she watched him close the book, putting it back on the shelf, she realized that it wouldn't be too many more years before everyone would guess Gar's true parentage, because the older he got, the more he looked like his real father. By the time he was full grown, he was going to be the image of Jarrod. Only, unlike Jarrod, he was even-tempered and happy-go-lucky most of the time, rarely rebeling against anything asked of him. Rhetta continued to study him as he came back and straightened some pencils and papers on his desk, then walked ahead of her when they left the schoolroom and went on upstairs. Sometimes she was afraid perhaps he had inherited Jarrod's mother's weakness, a weakness she hated, and one that had quickly taken Jarrod's mother's life under the demanding personality of her husband. Well, that couldn't be helped. After all, what could she expect from her son, having to live most of his life in a household of women while the men were away fighting a war.

When they reached his bedroom, he stood quietly while she helped him on with his jacket; then she handed him the wide-brimmed hat that was so much like Griff's.

"Now, go downstairs, find Cinnamon, and have him bring the buggy to the front door," she said as she finished buttoning his jacket and straightened. "I'll meet you by the front steps."

"Where are we going?" he asked.

"You'll see." She turned him toward the door. "Now, scoot," and she gave him a pat on the rear, then followed slowly after he left the room, making certain he was on his way through the foyer, headed for the kitchen, by the time she reached the top of the stairs.

She stopped on the landing and looked around, just to make sure. Not a soul was in sight. Good. Turning quickly, she opened the door to the master bedroom, took one last look for good measure, then slipped inside, closing the door swiftly behind her. She was going to need as much money as she could to get out of this mess, and Griff always kept enough money in the house to cover household expenses and any extra ones that might come up, without having to travel all the way to the bank in Raintree. But where was it?

She stood just inside the room, her eyes sifting over

everything. It had to be in one of the dresser drawers. Moving quickly, she tried them all, stopping at the middle drawer, which was the only one locked. She had to get it open, but how? Turning slowly, looking around, she spotted a letter opener on the stand beside the bed and grabbed it, then turned back to the drawer with a vengeance.

It took only a minute or so to pry the drawer open, and she straightened, breathing heavily. After shoving a bunch of papers aside, she opened the small strongbox beneath them, scooping out all the money, counting it hurriedly. Eight hundred in gold coins, with only a few paper bills. Not enough to make up for everything she was losing, but enough to get her and Gar safely out of Texas.

Her fingers closed tightly around the coins and bills and she reached into the other end of the drawer, grabbing one of Griff's bandannas. After tying the money inside, she shut the drawer and hurriedly left, heading for her own room in the other wing of the house, where she stuffed the bandanna full of money into her handbag, picked up her cape, and fastened it as she headed for the door, then went on downstairs to meet Gar.

She could take nothing with her except the clothes on her back, and as she reached the foyer, she hesitated momentarily, looking around. Again tears came to her eyes. She didn't want to leave. This was home! Her house, her life . . . everything was happening too fast. Her eyes darkened savagely, every instinct inside her fighting against what was happening. Suddenly everything in the room came into sharp focus, blurred only by her tears.

Money, power, prestige—they'd been a part of her life for so long. How was she to survive without them? She gulped back a sob, remembering how she and Griff had gone to Austin before the war and been guests of the governor, and probably would have been invited again, too, if only . . .

It wasn't fair, and suddenly as the tears rolled down her cheeks, a wave of bitterness swept over her. She'd had it in her grasp, been part of it, but never again. Her lips pursed as she pulled a handkerchief from her handbag, then wiped her eyes and straightened angrily, a hateful look in her eyes.

Hate could make even a coward strong, she told herself silently, and right now she hated Griffin Heywood more than she'd ever hated anyone in her life, except perhaps Jeanine Grayson. They'd pay, that was for sure. For now she had no choice but to leave, only somehow, some way she'd come back when they least expected it, and see that they both paid. Oh, how she'd get even!

Whirling abruptly, she shoved the handkerchief back in her handbag, opened the front door, and stepped outside, hurrying down the steps to the buggy where Gar was waiting and Cinnamon was holding the reins for her.

"You sure you don't want me to drive, Missus Heywood?" Cinnamon asked as he helped her into the buggy.

She sat rigid, her face an unreadable mask. "Not today, Cinnamon," she answered curtly. She knew her eyes were red from crying, but it was none of the old man's business. "I can handle the buggy fine by myself."

He handed her the reins. "Is there anythin' else I kin do?" he asked kindly. "I could come along—"

"No, thank you," she snapped. "We'll go alone!"

He shrugged, frowning as he backed away toward the side of the drive. "Shore nuff, ma'am," he said, then watched curiously as she flicked the reins, maneuvering the buggy down the long drive, beneath the huge sycamores that stood like sentinels on each side, and on toward the main road. Then, just before reaching the spot where the drive curved, taking its occupants out of sight of the ranch house, Rhetta pulled back on the reins and the buggy stopped abruptly.

Still sitting stiffly in the seat, she took a deep breath, then turned slowly, looking back at the house.

"What's the matter, Ma?" Gar asked from beside her.

She didn't answer. She couldn't. How could she tell a boy of seven to say good-bye to the house he'd always loved and the people who made up that house? The people who'd loved and coddled him since he'd been born. The people who were soon going to hate him when they dis-

covered he wasn't Garfield Heywood's son and that his
mother was a murderess. How could she? She couldn't,
and as the late-afternoon sun touched the log house with a
golden glow that made it shimmer like a mirage in the
distance, she gnashed her teeth together fiercely and whirled
back around in her seat, then whipped the horse quickly
into a gallop, while Gar, terrified, grabbed for something
to hold onto. Giving the horse his head, she let him plunge
on recklessly, careening the rest of the way down the
drive. Then the buggy swerved, sliding into the dust of the
main road, and she had to fight the reins momentarily to
keep them upright.

"Don't worry, Gar!" she shouted angrily as the horse
continued to bolt headlong down the main road. "Mother's going to take good care of us from now on, you'll see.
Just trust me!" and as she urged the horse on, making him
go even faster, Gar held onto the side of the buggy, tears
rolling down his cheeks, wondering what it was all about.

Gar's heart was in his throat. He'd seen his mother
upset and angry before, but never like this. There was
something frightening about her strange behavior, and he
was so scared. More scared than he'd ever been before in
his whole life, yet all he could do was hang on and pray.

Rhetta slowed the team only a few times, but not sufficiently that Gar felt secure enough to loosen his hold on
the side of the buggy or ask her what was wrong, and by
the time the buggy rattled into view of the old house at the
abandoned mine and Rhetta finally slowed, then brought it
to a stop in front of the rickety porch, Gar was no longer
just scared, but in a mild form of shock.

The reins felt like they were cutting into Rhetta's flesh
as she pulled on them, making sure the horse would stay in
place; then she slapped them around the bar at the front of
the carriage and pulled, tying them into place. It was
almost dark now and as she looked toward the house, she
stared apprehensively at the men, who were sprawled around
on the porch, watching her.

"Where's Jarrod?" she called, not wanting to get down
if he wasn't there yet.

Burke was sitting on the porch rail, rolling a cigarette, and he leaned back against one of the posts that held up the roof, glancing over at Red, who was in the open doorway.

"Go tell Jarrod he's got company," he said, and licked the length of the cigarette paper as Red turned and disappeared into the house.

Rhetta felt self-conscious as she waited, knowing Burke was studying her closely while he finished with the cigarette; then he shoved it between his lips and lit up. She didn't know which of these men she liked least, but one thing for certain, she didn't trust any of them, Burke included, but she tried not to let him see that his scrutiny of her was unnerving.

Burke took a long drag off his cigarette, then flicked the match away as Red came back out, followed by Jarrod, who had shaved and cleaned up some while he'd been waiting for her. However, he was still wearing the same clothes he'd had on the day before, and their rumpled condition made him appear rather unkempt.

"It's about time," he said as he ambled fluidly down the steps and walked up to the carriage, his spurs softly jingling with each step. He reached up to help her down.

"I have to talk to you—alone," she said as she stepped to the ground, then turned to her son.

Gar was crouched at the other end of the buggy, still hanging onto its side, his face pale.

"Get down, Gar," she said firmly, but he shook his head, still cowering. "I said get down," she repeated,

The boy still didn't move.

She leaned forward, toward him, holding her hand out to him. "Please, Gar," she pleaded.

His eyes shifted nervously from his mother to the men on the porch. Their clothes were dirty, and they looked rough and mean. "I'm afraid," he whispered shakily.

He wasn't only frightened, but bewildered, and Rhetta knew there was nothing she could do to ease his fears. "Gar, please, do as Mother says," she ordered anxiously, then her voice softened as she tried to make him feel a little better. "Please, dear, nothing's going to happen, I promise you." She gestured with her fingers for him to take her hand. "Now, come along."

"Why did we come here?" he suddenly asked as he looked straight at her, and Rhetta saw tears glistening in his eyes.

"Trust me," she answered solicitiously. "Please, Gar, now give me your hand." Her patience was wearing thin. "I don't want to have to get angry with you. Please, dear!" she pleaded more forcefully.

He seemed to concentrate for a minute, as if pondering what to do, then reluctantly gave in and let her help him from the buggy. When they reached the porch, she sat him on a chair, instructing him to sit quietly and wait for her; then she and Jarrod went on into the house, closing the door behind them.

The kitchen of the old house looked as cluttered as it had the first time she'd seen it, and she stood just inside the door, staring at Jarrod, who walked over and began turning up the lamp on the table.

"I hope you've made some kind of arrangements," she said as she toyed nervously with the handbag hanging from her wrist.

He watched the flickering light get brighter, then turned. "What kind of arrangements?"

"What kind . . .? Good Lord, Jarrod," she half-whispered, moving toward him. "Don't be stupid. We can't stay here, and you know it. Griff knows he can find us here."

"So?"

"So he'll come after us."

"With the boy here?" He smirked. "He wouldn't dare."

"You'd use Gar?"

"To get what I want, yes."

Her eyes narrowed. "What do you mean . . . ? What do you want?"

"I want safe passage out of here for both of us, and if it means using Gar, then we use him."

"He's my son too, you know."

"Look," Jarrod said, more confident than he'd been all day. "As long as Griff knows we have Gar with us, he'll be careful how he handles things, you know that. Besides," he said, his eyes gleaming unnaturally, "if we bargain right, we could end up with a nice bundle of cash to take with us when we leave."

"Bargain? You mean with Gar?"

"Why not?"

"Oh no." She shook her head. "I'll not give him my son."

"Not even to save your neck?"

She inhaled sharply, fear settling in her eyes, "It's come to that?"

"We sort of messed things up, didn't we, Rhet?" he said softly, and reached out, touching her face. "And I thought it'd be so easy." He ran the back of his hand down her jawline, his eyes searching hers. "It was all going so well, too. His death would have been blamed on the men who were trying to stop his cattle drive."

"And then she came along!"

"I'm afraid so."

She reached up, grabbing his hand. "I'm not a good loser, Jarrod," she said.

He sighed. "Neither am I." His arms went around her and he pulled her close. "I wanted you and Trail's End . . . it was all planned so perfectly."

"What do we do now?" she asked hesitantly. "Just wait?"

"Not on your life." His eyes were hard, unyielding, not the eyes of a defeated man, and he straightened, looking down at her. "If we use our heads, I think we can get out of this yet," he said, and she could almost see the brain working behind those eyes, sifting, sorting, rejecting. Trying to pick the best plan. "If Griff doesn't show up until tomorrow afternoon, we'll take the boy with us," he said thoughtfully. "We can catch the stage the other side of Raintree. In the meantime, tonight I'll ride to the Double V Bar and pick up some money I've stashed there so we can pay off the men."

"And if Griff comes before we have a chance to leave?"

"That's where we use the boy." He searched her eyes. "Even though he's my son, I could tell by the look on Griff's face that he loves the boy, so he won't take a chance on hitting Gar by riding in here shooting. So if we can calm him down enough to talk to us, I think he'll be willing to let us go, for the boy's sake. After all, I doubt he'll want Gar to learn the truth about us, and if we promise to keep our mouths shut and just disappear, he might be willing to pay."

"I said I wouldn't leave Gar, Jarrod."

"You won't have to." He smiled, trying to reassure her. "We'll tell Griff that we're going to take Gar with us only as far as the border, just to make sure Griff keeps his part of the bargain; then we tell him we'll leave the boy so he can take him back to Trail's End with him. Only once we reach the border, there's no way short of gunplay he can keep us from taking Gar across with us, and you know he won't risk Gar being hurt?"

"You're planning to head for Mexico?"

"Why not?"

"I hate Mexico." She frowned. "What if Griff follows us over the border?"

"I've got friends in Mexico."

"So does he."

"For Christ's sake, Rhetta, just once do what I ask without giving me an argument, will you?" he lashed out, and his eyes narrowed. "If you'd just done that right from the start, we wouldn't be in the mess we're in now, and you know it. But no, you had to talk me into doing things your way and starting rumors around that somebody was trying to stop Griff's cattle drive so that when he was found dead they wouldn't start looking in our direction. My way was too messy, you said. Too much of a risk to just shoot him without giving Sheriff Higgens a reason. You were so afraid he'd see the obvious." His arm tightened about her waist. "And it was your idea to get rid of the Grayson woman too. Don't forget that. I told you we should have just concentrated on killing Griff."

"But you went along with it."

"Not until I found out about her and Beacon. Even then, though, I was skeptical."

"Well, it wasn't my fault your men decided to let the Indians kill her instead of doing it themselves," she said bitterly. "You should have found out what they were planning, and maybe all this could have been avoided. Of all the damn Indians out there, they had to pick Chief Horse Back's men to give her to."

"Look," he said, his face set in a hard line, "it wasn't your fault, and it wasn't mine. It just happened, that's all." His voice deepened. "Things went wrong, honey," he went on, and cupped her face in his hand. "But we still have a chance as long as we stick together. Don't let's fight."

He leaned down, his lips eager to try to soothe her and take away some of the pain he knew she was feeling, but she pushed him back.

"Not now, Jarrod. For God's sake," she whispered. "Is that all you ever think of?"

"I love you, Rhet."

She sighed. "I know," and this time she let him kiss her long and hard, but as he drew his mouth from hers again, her hands once more pushed against his chest. "Jarrod, we don't have time for this now," she pleaded anxiously. "Please . . ."

His eyes bored into hers, but he knew she was right, and his arms eased from around her, letting her back away from him. "All right, I want to get everything straight," he said as he stared into her dark eyes, catching a hint of the fear she was trying to keep under control. "Do you have any money at all?"

"Some."

"How much?"

"I managed to take about eight hundred Griff had at the house."

"That's a start." He frowned. "But I promised Burke and the others I'd pay them off when we leave, so we're going to need more." He straightened, gazing off over her head toward the closed door behind her. "Like I said, it won't take me long to ride to the Double V Bar. You and the boy can wait for me here."

"With those men out there?"

"They'll stay put."

"They'd better!"

He took out his gun, spun the barrel to check the ammunition, then slipped it back in its holster. "I'll be back as soon as I can," he said. "And we'll try to leave by daybreak." He walked over and opened the door. "Now, call Gar in here."

Rhetta moved to the doorway and called to Gar, who climbed gingerly off the chair where he'd been waiting and walked slowly into the room, eyeing the men outside on the porch warily as he left them; then he stood close beside his mother, staring hard at Jarrod.

"Don't look so worried, son," Jarrod said as he studied the boy. "Everything's all right."

"I'm not your son," Gar threw back angrily.

"You're not my . . ." Jarrod's eyebrows raised and he glanced at Rhetta.

"Jarrod!" she cautioned.

"Well, now, I'll tell you, boy," he began, and once more Rhetta cut him off.

"For God's sake, Jarrod, not now." She was almost yelling, yet trying to keep herself under control.

Their eyes met and Jarrod saw the anguish she was feeling. He couldn't hurt her. He loved her too much, so instead he backed off. There'd be time later.

"Your mother's right, son," he told Gar reluctantly. "It can wait for now." He reached out to ruffle the boy's hair, but Gar shrank back, hiding behind Rhetta. "If that's the way you want it." Jarrod straightened, then hitched the gunbelt more comfortably onto his hips. "But for now you've got a job to do. I have to ride out for a while and I expect you to take care of your mother while I'm gone, understand? Then, when I get back, we're all going on a nice long trip."

Gar's eyes widened frantically as he clutched at the back

of Rhetta's skirt. "I don't wanna go no place, Ma!" he yelled. "I wanna go home!"

Rhetta turned and stooped down, her hands on his shoulders. "Gar, please," she pleaded. "It'll be all right."

The boy was shaking. "I wanna find Pa!" he cried. "I don't like it here, I wanna find Pa!"

She had to think of something. Anything to keep him from trying to run off. He was headstrong and could be willful at times.

"Gar, Pa's dead," she lied hurriedly, then winced at the stunned look on his face. "The Indians killed him," she went on in desperation. "Your pa's dead, Gar. Now, please—"

"No!" Tears flooded his eyes. "No, Ma, no. They didn't . . . they wouldn't," he sobbed breathlessly. "They were his friends."

"Not anymore." Her fingers clenched harder on his shoulders. "Gar, listen to me, please," she begged. "Pa's gone and so is Miss Grayson, so now I'm making the decisions, do you understand? And I say we're going away, to try to forget."

"But Crystal and Mrs. Brandt . . . ?" He gulped back a sob. "Aren't they coming?"

A pang of guilt tore through her and she suddenly felt angry. Angry at herself, Jarrod, Griff, and the way her whole life had turned out. She pulled him into her arms, hugging him, letting his tears wet the bodice of her dress and not caring for the first time in her life whether he was ruining it or not. "Gar, things happen, and life changes," she tried to explain, in an effort to soothe him. "And sometimes there's nothing we can do except go on as best we see fit." Her arms tightened. "I want you to be a big boy, Gar, and someday, when you're older, I'll tell you about everything, but right now . . ." She backed away, looking steadily into his face again. "You've got to trust me, dear, please," she pleaded. "Pa wouldn't want you to act like this." She was close to tears herself. "Remember how Pa always said to be brave, no matter what?" she asked.

He nodded, sniffing.

"Then that's what we expect you to do." She released him, then stood staring down at him. "Now, are you going to be brave?" she asked firmly.

Gar stared up at her for a few seconds, then sniffed again, wiping his nose on his sleeve and streaking the tears and dirt across his cheeks with his fingers as he straightened.

"I won't cry no more," he sniffed, gulping back, and stared hard at his mother, as if waiting for her to praise him for trying so hard when his heart was breaking inside him. Instead, it was Jarrod who spoke.

"That's the way, kid," he said, and Rhetta smiled slightly, nodding, showing her approval; then Jarrod glanced at her quickly. "Now, I'll be back as soon as I can." He started for the door. "Take care of your mother, Gar," he told him. "And don't you worry. Everything's gonna be fine." Then he walked out, closing the door behind him, leaving them standing alone in the room.

Rhetta's eyes moved from her son to the door that had just closed, and for a minute she stood motionless staring at it. She could hear Jarrod outside giving orders to his men, but still didn't move. Then slowly, after hearing him say good-bye, she turned and walked to the table, watching the flickering light from the kerosene lamp as it cast shadows about, and she reached out, turning the wick even higher, hoping to dispel some of the gloom that had crept into the room, trying to make it a little more pleasant for them in spite of the dirt and filth. However, a few seconds later, as she glanced back once more at Gar, still standing straight and tall, trying to prove he was strong and brave, then listened to the hoofbeats of Jarrod's horse fading in the distance, she suddenly knew that for just that one brief moment she hated herself even more than she hated Griffin and Jeanine.

14

Jarrod pulled his hat down tighter on his head and spurred his horse harder. He was covering ground fast, but even at this pace it would take hours for him to do what he had to do. He'd told Rhetta he'd be back for her, and he would, but the money he told her he had, didn't exist. He'd already spent everything they'd stolen when they robbed the messenger carrying the Trail's End payroll. Now he needed money fast, and there was only one place that carried enough cash. The bank in Raintree was small, but it was better that way.

Even though he pushed his horse hard, it still took a little over three hours for him to reach town, and by that time it was eleven-thirty. He reined in behind the livery stable and sat for a while contemplating. The town was fairly quiet, except for some music and laughter from the Golden Cage, and he was glad he'd decided to carry the thing off alone.

Harlin Winslow, the banker, was a good friend of his father, and the thought of what his father was going to think almost stopped him, until he remembered he was fighting for their lives. He'd tried to get Rhetta out of his system years ago, but had never been able to. Even went to Mexico to forget. But then, one glimpse of the boy . . .

He quit daydreaming and nudged his horse forward, walking him along the back of the buildings until he came to the bank. Reining up, he climbed down and tethered his horse on the railing at the back steps, then quietly melted into the alley that ran alongside the bank, keeping in the shadows until he reached the main street of town.

Winslow was a widower and lived alone in a small house just a few streets down. Jarrod glanced about furtively to make sure no one was about, then began moving stealthily, trying not to let his spurs jingle, as he kept close to the buildings, until he reached the street he wanted. Then he moved down it until he came to a white picket fence with a gate that he easily slipped through, cautiously approaching the front porch.

Ordinarily the banker would have been sleeping by now, but tonight his arthritis was acting up and he was just starting to climb out of bed to get some liniment when Jarrod came through the open bedroom window with his gun drawn.

"Sit right where you are and don't move," he ordered quietly when he saw a slight movement in the bed, and he swung his legs the rest of the way into the room, over the windowsill, while Winslow stared at him, startled.

Jarrod was silhouetted against the window, so the banker was unable to tell who it was, and he clutched the covers to his chin, trembling. "Who's there?" he asked nervously.

"Only an old friend, Harlin," Jarrod answered, then slowly walked toward him. "Now, get out of bed and put on your clothes. We're going for a walk."

"But . . ."

"I'm not playing games, old man. Move!" Jarrod ordered, and Winslow heard the distinct sound of a gun being cocked.

He slid ungraciously from the covers and stumbled in the dark, finding the chair by the dresser, grabbing what he hoped were his pants off it, and pulled them up over his hairy legs, then tucked his nightshirt into his pants. Bending over, he rummaged around until he found his stockings and boots, then sat down, pulling them on, while Jarrod continued to watch.

Winslow's hands were shaking, but he managed to stand

up again and grab his jacket from the back of the chair, slipping it on; then he faced the dark silhouette that was moving toward him again.

"Now, let's go," Jarrod said, and shoved his gun against the old man's ribs, this time prodding him toward the bedroom door.

"Jarrod?" Winslow gasped breathlessly as he finally recognized his intruder. "It is you, isn't it, Jarrod?" he asked.

"That's right, it's me," Jarrod answered. "So what?"

"So what . . . ? Is this some kind of a jest?"

"It's no jest, Harlin," Jarrod answered viciously. "So get that straight. I know exactly what I'm doing." The gun rammed tighter against Winslow's ribs and he could feel Jarrod's breath hot on his cheek. "Now, I don't have time for any more nonsense," Jarrod said. "So no more questions," and the gun dug even deeper. "This is what we're gonna do. We're gonna walk to the back door of the bank, and you're gonna open it for me, understand? Then we're gonna go inside, and you're gonna open the safe so I can take out all the money. Have you got that?"

Harlin sputtered, starting to protest.

"Shut up!" Jarrod ordered angrily. "I don't have all night. Now, come on." His brooding eyes narrowed as he shoved the old man ahead of him through the dark house toward the front door, the gun kept steadily against him.

The streets were still deserted as they left the house and threaded their way to the back door of the bank, where Winslow fumbled nervously with the keys before finally getting the door open.

"All right, inside," Jarrod said as the door swung open, and he followed the banker into the darkened office, then ordered him to stay put while he pulled down the shades and lit a kerosene lamp, keeping the wick low.

"Now," he said as he sat on the edge of the banker's desk in the dimly lit office and waved the gun at the old man. "Open the safe."

Winslow had been trying to get his eyes adjusted to the flickering light and he stared at Jarrod curiously now, hoping maybe this wasn't real and he was in the middle of some sort of nightmare.

"This is madness, Jarrod," he said, trying to dissuade him. "Why would you want to rob me?"

"Why else, I need money."

"But your father . . . you don't need my money."

"My father's got stocks, and cattle, and a ranch." He leaned forward, the gun leveling steadily on the old man. "I need cash, Harlin. Cold, hard cash," he stated. "Now, open the safe and be quick about it," and this time the gun moved toward a spot right between Winslow's eyes, and the banker knew it'd do no good to argue any further. He turned hesitantly and stooped down to open the safe.

Jarrod grabbed an empty bag off a file cabinet next to the safe and tossed it down to the old man. "Put the money in here," he ordered curtly, then watched eagerly as Winslow pulled the door to the safe open and began stuffing money into the bag.

When the safe was finally empty, Jarrod grabbed the bag, then dragged the old man toward the back door, blowing out the lamp on the way. When he was sure no one was outside, he ordered the old man out, shut the door, and left, stopping at the foot of the steps.

"All right," he said as he untied his horse. "Get on."

Winslow gawked at him, startled. "Me?"

"That's right, you're going with me. Now, like I said, get on, and no funny business."

The old man complied reluctantly, wondering what the hell Jarrod was up to now, and his curiosity was further piqued when Jarrod mounted behind him after first putting the bag full of money into his saddlebag. He'd kept his gun trained on Winslow the whole while, but now it was rammed against his ribs again, and Jarrod managed the reins with his other hand. Winslow felt Jarrod nudge the horse, urging him forward, and they slowly moved away from the building, skirting the rest of the town slowly, until they reached the livery-stable corral; then Jarrod reined the horse into a loping canter and they headed away from Raintree, moving cross-country instead of using the road.

"You'll never get away with this," Winslow said as Jarrod slowed the horse again a few minutes later to ford a small creek.

"That's where you're wrong," Jarrod answered, and dug his horse in the ribs again, but this time keeping him to a steady walk, deciding it would be too great a risk to move too fast with both of them mounted. He couldn't afford to have his horse give out on him, or end up with a broken leg.

They'd ridden for some time when Jarrod finally reined to a halt, glancing about curiously, then slid from the saddle.

"All right, get down," he ordered Winslow, and the old man hesitated, forcing Jarrod to ram the gun harder into his ribs again. "I said down!"

Harlin Winslow was trembling visibly as he climbed from the saddle and stood next to a scraggly bush, the cool night air raising gooseflesh on the back of his neck. They were in a small wooded area, and it was extremely dark because the moonlight couldn't penetrate the thick branches overhead. As soon as Winslow was on the ground, Jarrod mounted the horse again and straightened in the saddle, staring down at him.

"I . . . I can't walk home, Jarrod, and you know it," Winslow stuttered helplessly as he stared up at the younger man astride the horse. "It's too far, and I'm not as young as I used to be. Please, the night air . . . my arthritis . . . "

"Don't worry, Harlin," Jarrod assured the old man. "You won't ever have to worry about your arthritis anymore," and before Winslow could even make an attempt to stop him, Jarrod leveled the gun that was still in his hand directly at the banker's chest and pulled the trigger, watching with mixed emotions as the old man's eyes widened like saucers and he gasped, unbelieving, then crumpled to the ground in a heap.

"And just think," Jarrod said softly as he stared down at his father's old friend while quickly holstering his gun, "nobody even knows you left home." With a vicious sneer he spurred his horse off through the trees until he came to a small stream, then entered, walking partway up it so no one could track him, before finally heading toward the Double V Bar at a fast gallop. There was still more to do before the night was over, and he'd already lost precious time.

As soon as it was dark enough to move, Jeanine and Griff left their hiding place on the cliff, and now, after hours of struggling cross-country in the dark, through wild underbrush and untamed rangeland, they topped the crest of a hill and Jeanine sighed.

"Is that what I think it is?" she asked hesitantly as a silver reflection shone below in the distance.

Griff's arm went about her shoulder. "You mean Indian Rock? It sure is." He pointed overhead. "And look, the moon's high. It must only be somewhere around midnight."

"For a while I thought we'd never make it," she said wearily. "Especially when we spotted those men searching during the afternoon."

"I told you they wouldn't find us." His arm was still around her. "I know every rock and hill on Trail's End where a man can hide. That's why I pushed you so hard when we first set out last night, so we'd be on Heywood land by the time the sun came up." His arm tightened on her shoulders reassuringly as he glanced down the slope again toward the lake and Indian Rock. "Now, if you can just hold out a little longer."

"Try me," she said quickly, and this time his arm dropped from her shoulder so he could take her hand, and he led her cautiously down the hill toward Indian Rock and beyond, to the trail that led to the ranch house, and a little over an hour later, tired and weary, they reached the edge of the woods. Stepping out from the shelter of the trees into the moonlight, they stood gazing off toward the ranch buildings spread out below them.

"Strange," Griff exclaimed curiously. "It's so late, and the house is still all lit up."

She looked over at him, frowning. "Maybe they just couldn't sleep?"

"Let's find out." He took her hand again, leading the way, and they moved down the lane beside the pasture fence, both wondering what they'd find waiting for them. Then, as they reached the corner of the main barn, Griff stopped in the shadows and pulled her against him.

She stared up in surprise.

"Jeanine, we have to talk a minute," he said huskily.

"Go ahead."

"I don't know what's going to happen when we walk in there," he offered, concerned. "If Rhetta thinks we're dead . . . who knows how her mind works."

Her blue eyes softened. "As long as I know you love me, it won't matter what she does," she answered, and he sighed.

"I do love you," he said, and leaned down, kissing her deeply, and for a few brief moments they both forgot the ordeal that lay ahead of them. Then finally Griff drew his lips from hers. "Ready?" he asked.

She nodded. "As ready as I ever will be," and a few minutes later Griff swung the kitchen door open and ushered Jeanine inside, staying close at her heels.

Crystal was at the sink, with Cory beside her, both of them with their backs to the door when Griff and Jeanine walked in. Hearing the door creak, they whirled around, wondering who else was wandering about at this time of night.

"My God!" Crystal gasped as she grabbed Cory's arm, almost knocking a glass of water from his hand.

"Where the devil—?" Cory began, but was interrupted by Griff.

"You mean neither of you are glad to see us?"

"Glad to see you?" Cory said, absentmindedly wiping spilled water from the front of his shirt. "Hell yes, we're glad to see you." He started walking toward them. "But where the Sam Hill have you been? You were supposed to have been back two days ago. I was just about ready to go lookin'."

"And get yourself scalped?"

"Scalped?" Cory ran a hand through his hair. "Hell,

them redskins ain't seen a head of hair like mine for years, Griff. They wouldn't know what to do with it.''

"Don't count on it," Griff answered, and his eyes moved from Cory to Jeanine. He gestured toward the table. "Come on, you'd better sit down.''

"Oh heavens," Crystal said, finally finding her voice again. "What am I doing just standing here," and she hurried to the table, helping pull out chairs for them. "You two look terrible," she said. "You must have walked for miles.''

"We have," Griff answered. He and Jeanine both sat down. "And I'll explain, don't worry. But right now, all we want is some food. We haven't had a thing to eat except dried jerky since shortly after leaving the Comanche, and that was the day before yesterday.

Crystal poured them both coffee first, then set cold chicken, biscuits, butter, and jam down on the table.

"What happened?" Cory asked as he straddled a chair backward, resting his hands on the back of it while he watched them starting to devour the food.

Griff swallowed three or four bites; then, "First of all, where's Rhetta?" he asked.

Cory and Crystal glanced at each other, reluctant to answer.

"Well, where is she?" he asked again.

Crystal's green eyes sparked. "You tell him, Cory," she said. "I'll go get Mrs. Brandt.''

Cory cleared his throat while Crystal left the room. "Well, you see," he tried to explain, "earlier this evenin', about an hour before dinner, some fella came to the door with a message for her. Mrs. Brandt said right after that Rhetta had Cinnamon hitch up a buggy for her, and she took off. Said she was taking Gar for a ride, and she ain't got back yet.''

Griff flinched. "She's got Gar with her?"

"Yup.''

"You looked for them?"

"When I got home. But it was late and we lost their

tracks just this side of the Vance property when it got too dark to see."

Jeanine put her hand on Griff's arm. "The mine?" she asked, and he looked at her intently.

"It has to be."

"If she took him there, with those men . . ."

Griff's hand covered hers, holding it tightly. "Don't worry. She loves the boy," he assured her. "She won't let anyone hurt him."

"I hope you're right."

Cory frowned. "Mind letting me in on it?" he asked curiously. "Or isn't it none of my business?"

Griff squeezed Jeanine's hand again, then looked over at Cory. "It's messy business," he said, his voice deepening with emotion. "But I think you have a right to know, since I'm planning to ask you to help."

"Help with what?" asked Mrs. Brandt as she stepped through the kitchen door from the dining room, with Crystal close behind, and Griff saw that although she looked quite composed, her eyes held a spark of relief at seeing him alive and well.

"If you sit down, I'll tell you," he answered quickly, and for the next few minutes he proceeded to go over everything that had happened since he'd left Trail's End in search of Jeanine, leaving out only what he thought unnecessary, which was his Comanche marriage to Jeanine in exchange for her freedom.

"I had a hell of a time talking Chief Horse Back into letting me bring her back," was his only comment on the matter, and Jeanine was grateful. But the rest of it—Jarrod's men kidnapping them and planning to seal them in the old mine, his confession about being Gar's real father and the part Rhetta had played in his brother's death—he told it all, and when he was through, the kitchen was so still they could hear each other breathing.

"It's only a guess," Griff finally said, breaking the silence, "but I'd say that Jarrod evidently got word to Rhetta that we escaped. If I'm not mistaken, she's probably at the mine right now."

"So that leaves you where?" asked Cory, and Griff's eyes narrowed.

"That leaves me a tool to bargain with."

"Bargain?" Mrs. Brandt stared at him, dumbfounded. "You're going to bargain with her?"

"Do I have any choice?" His eyes hardened. "She killed my brother, yes, but she's also Gar's mother, and I love the boy. I won't see him hurt. And if he knew his father was really Jarrod Vance, who knows what he might do."

"So you'll just let her go?" Mrs. Brandt couldn't believe it.

"For keeping her mouth shut and giving me my freedom, yes," he answered. "If either Rhetta or Jarrod ended up behind bars now, they'd never stop telling the world the truth about Gar, and what would that do to the boy?"

Mrs. Brandt's eyes were intense as she stared at Griff. "I love Gar too," she said bitterly, "but it doesn't seem fair that she should go unpunished, or Jarrod either for that matter."

"I know." Griff's jaw tightened stubbornly. "But it's the only way out, as far as I can see."

"And if they won't go along with it?"

"They will. They have to." He turned to Cory. "Roust the boys, Cory," he said, coming to a quick decision. "We'll go after the boy tonight, but first we'll ride to the Double V Bar to let Miles know what Jarrod's been up to. We won't tell him about Jarrod being Gar's father, but he has to know all the rest. And since there's a chance we could have trouble, it just might be good if we ask Miles to go along. Then we'll go on to the mine. I intend to settle things before the night's over, so tell the boys we'll be riding as soon as they're saddled."

"I presume I'm not invited, then?" Warren suddenly asked from the dining-room doorway, and they all glanced over in surprise, wondering how long he'd been standing there.

No one had seen him come in, but he had to have been there long enough to hear everything by the look on his face, and he was cradling a bottle in his arms as if it were a baby. His face was flushed, eyes bloodshot, as he looked right at Griff, and it was obvious he was feeling no pain. "I guess I can't really blame you for not wanting me here when you told everyone your little story," he said, making his way to the table. He sat down on one of the chairs, putting the bottle out in front of him gently, as if it was something precious. "And what a story, my God!"

Griff watched him closely. "I wish you hadn't heard, Warren."

"Oh, I don't doubt that." Warren's words were slurred. "I never heard such a pack of lies."

Griff straightened. "They weren't lies, and you'd know it too, if you weren't so drunk."

"Drunk? Hell!" Warren sneered. "I never have enough to get drunk on."

"Well, you're not getting any more." Griff made a quick decision, and reached over, snatching the half-full bottle off the table.

"Hey! What the hell . . ." Warren grabbed for the bottle but missed. "That's mine!"

"Not anymore it isn't." Griff handed it to Crystal. "Pour the damn thing out," he said disgustedly. "And don't let him have another as long as he's under my roof."

Warren's mouth dropped and he stared at Griff in complete surprise, because Griff had never interfered with his drinking before. Then suddenly he closed his mouth, his eyes narrowing, and he looked at Jeanine. She wasn't disguised anymore, but he still wasn't positive whether she was really Jeannie Gray, and there was no way he could prove it, even if she were. But she was a woman, and he'd seen the way Griff looked at her. "Oh, I see," he said after a few seconds, and he glanced back at Griff. "You're the only one allowed any vices, is that it, dear brother-in-law?" he said.

Griff frowned. "What are you talking about?"

"Her!" Warren answered as he glanced directly at Jeanine again for a second, then looked back at Griff. "I've seen the two of you together . . . I know what's going on, and so does everyone else," he went on. "It's a nice setup, isn't it? Get the wife out of the way by accusing her of murder, then the two of you live happily ever after. What an idea." He leaned forward. "But it won't work. I always knew you were too good to be true." He sneered. "Griffin Heywood . . . ideal husband . . . what a laugh!" His eyes sparked dangerously, his words losing some of their slur. "I knew you and Rhetta weren't hitting it off too well since you got back. I could understand that, you being gone for so long and all . . . but I never thought you'd hate her so much you'd make up a cock-and-bull story about her killin' your brother, then tryin' to kill you. What's the matter, divorce too messy for you, Griff? Afraid you'll come out on the wrong end and lose everything?" He stood up, lurching backward, almost knocking over a chair, then caught himself and gazed around at the others. "And to think you'd all believe him!" He looked directly at Mrs. Brandt. "You know very well Rhetta's not capable of murder."

"Do I?" The housekeeper's face was drained of color, her eyes glinting a dark golden brown. "Your sister's capable of anything, Warren, anything!" she answered.

"Well, I don't believe it!" he yelled drunkenly. "I know she's no angel, but murder?"

"Warren, why don't you sleep it off?" Griff suggested as Warren started to leave the table.

"Sleep? Hell, who needs sleep?" He turned, grabbing his hat and coat from the rack behind the door, starting to leave.

Griff's eyes followed him. "Where are you going?"

"Out!" Warren's eyes darkened. "To ride it off," he sneered viciously. "Like you said, I'm probably drunk, but I'm also gonna go see Rhetta and find out just what the hell's going on," and he stumbled across the threshold, slamming the door behind him.

Cory stood up. "Want me to stop him?"

"No, let him go," Griff said as he stared hard at the closed door. "He's boozed up and angry, that's all. Maybe the night air'll cool him off and sober him up some."

"I'll get the boys, then," said Cory, and pushed the chair in at the table before leaving.

Griff leaned back in his chair, pushing the rest of the food away from in front of him. He just wasn't hungry anymore.

"Don't take Warren's anger too lightly, Griff," Mrs. Brandt said wisely, as she saw how unconcerned he seemed to be over Warren's actions. "He doesn't like the idea of the safe little world he's been living in here being disrupted."

"Neither do I," Griff said. "But life isn't always that accommodating and he has to learn that." He straightened and turned to Jeanine. "Now, there's something I have to check on before I leave," he said hurriedly. "Will you come with me?"

Jeanine couldn't eat any more either, so she accepted the invitation and followed him from the kitchen while Mrs. Brandt stayed at the table contemplating and Crystal started to clear things away.

When he and Jeanine reached the top of the stairs, Griff swung open the door to the master bedroom and gestured for her to go inside.

"I have a feeling Rhetta's decided to make a run for it," he said as he followed her in and lit the lamp on the stand by the bed; then he strolled to the dresser, nodding as he realized the lock was broken. "Just as I thought."

When he opened the drawer and checked, the strongbox was empty.

"How much did she take?"

"About eight hundred. All I had." He closed the drawer. "Now I know I have to get to her tonight."

"I'm going with you, Griff," she said firmly. "In case there's trouble."

"Don't be crazy," he answered. "You could get hurt." He frowned. "Besides, even if there was trouble, how would your coming help?"

"Gar's there," she reminded him, hoping he'd understand. "He's probably frightened enough as it is. When you turn on Rhetta, his whole world's going to collapse. Maybe if I'm there, I can help him pick up the pieces."

"No, Jeanine . . . it's no good," he said. "It's too risky. You know what those men are like."

"Please," she pleaded. "Let me go with you. I can't stay here and just wait. Please, Griff."

He stared into her eyes for a long time, weighing the decision, then sighed, hoping he'd made the right choice. "All right, you win," he answered huskily, and reached out, pulling her into his arms. He bent to kiss her, but she pushed him away.

"No, Griff, no more, please," she said, suddenly taking him by surprise, and there were tears in her eyes. "We've only been fooling ourselves and you know it," she went on unhappily, her hands still on his chest, keeping him back.

His eyes hardened as he searched her face. "How? What do you mean?"

"By pretending we can come out clean in all this." She toyed with the fringe on his jacket and continued to stare up at him. "Don't you see? No matter which way we try to move, she has us stopped," she went on. "You said you'd bargain with her, her freedom for your silence about what she and Jarrod have done and about her killing your brother. But let's face it, Griff, even if you tried to accuse either of them of anything, it'd only be our word against theirs, and how far do you think we'd get? The husband and the other woman! The people in Raintree know nothing about her and Jarrod, so unless we could get Burke and the others to talk, there's no one to back us up, and they aren't about to stay around to get arrested. Besides, all she has to do is threaten to tell Gar who his real father is if you don't take her back, and you'd have no choice."

"I'd kill her first!"

"Griff!"

His eyes were troubled. "Well, good God, Jeanine, how much am I expected to put up with?" he asked bitterly. "My brother, my life . . . she's taken it all. I can't give her any more. I won't." His jaw set hard, unyielding. "Goddammit, Jeanine . . ."

She reached up, touching his face, her fingers caressing

his cheek, moving lightly along the rigid edge of his jawline. "And I vowed to stay away from you." There were tears in her eyes.

This time he did kiss her, and the kiss was hard, yet sweet, filled with all the anguished yearning both of them shared.

"I'll not give you up, Jeanine," he whispered passionately as he drew his mouth from hers. "I can't!" and his lips brushed her neck, pressing against her ear. "I didn't want to love you, believe me. I don't now. It's torn me apart inside and made my life a living hell, but dammit, I can't help it. I never knew I could feel this way about anyone." His voice deepened sensuously. "I wish I had the answers for you and could promise you the world." He straightened, once more searching her face. "But I can't. All I can do is love you, and even that has to be kept secret."

"You think the others haven't guessed?" she asked.

"I imagine Cory, Crystal, and Mrs. Brandt suspect, yes, and Warren does, but we don't dare let anyone know for sure. Not until this whole mess is straightened out anyway."

"And who knows when that'll be."

"Tonight," he said with conviction. "One way or the other I'm going to find an answer tonight." He cupped her face with his hand. "There has to be a way. Somehow things have to work out." He kissed her lightly but lovingly. "Now, come on, trust me," and a few minutes later when they entered the kitchen, Cory was already waiting, with guns for Griff to replace the ones Jarrod's men had taken from him.

"Saddle a horse for Jeanine too, Cory," Griff said as he adjusted the guns in his gunbelt. "She's going with us." Then he glanced over and saw the look of surprise on the housekeeper's face. "I know it's dangerous, Mrs. Brandt," he explained briefly. "But if things don't go the way I want them to, Gar's going to need someone there besides me, and he trusts Jeanine."

Mrs. Brandt frowned. "I hadn't thought of that." She

looked at Jeanine, for the first time realizing that it wasn't just the way she was wearing her hair that made her seem different, but that she didn't have her glasses on anymore, and didn't seem to need them. She began to wonder, then brushed the negative thoughts aside, at least for now. Griff was right, Gar was more than just fond of the young woman. "Take good care of him," she pleaded anxiously, and Jeanine nodded, assuring her nothing was going to happen to the boy; then Mrs. Brandt turned to Griff. "And don't let anything happen to you either," she said, trying to appear stern but giving her feelings away by the tears at the corners of her eyes.

"Don't worry, I'll be all right," Griff assured her, and after making sure they were all ready, he, Jeanine, and Cory went on outside to where the men were already mounted and waiting, and he helped Jeanine onto one of the horses, then mounted the one beside it. And with Crystal and Mrs. Brandt watching, the group rode away from the huge log house, down the drive and off into the night.

Mrs. Brandt stood quietly, watching them disappear in the darkness, their echoing hoofbeats growing fainter as they carried back to them.

"He's in love with that woman," she whispered softly to no one in particular, and Crystal glanced at her in surprise.

It was the first time anyone, even Mrs. Brandt, had had the courage to voice aloud what they'd all been thinking, except for Warren's drunken outburst a short time ago in the kitchen.

"I wonder how it's all gonna turn out?" Crystal added, watching for the housekeeper's reaction.

Mrs. Brandt looked over at her and frowned. "God only knows," she answered unhappily. "I only hope Griff won't regret what he's doing," and she straightened, inhaling sharply. "Now, let's go in. I have a feeling the rest of tonight's going to drag on, so we might as well find something to do," and as she opened the door for Crystal, then followed her back into the kitchen, Mrs. Brandt glanced quickly back down the drive, into the night, wondering if Crystal was praying as hard as she was for everyone's safe return.

It was a little after two in the morning when Jarrod pulled into the ranch yard at the Double V Bar and slid from the saddle, tethering his sorrel at the hitch rail. The house was dark except for a light in the kitchen. His father was often wandering around late at night. If he couldn't sleep, he'd get back up and have hot milk, a sandwich, or some other choice tidbit.

Jarrod moved along the side porch and opened the back door. His father was standing at the table, cutting into what was left of an apple pie, and his big stomach shook under his night shirt as he whirled around, momentarily startled by the sound of the door opening. He went back to his pie when he recognized Jarrod.

"Well, the wanderer finally returns," he said as he cut a huge piece. "Where the hell have you been anyway, boy?" he asked testily. "Haven't seen hardly nothin' of you for three or four days."

Jarrod stepped into the kitchen and stood watching his father for a minute, then moved over to the table.

"I'm leaving, Pa," he said quietly, and watching closely to see what effect it would have on him.

Miles went right on fixing his snack. He put the piece of pie on a plate, then sat down, picked up a fork and began eating, seemingly unconcerned over his son's statement.

"Didn't you hear me, Pa?" Jarrod asked.

"I heard you, boy." Miles mouthed another bite.

"Will you stop that, Pa!" Jarrod yelled angrily. "I'm not a boy anymore, Pa. I'm thirty years old."

"I know, I know," his father said impatiently, and gestured for him to sit down. "Don't be impatient, you've been to Mexico before."

"But this ain't like before."

"Well, sit down then, and we'll talk it over."

"There's nothing to talk over." Jarrod was talking slowly

and deliberately. "I couldn't stay now, even if I wanted to."

Miles glanced up from his food, and suddenly he saw something in his son's eyes he'd never seen before. Jarrod had always been a little wild, and at first he thought he was just getting itchy feet again and that he could talk him out of going to Mexico if that's what he had planned. Now he wasn't so sure. There was something different about Jarrod this time.

Miles frowned. "What do you mean?" he asked hesitantly.

"You may as well know, Pa," Jarrod said nervously, and his hazel eyes were hard and coldly unfeeling as he studied his father. "You'll find out anyway before it's all over."

"Find out what?"

He squared his shoulders, resting one hand on his gun butt, slipping the other in the front of his gunbelt. "I tried to kill Griffin Heywood, Pa," he confessed openly. "Only it didn't turn out the way I'd planned."

"You?" Miles's face paled, and his hand descended hesitantly with the fork still in it, the hunk of pie on the fork uneaten.

"That's right, Pa," Jarrod went on. "I'm the one behind all his trouble."

Miles felt sick. "But why?" he asked, the pie suddenly forgotten.

"Why not?" Jarrod's eyes flashed arrogantly. "I only tried to do what you didn't have guts enough to do to his old man. If you'd had enough backbone you'd have killed Zeb and taken over Trail's End years ago."

Miles's fist slammed on the table. "Jesus Christ, boy!" he yelled. "You don't just go around killin' people whenever they get in your way!"

"You do!"

"Not unless they draw first."

"So that makes you a hero, I suppose."

Miles's face reddened and he stood up. "Don't get smart, boy!"

"I told you, Pa. I'm not your little boy anymore."
Jarrod's head tilted arrogantly. "I haven't been for years."

"And you think 'cause you're growed you can do whatever the hell you please?" Miles's knees were shaking and he was forced to sit back down. "What the hell did you want Trail's End for anyway?" he asked angrily. "What's wrong with this place?"

"This place is yours, Pa, not mine."

"Well, Christ, boy! What made you think Trail's End would be yours with Griff out of the way? He's got a wife and son who'd inherit. Where'd you come in?"

"I wanted Rhetta, and she wouldn't leave Trail's End. It was the only way."

Miles shook his head in disbelief. "Jesus, I thought you'd forgotten about her years ago. You said that's why you went to Mexico." His eyes hardened knowingly. "I should have known you couldn't keep your hands off her." He paused a second, then went on. "And I suppose you've been carryin' on with her every time you came home," he said as he watched Jarrod's face and knew he'd come close to the truth. He stood up again, starting to pace the floor, blustering furiously. "Maybe we can talk to Griff . . . make a deal . . . he might be willing to forget the whole thing . . ."

"You don't understand, Pa!" Jarrod countered, forcing the issue further. "It won't work! I've killed four men, and two never even carried guns. They call that murder, Pa. There's no going back. Not this time! Not ever!"

Miles stopped, standing motionless, his face drained of color again, and he stared at his son. Where had he failed? He'd built the ranch up for Jarrod to have someday, and he was proud of the Double V Bar. Next to Trail's End it was one of the best ranches on the frontier, or had been before the war. It wasn't the ranch, though. That was only a part of it.

It was that woman. That goddamned woman! She was the kind that got into a man's blood and tore him inside out for want of her. At least he could understand how Jarrod felt. Hadn't he felt the same way about Griff's mother years ago? Only Jarrod was right, he'd never had the belly to do anything about it, except take second best after Zeb when she was willing. Lord knows he'd thought of killing Zeb until his guts ached, but folks whispered about him and Lucy enough; he wasn't going to take a chance on hanging. Besides, he'd never had the stomach for cold-blooded murder. Self-defense was one thing, but . . . He continued to stare at Jarrod as if suddenly seeing his son for the first time as a man.

"Who'd you kill?" he asked abruptly.

"The man carrying the Trail's End payroll, Jake Harper, Homer Beacon, and Harlin Winslow."

"Harlin? But he ain't . . ."

"He is now. I needed money, Pa, and now I've got it. I just stopped by to tell you why and say good-bye before I go get Rhetta and the boy."

"But, if Griff's not dead. . . ?"

"Pa, Rhetta's in it with me, don't you see? We planned the whole thing together. And you might as well know, Gar's my son, Pa, not a Heywood."

"Gar's . . ."

"That's right, my son. I never even suspected anything until I came back from Mexico last year and happened to get a good look at him. I'm surprised you didn't notice, but then you never did pay much attention to things like that." He saw the stricken look on his father's face, yet went on. "She never told me, because she wanted to be a Heywood and live at Trail's End. Well, now neither of us will have Trail's End, but I'll win anyway. I'm headin' for Mexico with Rhetta and my son."

"If they don't hang you first!" Miles was still pale and his knees felt funny.

"They'll have to catch me, Pa," Jarrod answered belligerently. "And I don't catch easy." His hazel eyes darkened and he stared at his father for a long time, then suddenly straightened, whirled around, and left the room, heading for his bedroom to gather up the few belongings he'd have to take with him, before coming back to the kitchen to say a last good-bye to his father.

Miles lowered himself onto the chair where he'd been sitting before, and glanced down at the half-eaten piece of pie on the plate in front of him, realizing the hunger that had driven him to the kitchen earlier was completely gone. Now, instead, he felt horribly sick inside, his stomach twisting into a ball of fire that felt like it was going to tear him in two as he waited for Jarrod to come back. He was waiting to say good-bye to the boy he loved and the man he'd now become. A man who was now a stranger to him. A stranger who'd ride off into the night hoping to escape the end of a rope. Suddenly tears crept into his eyes, and Miles felt far lonelier than he'd ever felt before in his whole life. And while he sat in the kitchen, bewildered, his heart breaking, he had no idea that outside in the dark, a group of riders was quietly approaching the Double V Bar.

It was a little after two-thirty. Griff raised a hand to slow his men down to a walk, and when they reached the big wooden gate with the V emblazoned on it, he reined his horse to a halt, with the men following suit. The gate was open and Griff glanced toward the long low house spread out before them in the lowering moonlight. There was a side porch outside the kitchen door, at the left, and a veranda on the other end, near the front door.

"Looks like we won't have to wake Miles," Griff said as he spotted a light flickering in the kitchen window.

Cory grabbed his arm, pointing to the hitch rail near the edge of the porch, where moonlight shone on a sorrel with a white blaze on its forehead.

Griff inhaled sharply, tensing. "Jarrod!" He straightened in the saddle, more alert now. "I'd better go in alone." He turned to his foreman. "Stay here, Cory," he whispered. "And keep Jeanine and the men with you. Jarrod may not take too kindly to seeing me."

Cory nodded, and Griff threw Jeanine a quick smile of assurance, then nudged his horse forward, easing him through the open gate and on toward the house, while the rest of the riders patiently waited, and Jeanine's lips moved silently as she prayed harder than she'd ever prayed before in her life.

Meanwhile, inside the kitchen, Jarrod was heading for the door, while his father stood helplessly by, watching him go. Suddenly he stopped, listening, then turned back to his father.

"Douse the light!" he yelled, trying to keep his voice low.

"Why?"

"Douse it!" Jarrod's gun was out already. "I hear a horse."

Miles reached over and blew out the lamp, then squinted, watching as Jarrod pulled back the edge of the curtain and peered out just in time to see Griff slide from the saddle and make a loping run for the watering trough.

"It's Heywood," he yelled over his shoulder, and Miles stiffened as Jarrod broke a pane of glass in the window and leveled his gun, aiming it outside.

"What the hell are you doin', boy?" Miles gasped incredulously.

Jarrod had spotted riders at the gate seconds after seeing Griff leave the saddle.

"He's brought a posse with him, Pa," he yelled, panicking. "He ain't even gonna give us a chance to bargain. Damn his hide!" and before Miles could try to reason with him, Jarrod squeezed the trigger, trying to pick off Griff before he reached the watering trough.

Griff hit the ground hard, his own gun in his hand now. Relieved that he wasn't hit, he grabbed his hat off his head before peering over the top of the watering trough, his eyes scanning the kitchen windows.

He knew the second the light went out that he'd been spotted, and was glad now that he'd headed for cover. Suddenly another flurry of shots broke the silence, thudding uselessly into the wooden trough, and he ducked low again.

Cursing angrily, he waited for the firing to stop, then made his decision. He'd been hoping to persuade Jarrod to talk, but wasn't about to get himself killed in the process. So, resting the barrel of his gun on top of the trough, he eased his head up, took a bead on the window from where the shots had come, and pulled the trigger, just as he heard Cory and the others riding up from behind to help out.

Jarrod saw the flash of Griff's gun, but never heard it. Instead, all he heard was his father shouting something from behind him, then felt the sudden burning pain in his chest. He clutched viciously at it, trying to stop it from hurting, but it was no use, and seconds later, as Miles squinted in the darkness, staring helplessly, unable to move, Jarrod reeled backward, hit the table, rolled against a chair, then sprawled on the floor at his father's feet.

Miles's breath choked him, and for a minute he couldn't breathe or even move as he stared down at Jarrod. The room was so dark and quiet now, as if time were standing still. Then gradually, knees shaking, Miles lowered himself to the floor, oblivious of the rough wood against his bare legs and the fact that his nightshirt was getting blood on it, and slowly, as if in a daze, he picked Jarrod up in his arms and turned him onto his back. Miles's arms went around his son, and he cradled him as if he were a baby, crooning to him, telling him not to worry, everything would be all right.

Suddenly he stopped and stared at the limp body in his arms, waiting for some kind of response, anything to show him that Jarrod was still alive. But there was nothing. His son was no longer breathing, and with an agonized groan Miles pressed Jarrod's lifeless body to his chest and began to sob as if his life too was ending.

Outside, Griff waited for answering fire, but there was none. Then he motioned for Cory and the others to stay back when he saw lights starting to go on in the bunkhouse across the drive. Very gingerly, ready to duck back down at any moment if need be, he stood up. Still nothing. All he could hear was a wailing moan that sounded sad and woeful.

He turned to see Cory dismounting a short distance from him. "Stay outside, Cory," he told him. "I'll go take a look," and he moved cautiously to the back porch, then reached down, turning the doorknob, swinging the door open wide.

The room was quite dark, but with his eyes accustomed to the night, and with faint moonlight filtering in through a side window, he could see well enough to know what had happened. Miles Vance was sitting on the floor in his nightshirt, holding Jarrod in his arms, and Griff knew instinctively that Jarrod was dead.

Miles gulped back a sob, suddenly sensing Griff's presence. He glanced toward the door, tears flowing down his ruddy cheeks into his beard. "You killed my boy!" he cried angrily, his fat jowls shaking with emotion. "You shot Jarrod! Oh God, Griff, you shot my boy!"

Griff's stomach tightened and he took a step into the room, then stood staring down at Miles, his voice low as he answered. "He shot first, Miles, and you know it."

Miles only shook his head. "He thought you brought a posse, and you shot him!" he wailed, as if he hadn't even heard Griff. "It's all her fault, that wife of yours. I wish he'd never laid eyes on her!" He buried his face against Jarrod's head. "Oh God, my boy, my boy! Griff, you shot my boy!"

Griff's eyes hardened, and for a minute he almost felt sorry for Miles, but as he stood there watching him grieving over the loss of his son, he suddenly remembered Gar and Rhetta and the part Jarrod had played in ruining his life. And he thought back over the years. How Miles had always spoiled his son and tried to give him everything he wanted from life. No wonder that when all else failed, Jarrod tried to take what he wanted in his own way. There was no way he was going to feel sorry for a man like Miles; he couldn't afford to. Without saying another word, Griff turned and left, not even bothering to close the door behind him.

He mounted his horse, then joined the others, including Cory, who was mounted again, and as the Double V Bar crew began staggering and stumbling out of the bunkhouse in various states of undress, trying to collect their senses and figure out what was going on, Griff raised his hand, motioning for everyone to follow, and with Jeanine at his

side, he led his men back through the gates of the Double
V Bar, then on down the road, at a gallop, heading toward
the old abandoned copper mine, Miles's presence with
them no longer needed.

15

They kept to the main road all the way, afraid to use the old cutoff after dark, since none of them were too familiar with Double V Bar land, and as they rode along, Griff began to wonder. What would Rhetta do when she discovered Jarrod was dead? Evidently he'd returned to the Double V Bar either to say good-bye to his father or to try to talk him into giving him money to add to what Rhetta had, so they could get away. Now, with Jarrod dead . . . He was certain she didn't love Jarrod, but there was a bond between them, and that alone was enough to hold her to him.

He glanced over at Jeanine beside him, moonlight playing on her fair hair as she reined her horse along the dusty roadway, and his thoughts began to wander back to their conversation earlier in his bedroom back at Trail's End. What if Rhetta did demand to be taken back, using Gar's true parentage as a threat? Could he do it? Could he take her back and go on pretending, if only for the boy's sake? He shuddered, suddenly knowing full well he couldn't. He'd rather take a chance on telling Gar the truth than live under the same roof with her again. But then, what would the truth do to the boy? Did he have a right to risk it? Rhetta had to talk to him, come to some sort of agreement, and bend to what he wanted for a change. She'd had her own way too long; this time he was going to do the demanding, and as they followed the road around a bend, then broke to the crest of a low hill, slowing their horses as they neared the abandoned mine, his jaw set hard. His mind was made up. This time he'd have things his way.

They rode a hundred or so yards closer, their horses at a walk; then suddenly Griff ordered the men to stop again. Spider and Luke wanted to stay close to Cory, but Griff told them to stick with the rest of the crew and see that the men spread out, just in case there was trouble from the men who were working for Jarrod.

"I'm going to try this alone first," he told them all as they gathered close for instructions. "We haven't told you why you're out here, but believe me, there's a reason, and a good one." He straightened in the saddle. "This much I will tell you. There's an old mining camp ahead, nestled at the foot of those hills, and some men Jarrod Vance hired are there with my wife and son, and I'm going to try to get them out, but I might need help. That's where all of you come in." He glanced at Jeanine. "I'm going to take Miss Grayson and Cory on ahead with me, and I want the rest of you to stay here and see if you can find some cover. Spider and Luke have been around, and should know the area some, so stick close to them. If I need help I'll send Cory back for the rest of you, but even if it comes to that, I want you to come in slow, understand? I don't want the wrong people hurt."

The men all nodded agreement and started dismounting, checking their guns.

"Good. Now, find a spot and hold to it," Griff ordered. He motioned to Cory and Jeanine, who joined him, reining their horses forward, while behind them the crew started melting into the shadows.

"Since you two know what's really going on, I want you with me," Griff said a short while later as they dismounted and tethered their horses at a nearby bush. "Now, come on," and they began moving forward on foot, trying to keep in the shadows.

When they were about two hundred feet from the house,

Griff suddenly stopped, Jeanine and Cory drawing up close behind him.

"What is it?" Cory asked, whispering as his eyes scanned the area.

Griff kept his voice low. "I'm not sure. But I have a feeling something's wrong."

Jeanine was close at his side. "What?"

"Look," and he pointed ahead toward the porch he knew was just off the kitchen. There was a dim light on inside, but with the moon riding low in the sky and giving just enough light, they could see that the place looked deserted. "No horses at the hitching rail, no men. They should be all over the place, yet I don't see a soul around."

Both Cory and Jeanine squinted, straining their eyes. Griff was right, the place looked deserted.

"Let me take a look around first," Griff suggested, still whispering softly. "If I need you, Cory, I'll signal. You know how."

Cory nodded, and Griff looked down at Jeanine.

"Take care of her too, just in case," he said, and Jeanine took his arm.

"Be careful," she cautioned.

Their eyes met momentarily, and he wished he could hold her for just a moment and tell her not to worry, that everything was going to work out. Instead, he just stared at her hard for a minute and tried to smile reassuringly.

"I'll be all right, don't worry," he answered, and she let go of his arm. He turned, walking away, and in seconds the darkness swallowed him up.

Jeanine and Cory moved quickly over to hide behind some bushes that were so low they ended up sitting on the ground. Even sitting, though, Jeanine was a great deal shorter than Cory, and he was the only one who could see over the top of the bushes.

"Do you still see him?" Jeanine asked.

"Nope. But don't worry, he moves like an Indian. Quiet and deadly." Cory turned, with his back to the bushes, settling down comfortably, and glanced over, watching Jeanine as best he could in the darkness.

Cory and Griff had been close for years, and although Griff was rather noncommittal about some things, the foreman knew him almost as well as he knew himself, and he sensed that his friend had been in love with Jeanine for some time, even though he'd never admitted it. He could tell by the way they acted around each other, and now he had a strange feeling that something had happened to them during the past few days to strengthen those feelings even more, and he dreaded to think what it might be, because now there seemed to be a quiet intimacy in the looks that passed between them. An intimacy that had been missing before. He'd noticed it the minute he'd laid eyes on them when they'd walked into the kitchen earlier, and he swore silently to himself as he studied her.

He hadn't had a chance to talk to Griff alone about anything since their return, but it was evident that the Jeanine Grayson who came back to Trail's End with Griff looked nothing like the timid, plain little schoolteacher who'd ridden out toward Indian Rock and ended up getting herself kidnapped just a few days before. And as he watched her now, he wondered if she could possibly be the Jeannie Gray Warren was always talking about. But then, even if she were, it wouldn't change things, and he frowned as he looked off into the darkness once more.

They waited quietly for what seemed like an eternity, Cory stoically listening and watching, his eyes scanning the area intently, while Jeanine sat on the ground beside him, fidgeting nervously.

Suddenly a bloodcurdling scream cut the night air, ending in a garbled, choking cry, then silence.

The hair on Jeanine's neck rose, and she dug her fingers into Cory's arm. "Cory?"

"Come on," he whispered, his voice barely audible, and they got to their feet slowly, cautiously, beginning to make their way in the direction where Griff had disappeared, which was also the same direction the scream had come from.

The moon had been low in the sky before; now it was gone completely, and as they moved forward, trying to penetrate the darkness surrounding them, Cory headed toward the only movement he could see. It was near a patch of light that was coming from the house.

"Over here," Griff called when he heard them approaching, and Cory moved off toward the light, making sure Jeanine kept with him.

A few seconds later they both stopped, and Jeanine gasped, startled as they almost bumped into Griff, who was kneeling at the edge of a clump of briar bushes a few feet from the porch, almost directly below the kitchen window from which a dim light filtered down. Beside him, crumpled in an awkward heap, her dark hair tangled where it was caught in the briars, was Rhetta. Her mouth was open, eyes wide, staring straight ahead, and Griff's hunting knife was protruding from between her breasts, where blood was still seeping slowly onto the bodice of her lavender dress.

"Oh my God!" Cory's face was ashen and Jeanine looked sick.

"Griff!" she managed to gasp, and his eyes settled quickly on her face.

"I didn't touch her!" he said, his voice strained.

Cory frowned. "But how?"

Griff stood up hesitantly and looked back down at the body of his wife. "I wish I knew." He took a deep breath and straightened, his eyes trying to search the darkness around them before once more resting on Jeanine. "I heard talking, and started toward the voices," he began. "I was trying to keep from being seen, so I was keeping low. Then I heard her scream."

"Did you see anybody?" asked Cory. "Anybody at all?"

"Not a soul, but I heard someone moving off in the underbrush, and I swear that just before you two got here, I heard a horse whinny somewhere close by, then the faint sounds of hoofbeats off toward the old barn the other side of the mine entrance." Griff cocked his head. "Listen, someone's coming."

Their heads turned in the direction of the rickety porch

from where the easy gait of a horse, walking slowly, echoed in the cool night air, and they waited for the rider to come into view.

Finally the horse was reined past the corner of the porch, then pulled to a halt when the rider saw movement under the window.

Jeanine inhaled sharply. "It's Warren!" she exclaimed, recognizing his familiar figure in the saddle.

Warren stared at all of them for a minute, then dismounted lazily. But just as he did so, he caught sight of the crumpled body on the ground, and his eyes narrowed warily. He took a step forward; then suddenly a sob caught in his throat.

"Rhetta?" He fell to the ground beside her, staring in disbelief. "My God, Griff! What have you done?" he cried, and Jeanine, who had looked up into Griff's face only moments before, saw him wince.

"I didn't do anything," he snapped.

"The hell you didn't!" Warren stood up, facing Griff, his eyes blazing angrily. "And I used to respect you!" He glanced at Jeanine, then back to his brother-in-law. "Well, was she worth it?" he asked. "Is she worth hanging for, Griff?"

"I said I didn't kill her!"

"You expect me to believe that?" He opened his mouth to go on, then suddenly stopped, as once more all heads turned, this time toward the main road that led past where Griff's men were hidden, from where they could hear the sound of a carriage hurriedly approaching.

"Now who?" asked Cory, and as all of them stared, waiting, Mrs. Brandt drove into view, pulled the buggy she was driving to a halt when she saw movement in the shadows near the porch, then got down and came forward, stopping to study the faces looking back at her.

"What's wrong? What is it?" she asked, frowning, and Warren was the first to break the silence.

"Griff killed Rhetta," he stated boldly.

"I did not!" Griff saw the housekeeper's eyes lower deliberately until they rested on Rhetta's body, still tangled partway in the briars; then she moved forward slowly and knelt beside it, looking it over for quite some time. The housekeeper's eyes were hard, her expression noncommittal as she stared at the body of the woman who'd made Griff's life so miserable for so many years; then finally she reached out firmly and ran her fingers down over Rhetta's eyes, closing them. Afterward, she wiped her hand across the skirt of her black dress and stood up again.

"Griff?" she questioned.

"You know I didn't do it," he answered.

"Yes, I know."

"Liar!" Warren yelled. "You were the only one here."

"What about you?"

"Me?"

Griff studied Warren curiously, suddenly realizing he was more sober than drunk. "That's right, you," he answered. "Where were you for the past few hours?"

"Like you suggested. I was riding around, trying to clear my head." He glanced down at his sister's body again, then back at Griff. "And besides," he went on, watching Griff closely, "it isn't my knife killed her, it's yours. I'd know it anywhere."

"And that proves I put it in her, I suppose?"

"Not necessarily. I'll let the sheriff prove that." He started for his horse.

Cory stopped him. "Where are you going?" he asked.

"Like I said," Warren answered Cory defiantly, "I'm going after the sheriff, and by God, if Griff's not here when I get back, I'll turn hell inside out to find him." There were tears in his eyes as he turned back to his horse, mounted, and rode off.

Griff glanced at the others. "It doesn't look good, does it?" he said.

Cory sighed. "I'm afraid there's lots of folks who'll believe the way Warren does."

"Where were you when it happened, Griff?" Mrs. Brandt asked hurriedly.

"About twenty feet away."

"And you didn't see anything?"

"Not a thing."

"But he heard someone running off," added Cory.

"At least that's a help." She glanced down at the body again, and this time her lip curled distastefully. "If only . . ." she mused softly, but didn't finish, and Jeanine, who'd been standing quietly listening to it all, suddenly looked up at Griff.

"No one will ever believe you," she said, her eyes troubled. "You know that, don't you?"

He looked directly at her, his eyes boring into hers. "You believe me, don't you?" he asked.

Did she? His heart was open to her, she could tell that by the look in his eyes, and yet their conversation in the bedroom, and his angry threat to kill Rhetta, kept haunting her. Griff was a strong man, and he'd been betrayed cruelly. Was that betrayal sufficient for him to carry out the threat? Had Rhetta refused to bargain with him?

She wanted to believe him, and every precious feeling she had for him begged her to forget the threat, that it had been only the logical action of an angry man, and slowly, as she delved into the depths of his blue eyes, her own softened with warmth, and she was suddenly so sure he could never have done it.

"Yes, I believe you," she whispered. "But no one else will."

He stared at her for a minute, then reached out, putting his arm about her shoulder. He led her away from Rhetta's still body, going deeper into the shadows by the porch, and once there, he pulled her close, both arms around her, so he could look down at her. "As long as you do," he said.

She flushed, embarrassed in front of Cory and Mrs. Brandt. "But, Griff . . . you said . . ."

"I know, I said no one was to know." His eyes darkened unhappily and he looked over her head at Cory and Mrs. Brandt still standing next to the body. "If they don't like it, they can go to hell," he said curtly. "Right now I don't give a damn, because I need you. I need your strength to get me through this."

"She's right about no one believing you, Griff," Mrs. Brandt said thoughtfully, her eyes studying the vague outline of the back of Jeanine's head in the darkness. "So if I were you, I'd be careful about letting any other folks know that the two of you are anything more than just friends." She drew her eyes from Jeanine and looked over at Cory, then surveyed the house and grounds, spotting the first faint rays of dawn beyond the hills to the east.

"I wonder where the boy is," she suddenly said, changing the subject, and Cory nodded toward the house.

"Probably in there."

"Then I think you and I had better go make sure he's all right," she said. "And if Griff doesn't mind, I think I'd better take him home."

Griff's arms eased from about Jeanine, and they both faced the housekeeper. "I don't mind at all," he said, thanking her with his eyes. "In fact, I'd rather not have to face him just yet. But please, Mrs. Brandt, whatever you do, don't tell him about his mother tonight. I'll tell him later myself, in my own way, if it's at all possible."

"As you wish," she answered, then motioned to Cory, "Come along, Cory. I may need your help," and they both turned to leave. Then suddenly Mrs. Brandt retraced her steps. She stood over Rhetta's body, staring down reflectively again for a minute; then, without saying a word, she removed the cloak from her shoulders, covered the body as best she could, and rejoined Cory at the porch steps and followed him into the house.

Griff looked down at Jeanine, and his arms tightened instinctively. "Just let me hold you, that's all I ask," he whispered softly.

She sighed. If only they could be alone, truly alone. She could feel his heart pounding in rhythm with hers, his hard muscles flexing beneath the buckskins.

"I was going to talk to her," he confessed, his voice raw with emotion. "Demand that she set me free."

"And if she hadn't accepted your demands?"

"Then I'd have begged." She felt his arms tighten. "I was willing to give her Trail's End and go away someplace, just you and I, if I had to. Anything, just so I had my freedom, so I could have you."

Her eyes were misty with tears. "You're free now," she said softly, but his face was troubled.

"Am I?" he asked, and she knew what he meant. Warren wasn't the only one who was going to accuse him. He wasn't free. He'd never be free until this whole mess was cleared up. "I love you," he whispered helplessly, and while he drew her closer, his lips covering hers, Cory stepped off the porch steps behind them carrying a sleepy Gar in his arms, then settled him in the buggy beside Mrs. Brandt, who had preceded him from the house. And as the sky grew lighter in the east, golden rays of sunshine streaming heavenward beyond the hills, Cory watched the housekeeper flick the reins, maneuvering the buggy around in the dust, and she headed down the only road that led out of the valley. Cory had told her where they'd left the men hiding and instructed her to stop and take a couple along as an escort, after berating her for leaving Trail's End alone. Now, after watching the buggy disappear into the predawn darkness, and waiting until the rattling noise from it faded in the distance, he turned toward Jeanine and Griff, who were talking quietly, their arms still around each other.

He hated to interrupt them, but it was time he found out what Griff wanted him to do about the men. After all, they couldn't stay hidden down the road forever waiting, because there was nothing to wait for anymore, except the sheriff. And besides, he glanced off toward the other buildings near the mine, he and Griff might as well put their time to good use while they were waiting for the sheriff and nose around a bit. Who knew what they might find. He straightened decisively, heading toward them.

It was early afternoon when the weary procession rode into Raintree, with Rhetta's body wrapped in an old blanket and strapped across a horse. Griff had wanted Jeanine to ride back to the ranch with Luke, Spider, and the rest of the crew, but she'd insisted on coming, and now, as he glanced over at her, he realized the toll all this was taking on her. She looked tired and worn out.

The news of Rhetta's death had spread fast, and as they rode slowly into town along the side street where the livery stables and corral were, then past the feed store, and on toward the sheriff's office, everyone seemed to be out and about, in doorways, and at windows, watching them curiously.

"I'm frightened, Griff," Jeanine said as Griff caught her eye, and he smiled, trying to be reassuring, but the smile didn't ring true.

Sheriff Higgens hadn't said too much, but Griff hadn't liked his attitude. They'd been friends for years, and now suddenly he was acting as if Griff were a stranger. Of course the fact that he'd been listening to Warren didn't help.

When the procession reached the sheriff's office, one of the deputies took the reins of the horse Rhetta's body was on and headed toward the undertaker's with it, while the rest of them dismounted and went inside.

To the sheriff's surprise, Bart Hendrix, the bank teller, was sitting in the sheriff's chair waiting for him when they walked in, and he stood up quickly as Dave Higgens flung his hat on the desk.

"What're you doin' here, Bart?" Higgens asked as he started around the desk to get some papers from one of the drawers.

"Bank's been robbed," Bart answered, and Dave Higgens looked startled.

"Hell it has!"

"Winslow's gone too," the teller added smugly.

Griff glanced over at Cory, frowning, then back to the sheriff, who was leaning over his desk now, staring curiously at the young bank teller.

"You mean Winslow ran off with the money?" he asked in surprise.

"What else?"

"No signs of robbery or nothin'?"

Bart Hendrix liked sounding important. "Went over to

his house and found the door wasn't locked," he went on. "And that gray suit he wore yesterday is missin', along with his boots. And there ain't no signs of the bank door bein' jimmied, either."

"The safe?"

"Wide open."

Sheriff Higgens stared at Bart Hendrix thoughtfully for a minute, then sighed as he sat down behind the desk. Dave Higgens wasn't too big a man, but he was stocky and muscular, his sandy hair prematurely touched with frost at the temples, and dark blue eyes that were often bloodshot from loss of sleep. He looked up at Griff.

"Well, Griff, looks like more'n one of our fair citizens has got himself in trouble, don't it?" he said.

Griff's jaw tightened angrily. "Meaning what?" he asked.

"Meanin' I ain't gonna be able to let friendship sway my thinkin' on this," Higgens answered. "So if you've got anything more to add to what you told me out at the mine, now'd be a good time to speak it."

"There's nothing more," Griff answered quickly.

The sheriff shrugged. "Have it your way."

"Then we can go?" Griff asked.

"For now. I can make the report out without you bein' here. Only stay close. I don't wanna have to ride out to Trail's End every time I get a notion to ask you somethin'." He glanced first at Jeanine, then Cory. "And that goes for the teacher here too," he added, then turned his attention once more to the bank teller. "Now, when did you discover Harlin missin'?" he asked as Griff nodded to Jeanine and Cory and the three of them headed for the door, leaving Warren staring after them while he listened to Bart Hendrix telling the sheriff all about the robbery.

"Warren's fuming," Cory said when they finally had the door closed behind them.

"Can you blame him?" Griff said. "He was hoping I'd end up behind bars. Too bad."

"Well, what do we do now?" Jeanine asked, flushing as she realized they were being stared at by a number of people who had congregated.

"We get some sleep," Griff answered wearily. "Come on," and they headed for the Empire Hotel, with Cory clearing a path for them through the crowd. When they reached the door to the hotel lobby, however, Griff stopped and turned to Cory.

"You too tired to run an errand?" he asked hopefully.

Cory shook his head, so Griff gave him instructions to go back to the ranch and tell Mrs. Brandt how things were going, see how Gar was doing, then get some sleep before coming back. He also decided to let Cory and Mrs. Brandt break the news to Gar about his mother, since he had no idea when he might get back to Trail's End again. Then, after watching Cory head for his horse, which was still in front of the sheriff's office, Griff and Jeanine went on into the hotel alone.

People were still staring at them, but Griff didn't seem too disturbed by it, figuring they probably felt they had reason. He and Jeanine were still wearing the dirty old buckskins, and it was the first time anyone in town had ever seen her without her usual glasses and with her hair falling free, and he could almost put words to the questions forming behind the townspeople's inquisitive eyes as he ushered her to the clerk's desk and they waited for Mr. Ed to finish with another customer.

A few minutes later, after saying good-bye to Griff, Jeanine closed the door to the room he'd gotten for her and leaned back against it, sighing for a moment, then walked over and sat wearily on the bed, starting to remove her clothes.

Griff had said to get some sleep, but how could she? It wasn't that she wasn't tired. Her eyes were drooping heavily, and every muscle in her body ached, but her mind was still racing from one thought to another. Well, at least she could get undressed and try. The buckskins felt like they were being peeled from her body, she'd had them on so long, and after tossing them aside in a chair, she climbed into the bed. The sheets felt cool against her naked body and she lay staring at the ceiling for a long time, trying to go over everything that had happened. Then slowly, in spite of the turmoil her thoughts were in, she finally dropped off into an exhausted sleep.

Meanwhile, in the room next to hers, the same room she'd been in the night he'd walked her home from the dance, Griff lay on the bed trying to think of something he might have missed seeing. Anything that would help prove he hadn't killed Rhetta. But no matter how hard he racked his brain, all he could remember was the terrifying scream, then a silence broken only by the soft crushing of underbrush and the faint echo of a horse's hooves in the distance. Even the voices he'd heard before her scream weren't distinctive enough to pinpoint. Rhetta could have been talking to anyone, and as the afternoon sun streamed in at the window, warming the room, he too finally closed his eyes, but slept fretfully.

It was dark when Jeanine woke. She must have slept the rest of the day away, and as she stirred in the covers, nestling a little deeper in their warmth, the sound of music and laughter from the saloon across the street floated up to her through the open door that led onto the balcony at the front of the hotel.

Suddenly she froze as she saw a movement in the shadows out on the balcony, and she held her breath as a figure was suddenly silhouetted in the doorway and a man leaned against the frame, watching what was going on down in the street below.

"Griff?" she asked, relaxing a little, certain she'd recognized him.

He turned and sauntered into the room. "I've been waiting for you to wake up." He sat on the edge of the bed.

"What time is it?" she asked.

"Close to eleven." He paused, then went on. "Mayor Talbot came to see me about an hour ago."

"Oh?"

"He said Higgens will be over to arrest me in the morning."

"They can't, Griff." She was trembling. "They just can't."

"Oh, but they can. We're good friends, yes, but as Talbot said, murders of passion aren't any too discriminating." He reached out, taking her hand, gently stroking her fingers.

"Who do you think did it?" she asked.

"I haven't the faintest idea." He squeezed her hand, not wanting to break the link between them. "And the sad part is, I can see everyone's reasoning. She was my wife, it was my knife, and I was bending over her body barely seconds afterward. I guess I can't blame them. Even you heard me threaten her."

"But you didn't mean it."

"Didn't I?" He looked pensive. "Sometimes I wonder. After all, most folks think of me as being part savage." He sighed. "Maybe I would have been capable of killing her, I don't really know." He shrugged. "It's possible I could have gotten mad enough."

"That doesn't make you guilty."

"Not in your eyes, and I'm glad," he said. "But you aren't going to be on the jury."

"You think it'll come to that?"

"I'm afraid it already has. Talbot said they've already sent a man to Fort Belknap and wired for a circuit judge, so it's only a matter of time."

She stared up at his vague form in the darkness, the smell of spicewood still clinging to him, bringing memories she never wanted to lose.

"I love you, Tosi Nuit," she whispered softly, and felt him tense; then slowly he began to relax and he bent over her, his voice deepening.

"Nei mah-ocu-ah," he answered huskily, and she frowned.

"Which means?"

"My wife."

"But—"

His fingertips touched her lips, stopping her protest. "You speak Comanche, and I married you in a Comanche ceremony," he said tenderly. "Or did you forget?"

"How could I?" she answered passionately, and reached up, pulling him down until his mouth met hers, and with her body yielding shamefully, she surrendered to the hunger that gnawed deep inside her, pleased to let him love her, yet terrified that it might be for the last time.

Griff kissed her back, then slipped hurriedly from his buckskins, and as he climbed in beside her, feeling her flesh soft and pliant against his, he knew that no matter what happened from here on, he'd never love anyone but Jeanine.

His lips found hers again in the darkness, and he drew her close against him, the joy of holding her so sweet he trembled.

"Are you cold?" she asked moments later when he drew his mouth from hers.

He sighed. "Hardly . . . I'm in love. So in love I never want to let you go." His hand played down the length of her body, and he rolled over onto his back, carrying her with him, so it was she who was stretched out above him, and as she kissed him, her tongue teasing him with sweet abandon, her body captured his hardness to her in a savage rhythm that seemed to come naturally, with little coaxing, and stifling the cries of delight that tried to escape her lips, Jeanine loved him with every movement of her body, every soft caress and driving need, until, this time, it was she who brought them both to a wild moment of ecstasy that tore through them like an all-consuming fire. Then, spent and breathless, her body still throbbing from the aftermath of their lovemaking, she let him slide her gently back to the smooth bedsheets, where he lay looking down at her, his eyes filled with love.

"We should clean up," he said softly, but she only smiled.

"I'll wash in the morning." Her eyes were suddenly troubled. "I don't want to let you go, Griff, it's too painful," she whispered softly, and her hand reached up to touch his shoulder, then moved to the scars on his chest.

"You think it's not for me?" He kissed her gently, his lips sipping at hers. "The pain cuts just as deep." He lowered his head to the pillow, then pulled her close in his arms. "But there'll be time enough to worry in the morning," he went on roughly. "For now just let me love you, and love me back, before we have to face the dawn again," and as the inappropriate music from the piano floated up to them from outside, the strains of "Dixie" filling the room, Griff lost himself in loving her again. Then, afterward, content with that love, he held her close to him until it was almost morning, stealing stealthily back to his own room just before the first faint streaks of sunlight illuminated the dawn sky.

By the time the sheriff arrived, shortly after sunup, with Warren at his heels, Griff was dressed and waiting in his room, anger and resentment mirrored in his eyes, and he was glad Jeanine wasn't up yet as the three of them made their way downstairs and on toward the jail. But the rest of the town wasn't as exhausted as Jeanine, and more than a dozen onlookers followed them all the way down the street, staring curiously as they moved along. Griff was irritated, but could easily understand why they were so inquisitive. It wasn't often one of the leading citizens of Raintree was arrested for the murder of his wife.

He frowned as they neared the jail, then suddenly stopped and stood erect, staring straight ahead at a sight he was hoping he wouldn't have to see.

Miles Vance, his face filled with hate, eyes racked with pain, was riding his horse right down the center of the street toward the sheriff's office, and he was leading a black-and-white pinto with Jarrod's blanket-wrapped body strapped sideways across it.

Sheriff Higgens stopped beside Griff, while Warren went on to the door to the sheriff's office, then turned, waiting, and they all watched Miles approach. When he was only a few feet away, he reined the pinto to a halt and stared hard at Griff before turning to the sheriff.

"My son's dead, Dave," he said bitterly, then pointed to Griff. "And that's the man who shot him."

Dave Higgens stared at Miles for a minute, then frowned.

"I've been expectin' you, Miles," he said. "Griff told me all about it."

"I bet he did," Miles said angrily, and dismounted, tying both horses to the hitch rail in front of the jail. "Did he tell you he rode into the ranch yard at the Double V Bar and started shootin' for no reason at all?" he asked.

"He said Jarrod shot first, and I'm afraid Miss Grayson and his foreman backed him up."

"Liars, all of them," Miles yelled. "He rode in at two in the morning and just opened fire, killin' my boy!"

"Well, right now I'm lockin' him up for killin' his wife," the sheriff said, and Miles looked startled.

"For what?" he asked.

"You heard me. Rhetta Heywood was murdered last night, and since Griff's knife was used as a murder weapon and since he was the only one with her at the time, it seems logical he was the one what did it, now don't it, Miles? So let's take just one killin' at a time to start with, if you don't mind," and he turned to Griff. "Might's well get it over with," he said. "Come on," and he joined Warren at the door to his office, holding it open for Griff, who glanced briefly at Miles, then went inside.

Miles's eyes followed the three men as they entered the jailhouse, his jaw working angrily; then he climbed into the saddle again and headed toward the undertaker's with the pinto and Jarrod's body in tow. So they had arrested Griff. Well, good. Now all he had to do was make sure they pulled the noose good and tight. After all, it didn't matter to him really whether Griff hung for Rhetta's murder or Jarrod's. The only thing he cared about was that Griff would hang.

At the hotel, the morning dragged by for Jeanine. She learned of Griff's arrest from Mr. Ed when she came downstairs for breakfast, and it didn't help her appetite much, nor did the news of Miles's arrival in town. Besides that, wherever she went she was being stared at, not only because she was no longer wearing the dowdy clothes and wire-rim glasses they were used to seeing on her but also because rumors were already being whispered about that she was the reason Griffin Heywood had murdered his wife. So after breakfast she went back to her hotel room and hibernated, waiting for Cory to return from Trail's End.

It was early afternoon when she stood on the balcony of the hotel and watched Cory finally ride into Raintree, but it was almost an hour later when she saw him leave the jail, heading toward the hotel, and she was anxiously waiting at the door when he reached it.

"How's Griff?" she asked after closing the door behind him.

Cory's hat was in one hand, a bundle in the other, and his dark eyes looked tired. "As well as can be expected, I guess. He's not the sort to be caged up."

"And Gar?"

"He's a pretty mixed-up little boy. I'm glad Griff changed his mind and decided to have us tell him about Rhetta, only we've been having a hard time convincing him." He watched as she walked over and sat on the edge of the bed, leaning against the bedpost, and he knew she was worn out too. "You know Rhetta had him convinced that the Indians killed you both," he went on angrily. "It's no wonder we've had such a hard time with him. First he's told his father's dead, then he's alive . . . now he doesn't believe his mother's dead." He shook his head. "Griff thinks it's wise if we bring him in for the funeral so he can see for himself. After all, his mother lied about his father's death, so now, Griff says if he doesn't see that she's really dead, he'll never believe us."

"Poor Gar." Jeanine frowned. "Has he asked where Griff is?"

"Since Griff doesn't want Gar to know he's been arrested, I told him his father couldn't come home just yet because of Rhetta's death, that there were too many arrangements to be made. He seemed to accept it, and Griff and I are trying to talk Dave into letting him be at the funeral."

"You think he will?"

"Who knows? Dave's been throwing his weight around ever since we came back from the mine."

"But he's supposed to be Griff's friend. Griff and Rhetta even stayed at his house the night of the dance."

"I know, but I'm afraid he's decided not to let his private life interfere with his duties as sheriff."

"How nice."

"Don't worry," Cory assured her. "We'll figure something out if he doesn't." He reached down, taking the bundle from beneath his arm. "I almost forgot," he said, handing it to her. "Crystal sent in some clothes for you."

She took the bundle from him, holding it in her lap. "Thanks," she said thoughtfully. "But I don't think I'll be needing them." She set the bundle on the bed and stood up, walking to the door that led to the balcony, and stood for a minute staring down the street toward the jailhouse. "I want you to ask Sheriff Higgens if I can go back to Trail's End now that they've arrested Griff," she said, then turned back toward him. "I think it'll be better for me out there, and besides, Gar needs me."

"They're going to talk about you and Griff no matter where you are, Jeanine, you know that, don't you?" he said.

"Yes." She walked back over beside the bed again, one hand resting on the bedpost, fingering it absentmindedly. "But at least out there I won't hear them, or have their eyes following me wherever I go, and I'll be with friends." She hesitated, studying his face. "I will be with friends, won't I, Cory?" she asked.

Cory flushed beneath his crop of auburn hair, his mustache twitching nervously. "Yes, ma'am," he answered, his dark brown eyes steady on her. "You'll be with friends."

She smiled. "Thank you, Cory."

He rubbed his mustache self-consciously. "Jeanine, have you heard about Miles?" he asked, changing the subject.

"You mean that he wants the sheriff to charge Griff with murdering Jarrod too?"

"I heard Miles spoutin' off when I was on the way over." He shook his head. "But there's no way in hell

he'll ever get what he wants because I let Dave know right
from the start that we can haul the whole Trail's End crew
in to back up our story if we have to. Griff never said he
didn't shoot Jarrod, all he told Dave was that Jarrod fired
first, so it's our word against Miles, and I think our
word'll carry more weight when all the facts are in.''

"But Mr. Ed's son Jasper said Miles has been telling
everyone in town that Griff fired first. What if they think
the rest of us are lying?''

"You didn't think he'd admit Jarrod did anything wrong,
did you? Miles is a proud man, and he wouldn't think
twice about lying to cover for Jarrod. Besides, he's taken
second best from the Heywoods for too many years, and
now he's finally got a chance to get even. I figure he'll
probably find a few more incriminating things to mouth off
about before he's through, too, but don't worry. More than
anything, he's only making a fool of himself.'' He straightened and started for the door. "For now, I'm gonna stop
by and see when John Scott's due back in town.'' He
reached for the doorknob.

"Cory?''

"Yeah?''

"Has Griff told anyone yet what really happened?'' she
asked.

His eyes hardened. "Nope. All he's told Dave is what
he told him at the mine. That he didn't kill her.'' He
paused a second, then went on. "He's waitin' to see what
John says first, because right now, the way things are, he
knows damn well nobody'd believe the truth anyway.'' He
straightened for a second, his face troubled. "Do you
realize,'' he said, "that everything that's happened has
happened just to you and Griff, no one else? It'll be your
word against what the folks in Raintree will consider facts,
and that ain't good, because Rhetta and Griff put on such a
good show all these years, it's gonna be hard convincing
the people of this town that Rhetta was trying to kill the
two of you.''

"But they're willing to believe he killed her!''

"Look at it from their viewpoint, Jeanine.'' He used his

hand, turning it over, gesturing. "You're alive . . . she's dead. If he opened his mouth now, without talking to John first, it'd only make matters worse."

"It really looks bad, doesn't it?"

"Don't see how it could be any worse. And the fact that it was Griff's knife doesn't help either."

"But he didn't have it with him. Those men working for Jarrod took it when they took his guns, before they took us to the mine. You saw, Cory, it wasn't in the sheath of his gunbelt when we were at the house."

"That's just the trouble," Cory said, disgusted. "Like I told Griff. I never even noticed. His guns were gone, but I didn't pay any attention to whether the knife was there or not, so I wouldn't be able to swear to it."

"Oh, fine." She sighed, realizing the situation they were in. The knife was Griff's, but if he told them he hadn't been wearing it, he'd have to tell them who did have it, and the whole sordid mess would be out in the open, and the problem was, how much could they dare tell and still be able to protect Gar from learning about his real father?

"Well, like I said, I'd better see what I can find out about John." Cory started to leave again. "And I'll let you know what the sheriff says about you going out to Trail's End." He opened the door. "Meantime, it wouldn't hurt any for you to get yourself a bath and change into them clothes I brought, and if Dave says yes, I'll get a buggy from the livery and drive you out. I'll also stop downstairs and tell Barney to bring up a tub and some water for you, how's that?"

"You don't mind?"

"Hell no, what're friends for?"

She smiled, and he smiled back.

"I'll give you an hour," he said, then left.

Jeanine was ready before the hour was up and they left for Trail's End without her saying good-bye to Griff, on his orders, relayed to her by Cory. Griff told Cory there was enough talk already without openly admitting there was anything between them, because to most people a man who no longer loved his wife was automatically capable of murder, and the fact that Griff, and his father before him, had helped build the town would have little influence on people's reasoning. Especially with the hate campaign Miles was starting to conduct.

The next couple of days were hard for Jeanine, even though Crystal and Mrs. Brandt politely welcomed her back to Trail's End. At least Mrs. Brandt was polite; Crystal was a little more enthusiastic, and acted like it was nothing unusual for Jeanine to take over the full care of Gar, almost as if she were his mother.

And Gar was so glad to see her. He was forlorn, though, and Jeanine had a hard time trying to keep his spirits up. They went over his schoolwork, when he was able to keep his mind on it, went riding, weather permitting, and she read to him by the hour. However, every time Cory or one of the men came back from town, the news was worse and Jeanine had a hard time keeping her own spirits up as well. Griff's past reputation was quickly being forgotten and the stories linking her with the owner of Trail's End were beginning to grow.

The worst part of it for Jeanine was that some of what the people in Raintree were talking about was true. She and Griff were in love, but the rest of it . . .

The third day after her arrival at Trail's End, Jeanine sat beside Gar in the closed carriage as it made its way toward town, the usual escort leading the way, with two more riders bringing up the rear, Cory being one of them. Rhetta was being buried today and Cory had told her that Dave Higgens promised to let Griff attend the services. For that she was thankful.

She glanced over at Gar. Ever since they left the house he'd been nervous and fidgety. Crystal had refused to come, and so had Mrs. Brandt, the housekeeper, stating that she was too old to start playing the hypocrite by pretending she had any feelings for Rhetta. "In fact, the world's probably better off without her," she'd told Jeanine shortly before she and Gar left the house, and it was hard for Jeanine to forget the look that crept into the housekeeper's eyes when she said it. "The only bad part about the whole episode is that Dave Higgens is stupid enough to think Griff could have done it," Mrs. Brandt had continued, and she'd gone on exclaiming about the sheriff's stupidity, and how it was a terrible way for him to treat a man he'd always considered his friend, and by the time Jeanine and Gar had climbed into the carriage, Jeanine began to wonder if perhaps they hadn't all misjudged Mrs. Brandt.

Now, as she sat in the carriage and watched the troubled look on Gar's face, she wished she didn't have to go either.

A light drizzle started when they were halfway there, which did little to help Jeanine's melancholy mood, and the air had cooled considerably, so she had to pull her cloak tighter for warmth.

"Are you cold?" she asked Gar as they jounced along in the carriage.

He turned from the window, where he'd been watching the rain bouncing off the parched earth. He'd been wondering if it'd rain enough to really wet the ground for a change.

"No, ma'am," he said quietly, then frowned, looking away again, and for the rest of the ride Jeanine let him keep to himself as much as he wanted, only praying he'd be able to accept his mother's death bravely.

When they finally reached town and the carriage pulled up in front of the large white building that was used for the church on weekends, and she saw the crowd of people gawking, she was glad that they'd kept Gar home for the past couple of days. As it was, today was going to be bad enough for him to get through.

She took his hand as they left the carriage, trying to keep beneath the umbrella Cinnamon was holding for them, but once inside, he let go of her and let out a soft cry when he saw his father coming toward him from the other end of the large hall where people were seated, waiting for the clergyman to begin the eulogy. Griff stooped down, arms outstretched, and pulled Gar close, hugging him hard while

Gar buried his face against his father's chest and cried, tears dampening the front of the black suit Cory had brought in for him the day before so he didn't have to wear buckskins for the funeral.

Griff's arms stayed around Gar for a long time; then he slowly looked up, his eyes catching Jeanine's, and she wished she could hug him too. It was frustrating, because instead, she just smiled coolly, and when Griff finished hugging Gar and stood up, she remarked calmly about the rain, and how it was a shame they had such a nasty day for the funeral.

They exchanged a few more polite words, trying to pretend there was nothing between them; then Griff took Gar's hand and they walked to the coffin, where the boy stood in awe, gazing at his mother's still body. Griff stooped down a few times, talking to him softly, hugging him once more when he started to cry; then later Jeanine was surprised when Sheriff Higgens let Griff ride to the cemetery in the carriage with them. Naturally he rode along, pretending for the boy's sake that he was along just as a friend, but as the carriage ambled down the muddy road, rain resounding off the roof, and she watched the intimacy between father and son, she didn't care what had motivated the sheriff. She was just glad he'd let Griff come along.

Even though it was raining, the funeral procession for Rhetta Heywood was one of the longest the residents of Raintree had ever seen. According to Cory, however, who stood next to Jeanine during the graveside services, holding the umbrella to help keep the rain off her, most of them were there out of curiosity rather than respect, and Jeanine wished she could tell them all to go home and leave them alone.

She watched rain spattering the coffin, crushing the delicate petals of some flowers a few people had placed there, and saw rivulets of water snaking trails as they soaked into the mud that had been parched earth only hours before, and she suddenly felt sad. Not for herself or Griff, or even Gar, but for Rhetta. She had been such a beautiful woman, and could have had such a good life, if only . . .

The minister's "Amen" broke off her daydreaming, and Jeanine glanced over at Gar, seeing the countless questions waiting in his eyes, questions she tried to answer a short time later as they once more headed back toward Trail's End.

The boy seemed to be in a rather strange mood as they rode along in the carriage. "Mama acted so funny that day," he said, his voice unsteady. "And I was so scared."

She reached over and took his hand. "I know," she answered.

"It was like . . . like she wasn't really Mama. Like today," he went on. "That didn't really look like Mama, did it?" he asked.

Her heart went out to him. "Oh, Gar . . ."

"It's all right, Miss Grayson," he said, acting quite grown-up. "I don't mind talking about it now. I won't cry as much no more either. Not about that anyway." He frowned. "But there is somethin' . . . Miss Grayson," he asked, "now that Mama's with God, why can't Pa come home? He don't have to make arrangements no more, does he?"

"I'm sure he'll come home soon, dear," she answered. "But it takes time."

He eyed her skeptically, then shook his head. "No," he finally said. "He won't be home, and I know why. Really I do." She saw tears in his eyes. "They think he killed Mama, don't they, Miss Grayson?" he suddenly blurted out, and she wished he hadn't.

Rain was falling harder now, a steady deluge, and she was glad they were in a covered carriage because outside Cinnamon and their escort were feeling the brunt of it. She flinched. Not only from the force of the wind whipping against the carriage, where it rattled the side curtains, but from the question he'd just asked that she wasn't sure she could answer, and the flickering kerosene light inside the carriage danced shadows across his worried face. She studied him closely. He was trying to stay calm, but was still so upset.

"What makes you say that?" she asked when she'd managed to settle her own nerves a bit.

He sniffed, and she knew he was trying not to cry. "I heard people talking and whispering," he answered reluctantly. "And Sheriff Higgens was with Pa all the time. He didn't think I noticed, but I did. He arrested him, didn't he, Miss Grayson?" he asked.

She shook her head. "Gar, don't—"

"He didn't do it, Miss Grayson, he didn't!" he cried, suddenly breaking down. "He didn't, I know he didn't," and tears flowed down his cheeks. "Please tell them he didn't, Miss Grayson," he pleaded. "Pa wouldn't kill Mama, he wouldn't. I know they argued lots, but I know he wouldn't!"

She reached out frantically, pulling him into her arms, hoping to comfort him. "You poor boy," she crooned softly, her own eyes hot with tears. "You poor little boy." Her voice faltered. "No, he didn't kill her, Gar." She leaned her head down, resting her cheek against the hat he was wearing, the one that was so much like his father's. It was damp against her cheek, but it didn't matter because her own tears were joining the rain that had soaked into it. "It's all a mistake, Gar, a big mistake," she went on, cradling him close. "You'll see, they'll let him go, they'll have to," she said. "They'll just have to." She kept her arms around him all the rest of the way to Trail's End, while she prayed her words would be prophetic, because if they weren't, there was no way she could stand to see Griff hang for murder without dying inside herself.

16

The rain had finally slowed down to a light drizzle, but wind was still whipping around wildly as Cinnamon drove the carriage up to the front walk and stopped, then climbed down from his seat to help Jeanine and Gar.

Peggy and Beth were waiting at the top of the steps, just outside the front door, with umbrellas, but Jeanine was reluctant to let go of Gar, even when the carriage door opened. They had both quit crying, but she could tell by his eyes that anger, fear, and frustration were still very much a part of him.

"Be careful," she cautioned as she handed him over to Cinnamon; then she followed him out herself, closing her eyes slightly, to ward off the sting from the tiny drops of rain on her face.

Peggy and Beth had umbrellas over them only seconds after they reached the ground, but Jeanine looked back for a minute, calling to Cinnamon, who'd regained his seat on the carriage.

"Cinnamon, will you please tell Cory to come to the house when he's through with his horse?" she yelled up to him, and Cinnamon nodded, then flicked the reins, and as he started heading the carriage out back, they all made a dash for the front door.

"Did anyone ask where we were?" Beth asked Jeanine

curiously, once they were inside, and Jeanine shook her head, trying to catch her breath.

"Not a soul."

Beth shrugged. "Stands to reason, I guess," she said as she leaned the wet umbrellas up against the umbrella stand to dry off a bit before putting them away. "I think everyone knows why we weren't there." She joined her sister, who was using an old rag to wipe excess mud from Gar's shoes, only she still kept on talking to Jeanine. "And I bet you got stared at a lot too," she went on. "After all, you ain't wearin' the glasses no more, and it makes you look different." She took a breath, but only a quick one. "And Peg and I think it's just awful the way the folks in town are gossipin' about you and Mr. Griff. Why, the Kid came back last night and said—"

"Beth!" Crystal was halfway down the stairs to the right of the front door, and now, as she came the rest of the way, her face was livid. "What in the world . . . ? For heaven's sake, girl," she admonished, "will you stop the rattlin'. Jeanine's upset enough as it is. Ain't no use repeatin' gossip."

Jeanine looked at Crystal thankfully, then glanced down at Gar, while Beth blushed, all too aware she'd opened her mouth too much again.

"You'd probably better take Gar into the kitchen and fix him something warm," Jeanine told the girls hurriedly while she took off Gar's hat and smoothed his hair affectionately. "It's been rough for him, and he's still pretty upset."

Peggy handed Jeanine the rag she'd used to clean Gar's shoes with; then she and Beth hovered over the boy solicitously as they began ushering him toward the back of the house, only this time Beth let Peggy do most of the talking.

"I'm sorry," Crystal told Jeanine when the girls were out of earshot.

Jeanine sighed. "It's all right, really. They don't realize . . ." She reached up, unfastening the cloak about her neck, and let Crystal take it from her, so Crystal could shake it off some before hanging it up; then Jeanine tried to brush some of the mud off the hem of her skirt. She had already scraped most of the mud from her shoes just outside the door before coming in, so it took only a few seconds more to clean them the rest of the way with the rag Peggy had handed her.

"I'll take that," Crystal said once she'd hung Jeanine's cloak up, and she frowned a little. "How's everything goin'?" she asked after Jeanine handed her the rag, and she wadded it up, trying to keep the mud on it from dropping to the floor.

Jeanine straightened. "I don't really know. I haven't talked to Cory yet." She wiped a wet curl from her forehead, trying to tuck it back and smooth it down so it would become part of the bun she was again wearing at the nape of her neck. "In fact, that's what I was going to ask you. I told Cinnamon to have Cory come in when he was through with his horse. Do you suppose we could have some coffee brought in?"

"Where?"

"The parlor, I guess. I just hope there's a fire in the fireplace."

"There is." Crystal walked as far as the parlor door with her before heading into the kitchen.

Jeanine didn't have to wait long for Cory, and she was warming herself near the fireplace when he came in. He'd left his boots and slicker in the kitchen, but rain was still clinging to the edges of his mustache.

"It's gettin' nastier out there again," he said as he joined her. "Wouldn't be surprised to see the creek in toward town overflowin' if this keeps up."

Jeanine was near one of the windows, and she glanced out. "Does it rain like this often in the winter?"

"Only occasionally." He bent toward the flames, warming his hands. "But the summers make up for it."

Jeanine stared at the deluge of rain outside. It was still supposed to be daylight, yet the sky was so dark . . . and there was a slight yellow cast to everything, making it look weird. She straightened pensively, and was just about to say something when Mrs. Brandt came in.

"Well, I'm glad you're finally back," she said in her usual crisp manner. "It's just terrible, being out here, not knowing what's going on."

"There's really not much of anything going on right now," Cory offered. "Without John here, we're workin' with blinders on, so Griff's just keepin' his mouth shut and lettin' everyone else do the talkin'." He took a deep breath. "There is one thing, though. He said none of us are to tell anybody anything about what he told us that night he and Jeanine came back. Not the crew, the sheriff, nobody."

"What about Warren?" the housekeeper asked. "He hasn't been back since that night, except to get a few clothes. He's been staying in town, I guess, and from what some of the crew are saying, he's blabbing everything all over the place."

"Don't worry about him," Cory assured her quickly. "He's only tellin' what he wants people to know, and he ain't said nothin', or even hinted that Griff might not be Gar's pa either, and I don't think he will."

Jeanine was surprised. "That's strange," she said. "Why, he was mad enough that night to do almost anything to get even with Griff."

Cory grinned knowingly. "Griff said he's got Warren all figured out. He said Warren figures that if folks learn Gar is really Miles Vance's grandson, then if Griff's hung, Miles ends up bein' his closest next of kin and Trail's End could be lost to the boy, 'cause he ain't really a Heywood, and that could leave Warren with no place to stay, 'cause Miles sure wouldn't put up with havin' him around. But if folks don't know who his real pa is, then if Griff's hung, Gar would stay right here at Trail's End, and Warren could walk right in as next of kin and live here for the rest of his life like a king."

"So that's it." Jeanine's eyes darkened. "No wonder he hasn't said anything."

"Stands to reason, don't it?" Cory moved a little away

from the fireplace now that he'd warmed up some. "Griff said what we really have to do is see if we can find those men Jarrod hired."

Jeanine looked defeated. "Do you know how hard that's going to be?"

"Like lookin' for a snowflake in hell, but I sure aim to try." Cory eyed her, frowning. "You been teachin' Gar to draw pictures with his schoolin' ain'tcha?" he suddenly asked, surprising her, and Jeanine nodded.

"It's part of the schoolwork."

"Then that's it," he said abruptly.

"What's it?" Mrs. Brandt asked, wondering what he was up to.

"Well, look," he began, hoping it'd work. "Since Griff and Jeanine are the only ones who know who those men were, then they gotta tell us what they look like. And the best way to do that is to draw their pictures. Now, Griff can't draw a straight line, but if the teacher here thinks she can come up with somethin' . . . hell, we can't just go out lookin' for a fella with a scar on his face. That'd cover half the men in Texas. But if we had a picture that looked enough like him . . ."

Jeanine smiled. "Cory, you're an angel," she said quickly. "I think I can maybe draw good enough likenesses of a couple of them. Especially the one named Burke." Her smile faded. "I'll never forget his face."

"How about the others?"

"I'm not too sure. Maybe the one they called Red."

Cory was pleased, and he and Mrs. Brandt followed Jeanine to the schoolroom, where she found pencil and paper, then sat at the desk sketching what she could remember of their faces, while Mrs. Brandt stared out the back window, watching some trees near the pasture bending with the wind and rain, and Cory spent the time roaming around the room, perusing some of the schoolbooks.

Jeanine continued drawing at the desk, and as she finished each picture, she added a description at the bottom. However, she was only able to do a really good likeness of

Burke, although the one of Red was close enough that when Mrs. Brandt saw it, she recognized him immediately.

"That's the man who brought the notes to Rhetta," she exclaimed. She glanced down at the description. "I think if I remember right, his eyes were blue, though, not gray. And they were so pale blue they looked like they had white flecks in them. The kind of eyes that could make your hair stand on end if they decided their owner didn't like you."

"Nice fella," Cory said as he looked over Mrs. Brandt's shoulder; then suddenly he frowned. "You and Griff were right, Jeanine," he said. "I remember seeing him around town. And the other one too."

"I wish I could have remembered enough to draw pictures of all of them," she said. "It was so dark, though, and when we got to the mine, they put us in that back room right away. But at least these two are a start."

Mrs. Brandt handed the pictures to Cory. "What will you do with them now?" she asked.

"Well . . ." Cory frowned as he studied them for a few minutes, then folded them and put them in his shirt pocket. "My best bet is to show them to Spider, Luke, and Dustin. They'll not only keep their mouths shut, but I know we can trust them. If they start searchin' right away, maybe we can learn enough by the time John gets back to town to force Dave to let Griff go."

"But will that be wise?" Jeanine asked. "When, and if, your men find Burke and the others and bring them back, if they do tell the truth, there's no way we'll be able to protect Gar from finding out who his real father is."

"You think they know?" Mrs. Brandt asked.

Jeanine shook her head. "I don't know, but even if they don't know about Gar, they know all about what Rhetta and Jarrod were doing, and how can we explain all that without bringing Gar into it?"

"I'm sure it can be done," the housekeeper answered. "At least it's better than just sitting around speculating."

"And who knows what we might learn," added Cory.

Jeanine frowned unhappily. "I know you're probably

right," she said. "But I wish there was some other way." She hesitated for a minute and picked a paper up off the desk in front of her. It was a picture of a horse that Gar had drawn the day before. "By the way," she said as she glanced up from the picture. "I thought it'd be best to tell you that Gar knows his father's in jail."

Mrs. Brandt's hand flew to her breast. "Who told him?"

"He heard the whispering in town. It was hard for him not to."

"How'd he take it?" asked Cory.

Jeanine remembered Gar's sad face in the carriage on the way home. "How else? He loves Griff. He keeps telling himself his father isn't guilty, that he couldn't have done it, yet I think he senses his parents were having problems and that there was really no love between them."

"It's outrageous, them arresting Griff," Mrs. Brandt said abruptly, and she turned, walking to the back of the schoolroom again, once more staring out the window. "Why, the Heywoods have been the lifeblood of this town," she went on. "Without them, Raintree probably wouldn't even exist. At least not the Raintree they know. The schoolhouse and meeting hall, Empire Hotel, livery stable, none of it would have been built without Heywood money." She turned back, facing them. "Even the jailhouse," she stated ironically, then straightened. "Ridiculous, isn't it?" She sighed and reached up, shoving one of the hairpins harder into the braided coronet atop her head where it had started to loosen, then clasped her hands forcefully in front of her. "Well, he may be there," she continued crisply. "But he certainly won't be convicted. They wouldn't dare!"

"Don't be so sure," Cory cut in. "All they know is that Rhetta's dead and Griff's knife killed her. What more do they need?"

"What about his friends?"

"In Raintree?" Cory was cynical. "He's been gone four years, and folks change. I wouldn't count on any help from that quarter."

"Oh dear." The housekeeper frowned. "You're sure?"

she asked hesitantly. "Talbot, the others . . . they really think he's guilty?"

He shrugged. "Let's put it this way," he answered, watching her topaz eyes darken to a deep amber. "If a jury finds him innocent, they'll probably shake his hand and go on just like nothin' happened, but if he's found guilty, there ain't a one gonna lose sleep if he's hung."

Mrs. Brandt shook her head slowly. "I never thought . . . If I'd known it would turn out like this . . ." Suddenly she seemed to pull herself back to the moment and glanced quickly first to Jeanine, then Cory, then back to Jeanine again. "Oh, I'd better tell Crystal to bring the coffee in here," she said, her voice once more ringing with authority. "Or are you going back to the parlor?"

"Here will be fine," Jeanine said, wondering why the housekeeper seemed to have been befuddled for a moment, and she suddenly felt the emotional impact of another intense look from the housekeeper's strangely vibrant eyes; then she and Cory both watched as Mrs. Brandt excused herself and left the room, closing the door firmly behind her.

There was an awkward silence in the schoolroom right after the housekeeper left, and Jeanine and Cory both felt it strongly, but before either had a chance to say anything, Crystal came in.

"Mrs. Brandt said you was in here," she said as she set the tray with the coffee and cups on Jeanine's desk.

"That's all right, I'll pour," Jeanine said when Crystal started to reach for the silver coffeepot. "You probably have things to do in the kitchen."

"Amen to that," Crystal agreed. "Everyone's been trackin' mud in the back door, and the kitchen's a mess." She glanced down at the tray. "There's some sweet biscuits, if you want," she said, and glanced over at Cory, who was watching her appreciatively. "Your favorites," she said as she headed for the door, then threw back over her shoulder, "Just don't eat too many."

They watched the door shut behind her, then Jeanine stood up, glancing over at Cory. "Coffee?" she asked.

"And just a couple of biscuits," he replied. "I think Crystal's been keepin' track of my waistline lately."

Jeanine smiled as she poured them both coffee; then she watched Cory start nibbling on one of the frosting-covered biscuits.

"I saw you and Griff talking quite a bit right after the services," she said after a few minutes. "Did you ask him?"

"I did," he answered. "And he said he'd like more than anything in the world to see you. But until John gets back, it's best the two of you stay as far from each other as possible. He did send a message, though." His face tinged with pink. "He said to tell you not to worry, that things will work out." He paused and now suddenly the pink tinge on his face turned to crimson. "He also said to tell you he loves you very much, and always will, no matter what happens."

Her eyes fell before his embarrassed gaze; then she slowly looked back up at him. "You think it's wrong, don't you, Cory?" she said hesitantly.

"It ain't up to me to say one way or the other, Jeanine," he replied. "But I saw it comin'." He blew over his coffee, cooling it a little more. "Griff and I've been friends a long time and I can read him like a book. We've been close friends since long before his marriage, and I guess besides Crystal, Mrs. Brandt, and John Scott, I'm the only other person who knew Gar wasn't his son. In fact, when he told me what he was planning to do, I tried to talk him out of it. I told him that someday he might meet somebody and things could get complicated, but he swore there wasn't a woman out there he couldn't walk away from. I knew he was lying the day you came along, but it was too late for him to do anything about it. You don't just throw away eight years of marriage, even to the wrong woman, without weighing the consequences first, but I guess he'd finally made up his mind." He studied her face for a minute. "There's only one thing I want to know, Jeanine," he went on. "Do you love him enough to stand by him through all this mess?"

Jeanine stared back at him. Cory was a big man, and gruff at times, but he was also sensitive in many ways, and she understood why Crystal felt the way she did about him. Her blue eyes glistened warmly and her voice was hushed.

"I'd gladly give my life for him if I thought it'd help, Cory," she said softly.

He sipped the coffee. "And your reputation?" he asked, then shoved one of the small sweet biscuits in his mouth.

She laughed spitefully. "What reputation? By now I'm probably the most notorious woman in Texas." She walked toward the back of the schoolroom, carrying her coffee with her, sipping on it occasionally, then glanced out, watching the rain still driving hard against the glass. "When I first came here, Cory," she began, "I was afraid. I guess instinctively I knew I shouldn't stay, yet something made me. Maybe if I hadn't come Griff would be dead now and Jarrod and Rhetta would be running things here at Trail's End, I don't know. But one thing for sure . . ." She turned to face him. "If my being here and loving him helped save his life in any way, then I'm glad I came, regardless of anything else. And when you see Griff again, give him my love and tell him I'll stay away since that's what he wants, but tell him I miss him terribly, will you?"

"Sure will." Cory sauntered over to the desk and popped another biscuit in his mouth.

"When do they start the proceedings?" she asked. "Or isn't it set yet?"

"The judge is due sometime this week."

"That doesn't give us much time to figure out some way to help Griff, does it?"

"Sure don't." He finished the rest of his coffee, then set the cup down. "Let's just hope John gets back soon," he said. "Otherwise we don't have just a few problems, we've got a big pack of trouble. Now"—he licked a bit of frosting off one finger—"do you need me for anything else?"

She shook her head. "Not now, Cory," she said. "And thanks for bringing the message from Griff."

"My pleasure," he said, then started for the door. "You know, it's really strange." He hesitated with his hand on the doorknob. "One day the people in Raintree are lookin' up to Griff as if he's someone special, and the next they're waitin' to crucify him." He shook his head. "It just don't make sense, does it?" He was shaking his head as he left.

Jeanine stared after him, the quiet in the schoolroom broken only by the spattering of the rain against the windows and the howling wind. Cory was right. If only she could wake up and discover this whole thing was nothing more than a horrible nightmare . . . But it wasn't that easy, and she knew it. Life never was, and she sighed, turning back again to watch the storm outside.

John Scott finally arrived back in town two days later, riding in shortly before midnight, and went right to the rooms he had over his office, since he knew nothing about what had been going on in Raintree during his absence. The news of Rhetta Heywood's death and Griff's arrest never reached the newspapers in St. Louis where he'd been, and it wasn't until morning that he heard about it. Now he sat on a hard cot in Griff's jail cell, leaning back against the wall, eyeing his client curiously. He'd known the Heywoods for so long, he almost felt like one of the family, and now the task of defending Griff was heavy on his shoulders.

He continued to stare at his client. Griff was a strange man. He'd never made friends very easily, or let anyone know what was really inside him, yet most people respected him instinctively. John attributed it to the fact that he'd lived with the Indians in his earlier years. It had not only taught him integrity but also made him seem almost part Indian, and more often than not it was hard to read his thoughts by the look on his face, and right now John was having a hell of a time trying to get past the hard glint in Griff's brilliant blue eyes.

Griff had just finished shaving, a task the sheriff usually watched. This morning John had the privilege.

"As I said, I have to know the truth before going into a courtroom," John said as he watched Griff wipe the excess lather off his clean-shaven face with a towel.

Griff finished wiping his face dry, then rubbed his hand across his smooth chin. The shave had been refreshing and he was glad Dave let him shave every morning. The thought of even a day's growth of beard was repulsive to him. Another throwback to his Indian days, he assumed. He glanced over at John.

"Where do you want to start?"

"At the beginning," John instructed him. "I heard the town's version on the way over here." He relaxed, leaning back more comfortably against the wall. "Now let's hear yours."

Griff studied him thoughtfully for a minute; then, after dumping the water from the basin out the window, splashing some of it against the bars, and wrapping the razor and soap in the towel, he called Sheriff Higgens in, gave the things to him to put back, and turned toward John while the sheriff went back into his office at the front of the small building.

"You sure you want to go through with this, John?" Griff asked. "It's not going to be easy, you know."

"Would I be here if I thought you were guilty?"

"You could just be curious, like everybody else."

"Dammit, Griff! Don't make me mad," John retorted. "You've known me long enough to know better than that. Now, out with it . . . beginning to end."

Griff walked over toward the window, glancing out between the bars, then began pacing the cell as he related the past few days' events. When he'd finished, at first he thought John had fallen asleep, and he stared at him, frowning; then John slowly opened his eyes and straightened, leaning forward on the cot.

"That's it?" he asked.

"That's it," Griff repeated, and John looked pensive as he stretched, then ran a hand through his hair. It was dark and curly, but getting a little sparse on each side just above the temples, with white frost tipping the low sideburns, and his dark green eyes often faded toward gray when he was angry. At the moment though they were exceptionally green and they studied Griff closely.

"All right, now let me get this straight," he said, trying to put things together. "You say after Mrs. Brandt left in the buggy with Gar, that you and Cory looked around and found the horses in the barn?"

"And the buggy from Trail's End that Rhetta had used when she and Gar left that day shortly before dinner. We had some of the boys take them back to the ranch after the sheriff arrived. Only, John, they weren't the right horses, that's what I'm trying to tell you." He faced John squarely. "When I left to get Jeanine, I was riding Che-ak, and I still had him when we were kidnapped. The only horses in that barn were Blossom—Jeanine had been riding her—the horse from Trail's End that was still hitched to the buggy, and a lame horse, a scrawny sorrel I'm almost certain belonged to one of the men who'd been working for Jarrod. It had a Mexican brand on it."

"There was no sign of your stallion?"

"None."

"Then we'll have to presume one of the kidnappers exchanged his lame horse for Che-ak."

"That's all good and fine, John," Griff replied. "I can go along with that. But what I can't understand is why Jarrod's men had already left." He sat down on another cot opposite the one John was on, and leaned toward him. "While we were on our way to the mine that night with the kidnappers, after we guessed that Jarrod was the one behind everything, Burke and the others kept talking about all the things they were going to do with the money they'd make when they started work at Trail's End. I guess Jarrod promised Burke the foreman's job when he took over."

"In other words, they weren't just working for money."

"Right, and Burke kept bragging about how he was ramrod at a place down near the border some years back and how anxious he was to be top dog again. Now, why would they take off?"

"Maybe because Jarrod was dead, Griff," John reminded him. "That meant their plans to work at Trail's End were dead too."

"But they didn't know Jarrod was dead, John. And that's what I don't understand." Griff's eyes narrowed shrewdly. "Why would they leave?"

"Jarrod had probably been there earlier and told them the plans had fallen through. It only makes sense that they were probably running, that's evidently what Rhetta and Jarrod were planning to do. Since he couldn't come through with the jobs for them, Jarrod probably paid them off instead, and they must have left when he headed for the Double V Bar to get his things."

"Cory said that Gar told him the men were still outside waiting when he lay down to go to sleep, and that was quite a while after Jarrod left."

"So where does that leave you?" John asked.

Griff's eyes darkened. "Confused." He sat up straighter on the cot. "I just can't see men like that leaving empty-handed, and yet Dave said the eight hundred dollars Rhetta stole from my bedroom drawer was still in her handbag."

"Maybe they're the ones who robbed the bank that night?"

"And Winslow?"

John shrugged, then stood up. "Maybe they took him along as a hostage, in case anything went wrong." He stretched. The jail smelled musty and rank, and he walked over to the window for a breath of fresh air. "In any case, the fact that they weren't there has nothing to do with the fact that you were, and that you were kneeling over Rhetta's body only seconds after she was killed."

Griff's eyes hardened. "But I didn't kill her."

"Then who did?"

"That's what I've been trying to figure out!"

John walked back over and sat on the cot again, facing Griff. "Unfortunately, you're the only one with a motive, Griff," he said unhappily.

"I was wondering when you'd get to that." Griff leaned back against the bars of the empty cell behind him.

"You're in love with her?" John asked.

"That's right," he answered irritably. "I'm in love with her."

"Does she know?"

"Yes."

"That's what I was afraid of." John looked apprehensive. "How far has it gone?"

"What do you mean by that?"

"Just what it sounds like." John leaned forward. "Griff, have you made love to her?"

Griff's eyes darkened, and he straightened, then stood up. "No," he lied, and strolled to the window, staring out.

"You're lying, Griff."

Griff whirled on him. "Prove it."

"I don't have to, the prosecutor will."

"He can't."

"Don't bet on it." John was troubled. "Griff, all he has to do is put Jeanine Grayson on the stand and wear her down. Do you want that?"

"Goddammit, John," Griff shouted. "Why do you have to know everything?"

"In order to defend you." John's eyes were troubled. "I don't want any surprises to pop up without warning. This is a small town, and we'll be lucky to find enough unbiased people for a jury as it is, so the least we can do is be ready for anything that might come along."

"You make it sound cheap, John."

"They'll make it sound worse." John saw the pained look in Griff's eyes. "Where and when, Griff?" he asked.

Griff turned his back on John momentarily and stared out the window again. It had rained the day of Rhetta's funeral, but already the ground was almost powder dry again. A small bird flew off the roof of the building next door to the jailhouse, landing on the seat of an old buckboard parked in the alley between the two buildings, and Griff wished with all his heart that he could be so free. Suddenly he squared his shoulders and turned to face John again.

"You know the Comanche marriage ceremony, John?" he asked.

John frowned, puzzled. "I know it, yes."

"Well, it was the only way I could get Chief Horse Back to release her."

John whistled softly, shook his head, then looked over at Griff. "Does anyone else know?"

"The Indians."

"Thank God." John sighed. "Let's hope it stays with the Indians, but I doubt it will." Suddenly he saw something in Griff's eyes. "Griff?" he asked suspiciously. "Is that the only time?"

Griff's face reddened and John was sure he'd read it right the first time.

"All right, where and when?" he asked again.

Griff's eyes shifted from John's face and he studied the small brown flecks in the lawyer's tweed suit, noticing that the edges of the sleeves were getting threadbare and that John had lost a little weight on his trip to St. Louis; then he turned to stare out the window again.

"Griff?" John was insistent.

"My God, John, do you have to know it all?" he pleaded angrily. "Isn't that enough?"

John didn't answer, he didn't have to, because Griff already knew the answer. John had to know it all, and slowly Griff turned, facing him again. He cleared his throat. It wasn't fair! It was sacrilegious to tell someone else something so intimate. Jeanine was something he'd thought he'd never find, she wasn't some barroom whore or mistress that a man could brag about in order to boost his ego. He was in love with her. Damn John anyway!

"Where?" John demanded this time, and Griff's eyes narrowed savagely, his voice dropping to barely a whisper.

"At the hotel, the night we brought Rhetta's body in . . ."

"The hotel . . . ?" John was livid.

"Shhh . . ." Griff cautioned, warning John to keep his voice down. "Dave'll hear you."

"Good God, Griff!" John gasped. "What the hell . . ."

"Don't worry, I went to her room from the balcony. No one saw me."

"I sure as hell hope not." John shook his head. "Whatever possessed you . . ."

"I wanted to tell her that Dave was going to arrest me in the morning."

"And you just couldn't keep your hands off her, I suppose." He was furious. "All these years you could take women or leave them, now suddenly you can't control yourself? It doesn't make sense."

"Good God, John!" Griff's eyes were blazing. "I'm in love with her. She was in bed. I wasn't . . . She had nothing on . . . I couldn't . . ." It was the first time John had ever seen Griff rattled, but then suddenly Griff seemed to get hold of himself. "Dammit, John," he yelled, half-whispering, "I am human, you know."

John threw up his hands in disgust. "You sure picked a hell of a time to prove it," he said dejectedly, and neither man said anything for a few minutes. The air between them had been explosive, and now there had to be a settling.

Finally, his eyes still smoldering, Griff gazed over at John. "Is loving a woman such a terrible thing, John?" he asked solemnly. "Is it something to hang a man for?"

"It is if the man already has a wife and somebody kills her."

Griff walked back over and sat down again on the cot.

"I've been asking questions all morning, ever since I learned about this whole mess, Griff," John said, watching him closely as he settled back on the cot again. Griff had changed clothes after the funeral and was wearing buckskin pants again, but Crystal had sent a blue shirt in the day before, and he was wearing a buckskin vest over it, the sleeves of the shirt rolled down against the chill in the cell. "Infidelity is one thing few people every condone, Griff," John went on, "no matter what the reason, and they're already speculating about you and the teacher. If they ever learn about this, you won't have a chance."

"Then I'm not really on trial for murder, but infidelity."

"That's about the extent of it." John looked troubled. "I've seen it happen before," he said. "They seem to think that any man capable of cheating on his wife is just as capable of murdering her, and if they discover just how far your involvement with Miss Grayson has progressed, I'm afraid we're going to have to try to prove otherwise, and it won't be easy."

"You know I didn't kill her, don't you, John?" Griff asked.

John stared hard at him for a minute, then nodded. "Yeah, I know you didn't do it." He stood up, then stretched and looked back down at Griff. "I think maybe you were mad enough, and you had a damn good reason to want her dead, but I just can't imagine you killing anyone unless it was in self-defense. Besides," he sighed, "I know you don't lie, and you told me you didn't."

Griff smiled amiably. "Thanks, John," he said, and for the rest of John's visit they tried to figure out some sort of defense. The circuit judge hadn't arrived in town yet, but John knew he had his work cut out for him, and after leaving Griff at the jail, he spent the rest of the afternoon wandering around town, listening and asking questions here and there.

Evening, however, found him out at Trail's End, standing in the library, facing Gar's teacher, Jeanine Grayson. He'd already talked to Cory, Mrs. Brandt, the crew, and even Gar. Now he'd asked to see her alone, so they'd left Mrs. Brandt, Gar, and the twins in the parlor. But he was having a hard time choosing the right words.

Jeanine was dressed in pink, making her look delicate and fragile, yet there was a strength about her that was hard to define. He had seen her a few times before, and had met her at the Mexican Independence Day celebration dance. On those occasions she'd been wearing glasses and her hair pulled back severely in a chignon. This new version had come as a complete surprise and he liked it. She was a lovely woman, not exceptionally beautiful, but soft and desirable with a lovely pair of blue eyes that were captivating. He could easily understand Griff's feelings.

He cleared his throat. "I hope you don't mind talking to me without the others present," he said calmly. "But I'm not sure how much Griff may have confided in them."

"They know the whole story, Mr. Scott," she answered.

His green eyes twinkled devilishly. "I doubt that, Miss Grayson."

"Oh?"

"That's why I said alone. I'm sure there are a few things you'd rather not have them know."

She blushed. "Do go on, Mr. Scott," she said apprehensively. "Just what did Griff tell you?"

His eyes softened. "I wasn't just prying, Miss Grayson, believe me," he answered apologetically. "Only I have to know everything. And don't blame Griffin, I forced it from him."

She stared at him, scowling, wondering. Did he really know, or was he fishing for information? She hadn't talked to Griff since his arrest, and she hardly knew John Scott.

"I know about the Comanche wedding ceremony, my dear," he finally said, sensing her reluctance to confide in him. "So please trust me."

He saw her face turn from red to white, and knew by the way his admission had shaken and embarrassed her that Jeanine Grayson wasn't a loose woman used to promiscuous affairs. Good. He'd been worried after his talk with Griff, and was praying that Jeanine Grayson's feelings for Griff equaled his for her.

"It isn't fair," she murmured softly, and walked over to the fireplace on the inside wall, absentmindedly watching the glowing embers. "You had no right," she said, then turned to face him, her eyes misty with tears. "What happened is between Griff and me."

"Is it?" he asked, trying to make her understand. "If you were asked in court if Griffin Heywood ever made love to you, what would you answer, Miss Grayson?" he asked simply.

She hesitated.

"You'd tell the truth, and you know it."

"What makes you so sure?"

''Your eyes.''

''Eyes can be deceiving,'' she answered, and her chin tilted up stubbornly. ''I've lied before. My life has been nothing but lies. I guess I can lie again if need be.''

''Under oath?'' He studied her carefully. ''I doubt that very much. No . . .'' He shook his head. ''You'd tell the truth under oath, and I don't want any surprises thrown at me.''

''Then maybe there's something else you ought to know, or did Griff tell you that too?'' she asked.

''Tell me what?''

For a minute Jeanine regretted her sudden outburst, not quite sure whether she should have opened her mouth or not. Maybe Griff didn't want John to know, but then, if he had to know everything . . .

''Miss Grayson, if there's something Griff hasn't told me that I should know . . . something that might come up later and cause problems . . .''

Jeanine straightened, leaving the warmth of the fireplace, and strolled to the French doors. They were shut, the evening being cool, and the darkness outside looked foreboding. If only Griff were here to help her decide . . . but he wasn't. Well, since he wasn't, and since John Scott hadn't mentioned it, evidently Griff must not have told him, so maybe it was best she wait too. She turned, sighing.

''There's nothing else, really,'' she answered.

''But you said. . . ?''

''I shouldn't have said anything,'' she told him anxiously. ''What happened before I came here . . . well, I guess it's really no one's business.''

His eyes narrowed as he stared at her curiously for some seconds, then suddenly he nodded. ''Aha, I think I know what you're referring to, my dear,'' he said knowingly. ''But you have no worries there. He told me all about Jarrod being Gar's real father, and believe me, it is important, but it's something we're not going to use unless we have to. In the first place, all it would do is give him another motive for hating Rhetta, and tear Gar apart, and we've got enough problems already.''

Jeanine began to relax the minute she realized what John was talking about, and now she took a deep breath, relieved, because it was apparent Griff hadn't revealed her true identity, and if he hadn't, there was evidently a reason. Thank God she didn't say anything. For now, she'd just wait to talk to Griff first.

''Then he did tell you,'' she said, pleased he'd found an out for her.

''Like I said,'' John answered. ''He knew I had to know everything.''

They talked a while longer, going over some of the things Griff had told her, then Jeanine walked to the door with him.

''I was wondering,'' he said as she handed him his hat. ''Griff said you hadn't been to see him since he was arrested. Is that right?''

''We didn't think it wise.''

''Well . . .'' He cleared his throat. ''I think maybe it might be the best thing you could do.''

''Oh?''

''I've been thinking.'' He was holding his hat by the brim, turning it absentmindedly. ''Griff said he intends to tell the truth, as far as it's possible, that is, so if we want people to think Rhetta had a reason for killing him and getting rid of you, then we have to give them her reason.''

''You mean me?''

''Why not? Rhetta and Jarrod became lovers last year when he came back from Mexico, so when Griff returned, they decided to get rid of him and make it look like someone wanted to get rid of him because of the cattle drive. When you came along and started nosing into things because you'd fallen in love with Griff and didn't want to see him dead, they decided to get rid of you too, but it didn't work out that way. Things went wrong, and instead Rhetta and Jarrod are dead. If we tell the story that way, which, in itself, is the truth, I think we can keep Gar out of it, and by admitting that there is something between you ahead of

time, there'll be less reason for them to badger either of
you in court and maybe no one will find out how far your
affair has really gone.''

"You'll never get Griff to agree."

"I will if you talk him into it." His eyes darkened.
''Miss Grayson, right now Griff doesn't have much of a
chance. Before, when I was talking to the crew, Cory
McBride told me some of the hands left to see if they can
find the men Rhetta and Jarrod had working for them. If
they come back empty-handed, we have to have something
to work with, and unfortunately this is all we have. The
judge is due to arrive any day now, and if I have to go into
that courtroom without anything to back up Griff's story, I
might as well give up before I start.''

"You're sure there's no other way?"

"Not unless you know who really did it," he said
softly. "I asked Griff about Gar going on the stand and
telling about his mother's actions that day, but even that
wouldn't help us, except that she told the boy his father
was dead. The prosecution could come back at us and say
she did it to ensure the fact that the boy would go with her
and not want to stay with his father. Besides, Griff refuses
to let him testify, even if he could help. So this is all we
have. We'll be fighting for his life, and I've never known
the truth to fail yet." He took a watch from his pocket,
checking the time, then asked her, "Will you try?"

"If you're sure it's the thing to do."

"I'm not really sure of anything, but it's the best we've
got." He corrected himself. "It's *all* we've got."

She nodded, and he checked his watch again. "Now,
it's getting late . . ." He slipped the watch back in his
pocket and reached for the doorknob. "If you'll be in my
office in the morning a little after eleven, I'll take you to
see Griff.''

She agreed, then stood in the open doorway, watching
him leave, her thoughts troubled. As he donned his hat,
hefted the guns he was wearing beneath the jacket of his
tweed suit more comfortably onto his hips, and mounted
the horse he'd left at the hitching rail, riding off down the

drive, she felt the gooseflesh rise beneath the sleeves of her pale pink dress and wondered if she'd done right by not telling him her true identity, and the answer was still haunting her as she closed the door, heading for the kitchen, where she asked Crystal to wake her early and have an escort ready, because she had an appointment in town.

17

The next morning Jeanine left for town early, with Cinnamon driving the buggy and two hands from the ranch riding escort. Luke, Spider, and Dustin were still hunting for Jarrod's men and Cory had gone out on the range to check on the roundup, since Griff was behind bars. Most of the crew had gone back out with Cory, except for the Kid, and they'd left just a skeleton crew behind to run the ranch. Griff insisted they were to keep the roundup alive, because even if he were hanged for Rhetta's murder, Gar would need the sale of the steers to keep Trail's End going, and he'd made Cory promise to see it through for the boy, if need be.

Once in town their escort disappeared into one of the nearby saloons, while Cinnamon drove on down the street to John's office. When they pulled up in front, a few people wandering about stared at Jeanine as Cinnamon helped her from the buggy, but she tried not to let them intimidate her, and held her head high, the wide-brimmed blue bonnet she wore hiding her face from their view. Except for the day of the funeral, it was the first she'd been in town since Griff's arrest. She straightened the tailored jacket to her plain blue suit, then headed for the door to John's office, frowning as he opened it for her.

"I feel like I'm on display," she said nervously as he quickly shut the door behind her, and in spite of the fact that it was a cool day, she could feel perspiration making her petticoats cling, and beads of sweat moistening her camisole, so it too stuck to her.

"You'll get used to it after a while," he said, but she shook her head.

"Never. Not those looks." She'd left a parasol in the buggy, but pulled at her gloves self-consciously, hoping Griff would think she looked all right; then she clutched her handbag a little tighter. "Have you told him I'm coming in?" she asked.

"Nope."

"You didn't?"

"He'd have cursed me if I had." John reached for his hat. "I thought maybe he might take it a little better if you were there in person, to sort of soften the blow for him."

"He's going to be upset."

"Oh, I don't doubt that. But I still think I'm right. Now, shall we?" he asked as he opened the door for her, and they stepped out onto the boardwalk, heading for the jailhouse a short way down the street.

Cinnamon had left the buggy in front of John's office, then wandered to the general store to visit with a few old friends who were usually hanging around, and when John and Jeanine strolled past them, she saw Cinnamon frown distastefully at something one of his friends mumbled, and she flushed self-consciously.

Sheriff Higgens was sitting at his desk writing a report when they walked in, and he glanced up. His face was sullen.

"Something I can do for you, John?" he asked.

John was just as unfriendly. "We'd like to see Griff."

Dave looked at Jeanine curiously. "The lady too?"

"The lady too."

Dave made John relinquish the guns from his gunbelt, setting them on the desk, then John watched Dave Higgens reluctantly move from behind the desk, take a set of keys, and unlock the thick iron door that separated his office from the two cells in back, then gesture for them to go through.

"By the way, what was that commotion I saw over here a few minutes ago?" John asked as Dave shut the door behind them. "I was almost ready to come over, when I saw Miss Grayson's buggy coming down the street. Something happen?"

"Something happened, all right," the sheriff answered irritably. "One of the men from Jack Hadley's Circle J brought what looks like Harlin Winslow's body in. Said he found him out in the woods the other side of town. Looks like he was shot in the chest, but the body was in pretty bad shape. The doc's lookin' it over now."

Jeanine frowned, remembering the bank teller being in the sheriff's office when they'd brought Rhetta's body in. "And the money?" she asked, surprising them.

Both men glanced at her.

"Well, the bank teller said the bank's money was missing as well as Mr. Winslow," she explained quickly. "That's why Mrs. Brandt had to wait for the man from the bank's insurance company in Dallas to get here before she could draw any new drafts for household expenses."

Dave Higgens eyed the young woman, his dark blue eyes intense. "His pockets were empty," he answered hesitantly. "And he'd put his suit on right over his nightshirt. Men don't do that unless they're forced to."

"Then the money wasn't found?"

"Nope," he said, then gestured toward the short hall that led to the jail cells. "This way," he said, and John let Jeanine go first.

Griff was still the only prisoner, and except for an occasional drunk who was thrown into the cell beside him to sleep it off overnight, he had been the only prisoner occupying the cells since his arrest. He was standing near the window when they reached the cellblock, gazing out, watching the clouds drifting across the sky, and wishing somebody'd walk through the alley, just so he'd see a human being again. The window was high, but being six feet tall, he was able to look through the bars easily. He was wearing the same blue shirt and buckskins he'd had on the day before, and John gave Jeanine a nudge, motioning for her to step forward.

"You've got visitors, Griff," Dave called out, breaking the silence that seemed to hang in the air, and Griff whirled around, adjusting his eyes after staring into the sunlight; then his face drained of color.

"Jeanine?"

Their eyes met and he hesitated, continuing to stare, face puzzled.

John turned to Dave. "If you don't mind," he whispered, "we'd like to see him alone, Dave."

The sheriff glanced at Griff, then Jeanine, then back to John.

"It's a reasonable request," John reminded him, and Dave finally shrugged, then walked over, unlocked the cell door, ushered them inside, locked the door again behind them, and left, retracing his steps down the hall.

Griff didn't move until he heard the clang of the iron door echoing from the end of the hall; then he took a step toward Jeanine, unable to believe what he was seeing. When he turned, he'd been expecting to see only John.

"I've missed you," he said softly, his eyes boring into hers.

She sighed. "I missed you too."

They stood in the jail cell, staring at each other, hardly daring to breathe.

"You shouldn't be here," he finally said as he continued staring; then, "My God," he groaned passionately, "I never thought I could miss anyone so damned much," and his voice was hoarse, barely a whisper.

"Me either." She held her breath. If he'd only touch her.

He started to reach out, then fought the urge to take her in his arms, and straightened forcefully, whirling on John, his eyes suddenly blazing.

"What the hell do you think you're doing, John, bringing her here?" he asked angrily.

John faced him squarely, refusing to back down under

his sudden attack. "Now, calm down, Griff," he cautioned. "If you'll just give me a chance to explain."

"I'm waiting!"

John told him what he'd told Jeanine the night before, while Griff stood motionless, trying to ignore the fact that Jeanine was standing within arm's reach of him, removing the wide-brimmed bonnet she had on, to reveal the soft blond hair beneath. Hair he'd love to bury his face in. She set the bonnet down on the edge of one of the cots while Griff watched her closely; then, when John was through, Griff glanced over at his lawyer, his eyes hardening.

"Are you insane?" he asked helplessly.

"No, I'm not insane," John answered. "But I'm trying to build some kind of defense for you." He was annoyed, with reason. "For God's sake, Griff, the way it stands now, you don't have a prayer. They know damn well your feelings for Miss Grayson are anything but platonic, and by trying to hide it, you're only making yourself look even more guilty. But if we give Rhetta a reason for wanting Jeanine dead as well as you, at least we've got something to work with." John glanced at Jeanine, the longing in her eyes so revealing. "Now, Dave just told us they brought Harlin Winslow's body in a short time ago and the doc's taking a look at him, so I'm going to leave you two alone for a while and go find out what I can, all right? And by the time I get back, I hope you've thought over what I've said and changed your mind." He yelled for Dave to come unlock the door, and after both men had once more disappeared down the short hall, and the clang of the iron door echoed back to them, Griff, who had moved back to the window again, turned once more to face Jeanine. She felt awkward and out of place, and tears rimmed her eyes.

"How's Gar?" he asked casually.

She forced the tears back. "I'm afraid he knows you've been arrested."

Griff frowned. "I guess I expected it. He's a smart boy." He sighed. "How's he taking it?"

"He insists you couldn't have done it, yet . . ."

"Yet what?"

Their eyes met again. "I think he senses how it was between you and Rhetta."

"How's that?"

"Last evening when I was tucking him in, he said something that was rather a shock."

"Oh?"

Her voice was strained. "He said, and I quote, 'I wish Pa could have felt about Mama the way he feels about you,' unquote."

Griff flinched.

"The voice of innocence," she said bitterly. "When I said he was imagining things, he shook his head and insisted he'd watched you, and you looked at me so special." Tears were close to the surface again. "He insisted he could tell."

He stepped toward her slowly, and reached out, touching her for the first time, then drew her gently into his arms.

"I never realized it was that obvious," he offered, whispering.

She stared up at him, her misty eyes filled with longing. "Neither did I."

He studied her mouth, watching the way it curved, the soft sensuous tilt to the corners; then, "Dare I?" he asked huskily.

Her face flushed hot, and her knees felt like jelly as he slowly bent his head, and she closed her eyes. His lips were light on hers at first, like the kiss of a butterfly's wings, then deepened fervently, and she clung to him, never wanting to let go. One kiss blended into another, each one more wildly satisfying, as he kept trying to wrest his mouth from hers, yet couldn't seem to. Then, with all the strength he could muster, Griff finally managed to draw his head back.

"I love you," he whispered, gazing into her eyes.

"And I you."

He sighed. "But this isn't getting us anywhere. If I keep holding you like this, I'm only going to get myself in even more trouble."

Her eyes were shining; still, she had to feel him out, find out how he felt about what John was planning.

"Griff, what do you think of John's idea?" she suddenly asked, and saw his eyes darken.

"It stinks!" He let go of her, and her heart sank. "If he thinks I'm going to get up on the stand and openly let them drag you into it, he's sadly mistaken."

"But I'm already in it."

"How?" He shook his head. "You're my son's governess, and I rescued you, that's all."

"But that isn't all," she insisted.

"It is as far as this town's concerned." His eyes were glistening furiously. "If I got up on the stand and openly told them I loved you, they'd never give us a chance. Don't you understand?" He straightened stubbornly. "You said you'd never be my mistress—well, that's the first thing they'd accuse you of being!"

"Griff, all we do is tell them the truth, right from the beginning," she pleaded.

"You think they'd believe it?" He shook his head. "Never! What we have to do is convince them that when I went after you, I did it because you were my son's teacher and I felt responsible. You only happened to be with me when Jarrod and Rhetta made their play. It's the only way."

"It's the worst way, Griff," she pleaded. She had come to the conclusion last night that John was right. "If we don't admit it now, the prosecution will only drag it out on the witness stand, and it'll just make things look worse."

"Not if we convince them there's nothing between us."

"That's crazy, Griff, the whole town's already speculating and accusing. We can't avoid it."

"We can!"

"How?"

"Don't come see me again," he answered. "And don't look at me like that, it's a dead giveaway." His jaw tightened, and he saw tears in her eyes. "I'm not going to tell them the truth, Jeanine." He winced. "At least not all of it. I'll admit going after you, and I'll tell them Jarrod and Rhetta were trying to kill me, and you were inadvertently dragged into it, but I won't mention anything about Jarrod being Gar's father, nor will I admit loving you. Do you understand? I should never have let myself get involved with you in the first place. I told you before that I didn't want to love you. That you complicated my life, so why don't you get out now? For your own sake!"

"Griff!"

"No! I won't do it, Jeanine. It's too much of a chance. I've hurt you enough. I won't hurt you any more."

"They'll make me testify anyway."

"I know."

"I can't lie, Griff," she said. "If they ask me . . . I'll be under oath . . . I won't deny what I feel for you."

He stared at her. "Then don't, if that's what you want. But it won't matter. You wouldn't be the first woman to fall in love with a man who wasn't in love with her."

"Oh, Griff," she cried. "Why are you so stubborn? Don't you see what they'll do to us?"

"Us?" His eyes narrowed. "There is no more us," he said bleakly. "Us died when someone plunged a knife into Rhetta. I realize that now. Don't you see? It won't work, Jeanine. I was a fool for ever thinking it would. It's over for us, it has to be. And if anyone asks, I'll deny ever loving you."

"You can't, Griff, and you know it," she whispered tearfully. "You can say it all you want, but the prosecution isn't going to ignore the rumors, and when it finally does come out, it'll put the noose right around your neck. Please, Griff . . ."

Her mouth was quivering, her eyes pleading, and . . . Oh, God! How much he loved her. Suddenly the fight just seemed to drain right out of him, leaving only a warm glow of love for her in its place, and he felt flushed deep inside. What was the use? She was right, so was John. To try keeping their love a secret was just opening up their vulnerability, yet he hated to think of what might lie ahead of them, and especially for her.

"All right," he finally conceded. "You and John win,

I'll let the world know I love you, but it had better get no further than that. I don't want them finding out I made love to you, so John had better be right. I'm doing this against my better judgment, and I don't like it. Not one bit, but I'll do it.''

She sighed. Thank God! He was still angry but at least he'd given in.

"There is one thing more, though," he said, frowning. "As you've probably realized by now, I didn't tell John about Jeannie Gray."

Her eyes darkened. "Don't you think we should?"

"Not unless we have to."

"But John said he had to know everything."

"That's right. Everything that has to do with what happened here, not something that's been over for months. And what good would it do anyway? It'd only be something else for people to condemn us for. Besides, I don't know how John would take it. He's as much a diehard rebel as the rest of Raintree, and we need him." He shook his head. "No, we don't tell John about Jeannie Gray. Not yet anyway. Not unless we're forced to," and he reached out, pulling her into his arms to kiss her again, when they heard the iron door to the sheriff's office opening, and Griff's arms fell from around her. It was one thing to tell the world he loved her, but he'd be damned if he'd compromise her in front of Dave.

John greeted them casually, then waited until Dave left again. He turned to Griff. "Well, did you decide to try it my way?" he asked, his face unyielding.

Griff shrugged. "Why not? Either way, I'll probably hang."

"Griff, don't." Jeanine was upset enough. She looked over at John. "Did you learn anything about Winslow?" she asked.

He'd told both of them his theory that perhaps the men Jarrod hired had robbed the bank, and now he shook his head. "Doc says he's been dead close to a week, and since you said it happened the night Rhetta was killed, then whoever robbed the bank must have shot him as soon as they were far enough away, where no one would hear the shot.''

''Then if it is Burke and his men, the boys are going to have a hell of a time trying to find them,'' Griff said. ''They aren't about to stick anywhere close by, not if there's a chance they could hang for murder.''

John walked over and plunked down on one of the bunks, unbuttoning his suit coat so it wouldn't bulge over his empty gunbelt, and Jeanine almost smiled, watching him. Most of the lawyers she'd seen back east were all spit and polish, and it seemed strange to see one who toted guns.

''Come, sit down,'' he said, gesturing to the other bunk.

Griff glanced at Jeanine, then took her hand, leading her to the cot opposite John, and they both sat down.

''I've been thinking,'' John began. ''In fact, I was up most of the night with my thoughts . . .''

''Go on,'' Griff urged when he hesitated.

''All right, this is what we have. The only one who knows someone was trying to kill you, Griff, is Jeanine,'' he stated. ''She was there when the men attacked you in the alley. And when you were shot in the arm, she conveniently took care of the wound.''

''Mrs. Brandt knew I'd been shot.''

''Ah yes, the loyal housekeeper who treats you more like her own son.'' He frowned. ''That's one of the things that's been troubling me too. What was she doing at the mine that night, Griff?''

''Didn't she tell you?''

''She told me the same thing she told you, but . . . I'm just not quite sure I believe her.''

''Why not?''

''Well, Jeanine told her she was going to take care of the boy, so there wasn't really any need for her to go, right?''

''You don't know Mrs. Brandt.''

''Ah, but I do,'' John countered. ''That's just it. She hated Rhetta with a passion, we both know that, and I imagine after you told her about Rhetta killing Garfield and trying to kill you . . .''

"Mrs. Brandt?" Griff shook his head. "Never," he argued stubbornly. "She isn't capable of murder, and you know it."

"Do I?" His eyes darkened. "She considers you and Gar her family, Griff," he went on, trying to convince him. "Even a gentle cat can become a killer if she thinks she has to protect her family, and with at least half the people who've ever been hanged for murder, I bet I can wager you that somewhere there was always somebody who thought they weren't capable."

"Not her, John." Griff straightened, getting into a more comfortable position. "I'm glad you're trying to be helpful, but not Mrs. Brandt. Besides, she was at the ranch when we left."

"And could have driven to the mine while you were heading for the Double V Bar to talk to Miles."

"You'll have to do better than that."

"All right." John leaned forward. "What about Warren?"

"Warren?"

"Yeah, Warren. You said yourself that you intimated he might have had something to do with it that night, when he started accusing you."

"I was only grabbing at straws."

"Still . . . you may have made a point. After all, he showed up awfully soon after she was killed."

Jeanine was apprehensive. "But his own sister?"

"It's happened before."

"He has no motive," Griff reminded him.

"Oh, but he does."

Jeanine and Griff exchanged glances.

"Go on," Griff said, looking back at John.

"You told me you were planning to talk Rhetta into giving you a divorce and getting out of your life, right? Her freedom for yours. Well, with Rhetta no longer a Heywood, where did that leave Warren? He was probably mad enough at his sister for botching things up for him and making him the loser, who knows how his mind works, especially one pickled with alcohol. When he left Trail's End he told you he was going to find out just what was going on. Well, maybe he did. He and Rhetta quarreled all the time anyway, you know that. Maybe they argued again, Warren lost his temper, your knife was handy, and he used it without thinking. After realizing what he'd done, and hearing you close by, he could have run off to where he'd left his horse, waited just long enough to give you, Cory, and Miss Grayson time to find his sister, then pretended to ride in as if he had just gotten there.''

Griff and Jeanine exchanged glances again, then looked back at John, and Griff's forehead wrinkled into a scowl.

"At least that makes more sense," he said thoughtfully. "I know there were times when it was evident there was little love lost between the two."

"And Warren's crying louder for your neck than anyone else," John replied. "Unless maybe Miles Vance." He eased forward, stretching, then relaxed again. "And that leads us to another possibility."

"Miles?"

"Why not?" John took a deep breath. "Didn't you say he blamed Rhetta for what happened to Jarrod?"

"In a roundabout way," Griff answered. "But I'm the one who shot him. It's my head he wants on a platter."

"But you wouldn't have shot him if it hadn't been for his involvement with Rhetta. It was her fault he did what he did; your shooting him wouldn't have come about if he hadn't been messing around with your wife, and Miles is on a vengeance trail anyway you look at it."

"John, Miles was in his nightshirt when I left him."

"And he could have put on his clothes, taken a shortcut to the mine, gotten there before you, killed Rhetta, and left without you even knowing it. After all, he didn't bring Jarrod's body in till Sunday."

"That's all good and fine, except I doubt Miles could move that fast. Even taking a shortcut would be cutting it close."

"He could make it, though," John insisted.

"He could," Griff said thoughtfully. "At least it's a possibility."

"And what about the men who were working for Jarrod?" John asked. "Would one of them have been capable of killing her?"

Once more Jeanine and Griff exchanged glances, and Jeanine frowned, feeling her stomach tighten instinctively.

"I'm sure the one named Burke could have," she said, looking back at John. "But why would he want to?"

John studied her face for a minute. "Well," he answered slowly, "I got to thinking. Griff said yesterday that Gar told Cory the men were still there when Jarrod left. Now, Gar also told Cory that before he went to sleep, he heard Jarrod outside giving orders to his men and telling them he'd be back to pay them off. But what if Burke figured Jarrod wasn't going to have enough money, and he and his men wanted more? He could have sent his men in to rob the bank and kill Winslow while he waited to intercept Jarrod when he got back to the mine. Only, with his mind working the way it did, he might have decided to . . . ah . . . excuse me for my crudity, Miss Grayson," he apologized, and cleared his throat. "But he might have decided to enjoy the boss's lady while he was waiting, figuring since promises of the jobs had fallen through, and they had no use for Jarrod anymore, if Rhetta complained to Jarrod when he got back, and things got too sticky for him, Burke would just shoot the both of them and he and his men would take the money Jarrod brought, and what the boys got from the bank, and they'd head for the border. Only I figure Rhetta put up an argument, and with her usual cutting remarks probably made him mad enough that he lost his temper and ended up killing her. When he heard you coming, though, he probably thought it couldn't be Jarrod because he'd have no reason to sneak back in, and since he knew you and Jeanine had escaped, he was afraid it might be the law, so he lit out, circled the house till he reached his horse, which was probably in the shadows someplace where you couldn't see it, and took off. He knew the route his men took to town, so probably met them on their way back, and they could have either split up or just headed for the border.''

He saw the surprised looks on their faces.

"Well, it is possible, isn't it?" he asked.

"It's possible," Griff answered hesitantly. "And that'd explain the bank being robbed, but . . .''

"Griff, men like this fella Burke use women like most men use whiskey, for relaxation and fun, not because they care . . . and your wife was a very beautiful woman. Besides, wasn't Burke the one who took your hunting knife and guns?''

What John was saying made sense; in fact everything John said had made sense, about Warren, Miles—the only exception was Mrs. Brandt. There was no way he could even imagine her shoving a knife in Rhetta, and besides, where would she get his knife in the first place? But the others . . .

They talked for quite a while longer while John went back over his theories, trying to pick each one apart and figure out which was the more plausible.

"I'm going to try to do some investigating on my own, Griff," he finally said as he and Jeanine were getting ready to leave. "Maybe I can pick up on some little thing somewhere that'll make it fall into place. If not, then we've got a battle ahead of us. It's not easy to defend a man with no defense. Your boys out at the ranch can't even swear to whether Indians or white men really captured Miss Grayson. After all, Indians ride shod horses too sometimes when they've stolen them from white men.'' He shook his head. "I sure as hell hope the men Cory sent out come back with something," he said as Jeanine put her bonnet back on. "Because what we've got here is a mess.''

They were working their way toward the cell door. "I don't want to hang, John," Griff said, and his arm went about Jeanine's waist.

John saw the affectionate gesture. "Don't worry, Griff," he said. "I can't guarantee anything at this point, but I'll tell you one thing. I'll give them one hell of a fight." His eyes crinkled at the corners. "Now, give the little lady a quick kiss, and I'll call Dave to let us out of here,'' and he turned his back on them, facing the cell door, yelling for Dave.

"I guess John's right," Griff said as his arms went about her, and he gazed down into her face. "But I sure as hell don't like it."

"It's the only way," she answered.

He tried to smile. "When will you be in again?"

"When I can."

They heard the key turning in the big iron door down the hall, and Griff leaned down. The kiss was warm, filled with yearning, and when it was over, she eased from the circle of his arms reluctantly.

A few seconds later Dave watched them curiously as he unlocked the cell door; then John gestured for Jeanine to go ahead of him, said a last good-bye to Griff, and they started toward the hall.

"Tell Gar everything'll be all right," Griff called after them as they heard the cell door shut behind them, and Jeanine stopped, turning back.

"Don't worry, I will," she promised as Dave joined them. "Good-bye, Griff."

His eyes caught hers and held. "Good-bye," he answered, his voice strained, and she turned away again quickly, hating to have the last memory of her visit be an image of him staring at her through the bars.

When she and John stepped out onto the boardwalk in front of the jailhouse, it was not too far past lunchtime.

"You'd do me a kindness if you'd have a bite to eat with me at the Steak House before going back to Trail's End," he said, and she stared off down the street, contemplating his offer.

There were some things she wanted to talk to him about. She probably should.

"All right," she answered, making a quick decision, and a few minutes later they were sitting at a small table in the only restaurant in town, about a block from the jail, right next to the hotel.

It wasn't a fancy place. Nothing like the dining places in

the East. The strong smell of food cooking had assailed them the minute they opened the door, as well as the searching eyes of a number of patrons. The tablecloth was faded, the floor bare, and the young woman who came out and took their order looked tired and overworked.

"The town's growing," John said a short while later when they started to eat, and Jeanine glanced up from her soup. "This drive Griff and the others have started has brought a lot of men in," he explained. "Work's hard to find, what with the war just over, and some of them are bound to stay after the roundup and branding, since they won't all be needed on the drive."

"Is that good or bad?" she asked.

He shrugged. "All depends on what kind of men they are. Which reminds me." He set his fork down a minute, picked up the linen napkin, and wiped his mouth. "I know Luke, Dustin, and Spider took off to hunt for Burke, and Cory's doin' the ramrodin' for Griff, and that doesn't leave many men back at the ranch who are close enough to Griff to be certain of their loyalty. But I'll be needin' somebody to do some ridin' for me, and listenin' and askin' a few questions, and I'd like it to be somebody who won't be too conspicuous hangin' around town. Now, I figure you've been out at Trail's End long enough to spot the grumblers and complainers—they're usually the ones who can't be trusted too far. I would've asked Griff, but he's got a fool notion all the men he hires can be trusted. Maybe they can, I don't know." He picked up his fork again. "But I was hoping you could maybe think of someone."

"What kind of questions and listening are you referring to?" she asked.

"I'd like to try to find out which one of those theories I told Griff about holds the most promise of being right."

"Hmmm . . ." She thought for a minute; then, "I know he's rather young, but what about the Kid?" she suggested. "He's almost always trailing after Luke, Dustin, or Spider, and Cory thinks enough of him to trust him with the mail pickup in town and running drafts to the bank. So do Mrs. Brandt and Griff, for that matter. And if you want someone who can roam around town without people wondering why he's hanging around . . . he spends more time in town than he does on the range.''

John's eyes softened knowingly. ''I guess I forgot about the Kid. Then he didn't go after Burke with Spider and the others?''

''Not that he didn't want to.'' She straightened, looking very sure of herself. ''He said he'd ride through . . . Excuse me.'' She blushed. *''Hell,''* she said, ''if he had to, if it'd help clear Griff.'' Her face was crimson. ''Cory ordered him to stay at Trail's End, and he has, but he hasn't been happy about it.''

''Good.'' John ate a bit more while occasionally catching a quick peek across the small table at the schoolteacher; then he finally set his fork down again. ''Miss Grayson . . . Look, for all purposes, may I call you Jeanine?'' he asked.

She smiled. ''If you wish.''

He took a deep breath. ''Good,'' he said. ''Because, Jeanine, I'd like to ask if you could help me too.''

''Oh?''

''Griff says no, but I just can't get this thing about Mrs. Brandt settled and put aside. Somehow I have a feeling something doesn't quite ring true about what she was doing out that night.'' He took a quick swig of coffee, then wiped his mouth. ''In the first place,'' he said as he set the cup back down, ''I've never known Theola Brandt to drive her own buggy. Not that she doesn't know how, but the kind of woman she is . . . well, she figures she's too much a lady.''

''I didn't know her name was Theola.''

''Guess I'm the only one who ever calls her that, but then, Zeb used to, and I picked it up from him. You see, that's what I mean. She won't even let anyone call her Theola to her face. It has to be 'Mrs. Brandt.' But what I'm gettin' at is, she also knows how dangerous it is to be ridin' around alone at night, and especially off where the old Vance copper mine is. Now, if she was just bent on

helpin' with the boy, why didn't she have Cinnamon or
Venable go with her? Seems more logical to me that she'd
have someone along for protection of some kind. Griff said
that when she went back with the boy, Cory told her where
the men were waitin' and had her stop and take a couple of
them with her because he didn't want anything more to
happen. So I was hoping maybe you could sort of feel
things out, out at Trail's End, and see if you can find any
reason she might have had for doin' such a fool thing. It's
so unlike her, and you see, I happen to know the woman
knows how to use a gun and isn't afraid to, if need be. She
shot more than one Indian in her younger days, and people
don't always change that much, and with her hatin' Rhetta
as bad as she did . . . Think you can keep your eyes and
ears open for me, and maybe ask a question or two here
and there?''

"Griff won't like it."

"I don't aim to tell him, but we're fightin' for his life,
Jeanine, and anything I can find out to help him out of this
mess will be a blessing."

"Then count me in," she answered firmly. "I don't
know how much help I'll be, but I'll try." She paused a
second, then went on. "But don't you think, if she loves
Griff and the boy that much, that she would just speak up
now instead of letting Griff go through all this? That is, if
she were guilty?"

"Not necessarily. She could be hoping they'll acquit
him."

"That's true."

They talked a little more about John's unusual theories,
and Jeanine promised to send the Kid in to his office first
thing the next morning when he came to town for the mail.
So as soon as they were finished eating, John paid for their
lunch and they left. Once outside, however, Jeanine began
to feel the first full impact of her visit with Griff.

Afternoon always seemed to bring out more people in
Raintree. Maybe because by the time they got up, did
chores, and got ready, it took that long for them to ride to
town—she had no idea. But whatever it was, they seemed

to be everywhere this afternoon, and word of her visit to the jail had apparently traveled fast. As they crossed the street and began walking past the Golden Cage Saloon heading for John's office, some of the men who'd been lounging around out front began making crude remarks that could be construed no other way except as disrespectful.

"Pay no attention to them," John cautioned as he took her elbow, showing her his support. "They're just a lot of saddle tramps from the Double V Bar."

"That means Miles is in town."

"Probably," he answered. "But don't worry about him either, he'll only be repeatin' the same thing he's been sayin' for the past week, and from what I've heard, nobody's payin' too much attention to him."

"Apparently his men are."

"Like I said, those men are riffraff. They just don't know a lady when they see one."

Cinnamon was waiting for them when they reached the buggy, so John sent him down to the saloon at the other end of town to get their escort while he helped her in.

"Now, come on," he coaxed as he watched her settling back against the seat. "No more fussin' over the bad manners of a few cowpokes, all right?"

She smiled. "Thanks, John," she said gratefully. "Now I know why Cory said we could trust you."

He smiled back, then glanced behind her to where Cinnamon was hurrying toward them, while behind Cinnamon, back at the Lone Star saloon, the two men who'd ridden escort for the Trail's End buggy were mounting their horses at the hitch rail. Cinnamon was panting breathlessly when he reached them, and excused himself for taking so long, then climbed into the driver's seat and picked up the reins.

Suddenly, as he lifted the reins, ready to flick them, to turn the buggy around, heading back out of town, he glanced up and hesitated, the squeak, scrunch, rattle, and pounding hoofbeats of an approaching stage catching his attention as it did that of everyone else in town. And as Jeanine and John also watched the creaking stage lunge into sight, it began to slow down some, then flew by them at a fast clip, kicking up a whirl of dust that had Jeanine covering her face. A few seconds later, when the dust had cleared and she opened her eyes again, she turned in her seat, looking back behind her, just in time to see the driver pull up, stopping in front of the Empire Hotel.

While brushing dust from the jacket of her suit, she watched curiously as the driver reached behind him, grabbed a slightly worn carpetbag from among some of the other luggage, and carried it with him, climbing down from his perch; then he headed for the stagecoach door and opened it so he could help someone down.

Well, that's a change, she thought, realizing he hadn't just tossed the passenger's luggage in the dirt road. She squinted, shading her eyes a little, trying to see better, but whoever the passenger was, he or she was hidden behind the stage, since the hotel was on the opposite side of the street.

Then, to her further surprise, after helping his passenger alight, the driver carried the brocade carpetbag on into the hotel. A few seconds later, he came back out empty-handed, said something to the passenger, who was still standing on the other side of the stage; then, since no new passengers seemed to be waiting, he climbed aboard, settled himself comfortably on his precarious perch again, and whipped up the horses, disappearing down the road at the opposite end of town in another cloud of dust.

Jeanine drew her eyes from the spot where the stagecoach had disappeared and let them settle on the lone passenger the driver had treated with such consideration, unaware that standing next to her beside the buggy, John also was studying the newcomer.

The man was tall, at least six feet, with a silver-streaked beard covering his chin, and it was clipped neatly, a narrow mustache above it. Thick dark brows rested over a pair of deep-set hazel eyes that were perusing the town vigorously from one end to the other, missing very little, and Jeanine was certain she felt them resting on her for a brief moment before moving on. But it was hard to tell from such a distance.

His clothes were wrinkled from riding, but the black suit, although shiny in the seat, was well tailored, the shirt beneath its swallowtail coat sporting narrow ruffles that showed off his slim black tie, and a flat-crowned, wide-brimmed black hat helped shade his face from the afternoon sun. He had hooked his left thumb in the front pocket of his vest and was holding a hand-carved wooden cane in his right hand, with the tip of the cane touching the ground, and he was casually swinging it back and forth. Then, quite abruptly, he unhooked his thumb from his vest pocket, turned, looking up at the worn sign over the upstairs balcony of the hotel, and stood for a minute as if hesitant to go inside.

"Well, well, well," John exclaimed as they all stared at the man.

Jeanine glanced over at him. "What's the matter?" she asked.

John's eyes were still on the gentleman standing in front of the hotel, and Jeanine looked back at him too, then frowned, watching closely as the man slowly began to walk and it became apparent that the cane he carried was badly needed. As he took each step, using it to steady himself, she could see that his right leg didn't seem to want to cooperate and move forward with the same agile movement as his left leg.

John's eyes narrowed shrewdly. "That, Jeanine, is Judge Damian Worth, the circuit judge from Dallas," he said slowly as the distinguished-looking gentleman limped toward the door of the hotel, "I'd know him anywhere," and as Jeanine watched the man disappear inside, removing his hat as he went through the door, an unsettled feeling began to grip her, causing a chill to run through her, and she shivered.

This was the man they'd all been waiting for. The man who would oversee the people who would hold Griff's life in their hands. The man who would control some of the most important aspects of both their lives over the next few days, and suddenly she was afraid, because the man she had seen walk into the hotel, in spite of his limp, looked like a hard, domineering man, a man to be reckoned with, and a man who looked like the word "leniency" had never been a part of his vocabulary. And a few minutes later, after saying good-bye to John, Jeanine sat in the buggy, staring hard at the hotel, wishing as Cinnamon drove past it that the next few days didn't have to be.

It was close to dinnertime when Jeanine arrived back at Trail's End, tired but pleased over her visit with Griff. If only she could be as pleased about the rest of the day's events. Not only had the judge's arrival upset her, but during the ride out she was having second thoughts about her promise to John Scott, and the feelings she was having were contradictory. She wanted to do everything in her power to help Griff, yet the thought of spying on Mrs. Brandt, and that's just what she would be doing, spying again—the thought irritated her. Perhaps because, with the thought, came back all the ugly memories of what her life had once been. There had been some good times, yes, and Homer, bless him, had told her once that she seemed to thrive on excitement, but there was a difference between the thrill of outsmarting an enemy and the hurt that could come with knowing you'd betrayed someone who trusted you and considered herself your friend. And she had a strange feeling that in spite of the housekeeper's curt manner, Mrs. Brandt liked her. Well, she'd promised John, and it was important, so she'd have to go through with it. Still, as she stepped down from the buggy and made her way up the front steps of the ranch house, then went on into the foyer, where the twins were waiting to take her parasol, hat, and gloves, there was an emptiness inside her that made her feel melancholy and out of sorts.

"How's Mr. Griff?" Beth asked as Jeanine handed the things to her, and Jeanine was taken by surprise.

"You knew I went to see him?"

Peggy smiled sheepishly. "We heard Mrs. Brandt telling Ma."

"Oh . . ." Jeanine pulled on the tail of her suit jacket, straightening it, then smoothed a stray hair back from her face. "Where is Mrs. Brandt?" she asked.

Beth nodded toward the hallway to the right, at the foot of the stairs. "She's in the library doin' somethin', and Gar's in the kitchen helpin' Ma."

"Oh, I can just imagine how much help he is," Jeanine said, and was able to force a semblance of a smile. "How long before dinner?"

"About half an hour," Beth answered quickly, then asked the same question again. "But you never said how Mr. Griff is."

"Oh, he's fine," she answered. "That is, he's doing all right, but I think maybe he could probably use some clean clothes the next time one of us goes in." She turned suddenly to the other twin. "Peggy, would you mind doing me a favor?" she asked.

"What's that?"

"Is the Kid around outside anywhere?"

Beth laughed. "Now, what makes you think she'd know where he is?" she teased, and Peggy slapped at her playfully.

"Stop it, Beth," she scolded. "This is no time for funnin'. Can't you see Jeanine's not in any mood for your nonsense."

Beth made a face. "That's just the trouble," she said peevishly. "Everybody around here is too serious about everything. Now you're makin' Jeanine the same way." She glanced at Jeanine, then frowned, and her smile faded. "I guess maybe you ain't in much of a funnin' mood, like Peggy said, are you?" she asked.

"It's all right, Beth," Jeanine answered, not wanting to hurt her feelings. "I guess I'm just tired."

"Well, who wouldn't be," she went on. "I'll just take the things up to your room for you," and she headed for the stairs, taking them jauntily, whistling softly all the way.

Jeanine couldn't help smiling a little. "I think the Kid's down near the barn somewhere," Peggy said, answering the question Jeanine had asked her. "Did you want me to tell him somethin'?"

"Tell him that tomorrow morning when he goes into Raintree, I want him to go to John Scott's office. If John's not there, tell him to find him, and make sure he talks to him before coming back out to Trail's End. And I want you to specify to him that it's very important and that Mr. Griff's life could depend on it."

Peggy's eyes narrowed curiously. "It's that important?" she asked.

"It's very important," Jeanine answered, and was surprised when Mrs. Brandt asked:

"What's very important?"

Jeanine hadn't seen her coming down the hall, and she turned, facing her. Nothing ever changed about Mrs. Brandt, except that perhaps the style of her usual black dress did vary occasionally. Other than that, her hair was always the same, the coronet tightly wound, with the same small silver hoops in her ears, and her only other jewelry, the small cross, was always on the front of whatever dress she had on. Her sharp eyes sometimes made Jeanine feel a little uncomfortable.

"I was planning to tell you all about it," Jeanine answered, trying not to let her discomfiture show. "If you want, we can talk in the library."

Mrs. Brandt agreed, and they left Peggy, who promised to give the message to the Kid; then Jeanine and Mrs. Brandt retired to the library, where Jeanine proceeded to tell Mrs. Brandt about her visit to Griff and John's theories about who might be guilty, tactfully omitting his suspicions about the housekeeper herself.

"If we could just find the person who really did it," Jeanine exclaimed.

"I should tell them I did it," Mrs. Brandt said angrily. "Then they'd have to let him go." She saw the surprised look on Jeanine's face. "Well, they would."

"But they'd never believe a thing like that," Jeanine said, hoping Mrs. Brandt hadn't misread the reason for the startled look on her face. "They'd know you were only trying to protect him."

"Oh? Well, now, don't be so sure." She straightened, her chin tilting stubbornly. "I was out at the mine that night, if you remember," she reminded her.

"But you went there because of Gar."

"That's what I told Griff. But I could tell the sheriff that I went there to make sure Rhetta would pay for what she did to the Heywood family. For killing Griff's brother and ruining Griff's life."

Jeanine stared at the housekeeper, studying her closely while she talked. There was a depth in her topaz eyes, and something about the tone of her voice, as if she were reciting from memory something that had really happened.

"After all, I did go out there alone. I could tell them I had a gun with me and was planning to shoot her, only the knife was handy, and I didn't want to wake up the boy, who was sleeping in the house at the time." Her mouth curved into a rare smile as she stared off toward the French doors at the back of the library. "I should have done that right from the start," she said thoughtfully. "Then Griff wouldn't be in the mess he's in." She seemed to collect herself again and came back to the present and Jeanine. "After all," she said, once more in her usual crisp manner, "I doubt they'd hang a woman my age, don't you?"

"I doubt they'd even believe you," Jeanine said, only her words didn't necessarily convey the thoughts that were tumbling through her head. "Besides, even if you tried to make them believe you did it, it'd ruin everything, wouldn't it? Because you'd have to tell them how Rhetta ruined Griff's life and why Rhetta shot his brother, and we could never keep Gar out of it then."

Again Mrs. Brandt looked thoughtful, as if her mind was absorbed with something else; then, "You're right, of course," she agreed firmly. "It was just a thought. You see, Griff's like a son to me, and I'd do anything to see that he was happy, and it near kills me every time I think that he could hang."

"I know," Jeanine said, then sighed. "Well, at least we

won't have to wait much longer,'' she went on. ''The judge rode in on the stage today, so it won't be long now.''

''He's here?''

Jeanine nodded. ''Arrived just as I was leaving. John said his name is Worth, Judge Damian Worth.''

This time it was Mrs. Brandt's turn to look startled. ''Judge Worth? Are you sure?'' she asked.

''That's what John said. Do you know him?''

Mrs. Brandt took a deep breath and straightened, looking pleased for the first time in days. ''Well, at least that's a help,'' she said with a little more spirit.

Jeanine frowned. ''How's that?''

''Because, Jeanine, not only is Damian Worth a close friend of Griffin Heywood's, but Damian Worth wouldn't even be alive today if it weren't for Griff. He owes Griff his life, so maybe now he can repay the debt. Ah, yes, things are starting to look up after all, wouldn't you say? Now, if you'll excuse me, I know you'll want to freshen up before dinner, and I do have some things to do . . . and, oh yes,'' she said just before leaving, ''thank you for bringing me the best news I've had in days.''

Jeanine stood in the library alone, the housekeeper's astounding revelation still ringing in her ears.

18

Griff stood in his cell and stared at John. "But why Damian?" he asked angrily.

John shrugged. "Who knows? Maybe he asked for it. He didn't say."

"You know what everyone's going to think, don't you? They're going to think somebody's being bought off. There are just enough old-timers around to remember that I saved Damian Worth's life once, and now they probably figure he's here to save mine."

"So let them think what they want." John had been sitting on the cot. He stood up. "I just thought you should know."

"Thanks," Griff said, and walked over to the window, staring out between the bars. It was dark already, and he hated nights the most. "Did he say how soon it'd be?" he asked.

"He said another day or two. Things still aren't any too organized back in Dallas, what with the military bucking the local government, but they sent for Tom Frawley to be prosecutor, and Damian said he should be here by tomorrow. He's been down in Austin and he'll need at least a day or two to familiarize himself with everything."

"Why didn't they just ship me off to Dallas and get it over with there, John?" Griff asked bitterly. "That's what they usually do with something like this."

"I know," John sighed. "But from what Damian says, the docket was too full. And besides, we're too far out. It'd be hell tryin' to haul everybody back there to testify, so they decided the best thing to do was just handle it here."

"Great!" Griff exhaled disgustedly. "Only one thing bothers me, John," he said testily. "Like you said before, where the hell are they going to find twelve unbiased men in this town?"

He was right. Tom Frawley rode in the following day, and for the next three days they screened almost the whole town before coming up with a jury. However, it was three days well spent, because it gave John the time he needed to find out if any of the theories he had about Rhetta's murderer could be solid enough to be brought up in court.

When John first decided to investigate on his own, he had no idea what he might come up with. All he was sure of was that if Griff didn't do it, and he felt sure Griff hadn't, then someone else had, so he'd singled out the people most logically involved and tried to go from there. At first, when he'd started running the different possibilities over in his mind, it had been purely conjecture, and he'd even felt a little foolish, especially when suspicions of Theola Brandt began taking shape. But when a man's life's at stake, even the foolish possibilities can't be ignored, and now, two days after sending Jeanine back to Trail's End to learn anything she could about the woman's activities that evening, he was glad he hadn't just thrown the idea aside.

The Kid, after visiting John's office and agreeing to see what he could learn in town, was reporting every casual remark and loose conversation, but so far not one bit of information he'd given John had been incriminating enough to prove John's theories were any more than that. Just theories. Warren was still wandering around town lamenting his sister's death, and Miles and his men were still furthering their hate campaign against Griff. Jarrod had been buried in a quiet ceremony the day after Rhetta's burial, and Miles had spent little time at his ranch since then.

But now John sat in his office staring across the desk at Jeanine.

"Are you sure about this?" he asked, really surprised.

"I don't see why Crystal would lie."

He pushed his chair back and stood up, pacing to the door, then glanced back at her. "If it's true, then I could be right."

"But Crystal said she took a rifle," Jeanine reminded him. "Rhetta wasn't shot, she was stabbed."

"You don't see it, do you?" he replied anxiously. "If Theola Brandt was mad enough to take a rifle with her when she left Trail's End, and was threatening to make sure Rhetta couldn't hurt anyone anymore, then she could have been mad enough to stab her . . . and after what you say she told you . . . you know, she could have been reciting what really happened."

Jeanine's eyes were troubled. At first she hadn't wanted to tell John about her conversation in the kitchen with Crystal. But the more she thought it over, and the more she remembered what Mrs. Brandt had told her in the library, the more she realized she couldn't let her feelings for the woman overshadow her feelings for Griff. If Mrs. Brandt had killed Rhetta and was keeping quiet in the hopes that Griff would be acquitted, it was a cruel thing to do to someone you loved. Yet, perhaps she could understand the housekeeper's reasoning. It would be easier for Griff to stand the rigors of a trial than for her to take a chance on hanging. However, John couldn't count on the housekeeper confessing her guilt if Griff was convicted. She was no longer a young woman, and anything could happen between now and then. He frowned.

"There's only one problem now," he said, and walked back to sit at the desk. "Griff'll never believe she didn't take the rifle along to defend herself in case she ran into Indians."

"We saw a couple on the way in today," Jeanine said, "and when the Kid came back last night, he said they raided a place just northeast of here."

John nodded. "They never let up. I guess they decided

they didn't like the Quarter D being so close to the Wichita River. They've even been giving the men a hard time with the roundup, from what Cory said when he came in yesterday to see Griff.''

''Then there's no way you could prove she didn't take the rifle because she was scared she might run into some of them?''

''Not really.'' He leaned back. ''Except for what you told me Crystal said. That Theola was threatening Rhetta when she left the ranch.'' He had picked up a pencil and was fingering it thoughtfully. ''Well, at least it's something to start with.''

And by the time the trial started a few days later, he had even more to use, but not against the housekeeper this time.

The Kid's eavesdropping around the saloons had finally paid off, and he learned that after Griff shot Jarrod that night and left the Double V Bar, Miles was so distraught for a few minutes that he just didn't seem to know what to do. However, once he got himself under control, he laid his son's body back on the kitchen floor, went out onto the back porch, ordered his men to get a blanket and wrap Jarrod's body in it and tie the body on Jarrod's horse; then he went back into the house, saying he was going to get dressed. And according to his men, who were then ordered to stay at the ranch, within ten minutes he was riding through the front gate at the Double V Bar on his own horse, with Jarrod's horse in tow, claiming that he was taking his son's body to the sheriff.

John stood in his office the night before the trial was to start, staring at the report about Miles, and frowned. It didn't make sense. If Miles Vance left the Double V Bar so soon after Griff and the Trail's End crew left, then why did it take him so long to get to Raintree? Rhetta was killed on Saturday, shortly before dawn, and Miles didn't ride into Raintree with Jarrod's body until Sunday morning.

And then there was Warren. He had plenty of time to reach the mine before Griff and the others. John had mentioned both facts to Dave Higgens, but the sheriff hadn't seemed to be interested. The only fact he cared

about was that Griff was the only one bending over
Rhetta's body seconds after she screamed, and the murder
weapon was his hunting knife. Ah well . . .

John straightened and put all the papers he needed into
his briefcase. It wasn't the greatest material he'd ever had
to work with, but at least it was better than when he
started, and tomorrow would test whether he'd been wasting his time or not.

The next day the air was crisp and clear, with the sky
overcast. All morning, people had been making their way
toward the building in town where the trial was being held,
so that by the time Jeanine walked in with Cory, it was
packed. They were holding the trial in the same building
where the services had been held for Rhetta, the building
that alternated as meeting hall, school, and church on
Sundays. Unfortunately for the schoolchildren who used it
on weekdays, instead of school being called off, they had
made arrangements to hold classes in the now empty of-
fices of the *Beacon Journal*. Since Homer Beacon's death,
the place had just stayed empty while word was sent back
east trying to locate any relatives the man might have had,
and with the presses and other equipment utilized so they'd
hold books and papers, or else shoved out of the way,
there was plenty of room for the students.

Cory had ridden in to Trail's End from the range the
night before and had escorted the Trail's End buggy in
early this morning, then walked over to the hotel to meet
Jeanine. Now he ushered her up to the front of the room,
where they sat directly behind the chair Griff was to sit in.
Jeanine had arrived in town the day before and had gone
directly to the hotel, where John had reserved a room for
her; then, before settling down for the night, she had
visited Griff in jail. It was only the second time she had
seen him since that first day she and John had gone to see
him together, and it was the first time she had visited him
alone. Now, as she sat in the courtroom behind the defense
table where John was sitting, and stared at Judge Damian
Worth's stoic face, waiting for them to bring Griff in, she

remembered last night with feeling. Griff was her life now. He was all that mattered, and he just had to live. Her jaw set firmly.

Cory was sitting at her right, and Mrs. Brandt was sitting next to Cory; Jeanine leaned forward a little, taking a quick glance at the housekeeper.

If only she could read the woman's mind. Mrs. Brandt hadn't ridden in with Jeanine the day before, deciding to stay at Trail's End and come in with Cory every day for the trial. Her contention was that she was needed out at Trail's End, which was undoubtedly true, although after talking to her that night in the library, and remembering the things Crystal had told her, Jeanine was beginning to wonder if maybe John was right about the woman. One thing for certain, the housekeeper was determined that neither Trail's End nor the trial would be able to get along without her presence, and since the trial was to start every morning at ten, that meant she and Cory would be leaving Trail's End every day about sunup, leaving Crystal and the twins to take care of Gar and see that things ran smoothly at the ranch.

Jeanine knew Crystal would rather be at the trial, but someone had to stay at Trail's End, and since she wasn't directly involved, it was logical she'd be the one chosen. Besides, they still hadn't had any news from Dustin, Spider, and Luke, even though they'd sent a man to Fort Belknap to see if they could have sent a wire. The telegraph hadn't reached Raintree yet, but bypassed it to the south, and it was the only way they had to get word back to Cory if they did locate Burke or his men. Crystal told Jeanine not to get discouraged, because even if they did pick up Burke's trail, it was likely they'd be traveling through wild country where they'd be lucky to see a town, let alone a telegraph. So now Jeanine sat in the courtroom growing more nervous by the minute as the hands on the wall clock to the right of the judge's desk moved closer to ten.

It was two minutes to the hour when the side door opened and Sheriff Higgens stepped in, followed by Griffin Heywood, with a deputy close at his heels, and suddenly the courtroom became silent, all eyes on the tall rugged-looking rancher who was making his way to the chair beside John. He sat down, after first smiling warmly and mumbling a soft greeting to Jeanine, then winking at Cory and Mrs. Brandt.

Jeanine smiled back, and Cory and the housekeeper nodded; then all heads centered on the distinguished man at the front of the room, who was pounding his gavel vigorously on the desk.

The first witness was Dave Higgens, followed by Doc Theran. The sheriff's testimony was mostly routine about what he found when he reached the old Vance copper mine and about the murder weapon. Except, of course, when he volunteered to let everyone know that Gar Heywood's governess had been visiting the prisoner, which caused a mild stir in the courtroom. John's only cross-examination of the sheriff was to question him about the money found in Rhetta's handbag, verifying the amount. Then he did ask permission to bring him back if need be, as well as the doctor.

By eleven-forty-five, Tom Frawley had gone through most of the Trail's End crew Griff had taken with them that night, learning absolutely nothing, and now suddenly the courtroom grew silent, as if everyone were holding his breath, because the prosecution had just called James Spider to the stand.

When no one moved, and it was apparent that Spider wasn't in the courtroom, Damian Worth looked directly at John. "Mr. Scott, do you happen to know where the witness is?" he asked.

John stood up. "No, your honor." And he didn't. All he knew was that Spider, Luke, and Dustin had taken off to hunt for a man named Burke, but he'd told Judge Worth the truth. No one, not even Griff, knew where they had disappeared to.

"Then since the witness is undoubtedly a hostile one," Judge Worth said quite calmly, "I suggest the prosecution hire someone to find him and serve him with a subpoena."

"You can't be serious, Judge Worth," Tom Frawley protested. "No one's seen the man for days."

"Mr. Frawley," Judge Worth countered, his hazel eyes unwavering, "is he or is he not important to the prosecution of this case?"

"Yes, your honor."

"Then I suggest you do as I've instructed."

"Yes, your honor."

Judge Worth's eyes rested on Griff momentarily; then he glanced over once more to the prosecuting attorney. Tom Frawley was younger than John, and had been making quite a name for himself in the few months since the end of the war. He was thin and rather nice-looking, with brown hair that waved slightly to the edge of his collar, dark blue eyes, and a mustache that detracted from the unusually long length of his nose. He was a competent attorney, but the notoriety he'd been receiving lately had made him a trifle arrogant and it showed in the way he conducted himself, both in and out of the courtroom.

"Your next witness, Mr. Frawley?" the judge asked, and for the next few minutes the spectators had to watch Tom Frawley, Judge Worth, and John Scott repeat the same routine they had just gone through as Tom Frawley called Harold V. Dustin and then Luke Barnett to the stand.

Disgusted, and a little weary by now, Judge Worth straightened and looked at the clock.

"Since it's a little after twelve, I suggest we recess for lunch," he said. "We'll convene again at one-fifteen," and his gavel came down with a force that made Jeanine wince.

Jeanine stared at the back of Griff's head, then felt her heart sink as Sheriff Higgens stood up, motioning for Griff to stand too, and Jeanine watched unhappily as Griff and the deputies followed the sheriff out. She'd been hoping to have lunch with him, or at least get to talk to him during the recess. Now it was impossible, and she turned her attention to the judge, who, to her surprise, reached into one of the desk drawers, drew out a sandwich wrapped in brown paper, then gestured for someone to bring him a cup of coffee.

"Are you going to eat anything?" Cory asked, leaning close so Jeanine could hear him.

Since the judge had called recess, the room had erupted into a cacophony as people who didn't want to lose their seats also pulled out lunches and began speculating on who would be called next.

"I'd rather just have some fresh air," Jeanine said, trying to shut out some of the noise. "But I'm afraid we might lose our seats."

"Nonsense," the housekeeper said as she leaned around Cory, joining in the conversation. "They have to let us in, my dear, we're prime witnesses." She stood up. "I'd like some fresh air too. Shall we go?" Jeanine and Cory both got up, and Cory leaned over and asked John if he'd like to join them. He declined, saying he had work to do, so they followed Mrs. Brandt, who was threading her way through the crowd toward the back door.

Once outside, Cory decided fresh air wasn't enough for him and headed for the Lone Star saloon while Jeanine and the housekeeper worked their way toward the side of the building. It was almost as crowded out here as it had been in the courtroom. The newspaper office where the children were holding school was directly across the street, and they'd been let out for lunch too. Now, their sandwiches eaten, they had come over to play in the schoolyard, and were running about, getting in everyone's way. The girls were enjoying a game of Simon Says, but the boys' favorite game seemed to be playing sheriff, and at the moment they were pretending to hang one of their friends from a small tree near the back of the play yard. Jeanine watched them, then shivered, turning away.

"Don't let them bother you, Jeanine," Mrs. Brandt said when she saw the effect the children's play was having on her. "They're only pretending. Don't worry, he won't hang."

Jeanine stared at her, frowning. "How can you be so sure?"

"I have faith," she replied calmly. "Besides, Damian would never let him hang."

Jeanine wasn't so sure. Griff had explained to her how he'd saved Damian's life out on the range some ten years before when he'd been trampled by a wild mustang, and the two had become close friends. The accident had left Damian's right leg crippled, but it hadn't deterred him from finishing his law studies and going on to become a judge. But even though they were still friends, Griff told her he was certain Damian's integrity would never be compromised.

"All he'll do, Jeanine, is make sure the trial's a fair one," he'd said last night, and Jeanine was inclined to believe him, in spite of what the town and Mrs. Brandt thought.

"I wish I were as sure as you," she told the housekeeper. "But I'm afraid Judge Worth doesn't strike me as the sort of man who'd compromise his principles. Not even for a friend."

Mrs. Brandt's lips tightened. "Perhaps you're right," she said softly. "Who knows?" Then she looked directly at Jeanine, her eyes strangely warm. "You know, I'm not much for sentimentality, my dear," she said abruptly, "but there's something I've been wanting to say to you ever since this happened, and I hope you won't mind. You see, Griff's like a son to me, Jeanine. I've seen him waste so many years in a loveless marriage with that horrible woman. Oh yes, Rhetta was lovely to look at, I know, but . . . well, you were under the same roof with her long enough to know what she was like." Her eyes softened even more as she looked at Jeanine. The housekeeper was wearing a small black hat atop her braided coronet and it was tied beneath her chin, making her look strangely young. "When you first came, Jeanine, and I saw the way Griff looked at you . . . I warned him, my dear, but he wouldn't listen. Now, I know none of this was your fault, so all I ask is that you stick by him so that if he's acquitted, he'll have you to turn to. It'd be a shame if Rhetta's death accomplished nothing."

Jeanine frowned, puzzled by the housekeeper's sudden friendliness.

"Please, my dear. I know you love him, and I know he loves you." Her voice was low, hushed, so no one else would hear. "All I ask is that when this is all over, you make it up to him for the years he's lost." She reached out and took Jeanine's hand. "Will you do that for me, please?"

Jeanine nodded, unable to find words. Mrs. Brandt's sudden show of friendship was disconcerting, to say the least, and now Jeanine suddenly felt guilty for having told John about her conversation with Crystal that was so incriminating against the housekeeper. At least for a moment she did; then, a few minutes later, after Cory returned and they made their way back into the courtroom, she began to go over her conversation with Mrs. Brandt again, and after settling down in their seats, as Griff was ushered back in again, and the hands on the clock moved to one-fifteen, she just wasn't sure what she believed anymore, and she looked up abruptly as court convened and Tom Frawley called Cory to the stand.

It was late evening and Griff sat in his cell staring across at the empty cell beside him, letting his thoughts run back over the afternoon in court. Tom Frawley had torn Cory's testimony apart after only the first few questions, and Griff had been sick about it. He closed his eyes, remembering the look on Cory's face when the prosecutor had asked him where he was when he heard Rhetta scream. Naturally Cory told the truth, and as Griff thought back over it now, he realized that even the truth sounded incriminating, and he wished he hadn't let his guard down in front of Cory and Mrs. Brandt that night and taken Jeanine in his arms, because Tom Frawley had been quite adept at getting Cory to tell about that too, even though Cory did so reluctantly. But then, what did it matter? He knew now John had been right. Even if he and Jeanine had tried to keep their feelings hidden, it never would have worked.

Griff got up off the cot and strolled to the window, staring through the bars into the night sky. At least he could thank God John was able to undo some of the damage during his cross-examination of Cory so that the jury knew the true facts. Only the question now was: did they believe the truth when they heard it?

Cory and Mrs. Brandt had both come to see him earlier, just before leaving for Trail's End, and Jeanine had stopped by right after dinner. He thought back over her visit. If he didn't have her, he'd go crazy being cooped up in here. But just the thought that maybe a miracle would happen and he'd get out of all this and be able to be with her kept him going.

He frowned as he remembered Damian's cold eyes appraising him off and on during the trial. Damian hadn't come to see him since arriving in town, but Griff could understand his reasoning. It was bad enough the whispering had started the minute the judge arrived; if he'd come by to say hello to his old friend, they'd have protested all the way to the governor. As it was, they were watching the proceedings closely, ready to yell foul at the slightest hint that Judge Worth was being partial to him.

Griff walked back over and dropped onto the bed. He was weary and troubled, yet knew he needed sleep, because from what John said when they had gone over everything right after the day's proceedings, tomorrow wasn't going to be any better than today had been. He closed his eyes.

At ten the next morning, Griff sat next to John again in the courtroom and watched Mrs. Brandt walk to the witness stand. Her face was unreadable, eyes intense as she repeated the oath with her hand on the Bible, then sat down.

As usual, the first part of her testimony was routine; then Tom Frawley began his questions in earnest, and Mrs. Brandt didn't fare much better at his hands than Cory had. Griff tried to read the faces of the jurors during her testimony, but it was hard. Their eyes revealed little of what they might be thinking, and it wasn't until halfway through Tom Frawley's questioning of her that they showed signs that they were even listening to what was being said. Tom Frawley had just asked Mrs. Brandt how they happened to hire Miss Grayson, and Theola Brandt looked him straight in the eye without flinching.

"She was recommended by a mutual friend," she answered calmly.

"A friend of the family?"

"Not exactly."

"The friend's name, Mrs. Brandt?"

She hesitated a moment and looked directly at Griff before finally answering. "Philip Sheridan," she said quite distinctly, and Judge Worth had to call for the courtroom to quiet down as a buzz of whispering erupted.

"Philip Sher . . ." Frawley straightened in surprise, his eyebrows raised. "Do you mean General Philip Sheridan of the United States Army? The man who was just recently appointed military commander of the states of Texas and Louisiana?" he asked incredulously.

"Yes, sir," she answered calmly, and it was obvious Tom Frawley hadn't anticipated her answer.

"And how did this come about, Mrs. Brandt?"

"It's quite simple," she answered, her curt manner once more in control. "Griff and I happen to know General Sheridan from before the war, when Zebediah Heywood sold horses to the army. After the war ended, I wrote to him for Griff, hoping we could resume trading again since things weren't going too well at the ranch financially, and in the the letter I happened to mention that we were looking for a governess for Master Garfield. He suggested Miss Grayson, so we hired her."

"I see, and how did General Sheridan happen to know Miss Grayson?"

"That you'll have to ask her," she answered.

Griff knew Frawley was irritated by the way his eyes narrowed, and he was hoping the prosecutor would get off the subject of Jeanine's connection to General Sheridan, which he did. However, he didn't drop the subject of Jeanine, and Griff felt anger surging inside him as he sat at the defense table and listened to Tom Frawley trying to get Mrs. Brandt to admit that he was having an affair with Jeanine, even referring to her at one time as his mistress. A statement John quickly objected to, receiving a sustain from Damian, who was trying his best to be impartial.

Griff could tell that Frawley was frustrated. It was obvious he'd heard all the talk about town that something had been going on between him and Jeanine long before Rhetta's murder, yet so far he'd been unable to prove anything too incriminating on that score, and by the time he turned to John and said, "Your witness," he was glaring at Mrs. Brandt with hate-filled eyes.

Griff watched John stroll calmly up to the witness stand while Frawley went back to his seat.

"Mrs. Brandt," John began reluctantly, "you told the prosecutor earlier that you went to the mine the night of Rhetta Heywood's murder to help with Master Garfield Heywood, is that right?"

"I did."

"Why did you think you had to help with the boy?" he asked abruptly.

She was startled. "What do you mean, why?"

"Mrs. Brandt. . . ." John straightened, then looked at her squarely. "When Miss Grayson, Mr. Heywood, and the men from Trail's End left to go to the mine, didn't both Mr. Heywood and the governess tell you that she was going along specifically to take care of the boy?"

"Well . . ." She was a little rattled and he knew it.

"Well what?" he asked.

"You see," she began, then stammered for a minute before going on. Her eyes shifted to Jeanine, then back to John. "Well, I just wasn't sure she could handle it alone," she answered, her voice steadying some. "You know how it is with young people."

John watched her closely. She'd slipped by that one. Now what? "All right, then, Mrs. Brandt, why did you take a rifle with you that evening when you left Trail's End, and why didn't you have one of the hands drive the buggy for you when you left?"

"Really, John, what on earth are you trying to do?" she asked haughtily. "What kind of a question is that?"

"Just answer it," John said, and Mrs. Brandt looked over at Judge Worth as if waiting for him to tell her she didn't have to, but he didn't cooperate.

"Answer the question, Mrs. Brandt," he said, agreeing with John.

Mrs. Brandt's hands clenched tightly on the handbag in her lap. "I have to?" she asked nervously.

Judge Worth nodded.

"All right, I didn't take anyone with me because I just didn't think of it, and I took the rifle in case I ran into Indians."

That's what he'd thought she would say. "Mrs. Brandt," he said deliberately, "when you left Trail's End that evening, did you tell the cook, Crystal Eaton, that you were going to see to it that Rhetta Heywood paid for what she had done to Griffin Heywood?"

"What the hell are you trying to do, John?" Griff suddenly yelled as he stood up, and Judge Worth grabbed for his gavel.

"Sit down, Griff," he ordered.

"The hell I will," Griff yelled. He looked at John. "What are you trying to do to her?" he demanded. "She didn't have any part in this. I told you that before."

"That's right, you did tell me," John said angrily. "But Crystal Eaton said that after you and the others left, she and your housekeeper got to talking and Mrs. Brandt became furious over what was happening, and when she left the house, telling her she was going to the mine, she also told her she was going to see to it that Rhetta paid for what she did, and she made sure the rifle she took was loaded. Don't you see, Griff, she left in plenty of time to get to the mine before you."

"But she didn't kill Rhetta. She wouldn't!"

"She's killed before!"

Judge Worth's gavel was pounding furiously. "Griff, sit down! Mr. Scott! We'll have order here!" He stood up and leaned forward, staring at all of them, and Griff slowly lowered himself to his seat, while John stood stockstill, breathing heavily, and Mrs. Brandt fidgeted nervously with her handbag. Judge Worth sat down, then looked over at Mrs. Brandt. "Mrs. Brandt, you will please answer counsel's question," he instructed her sternly.

Mrs. Brandt's eyes narrowed. "All right," she said, and looked at Griff for a moment, her eyes pleading. "I was angry when I left the house, yes, and I think if Rhetta had been there I would have killed her, because that's what I was planning to do. But by the time I reached the mine, I'd calmed down and realized if I did, it would only complicate matters all the more." She took a deep breath. "Besides, when I got there she was already dead."

John stared at her curiously. "Mrs. Brandt, you left Trail's End in plenty of time to get there before Griffin Heywood and the others, and yet you didn't get there until after they arrived. Why?"

"Indians."

"Indians?"

Mrs. Brandt's voice was steady. She was definitely in control. "Yes, Indians," she repeated. "The road from Trail's End to the mine cuts through that arroyo near the northeast border where the water hole is, and there was a small party of them halfway up the hillside. I was afraid they'd see me, so I pulled off the road into the woods and watched until they left, then went on. I'm afraid they must have been there at least half an hour or so."

"I see." John wasn't sure whether to believe her or not, but for now there was no way to dispute her testimony. "That's all," he said, and walked back toward his seat, feeling Griff's eyes leveling on him viciously.

"John, I told you—" Griff began as John sat down.

"Shhh . . ." John cautioned him. "We'll talk later," and he motioned to Tom Frawley, who was calling Warren Granger to the stand.

Griff drew his eyes from John's face and glanced behind him to where Mrs. Brandt had just sat back down in the chair beside Cory. Her face was pale, lips trembling, and suddenly she looked so old; the lines about her mouth, permanently etched, were so severe. He'd never paid much attention to her age before, but knew she was in her early fifties, yet at the moment she looked twenty years older.

He watched her for a long time out of the corner of his eye, then turned all the way to the front of the courtroom again as Tom Frawley's questioning of Warren caught his attention, and for the next half-hour he listened to Warren trying his best to make his sister sound like a saint who had been betrayed by her husband because of his love for another woman. It wasn't that he actually made statements accusing Griff, but Tom Frawley had a way of distorting the truth during questioning, and Warren went along with him gladly. About the only thing Warren didn't do during the testimony was reveal the fact that he knew Jarrod was really young Gar's father, and when Tom Frawley turned Warren over to John for cross-examination, there was little left for John to ask about the murder itself, so instead he concentrated on the fact that Warren, besides living at Trail's End as a freeloader, not only argued regularly with his sister but also had the opportunity himself to kill her.

"Isn't it true, Mr. Granger," John asked as he paced back and forth in front of the jury, "that as Garfield Heywood's next of kin, you are under the assumption that if Griffin Heywood dies, you will be able to return to Trail's End and continue as you have in the past?"

"I . . ." Warren was flustered. "I guess."

"Well, I'm afraid you're assuming wrong, Mr. Granger," John informed him complacently. "You see, Griffin Heywood has made it very clear to me that if he is convicted of your sister's murder and sentenced to hang, he will make a will barring you from ever living at the ranch, or off its profits in any way."

"That's not fair!" Warren's face was livid as he stared at Griff. "You have no right!"

Judge Worth's gavel sounded over Warren's protest, and Warren finally settled back in the chair again, anger stiffening his body, making his amber eyes shine.

However, John didn't let up on Warren's cross-examination, and when he asked, "How long does it take to ride from Trail's End to the abandoned mine where your sister was killed?" Warren began to squirm.

"An hour or so, I guess," he answered belligerently, and John continued.

"On horseback?"

"Yes."

"Then how is it you didn't arrive until after your sister was dead, since you left before anyone else did?"

"I told Mr. Frawley before. I was drunk, and wanted to clear my head, so I rode around some."

"Or was it that you did arrive at the mine before your brother-in-law? You and your sister were known to quarrel a great deal, weren't you, Mr. Granger? Tell me, did you argue that night, Mr. Granger? Were you mad at your sister for ruining things for you? Is that why you killed her, then ran away and pretended to ride in again minutes later? Or was it because you knew the defendant was coming and thought if he were hanged for her murder, you'd be able to stay at Trail's End? For which reason did you kill her, Mr. Granger?" John demanded, and by now everyone in the courtroom was holding his breath, and Griff was surprised Frawley hadn't raised any objections. Maybe it was because Warren was sweating profusely, his eyes misty with tears and he looked guilty as all hell.

"No . . . no . . . I didn't kill her! I didn't!" he finally yelled at John, then slumped back in the chair, wishing he had a drink to wash away the dry bitter taste in his mouth. He swallowed hard, trying to moisten his lips a little.

"That's all," John said, and walked back to the defense table, seemingly oblivious of the whispering that had once more begun in the courtroom.

Warren tried to slip unobtrusively from the witness chair and make his way back to his seat, but all eyes were on him. Then suddenly the courtroom became silent again as Jeanine Grayson was called to the stand.

Jeanine was wearing her green velvet suit today, with the little straw bonnet she'd had on the first day she arrived in Raintree, and she could feel her underthings sticking to her in the stuffy room as she made her way to the stand. She took the oath, sat down, and set her hand-bag in her lap, trying to appear calm, but her heart was racing like mad.

"You'll have to remember, she's an extremely hostile witness," Frawley reminded the judge, and Worth nodded.

"Your name?" he asked.

"Jeanine Grayson."

"Fine. Miss Grayson, you came to the town of Raintree for the purpose of being tutor, or governess if you will, to Master Garfield Heywood at the ranch known as Trail's End, is that right?"

"Yes."

"Good. Now, during the time you have been at Trail's End, have there been occasions when you and the defendant, Griffin Heywood, have been alone?"

Well, he certainly wasn't wasting any time, she thought, but answered his question. "Yes, sir."

"And has the defendant ever put his arms about you in an intimate manner, Miss Grayson?"

She glanced quickly at John, who nodded, silently urging her to answer. "Yes, sir."

A slight buzz erupted somewhere in the courtroom; then everything grew silent again.

"All right, Miss Grayson, shall we go further? Has Griffin Heywood ever kissed you?"

Jeanine felt her stomach knot, and the lump in her throat made her almost lose her voice, so that when she answered, only the prosecutor could hear.

"Speak up, Miss Grayson," Frawley urged, pleased with himself. "The jury has to hear too, you know."

She straightened, trying to build up a little more courage. "Yes, sir," she said loud enough this time for everyone to hear.

"You mean, yes, he kissed you?"

"Yes, sir."

"How many times?"

He was irritating her now, with his snide manner, and it was giving her courage she didn't know she had. "How should I know?" she snapped back. "I didn't keep score!"

There was a laugh somewhere in the back of the courtroom, and Griff could hear someone nearby stifling a chuckle.

"Then where were you when he kissed you the first time, Miss Grayson?"

She remembered what John had said about telling the truth all the way. "It was in the harness room of the barn," she answered, and Tom Frawley's eyebrows raised.

"I see." He studied her for a second, then continued. "Tell me, was that before or after the night he walked you back to town from the Independence Day dance? He did walk you back to your hotel room that night, didn't he, Miss Grayson?"

"Yes, he walked me back that evening, and he kissed me after that," she answered.

"You mean he kissed you after walking you back to your hotel room?"

"No . . . he kissed me after the night of the dance."

"I see. Now that the night of this particular dance has been brought up, Miss Grayson, may I ask you what took him so long to walk you back to town that evening, since I presume everyone in this courtroom knows where the dance was held, and that it should have taken Griffin Heywood less than an hour to reach town and return. You see, it seems from what I've been told by people who attended the dance that he was gone a considerably longer time than necessary. Can you explain why?"

"Maybe because we didn't walk very fast. I don't really know."

"Then he didn't decide to join you in your hotel room, Miss Grayson . . . you mean nothing else happened?"

"No . . . yes."

"Well, which is it?"

"He didn't come into my hotel room, but something else did happen." She glanced quickly at John, who nodded, a slight smile playing about the corners of his mouth.

"What happened, Miss Grayson?" he asked smugly, and she glared at him.

"Someone tried to kill him!" she announced boldly, and again the courtroom came alive, so that Judge Worth had to call for order.

This was what John had been waiting for. He knew Tom

Frawley would stumble right into it, and he also knew it would sound better coming out during Frawley's questioning rather than under his cross-examination.

"Are you telling me someone tried to kill Griffin Heywood that night?" Frawley asked, surprised.

"That's what I said."

His eyes mirrored his disbelief as he asked, "When and where?" and Jeanine proceeded to tell him the whole story. When she was through, he stared at her curiously for a minute; then his eyes narrowed. "How do you know they were trying to kill him, Miss Grayson?" he asked when her story seemed to be over.

"They were attacking him savagely with their gun butts, and might have beaten him to death, only I don't think they'd counted on his being as strong as he is or of my showing up when I did."

"Miss Grayson, if the defendant was attacked, as you've just told us, then when he returned to the dance, why wasn't it apparent to the people there that he'd been in a fight?"

"I have no idea," she answered, more calmly now. "Except that Griff was doing a good job of defending himself, and the only severe blow was rendered to the top of his head, toward the back, so I doubt it was ever noticed."

"Then you saw who the attackers were?"

"No, sir, but I know who hired them."

Frawley frowned. "You know?"

"Yes, sir," she answered, sure of herself for the first time since taking the stand, and her voice rose so everyone could hear. "It was Jarrod Vance and Rhetta Heywood." Her voice echoed across the room like a pistol shot, igniting an uproar among the spectators that had Judge Worth pounding uselessly on his desk again, and the prosecuting attorney so flabbergasted that all he could do was stare at her and shake his head, stunned, while at the defense table Griff breathed a sigh of relief and relaxed. At last it was out in the open, and now maybe things would finally go his way for a change.

19

It took Judge Damian Worth almost a full ten minutes to get the courtroom quiet again after Jeanine's shocking announcement. Ever since Rhetta's body had been brought in, neither Griff, nor Jeanine, nor anyone else connected with Trail's End had given out any information about what had really happened, except to tell the sheriff that Jeanine had been kidnapped and Griff had rescued her from the Comanche. As far as Rhetta's and Jarrod's part in the kidnapping, or anything else that went on, they had said nothing. When Griff was arrested, he'd merely stated his innocence, and when John arrived back in Raintree, he'd decided it was better that way. Now Jeanine's statement had jolted not only the spectators but also Tom Frawley.

When the courtroom finally quieted down enough so that things could resume, the prosecutor looked at Jeanine skeptically. He was more composed now, the shock somewhat absorbed.

"Are you trying to tell this court that the deceased, Rhetta Heywood, had paid someone to murder her husband?" he asked incredulously.

"I am," Jeanine answered. "And they almost succeeded later on, too."

"Later?"

"Yes, sir. That's why Griff . . . Mr. Heywood and I

were in the harness room," she explained quickly. "Some-one shot him and I was dressing the wound."

"You were . . ." Frawley cleared his throat, distinctly disturbed again, yet knew he had to go on. If he didn't, not only would the jury be confused but also people would think his reputation as a lawyer was nothing more than just a lot of talk. He glanced at the defense lawyer and saw the gleam in his eyes. Damn the man anyway. He had known all along . . . Well, there was nothing he could do about it now. Taking a handkerchief from his pocket, Frawley wiped his brow, then stuffed it back hastily so he could continue. "You say you were dressing a bullet wound? Couldn't he have merely cut himself?"

"And shot his horse out from under himself and walked all the way back to the ranch, all because he cut his arm? No, sir. It was a gunshot wound. I've seen them before. The bullet went right through the flesh on his upper arm. If he showed you now, there'd be a scar there yet. It still hasn't healed all the way."

"Who else knew he'd been shot?"

Jeanine glanced at Mrs. Brandt. "He told me not to tell anyone, and at the time, I didn't think anyone else knew. But I learned later that he told the housekeeper, Mrs. Brandt."

"Didn't that seem strange to you?"

"That he'd tell the housekeeper?"

"No, Miss Grayson, that he told you not to tell anyone."

"Not really," she answered. "He felt that if only the two of us knew, and someone else were to mention it, we'd know that person had to be the guilty party."

"I thought you said Rhetta Heywood was the guilty party."

"I did, but at the time he was shot, we didn't know it."

"And since no one else knew he'd been shot, we have only your word it happened, right?"

"Yes." She shrugged. "I guess. Unless you intend to ask Griff and Mrs. Brandt."

Frawley ignored her last remark. "Miss Grayson, you say that's why you were in the harness room, to tend a wound. Are you sure you couldn't be mistaken? Isn't it more logical, Miss Grayson, that your sole purpose in being there was to have a clandestine meeting with the defendant?''

"No, sir," she answered stubbornly.

"Yet you say he kissed you. Why? For treating his wound?" He began to badger her. "Did he kiss you as payment for services rendered, or because you asked him to, or maybe because that's what he was planning to do all along? Tell me, Miss Grayson, I'd like to know, why did he kiss you?"

She drew her eyes from the prosecutor's face and looked beyond him to where Griff was sitting. She needed his strength, and as his eyes caught hers and held, the look that passed between them carried his love right to her heart. She straightened and looked back into the prosecutor's dark blue eyes, unafraid again.

"I guess he kissed me simply because he wanted to," she said defiantly. "I didn't ask him!"

He turned away from her belligerent gaze. "Isn't it true, Miss Grayson, that from the day of your arrival at Trail's End you tried in every way you could to seduce the defendant?" he asked.

"That's not true!"

"You are in love with him, though, aren't you, Miss Grayson?"

Her voice faltered, but only slightly. "Yes, I am, but—"

"The yes is sufficient," he interrupted, silencing her. "Now, shall we go to this supposed disappearance of yours? You were gone from Monday evening until Friday evening, is that right?"

"Yes, sir, I was—"

"I didn't ask for anything else," he said, once more cutting her answer short.

Griff tensed as he saw Jeanine glare at the man. He was doing it on purpose, so her testimony would sound more incriminating. Thank God John would be able to cross-examine.

"Were you and Griffin Heywood together all Thursday night, Miss Grayson?" he asked.

"Yes, sir."

"Wednesday night?"

She was getting nervous. "Yes."

"Tuesday night?"

"No, sir."

"Not on Tuesday night? Then your rendezvous was sometime during the day on Wednesday, right?"

"It wasn't a rendezvous!"

"I ask you, Miss Grayson. Did you meet up with the defendant on Wednesday?"

"Yes, sir!"

"Where?"

"At the Indian camp where I was taken after the men who kidnapped me turned me over to the Comanche."

Tom Frawley smirked. "Come now, Miss Grayson. Isn't it a fact that the defendant had you taken there so the two of you could be together for a while without anyone back at the ranch knowing?"

"That's ridiculous!" she answered furiously. "He knew nothing about it."

"Then how did he know where to find you?"

"He didn't. He had to hunt for me."

"Miss Grayson, I believe it's a known fact that the defendant lived with the Indians at one time, and was practically one himself. In fact, if my information is right, the camp where you claimed to have been held was presided over by the same chief who had practically adopted the defendant as a boy. Therefore, how do you know the defendant didn't just arrange the whole thing?"

"Because he didn't!"

"If it wasn't planned, then why were you allowed to leave with him?"

"Because . . . he bargained with them and . . . and made arrangements."

"What kind of arrangements?"

"I don't know exactly," she answered, a little less sure of herself. "I don't speak Comanche."

Tom Frawley knew he'd come to a stalemate with this line of questioning, so decided to try another tack. "All right, then, let's go to the night of Rhetta Heywood's murder," he said as he looked at the jury, then watched the defendant's reaction to the question he was asking. "Mr. McBride said you were with him, waiting, when Rhetta Heywood screamed. Tell me, did you hear Rhetta Heywood scream, Miss Grayson?" he asked, and drew his eyes slowly from Griff's hard, piercing gaze to look back at his witness.

She nodded. "Yes."

"Fine. Now, Miss Grayson," he went on, "was it possible . . . in other words, would there have been enough time, if the defendant were guilty, for him to have reached his wife before you heard her scream, plunge the knife into her, then be calmly waiting when you and Mr. McBride arrived on the scene?"

"You already asked Cory that."

"And now I'm asking you. Will you please answer?"

"But that's not what—"

"Miss Grayson," he interrupted, "was there enough of a time lapse or not?"

She licked her lips, then glared at him. "Naturally," she answered, and it was obvious she was upset. "But he didn't—"

"That's all, Miss Grayson." Frawley stared at her hard for a minute, as if he were puzzled about something. "Miss Grayson, I'd like to go back to the night of the dance we were discussing before," he suddenly said, and Jeanine frowned as Griff turned to John.

"What's he up to, John?" he asked. "And who told him about the dance anyway?"

John shook his head. "Shhh . . . he's probably heard talk. Listen, we'll find out."

"Miss Grayson, everyone I've talked to regarding that evening, either on this witness stand or when I was preparing this case, has told me that the defendant, Griffin Heywood, walked you back to your hotel room because Warren Granger, who had escorted you to the dance that evening, became drunk, caused a disturbance, and was rendered unconscious by the defendant, yet no one has told me what the disturbance was about, except that it did have something to do with you, Miss Grayson, am I right?''

Griff had seen Jeanine's face slowly lose color while Frawley was explaining the question, and now he held his breath, staring at her uncomfortably.

.''Miss Grayson, did you hear me?'' Frawley asked, surprised himself by how pale she suddenly looked.

''I heard you,'' she half-whispered, and he made her repeat the answer.

''All right, Miss Grayson. Since you heard me, then will you please answer the question? Did the commotion that evening have anything to do with you?''

She took a deep breath, then answered, ''Yes.'' She just couldn't perjure herself.

''In what way?'' he asked curiously.

She glanced over at Warren, then looked at John, her eyes pleading, but he looked as confused and anxious to hear her answer as Frawley was. Now she wished she and Griff had told him everything.

''I'm waiting, Miss Grayson.''

Her chin tilted upward. ''Warren Granger accused me of being someone other than who I am,'' she answered, trying to sound confident.

Frawley scowled, staring at her, rubbing his chin thoughtfully, as if trying to sort something out in his mind; then he wiped his hand across the top of his mustache. ''Miss Grayson,'' he finally asked, ''I was told by a number of people that when you first came to Raintree, and right up until the day of your supposed disappearance, you wore glasses, is that right?'' he asked.

Jeanine nodded. ''Yes.''

''What happened to them?''

''I lost them when I was kidnapped.''

''And you haven't had to replace them?''

''They have to be ordered from back east.''

''I see. You can see all right without them?'' he asked.

''Well enough.''

He seemed to ponder her answer momentarily, then went on. "All right, Miss Grayson, back to the confrontation at the dance. The information I have states that the defendant, Griffin Heywood . . . shall we say *interfered* with Warren Granger when Mr. Granger lunged at a gentleman named Homer Beacon, who was the owner of the newspaper in Raintree, is that right?"

"Why didn't you ask Warren?"

"Because I'm asking you. Now," he pressed the issue again, "did Warren Granger try to attack a gentleman named Homer Beacon?"

There was no way she could avoid answering. "Yes," she said reluctantly.

"That's better." The prosecutor strutted arrogantly toward where the jury was, at the right of the judge, where the choir usually sat for Sunday services; then he turned back to his witness. "Now, Miss Grayson," he said as he strolled back toward her slowly, "I also realize, after going over a few facts in my head, that the newspaperman, Homer Beacon, was accidentally killed the day after your supposed disappearance, and you know, I'm beginning to wonder if perhaps there wasn't some sort of a connection between the two of you. Was there, Miss Grayson? I'd like you to tell me the answer, please."

That was it. What course did she have to take? She put her head down and rubbed her forehead for a minute, trying to muster the strength to go on, then looked up again at Tom Frawley.

"Homer . . . that is, Mr. Beacon and I were trying to discover who was making the attempts on Griffin Heywood's life and I guess we got a little too close to the truth," she answered. "It wasn't until after Griffin Heywood rescued me from the Indians that we learned that Jarrod Vance had murdered Homer so he wouldn't talk."

"That's a lie!" Miles shouted from the end of the first row of spectators, and he stood up, shaking his fist. "You're lyin'! Jarrod didn't kill nobody!"

Again Judge Worth had to reestablish some kind of order while John turned to Griff.

"You knew this?" he asked.

This time it was Griff who cautioned John, "Not now. Listen . . ."

And as the room quieted, Frawley turned to Jeanine again.

"Miss Grayson, I'm puzzled," he said. "Why were you and Mr. Beacon trying to discover who was trying to, as you say, kill the defendant?"

"Because we were his friends."

His eyes narrowed shrewdly. "Miss Grayson, when did you first meet Homer Beacon?" he asked, and Jeanine glanced over at Griff, shaking her head dismally, then looked back at Tom Frawley.

"I've known him for a number of years," she answered reluctantly, and heard the whispering begin again.

"How did you happen to know him?"

"He worked as my manager and accompanist."

His eyebrows raised in surprise. "Explain that for the jury, please, Miss Grayson?" he asked, and she knew it was for his benefit, not the jury's. He realized he was stumbling into something the defense was evidently trying to keep secret, and he was enjoying seeing her squirm.

"I was a singer, and he played piano while I sang," she answered. "And he also took care of my bookings."

"Your bookings? But I was led to understand that you were, or are, a schoolteacher. Have you ever taught school, Miss Grayson?" he asked.

She sighed. "Only at Trail's End."

Tom Frawley's eyebrows lifted. "You're really a dance-hall girl?" He'd really been taken by surprise, and was just about to comment further on this new turn of events when Warren suddenly stood up, and Jeanine felt her heart drop to her stomach. Warren's eyes were on her, devouring her intensely, and she knew the charade was finally over.

"I knew it!" Warren cried triumphantly as his eyes locked with hers. "I knew it was you!" he yelled. "Homer said no, but I knew he was lying." He straightened arrogantly while Judge Worth tried to get his attention.

"Mr. Granger!" the judge said, addressing Warren, who was still standing staring at Jeanine. "Will you please either sit down or tell this court what you're talking about?"

Warren smiled, chuckling bitterly to himself, and Griff wished he could strangle him.

"Your honor," Warren finally said, addressing the judge, "and Mr. Frawley . . ." He was playing the moment for all it was worth and Jeanine hated him for it. "May I introduce the lady on the witness stand." He straightened arrogantly, eyes still bloodshot from last night's drinking. "May I introduce you to a Union spy and Confederate traitor, the woman who stole military plans from me, and who knows how many others like me. A woman I'm sure you've all heard of, a woman who should be hanged for her name alone . . . let me introduce you to the one and only infamous Jeannie Gray!" and he gestured dramatically toward Jeanine.

A hush fell over the courtroom and Jeanine felt all eyes centered on her; then she bit her lip, gulping back tears. She wasn't going to cry. She couldn't. She just couldn't let them know what they were doing to her.

The prosecutor was staring at her too, and now he scowled in disbelief. "Miss Grayson, is Mr. Granger right?" he asked as the unusual silence continued to pervade the courtroom.

"Yes, he's right," she answered helplessly, and John shot to his feet.

"Your honor, I request a recess," he said, his face livid, and without waiting for any further comments from anyone, since it was close to noon, Judge Worth called recess until one, and the moment his gavel hit the desk the whole room exploded in one big uproar.

John leaned over toward Dave Higgens, his eyes intense. "I'm expecting you to see that Miss Grayson reaches the jailhouse in one piece," he said hurriedly. "I'll go with Griff and your deputies. But I want her to be there as quick as you can get her there, understand?"

Dave nodded, and rushed from his seat to where Jeanine still sat in the witness chair watching the faces on the crowd that, although still in a mild state of shock, had suddenly become overly hostile.

Judge Worth stood up as quickly as he could with his bum leg, and scurried around the desk he was using, grabbing his cane from beside his chair on the way, and he moved over beside the chair Jeanine was in.

His eyes caught Sheriff Higgens. "I'll go with you," he said quickly, and Dave Higgens, taken by surprise, nodded; then, before Jeanine could sort out what was happening, she was whisked from the chair and escorted out the side door, down the steps, around to the back of the building, and toward the jail, with the judge on one side of her and the sheriff on the other.

It took Griff and John a little longer to make their way down the street and through the crowd, so that by the time they reached the jailhouse, Jeanine had calmed down some. But her hands were still shaking.

"I'd like to talk to Griff and Jeanine alone, if you don't mind," John told Dave once the outside door was shut.

Dave nodded. "It'll have to be back in Griff's cell."

"Then it'll be in the cell."

Judge Worth glanced at John. "I'd like to come along if I could, John. May I?"

John frowned. "It's not ethical."

"Hell, nothing about this whole trial's ethical," he remarked. "But I might be able to help."

"Come on, then," John said, and Dave led the four of them to the cell where Griff was being held, then left.

"You know what you're letting yourself in for, don't you, Damian?" Griff said as he watched his friend maneuver himself into a position so he could sit on one of the cots without his leg making him look too awkward.

Damian smiled. "I've had worse problems." He looked at Jeanine, who had taken off her straw bonnet and was staring into space absentmindedly. "Come sit down, Miss Grayson," he said, motioning toward the cot opposite him. "I'm sure John isn't going to make you stand up while we talk."

"No, go ahead, sit down," John said, then turned his

eyes to Griff, who was leaning back against the cell door
that had just closed. "Why?" John asked angrily. "Goddammit, Griff, why didn't you tell me who she really
was?" he shouted.

"What would you have done if I had?"

John took a deep breath, his eyes blazing.

"He's right, John," Damian cut in. "What could you
have done, except walked out and left Griff on his own?"

John glared at Jeanine. She was holding the straw hat on
her lap, fingering it nervously, her eyes cast down, and
he'd swear he saw a tear on her cheek. "How long have
you known, Griff?" he asked, looking once more at his
client.

"I suspected it right after she arrived, and she told me
on our way back from Chief Horse Back's camp." Griff
straightened and walked over, standing next to Jeanine.
"Don't hate her, John," he said. "She was doing her job
just like the rest of us, that's all."

"Was she?" he asked. "I wouldn't call betraying people who trusted her the same as fighting for your life on
the battlefield."

Jeanine glanced up at him. "I suppose the South didn't
have any spies in the North, is that it?" she asked, trying
to defend herself. "Are you trying to say the North is the
only one who played dirty? Mr. Scott, war isn't nice any
way you look at it. It never was. And I haven't always
been proud of the way I had to accomplish some of the
assignments I had, either. You must know that. But it was
the only way I knew to help my country when I thought it
needed help. And I'm sure if you had been asked to do
the same thing for the South, you'd have done it."

"Well, John?" Damian asked. "Would you have done
the same thing if you'd been asked?"

John stared at him. "Dammit, Damian, that isn't the
point. The point is that she helped us lose the war, and I'm
supposed to just sit here acting like she never did a damn
thing." He looked at Griff. "You can love her, knowing
what she's done?" he asked.

"That's your whole trouble, John," Griff said stubbornly. "To you everything has to be black and white, there's never any allowances for being human."

"That's not true."

"John, you're a lawyer," Griff reminded him. "You live by facts and rules. All right, then, I'll give you facts. Fact number one is that you liked Jeanine right from the first moment you met her, didn't you?"

John's eyes narrowed as he stared at Griff.

"And fact number two is that right up until the minute you learned who she really was, you still liked her, right?"

"Look, Griff," John answered, "this has nothing to do with whether I like her or not. This has to do with the fact that the war may be over on paper, but not to the people of this town, and you know it. We'd have gone on fighting until our last breath if we had to, and there are people out there who've lost sons because of her and others like her. I lost a brother. You can't just brush all that aside as if it never happened. It isn't that easy. There's too much hate for it to disappear as if it never existed."

Damian glanced over at Jeanine, then looked at John. "It won't disappear at all if you don't let it, John," he said. His voice was low and deeply resonant, and Jeanine glanced over as he kept talking. "Griff was right, you know, John," he went on. "Miss Grayson is the same woman now as the woman who took the stand a short while ago. I realize that for some people the war will be a long time ending. None of the rest of us like losing, any more than you." He frowned. "Do you think I like working with Yankees? Men that I know helped beat the Confederacy into the ground? But there's another side of the coin too. Before the war, this was one country and we got along pretty well, even though we had differences. We can do it again, too, only we aren't going to get any place unless we work at it. Loyalty is fine, but stubborn bull-headedness never got anyone anywhere. We're still the South, John, even though they've taken our name away. We always will be. But like Griff says, the war's over, and the forgiving and forgetting have to start somewhere."

John's dark green eyes had faded toward gray, and his

jaw was clenched hard beneath the frosted sideburns. "There are men out there who'd give anything to see her dead, Damian," he reminded him bitterly. "Can you ignore that?"

"No, I can't ignore it. But I can sure as hell try to keep them from accomplishing it. You know yourself, John, that hate never served any good purpose. So she was a spy. So were a lot of other people on both sides. So does that mean we should track every one of them down and hang them?" Damian's eyes glinted shrewdly. "And you can't tell me you can stand here looking at Jeanine Grayson, John, and not realize that when the war ended, Jeannie Gray ceased to exist too."

John ran a hand through his dark curly hair and straightened, taking a deep breath. He glanced over at Jeanine. She was watching him, her eyes misty and pleading. Dammit all anyway, why did something like this have to happen? Her eyes were such a beautiful color of blue, and right now she looked so vulnerable. Suddenly a pang of guilt ran through him. Damn! He'd conditioned himself to hate Yankees, and someone like Jeannie Gray . . . Yet, he had liked her . . . did like her.

He frowned. "All right, all right. I admit I can't go on hating forever." He flushed, and his voice lowered. "I guess I have to start somewhere, but it sure as hell goes against the grain."

Griff smiled sheepishly. "Thanks for understanding, John" he said.

John shook his head. "That's just the trouble, Griff," he said. "I don't understand. If you had just told me right from the start, maybe . . ."

"I probably would have, John, only I knew what your reaction would be, and I was afraid you wouldn't listen to reason. We were hoping it wouldn't come up during the trial."

John took a deep breath. "And now that it has?"

"I suggest you make sure someone keeps a close eye on Miss Grayson," Damian said. "As you reminded all of us, John, I'm afraid the rest of Raintree won't be as tolerant and reasonable about this as you've been."

"You're right there." John glanced over at Griff. "And I think we'd better have a long talk and go over a few things before we go back into the courtroom this afternoon. I don't want any more surprises thrown at me. This time I want to know it all. I don't intend to look like a fool again."

Damian stood up rather awkwardly, using the cane. "I don't think you'll need me anymore," he said.

Griff walked to the cell door with him, while Damian called for Dave to let him out. "I'm glad you're here, Damian," Griff said while they waited for the sheriff. "It helps."

Damian's face suddenly softened, his hazel eyes solemn. "When I saw your name on the report that came in, I didn't know what to do at first, Griff," he said, his voice filled with emotion. "I just couldn't believe it. You know how it is. You know someone for so long, at least you think you do. Then I realized that the years can change people, and besides, even close friends can't always know what's in another man's heart, not deep down inside, anyway. We all have secret parts to ourselves we don't let others see, and I know where love and emotions are concerned, anything's possible. So I decided the only way I could still show you that friendship doesn't always condone blindly, yet loves unselfishly was to see that your trial was fair. I decided that if you hang, Griff, it won't be because an ambitious lawyer wanted to make a name for himself, or a town needed a scapegoat, or a disinterested judge didn't want to take the time, or a corrupt judge could be bought off, or someone was just looking for vengeance. If you hang, Griff, it'll be because you're guilty, and only because you're guilty. I'll see to that."

"I didn't kill her, Damian," Griff said, his voice steady, and their eyes met and held as Dave came to unlock the door for the judge.

Damian drew his eyes from Griff. "Let's let a jury decide that, shall we, Griff?" he said abruptly, then straightened, his face like granite again, the warmth that had been in his eyes only a short time before replaced by a cold hardness that was unyielding.

Dave opened the cell door to let him out, and Griff watched Dave shut the cell door behind Damian; then he frowned, his eyes following his old friend as Damian limped toward the hall that separated the cells from Dave's outer office, Damian's last words running through his head. Let the jury decide? It was going to be even harder now, and he turned back, joining Jeanine and John Scott, who were trying the best they could to become friends again.

When court once more convened, a little after one o'clock, the atmosphere was far different from what it had been during the morning session. Hostility hung in the air, the spectators as well as the jury tense with emotion, as if waiting for something more to happen.

Neither Jeanine, nor John, nor Griff had eaten anything during the recess. Not that they couldn't have asked Dave to have something brought over from the Steak House, but after all that had happened that morning, food just didn't sound appealing to them.

Now Jeanine sat in the witness chair again, facing Tom Frawley, and suddenly wished she'd at least had some coffee or something hot, because her stomach was cramping and fluttering wildly as the prosecutor opened his mouth to begin the questioning again after it was determined that Jeanine was still under oath.

"Miss Grayson, excuse me," Frawley began, "but is Jeanine Grayson your real name, or is Jeannie Gray your real name?"

"It's Jeanine Grayson," she answered calmly. At least she hoped her voice didn't show the turmoil she felt inside.

"All right, then, Miss Grayson," he continued, "before we recessed, you told this courtroom that the altercation at the dance the evening of September 16 happened because

Warren Granger accused you of being someone else. Was
that someone else Jeannie Gray, Miss Grayson?''

"Yes."

"I see." Frawley straightened smugly. "And are you
. . . or should I say *were* you known at one time as
Jeannie Gray?"

"It was my stage name, yes."

"Your stage name." He cleared his throat. "And was it
also the name you used during the war in order to spy on
Confederate soldiers and—"

"Objection!" protested John. "The fact that the witness
was at one time known as Jeannie Gray has no bearing on
the case whatsoever."

"Sustained!" Damian replied, and Tom Frawley's eyes
narrowed viciously.

He'd have to think of another way to present it. "All
right, Miss Grayson, then when was the first time you met
Warren Granger, the murder victim's brother?"

"Objection!" John cut in again. "When Miss Grayson
met Mr. Granger has no relevance to the fact that Mr.
Granger's sister was murdered."

"On the contrary," Frawley argued. "It has every relevance since defense counsel himself tried to intimidate the
murder victim's brother, and it could very well be a factor
in establishing a motive for his sister's murder."

Damian frowned, then nodded toward Frawley. "Overruled," he said quickly. "Continue, Mr. Frawley."

For the next few minutes Tom Frawley took Jeanine
back over those three days in Richmond when her life had
touched Warren's so briefly, yet caused so much damage,
and when he was through, she suddenly realized that the
guilt she had been harboring earlier, over her part in the
war, had slowly been replaced by anger. Anger, because
as she glanced over at the intense faces of the jurors, and
the spiteful faces of the spectators, who were watching and
waiting for every little juicy tidbit they could condemn her
for, she knew in her heart that not one person in that room
had lived a life free from involvement in the war in one
way or another, and many may have done worse than she,

in the name of the Confederacy, and yet she was the only one who was being made to account for her actions. She tensed, her jaw tightening stubbornly, hoping Tom Frawley was through with her, but she should have known better.

He straightened, rubbing a finger across the top of his mustache again as he studied her for a minute, his eyes sifting over her pale gold hair that was once more in a tight bun at the nape of her neck. He took a deep breath.

"Miss Grayson," he asked, his eyes narrowing shrewdly. "you stated before that you are in love with the defendant, is that right?"

She eyed him apprehensively. "Yes."

"Then tell me, Miss Grayson, has the defendant ever told you that he's in love with you?"

She wanted to hit him. "Yes," she half-whispered so softly that the prosecutor could barely hear.

"Louder, for the jury please, Miss Grayson," he said, raising his own voice.

"I said yes!" she snapped angrily, and Tom Frawley smirked.

"Then let me ask you, Miss Grayson . . ." He was toying with her like a cat with a mouse, and she knew it. "Has the defendant, Griffin Heywood, ever made love to you?" he asked, and this time she clenched her mouth tight, refusing to answer. "Miss Grayson, I'm waiting," he said, and glanced toward the jury, pleased because they were all leaning slightly toward the witness, and he knew they were eagerly anticipating what she'd say.

"I already told you he kissed me," she answered belligerently.

"Miss Grayson, that's not what I mean, and you know it."

"I do not!"

"Then let me put it in simpler language, Miss Grayson," he said irritably. "I was hoping to avoid the use of carnal words for the act, for the sake of the women in the courtroom, but I guess I'm going to have to be blunt." He hooked a thumb in the vest pocket of his brown suit and slouched back a little in a rather self-satisfied manner. "I ask you again, Miss Grayson, did the defendant, Griffin Heywood, ever have intimate sexual relations with you?''

Jeanine closed her eyes. Her face was hot, and she knew it was probably beet red.

''Well, answer, please!'' he insisted. Then she heard Damian's deep voice penetrating the ominous hush that had fallen over the courtroom.

''Please, Miss Grayson,'' he urged her. ''You'll either have to answer or be held in contempt of court.''

Jeanine opened her eyes slowly, then gazed over at Griff, and suddenly her hand flew up, curling into a fist, pressing hard against her mouth as Griff stood up and addressed Damian.

''I'd like to know if I might answer that question instead of the witness, your honor?'' he asked.

Damian frowned. ''This is highly irregular, Mr. Heywood,'' he said hesitantly, and frowned, glancing at the prosecutor. ''Mr. Frawley?''

Tom Frawley's eyes were also on Griffin Heywood, and he studied him curiously. He was evidently trying to be a gentleman and save the lady any more embarrassment than what she'd already had to suffer. Oh well, as long as the outcome was the same, it didn't really matter who gave him his answer. Frawley thought a moment longer. In fact, perhaps coming from the defendant himself, the answer might even be more incriminating.

''Mr. Frawley?'' Damian asked again.

''I guess I have no objections to the defendant answering the question, as long as he's duly sworn in,'' he answered. ''And you, Mr. Scott?'' Frawley asked.

Griff looked down at John.

''Do you know what you're doing?'' John asked.

''It's better I tell it, John,'' he said roughly. ''There's a chance they might understand.''

John sighed. ''All right, Griff. It's your life.''

Griff turned back to the judge. ''Do you want me to take the stand?''

''Mr. Frawley?'' Damian asked.

"I don't think that'll be necessary. I'm sure he can answer yes or no just as easily from where he is."

Damian nodded. "As you wish." He had the Bible taken over to Griff, who took his oath; then Tom Frawley addressed him, while Jeanine sat quietly in the chair watching.

"All right, Mr. Heywood," Frawley asked loudly, "did you ever have sexual relations with Jeanine Grayson?"

Griff stood tall and erect, but instead of answering right away, he once more addressed the judge. "May I answer in my own words, your honor?" he asked.

"In other words, you don't want to simply answer yes or no, is that right?"

"That's right, your honor."

Again Damian looked at the prosecutor. "Mr. Frawley?"

"Yes or no will suffice," Frawley replied.

"Objection!" yelled John. "The defendant is on trial for his life, and since the outcome of this trial could weigh heavily on the answer to the prosecutor's question, I believe the defendant should have the chance to explain his answer."

"I didn't know there was any explanation that would justify adultery, Mr. Scott," Frawley quipped snidely.

John's eyes darkened to a deep gray as he tried to ignore the prosecutor's remark. "Your honor?" he pleaded.

Damian leaned forward a little and stared at the two lawyers, then answered, "The defendant will be allowed to answer the question in his own way."

He nodded to Griff. "Mr. Heywood . . ."

"As Jeanine . . . Miss Grayson testified," he began, "she was taken to Chief Horse Back's camp when she was kidnapped, and as everyone knows by now, I went after her and tracked her to the camp. When I arrived, they had plans all ready to make her a slave, and that would have meant that the Indian braves could have forced her to submit to them whenever they wanted her to. I couldn't let that happen." His eyes were on Jeanine now, and although his voice faltered for a brief second, he went on. "If I had told them she was my son's teacher they would have simply told me to get him a new one, so I told them she and I were planning to get married. Having not seen me too many times over the years, and believing me when I told them that rumors of my being married already were false, they believed my story, only the chief insisted we get married before leaving camp. It was his way of testing me, I know, so I had no other choice. It was either a Comanche marriage ceremony or admit I was lying and we'd both lose our lives. I couldn't let that happen, so we went ahead with the wedding, and I'm sure everyone knows the fundamentals of a Comanche wedding ceremony.''

Tom Frawley crossed his arms and stared at Griff, a sneer on his face. ''No, Mr. Heywood, I'm afraid we don't, at least I don't,'' he said sarcastically. ''What are the fundamentals of a Comanche wedding ceremony.''

Griff took a deep breath as he stared at the man, then answered. ''The ceremony starts with a feast, dancing, and storytelling; then the bride is taken to the tent of her family and put to bed for the night, with all of her clothes removed. If the bridegroom is able to slip by the sleeping members of the bride's family, take off his clothes, climb into bed with her . . . and make love to her,'' he said, his voice breaking slightly, ''when morning comes they are considered husband and wife.'' He paused for a moment, then went on, his eyes looking directly into Jeanine's again. ''Chief Horse Back chose his own tent and his own family for Jeanine, since she's not Indian.'' Again his voice broke. ''May God help me,'' he blurted huskily, ''I couldn't lie beside her all night without touching her!'' His eyes moved once more to Frawley. ''Yes, I made love to her!'' he answered, his eyes blazing with emotion. ''I slept with her, and I made love to her. So now you know!'' and the courtroom grew so silent Jeanine could hear the clock on the wall above the jurors' heads ticking loudly.

John held his breath, watching Frawley closely, wondering if he was going to expand on the question any further, and hoping to God he wouldn't. What Griff had just told the courtroom didn't sound half as incriminating as their night in the hotel would, and John sighed, relieved, as Damian asked the prosecutor if he wanted to ask the defendant any more questions. He declined.

"Then we'll go on," Damian said quickly, and ordered Griff to sit down, then turned the questioning over once more to Mr. Frawley.

The prosecutor stared at Jeanine for a minute, then sighed and turned to John. "She's your witness, Mr. Scott," he said curtly, and walked back to his seat smiling, satisfied that the jury now had their motive all wrapped up for them.

John's cross-examination of Jeanine was strained. Not only because of his own personal feelings but also because he felt as if he had betrayed them both by not being able to somehow stop Frawley from making it look like Griff had killed Rhetta so he could have Jeanine. Yet he had known before going into court that it was only a vague million-to-one chance that they could have avoided what had just happened.

What John had to do now, and he knew it, was try to salvage what they had going for them, and make the jury believe they were telling the truth. So the first part of her cross-examination by John carried her through the whole sequence of events from the evening Warren first brought her the message that was a trap and ended up with her being kidnapped, right up to the moment she and Cory found Griff standing over Rhetta's dead body at the old copper mine on the Vance property.

"Now," John went on, "let's go back to after you and Griffin Heywood returned to Trail's End after being held captive at the copper mine, where you say Jarrod Vance told you that he and Rhetta Heywood were in love, and had been trying to get rid of Griffin Heywood. You said Warren Granger left Trail's End first, and you said that after he left, the rest of you went to the Vance ranch, the Double V Bar, where Jarrod was shot; then all of you rode on to the mine. Tell me, Miss Grayson, what kind of mood was Warren Granger in when he left Trail's End that evening?"

"He was furious, and he'd been drinking."

"And did he threaten to do anything?"

"He said he was going to the mine to find out just what was really going on."

"Miss Grayson, you have been in this area long enough to know where Trail's End is located, as well as the Double V Bar. And you know where the abandoned copper mine is in relation to them. Now, do you think it was possible for Warren Granger to ride to the mine and arrive there before anyone else, kill his sister, then run off and double back, pretending he'd just gotten there after the rest of you arrived?"

"Objection!" yelled Frawley. "He's asking for an opinion."

"On the contrary," John said, addressing Damian. "I'm merely trying to find out, as Mr. Frawley did earlier with the witnesses, if there was a sufficient time lapse for it to be plausible."

"Overruled," Damian said, and lifted his hands, resting his chin on them as he watched John finishing his cross-examination of Jeanine.

"All right, let's clear up another mystery, Miss Grayson, if possible," John said. "Mr. Miles Vance has been telling everyone around town that Griffin Heywood rode into his ranch yard that night and began shooting, causing the death of his son. You were there at the time, were you not?"

"Yes, sir."

"Did you see who shot first?"

"I didn't see who was holding the gun, but as Cory McBride told the court earlier, the first shot was fired from one of the windows. Since I've never been in the Vance home, I have no idea which room the window was in. Cory and Griff said it was the kitchen."

"But the first shot came from the house."

"Yes."

"Then what happened?"

"Griff jumped from his horse and hid behind what looked like a watering trough near the well; then some more shots were fired from the house. Griff finally fired back; then everything got quiet, and some lights started to go on in another building the men told me was the bunkhouse. The rest of us had ridden in closer to see if we could help, but when Griff came out of the house, he said Jarrod was dead, so we rode on to the mine.''

John stared at Jeanine for a minute, then straightened, satisfied.

"No more questions," he said, and went back to his seat.

"Any rebuttal?" Damian asked Tom Frawley, but the prosecutor shook his head. "Then you may return to your seat, Miss Grayson."

Jeanine's legs felt wobbly as she finally stood up. She'd been in the witness chair for an extremely long time, and had had to go through so much that for a minute she had to steady herself, using the arm of the chair. Then, mustering all the courage she could, she finally made her way to her seat behind Griff. She could feel everyone's eyes on her, and it was hard not to just turn around and scream at them to get out of her life, to quit hurting her, that it wasn't fair.

"Do you have any more witnesses, Mr. Frawley?" Damian asked, and Tom Frawley stood up, causing some tittering laughter in the courtroom when he called the sheriff's wife, Alberta Higgens, to the stand.

Alberta was a plump woman, rather attractive, with hair the color of ginger, and big brown eyes. A few freckles still played across her nose, and there was a dimple in just one cheek. Being aware of it, she often smiled sideways, hoping it'd show. Most people liked Alberta, although her tongue did run away with her at times, and John frowned, watching her take the stand, wondering what the hell she had to do with Rhetta's murder.

However, once her name was out of the way and it was established that she was the sheriff's wife, he had his answer as Tom Frawley began questioning her, using Alberta to establish the fact that the Heywoods had been a close, loving couple.

"That is, they were up until recently," Alberta offered, and Tom Frawley looked pleased.

"Would you elaborate on that, Mrs. Higgens?" he asked.

Alberta fidgeted a bit, straightening her bodice and smoothing the skirt of her dark blue suit. She'd worn her church clothes today, and hoped they weren't too ostentatious for the occasion. Reaching up, she ran her fingers along one of the feathers in the front of her new hat. "Well," she began, and lowered her hand to her lap again, toying with the ties on her handbag, "the night of the dance that you were all talking about before, when Griff . . . that is, Mr. Heywood, walked the governess back to the hotel, he was gone well over two hours on a walk that shouldn't have even taken him an hour, going both ways, and when he got back I heard Rhetta ask him why he hadn't driven her instead. He said Miss Grayson wanted to walk, and he couldn't let her walk alone. That's when I heard Rhetta tell him she thought Miss Grayson looked quite capable of taking care of herself. Then she asked him what he was doing in Miss Grayson's hotel room that took him so long."

"Was she upset when she said it?"

"Upset?" Alberta rolled her eyes. "She was furious."

"What did the defendant do?"

"He just laughed. You know, sort of sarcastic like, and told her to quit trying to act like she was a jealous wife and behave herself, because she looked ridiculous. Then I'm afraid he saw me a short distance away and put his arm around her shoulder, trying to act like everything was all right. But it wasn't, I could tell," she added. "Rhetta was still fuming later on when the dance broke up and we all went to the house."

"Was that the first time you'd ever seen the defendant and his wife at odds?"

Alberta thought for a minute, then nodded. "Yes, sir, I believe it is," she answered firmly. "Everyone's always spoken of them as such an ideal couple. I know they didn't see much of one another durin' the war years. But she always said how he wrote so regularly, and since he came back . . . well, up until that night there'd never been any reason to even question that anything was wrong. They always seemed so much in love." She reached in her handbag and took out a handkerchief, wiping her nose. "Poor dear Rhetta," she sniffed. "It's so terrible."

"Thank you, Mrs. Higgens," Frawley said, and turned her over to John. "Your witness."

John knew now that Tom Frawley had called Alberta to the stand to prove that Rhetta had no reason for wanting Griff dead, and there'd be no way he could discredit her testimony, even if he tried. "No questions," he said, much to Frawley's surprise, and Damian looked over at Frawley.

"Your next witness, Mr. Frawley?"

"The prosecution rests its case, your honor," he said, and relaxed, smiling.

Now it's my turn, John thought as Damian asked him to call his first witness for the defense, and John turned, looking the courtroom over thoroughly. There was only one person in the courtroom who had been directly involved but whom Tom Frawley had conveniently neglected to call to the stand, and John was certain he knew why. The man's testimony, instead of helping, would no doubt be embarrassing to the prosecution. So now, determined to find the answers to all the questions that had been plaguing him, John called Miles Vance to the stand, and while everyone sat listening intently, John quickly took him back over the night Jarrod and Rhetta were killed. Only the answers Miles was giving regarding Jarrod's death were far different from testimony previously given by other witnesses when John had cross-examined them.

"You say the defendant fired the first shot, Mr. Vance. Why?" John asked, finally getting fed up with the man's lies.

Miles stared at him, frowning. "Why?"

"Yes, Mr. Vance, why?" John repeated. "What earthly reason would Griffin Heywood have for riding up to your ranch at about two or so in the morning to start shooting at your kitchen windows?"

Miles cleared his throat nervously. It was the first time anyone had asked him for a reason. Most folks in town had just taken his word for what happened. "You heard that Jezebel's testimony," he finally answered, trying to find a way out without incriminating Jarrod.

"Excuse me, by Jezebel, you're referring to Miss Grayson?" John asked.

"You bet I am," Miles answered. "She said Griff thought my son and Rhetta was havin' some kind of an affair. He was probably jealous."

"I see." John knew Miles wasn't thinking straight and was just latching onto anything that might make his son look good. "Do you think, then, maybe that's why the defendant went after his wife at the mine too?" John asked, trying to lead him on. "That he killed her in a jealous rage because he thought she was in love with Jarrod?"

Suddenly Miles realized the mistake John had caused him to make and he began to get flustered. "Well, hell no!" he blurted angrily. "Everybody knows he killed her so he could have the schoolteacher!"

"Then why would he kill your son, if all he wanted was Miss Grayson?"

By now Miles was really working on the brim of his hat, twisting it nervously. "Hell, I don't know why he done it," he yelled. "Maybe you oughta ask him!"

"I intend to, Mr. Vance. But I've already asked Miss Grayson, and not only she and Cory McBride but also the Trail's End hands who were there that night with Griffin Heywood have all stated on this witness stand that the first shots fired that night came from your house."

"They're lyin'!"

"All of them? Mr. Vance, why don't you just admit to this court that your son Jarrod stopped by the ranch to tell you that he and Rhetta were leaving town? That they had planned to kill Griffin Heywood and Jeanine Grayson, only things hadn't worked out right? And that he also told you the defendant and Miss Grayson had escaped and everything was lost? Why don't you tell the truth, Mr.

Vance?" John urged. "That Jarrod came to say good-bye to you, and when Griff showed up, he thought he'd brought a posse with him and started shooting?"

Miles was visibly shaken, and John was certain he saw tears in his eyes.

He took advantage and pressed Miles further. "Jarrod was killed because he was in love with another man's wife and had gotten himself into a mess over it, isn't that right, Mr. Vance?"

"Yes . . . no . . . well, not really," Miles finally broke down. "That's not the way it was. He was leavin', and because of Rhetta, but it was because Rhetta's husband was tryin' to get rid of her!"

"Are you saying that Rhetta went to your son for help because her husband was trying to kill her?"

Miles inhaled, taking a deep breath, relieved, catching at John's words. "That's right, yes, sir," he answered quickly. "That's it, that's the way it was."

"That's preposterous," John said. "Mr. Vance, how could Griffin Heywood be trying to kill his wife, when as far as anyone knew, he was still not back from rescuing Miss Grayson from the Comanche?"

Miles was shaken again. "Well . . . he was back," he said nervously. "Jarrod told me he came back without anyone knowin', and told his wife he was gonna kill her 'cause she wouldn't give him no divorce. Jarrod was tryin' to help her get away."

"Now, Mr. Vance, if your son was trying to help Rhetta Heywood get away from her husband, why did he leave her and her son alone and unprotected at the old copper mine?"

"He . . . he had to get his things from the house."

"I see, and did he need money too?"

"Money?"

"Yes, Mr. Vance," John said. "Money. Did Jarrod ask you for money, or did he have money with him?"

"I don't know."

"Did you look in his pockets before bringing his body to town?"

"Well, he had a coupla dollars."

"But it takes money to travel, and you said Jarrod had traveling to do. What was he planning to use, the money Rhetta had with her? Is that it?"

Miles shrugged. "I guess . . . I don't know."

"But, Mr. Vance, Rhetta Heywood stole that money from her husband's strongbox. Approximately eight hundred dollars was found in her handbag after she was murdered. If you remember, I asked the sheriff about the money earlier in the trial, and it tallies with the amount Jeanine Grayson said the defendant told her had been stolen from his bedroom at Trail's End the night Rhetta was killed. And yet you said Miss Grayson was lying. I think you're a little mixed up, aren't you, Mr. Vance?" John leaned closer to Miles. "Tell me, Miles, how long does it take to ride to the copper mine from your ranch?"

"A little over an hour, why?"

"Using the road?"

"Yeah."

"How about cross-country?"

Miles squirmed uncomfortably. "Not quite an hour, if you know the way."

"How long did it take you, Mr. Vance?" John suddenly asked.

Miles's eyes narrowed. "What are you gettin' at?"

"Mr. Vance, your son was killed Saturday morning around two o'clock and according to your hands who were there, they said you left the Double V Bar about ten minutes later with Jarrod's body tied onto his horse, stating that you were taking him to town to the sheriff. If you left the Double V Bar a little after two on Saturday morning, Mr. Vance, then how is it you didn't arrive in Raintree until Sunday morning, shortly after sunup? It took you over twenty-four hours for what should have been a two-hour ride?"

Miles's whiskers twitched back and forth and his face was pale, although it was hard to tell with his ruddy complexion. "I had things to do," he answered nervously.

"Oh, I bet you did." John straightened, making sure he

was in line with the jury, so they wouldn't miss a word. "And wasn't one of those things an act of vengeance, Mr. Vance?" John asked deliberately. "Isn't it true that after leaving the Double V Bar, you rode to the copper mine to confront Rhetta Heywood, argued with her, and killed her, just as the defendant arrived, then ran off, leaving the defendant to take the blame?"

"That's a lie! I wasn't near the mine!"

"Then where were you until Sunday morning?"

Miles bit his lip, then reached up, rubbing his whiskers, and tears filled his eyes. "My boy was dead," he answered, and choked slightly on the words. John wasn't sure whether it was for the benefit of the jury or if Miles really felt that bad. He went on, his voice unsteady. "My whole world was gone," he said, and sniffed, reaching in his pocket for a handkerchief. "You never lost a son, you don't know," he said, and tears started to well up in his eyes. "I rode around the Double V Bar for hours, not wantin' to give him up." He took a swipe at his nose again with the handkerchief. "I went to all the places where we used to go when he was a boy, when we'd go fishin' and huntin' together, and I just sat there rememberin'." He wiped his eyes with the handkerchief this time, then took another pass at his nose. "I lost my boy that night, Mr. Scott," he blubbered tearfully. "All I knew was that I didn't care no more whether I lived or died." He sniffed again, and pulled himself together some. "Then, after a while, close to mornin' on Sunday, I decided that life was worth livin' again, at least long enough to make Griffin Heywood pay for what he done. But when I rode into Raintree, I discovered the sheriff had already arrested him for killin' his wife. Well, fine, that way they'll both pay for what they done. I don't care whether he hangs for Rhetta's murder or Jarrod's." He glanced over at Griff. "All I want is to see the bastard hang!" he added viciously.

John knew there was no use trying to make Miles break. But then, maybe he wasn't guilty, and he glanced first at Warren, then at Mrs. Brandt, and frowned. Which one?

Maybe not any, and he wished to hell they'd hear something from the men Cory'd sent after Burke.

John sighed. "Your witness, Mr. Frawley," he said, but the prosecutor declined, and since it was so late, Damian called recess for the day, until tomorrow at ten.

John sat at the defense table a long time after the others had gone, trying to figure a way to keep Griff from hanging, because right now it didn't look good. The meeting hall was empty now, the only noise the sound of the clock ticking off precious minutes. Minutes he knew shouldn't be wasted. But what could he do? He looked down at the papers before him, then swore. It was here, it had to be here somewhere, why hadn't he caught it? One of them was lying, but who? Could Griff be guilty after all? He couldn't believe that. He wouldn't!

Angry with himself and the whole damn mess, he stuffed the papers into his briefcase, stood up, and was just ready to leave when Jeanine and Cory burst in the back door, and Jeanine was waving a piece of paper.

"They've caught him, John. It's a wire from Spider," she yelled breathlessly. "They're on their way back with Burke."

All John could do was stare at her, relief flooding over him. Maybe now they'd learn the truth.

20

They were at the Steak House and Cory sat across the table from Jeanine, with John at her side between them. Cory had let some of the other hands from Trail's End escort Mrs. Brandt back, deciding that with the atmosphere in town what it was, he was going to hang around for a few hours longer.

"I still don't think you should stay in town tonight," he said, glancing over at Jeanine. "I think you should be out at the ranch."

"Nonsense" she replied. "Everything's going to be all right. You'll see."

"He's right, Jeanine," John added. "You don't know these people like we do. You've seen them ever since this afternoon . . . hell, it wouldn't take anything to set them off, and with all the drinkin' they been doin' since court recessed for the day . . . don't you see, they're lookin' for a little excitement."

"I know," she answered. "But if I go with you to see Griff, then have you walk me to my room at the hotel . . . their catcalls and vulgar remarks won't bother me."

"And if they don't stop there?" Cory asked.

"Don't be ridiculous, Cory," she answered. "They wouldn't do anything foolish with Judge Worth here, and Sheriff Higgens has his deputies. Besides, they just wouldn't."

"I hope you're right."

She pointed out the front window. "Look, did you ever see anything so peaceful? It looks like any other day in Raintree. You're both worrying foolishly." She was right. A few people were wandering around here and there, and some cowhands making a ruckus down the street, but all in all, nothing that could be construed as being unusual. She leaned across the table. "Even in here, do you see anyone who looks ready to hang me?" she asked.

Both men glanced around the room. It was the dinner hour and the place looked no different than it did any other day. A few wranglers were savoring some good cooking for a change. Some couples were enjoying a night out, and the usual men and women who lived in hotel rooms and ate in restaurants were eating their dinners. Still, both men were on edge. It seemed to be something in the air.

"Besides," Jeanine went on, "I want to be close to Griff. You're having him testify tomorrow, aren't you, John?"

"I'm hoping maybe Cory might get back from Trail's End with Burke and his men before I have to put Griff on the stand. Where did you say Spider was when he sent the telegram?"

"He said they was headin' up from Fort Belknap," Cory answered. "If they been ridin' hard, they should make it to Trail's End before mornin'. When they left, I told them that if they found Burke, they were to go out there first, just in case. I didn't want them to maybe hit town and have somethin' go wrong."

John nodded. "Good." He set his napkin down and leaned back. "Then if you two are ready, we can stop by and see Griff before walkin' Jeanine back to the hotel." He looked at Cory. "Only, don't cut your time in bed too short, Cory," he said. "I don't want you stayin' in here too late and not bein' able to ride in tomorrow mornin'."

"Hell, John," Cory answered, "I can lose twenty-four hours' sleep and keep movin', you know that."

"Yeah," John agreed. "But will your eyes be open?"

Cory and Jeanine both laughed as the three of them stood up and left the restaurant.

It wasn't quite dark outside yet. They had walked over to the sheriff's office with the telegram from Spider after leaving the meeting hall, and had informed him that Spider, Dustin, and Luke were bringing in some of the men Jeanine had told about on the witness stand, and they would corroborate her story, which was the same one Griff was planning to tell from the witness stand the next day, only Dave didn't seem too excited. In fact, he took the matter quite calmly, which irritated John.

"You can bring any men in you want, but that don't mean they're tellin' the truth, John," he finally said, explaining his lack of interest. "You're gonna have to prove it. After all, people have been known to do anything to keep a man from hangin'."

Damian had taken the matter far differently. "I hope they can help Griff," he said after reading the telegram. "Because I'll be truthful: right now, the way things are going, I doubt Griff has a chance of being acquitted."

John hadn't been any too happy over Damian's remark, but knew it was true. Now, as he, Jeanine, and Cory strolled toward the jailhouse to visit Griff, he was hoping Griff was in as good a mood as he had been earlier when they'd told him about the telegram.

Griff's hopes were still high, but he was too worried about Jeanine, and told her so after they'd been there awhile going over the day's testimony and planning the next day's strategy.

"You're all worrying needlessly," she told them. "Nobody's going to risk trying to hurt me with the whole town watching. And anyway, what would they do, hang me? I've met the people in this town. They're stubborn, bullheaded, and prejudiced at times, but I can't see them resorting to something like that. Besides, I promise to stay in my hotel room with the door locked."

Griff hadn't liked it, but there was nothing more he could do. It was her decision to make; then John and Cory decided to leave the two of them alone for a little while and they called Dave to open the door for them, so they could wait for Jeanine in the sheriff's office out front.

"I wish you'd go to the ranch tonight," Griff said once they were alone. They were standing by the window of his cell looking out through the bars, watching the first few stars coming out in the night sky, while behind them the faint light from a lamp hanging in the corridor just outside the cell was casting weird shadows all around them.

"I'll be all right, don't worry," she answered. "And tomorrow, just think, when Burke tells his story, they'll have to believe you."

"I hope so."

Her eyes were shining. "Cory said he's going to bring Gar in with him tomorrow, especially since Dave Higgens intimated that Burke might be someone hired to lie just to try to get you freed. But if Gar confirms that he was one of the men at the mine . . . Cory said Gar knows you didn't do it, and he's been asking him and Mrs. Brandt to tell him everything that's been going on every day."

"Good God, I hope they haven't!"

She smiled. "Of course not. Just enough to keep him satisfied."

"And probably make him think I'll come out of this alive."

"You will."

He looked into her eyes, then reached out, pulling her into his arms. Her hair was still in the bun at the nape of her neck. She'd been wearing it like that ever since the trial started, and he reached up, smoothing it back, then cupped her face in his hand.

"I wish I could see it loose," he whispered softly. His eyes caressed hers. "It's always so pretty with the moon trying to hide in it, and the curls down to your bare shoulders." His thumb stroked her cheek lightly, sending shivers of delight through her. "How well I remember the first time I looked in your eyes and felt what I'm feeling now . . . that wonderful heady feeling. It frightened me then because I didn't want to feel it, yet now it thrills me, only I can't get enough of it. I ache inside for you, Jeanine.''

He kissed her softly, his lips caressing and sipping at her mouth, and she answered each kiss with love, until her whole body was bathed in the wonder of what they shared. It was a moment apart from all the agony of the past few days, and gave them hope that there could be a tomorrow.

''I love you, Jeanine,'' he whispered as he drew his mouth from hers, yet held her close.

''And I love you.''

His hands caressed her back, molding to every curve, then once more moving up until he held her face between his palms, staring at her as if seeing her for the first time.

''Thank you for coming into my life, Jeanine,'' he said huskily, and she frowned, her hands covering his.

''You can say that now?''

''Now, and always,'' he answered. ''Because if you hadn't come along, I'd never have known what love was.'' This time when he kissed her, it was a kiss filled with the promise of a tomorrow they hoped they'd both be able to share.

Suddenly Griff heard the key grate in the lock of the iron door that separated the sheriff's office from the prisoners' cells, and he drew his head back, looking down at her again.

''Be careful tonight, please, honey,'' he cautioned her. ''Raintree may look like a friendly little town, but it took guts to put roots down in this raw wilderness, and like anybody else, the folks here don't like to be deceived.''

''Please, Griff, I'll be all right,'' she assured him. ''I promise to stay in my room until Cory comes for me in the morning.''

He released her, but grabbed her hand and walked to the cell door with her as Dave stepped out of the hall.

''Guess that's it for tonight. Sorry, Griff,'' Dave said as he unlocked the door. ''Cory said he wants to see she gets back to the hotel all right before he leaves for Trail's End, and it's gettin' late.''

Griff squeezed her hand. ''Remember your promise.''

"I remember." She had picked her straw hat up off the cot on their way to the door, and she put it on, tying it under her chin as she looked up at him. She smiled, her eyes filled with love. "And you remember, Griff, tomorrow morning, when Burke's brought in, things are bound to change. Even if Burke didn't do it, there's a good chance he'll know who did. Someone had to be with Rhetta after he left and before we arrived. The truth has to come out."

"Sleep well," he said softly.

She nodded. "Tomorrow?"

"Tomorrow," he answered, and she walked out, then waited for Dave to close the cell door. She didn't want to leave. For some reason, leaving him tonight just didn't seem right. They should be together tonight to talk and make plans, because she just knew that tomorrow would be a new beginning for them. Her eyes held his while Dave shut the door, and she was still looking back at him as she reluctantly entered the hall to go back to the sheriff's office.

John had already left for his place, but Cory was waiting to walk her back to the hotel. They left the sheriff's office, crossed the street to the feed store, then started past the Lone Star saloon, and probably would have had to put up with a few crude remarks from some of the men lounging around outside if it wasn't for Cory's intimidating size and the warning looks he threw at them. Cory had been known to clear out a few saloons all by himself in his day, and there were few men willing to take him on under any circumstances, so they were keeping their mouths shut. But the looks were there, just the same. When they finally reached the hotel, he insisted on walking her all the way to her room, then came inside, checking to make sure everything was all right and cautioning her again on being careful, so that by the time he was ready to leave for Trail's End, Jeanine was beginning to wonder if maybe she should take their advice and leave with him. However, she decided she was just letting all the talk get to her, and tossed the notion aside, even though Cory's last act before leaving was to make sure the door to the balcony was locked.

After he was gone, Jeanine locked the door behind him, then stood in front of the dresser and took off her hat, setting it aside on the chair. The lamp on the dresser was low and she turned it up a little higher, staring at herself in the mirror. Her thoughts ran back over the past few months, and the mess she'd made of everything. But then, when she thought of what might have happened to Griff if she had turned tail and run that first day . . .

Sighing, she realized there was no use thinking of what might have been; all she could do now was pray that tomorrow would change things, and she walked over to the chair by the window where her suitcase was, reached in and pulled out her nightgown, then started to undress.

Down in the lobby, Cory stood looking out the front window of the hotel, trying to decide what to do. Before leaving the sheriff's office he'd told Jeanine he was anxious to get back to Trail's End so he'd be there when Spider, Dustin, and Luke arrived with Burke. Now he wasn't quite so sure whether he should leave or not, especially after walking her back to the hotel. He hadn't liked some of the looks she'd been getting, and sensed that things were a little too quiet. It was as if everyone was waiting for something, but what? He didn't like it. After a few minutes more of running the pros and cons through his head, he finally decided he was going to stick around about a half-hour longer, to look things over more closely, and as he left the hotel, instead of heading for the livery where he'd left his horse that morning, he headed for the Golden Cage across the street, since it was bigger and usually catered to a larger crowd than the Lone Star.

The saloon was a little more crowded tonight than usual, but at first glance nothing seemed out of the ordinary. A couple of girls in fancy dresses were throwing themselves around on the small stage in what was supposed to be a lively dance, while the boisterous piano playing bounced down from the high ceiling, echoing all through the place.

At the far end of the bar, just beyond the stairs that led to the balcony where a few couples stood looking down, a number of tables were filled with card players trying to concentrate amid all the noise, and the usual crowd was sitting at other tables or standing around drinking. Cory ordered a beer, then frowned as he studied the poker players for a few minutes. Miles Vance was at one of the tables, along with part of his crew, and although everything seemed all right, Cory had the strangest premonition that it wasn't.

The bartender poured his beer, and the dancers finished with a flourish, drawing a number of whistles and shouts from the crowd; then they left the small stage and began to mingle, laughing and joking, with the customers. Cory watched the proceedings with an experienced eye as one of the dancing girls sauntered between a couple of tables and moved over behind Miles, then bent down, leaning close, whispering something in his ear. Miles looked up, and they both glanced toward Cory; then the rancher's eyes narrowed, and he said something to the rest of the men at his table. They too turned, glancing his way, and suddenly even the piano became quieter, as others also turned to stare at Cory for a few seconds before going back to what they were doing.

Now Cory knew something was wrong. Usually the noise in the Golden Cage was at such a fever pitch that everybody was trying to outtalk everyone else, but tonight, although it was noisy, it was hard to distinguish what any one person was saying. Cory's frown deepened and he moved along the bar, trying to get a little closer to a couple of hands from the Circle J who were talking to one of Miles's wranglers. But the minute he got within earshot, their voices dropped in volume, then ceased as all three men looked at Cory.

"Something wrong?" Cory asked as they stared at him curiously, but nobody spoke. "I asked if somethin' was wrong."

"We was just wonderin' what kind of a fella would work for a traitor," one of the men from the Circle J finally said, then sneered.

He was almost as tall as Cory, but thin and wiry, with a narrow mustache and what looked like a two-day growth of beard, and his clothes were dirty enough to have been on his body as long as the beard had been on his chin.

Cory straightened, staring at the man, his muscles tense, fingers tightening around the sides of his beer mug. "If you're referrin' to Griff Heywood," he said, "I think maybe you'd better choose your words a little better, Mumford, don't you?"

Mumford laughed. "Hear that, fellas? McBride don't think I know what the word 'traitor' means." He turned. "Anybody in here who don't know what a traitor is?" he yelled so loud everyone could hear, and the piano playing stopped altogether as all heads suddenly swiveled toward the four men at the bar.

"Ain't that a lowdown snake?" somebody yelled from the back of the room.

"Yeah," piped in another voice. "That's a yellow belly who's more interested in what's under a woman's skirt than he is in bein' loyal to his friends and country!"

"Maybe he's color blind," someone else shouted. "He don't know the difference between blue and gray!"

"Or else he don't care!"

"And maybe he heard the war's over," Cory yelled back defiantly. He half-smiled as he stared at Mumford, then finished his beer. "You did know the war was over, didn't you, Mumford?" he went on after he'd wiped his mouth, and he made sure he was talking loud enough for everyone to hear. "But then, maybe you didn't. After all, you ain't too smart, Mumford, and sometimes you don't hear too good. Now, maybe if you'd get the horseshit out of your ears . . ."

Somebody close by laughed and Mumford's chin stuck out belligerently. "You ain't funny, McBride," he snorted.

"I wasn't tryin' to be." Cory straightened and casually laid a hand on his gun butt. "I'm tryin' to show the whole lot of you how stupid you're actin'." He looked around the saloon. "Ever since you all discovered Griff was messin' around behind Rhetta's back you've been so sure he hadda be the one who killed her, and yet there's hardly a married man in this place who ain't cheated on his wife at some time or another.'' He glanced up at a couple on the balcony, who'd come out of one of the upstairs rooms while the girls were dancing. One of the men was a small rancher just south of town. ''Hey, Dayton!'' Cory called up to him. ''Your wife know she's been sharin' you with Billie Jo?'' He glanced at the other couple beside Dayton and Billie Jo. ''And how about you, Jack?'' It was Hadley from the Circle J. ''You plannin' on goin' home and gettin' rid of Nell if she ever discovers you've been messin' around with Rosie?'' His jaw tightened angrily. ''Just because you've got a taste for somethin' else, and like it, don't mean you got the belly for killin' your wife, now, does it? Well, Griff ain't no different.''

''He's been protectin' a traitor!'' somebody yelled.

''He's been protectin' a lady who just happened to be on the Union side durin' the war. Now, if the war was still goin' on, I'd say you had a right to squawk, but it ain't. And besides, according to the Union, every one of you was a traitor, right along with me, and they ain't comin' out here to get even, so you don't have no right to be tryin' to get revenge!''

''You tellin' us what we can and can't do, McBride?'' Mumford asked.

Cory took a deep breath. ''Nope. I'm just warnin' you to go easy on who you're accusin' of what, because by this time tomorrow Griffin Heywood's gonna be a free man, and you might all hafta start eatin' crow.'' He turned, without waiting for anyone to answer, and walked out.

The doors swung shut behind him, but Cory didn't go any farther. He stopped on the boardwalk, waiting, one ear cocked toward the place. For a few minutes there was a lull, almost as if the saloon was empty. Then suddenly someone hit a chord on the piano, then another, and within minutes the strains of ''Dixie'' floated out through the swinging doors behind him. Cory shook his head, then stepped off the boardwalk, and as he strolled down the street, voices began to join with the piano, rising in volume, until he felt more like he was leaving a Confederate rally rather than a saloon.

He strolled down the main street toward the livery stable, music filling his head and uncertainty filling his heart; then he turned quite abruptly as someone called his name from the shadows near the corner of the street that ran alongside the bootmaker's, across from the Lone Star saloon.

"I thought you were still in town, Cory," the Kid said, trying to keep his voice low as he hurried to catch up with the foreman of Trail's End. "Can we talk?"

Cory resumed walking, with the Kid alongside him. "About what?"

"What you just said back there."

Cory stopped and stared at him. "How'd you know what I said back there?"

"Didn't see me, didya?" he said, and his eyes twinkled as he reached up and tried to stroke the straggly mustache he was so proud of.

"You were there?"

"Nobody pays much attention to me anymore, Cory," he informed him, rather pleased with himself. "I been hangin' around town so much lately, I figure they think I ain't workin' for Trail's End no more." He straightened, hefting his gunbelt more comfortably onto his hips. "That's why I gotta talk." He flushed. "I know some of the hands have been turnin' tail, and I guess I can't really blame 'em, they ain't been around too long, but I ain't runnin', Cory, and I just want you to know that I'll help any way I can, if you should need me."

Cory stared at him hard, and suddenly a thought crossed his mind. "You stayin' in town tonight, Kid?" he asked.

"You want me to?"

"I think maybe you oughta." Cory started walking again, with the Kid following. "Think you can keep your eyes and ears open?"

"For what?"

Cory stopped again. They were near the door to the livery stable, where a light shone out onto the dirt road, and he didn't want to be overheard, so he moved aside, closer to the corral where the horses were milling around.

"I don't like the atmosphere in town tonight, Kid," he said as he leaned against the top rail of the corral fence. "Listen." The music was fainter, but it still seemed to permeate the town, even drowning out the usual noise from the Lone Star. "They're drinkin' and they're talkin', and if they stay at it too long, things could get nasty." He looked straight at the Kid, his dark brown eyes studying the young man intently. "Now, I been thinkin'. If they do decide to start somethin', somebody's gonna have to be around to get word to the sheriff, 'cause I sure as hell don't want things to get out of hand."

"You goin' out to the ranch?"

"I was, but I ain't now. I figure I can do more good by ridin' out and meetin' Spider and the boys on their way up from Fort Belknap. They can't be more'n three or four hours out, and if I can head them off so they'll come here before goin' to Trail's End, we may be able to stop trouble before it starts, and prove to this town that Griff and Jeanine aren't lyin' about what happened. Now, here's what I want you to do . . .

A few minutes later, as Cory rode out of the Raintree headed south, hoping to intercept Spider, Luke, and Dustin before they bypassed the town and headed straight for Trail's End, although he was still restless and edgy, he felt a little better knowing the Kid would be keeping his eyes on things. He'd always liked the Kid. At almost twenty, he was responsible, trustworthy, and a hell of a fighter in a pinch. Quite a contrast to the puny kid who'd ridden into the ranch yard at Trail's End some six years before, with a mule under him, no saddle, and refusing to say who he was or where he came from. He'd worked hard, learned well, and now Cory was glad he could call him a friend, and as he dug his horse in the ribs, urging him into a gallop, leaving the town behind in a cloud of dust as he headed south, he was sure the Kid wouldn't let him down.

*   *   *

It was close to midnight. The Kid was sitting on a chair in a dark corner of the Golden Cage, his eyes on the men who were congregated at the bar. He had pulled his hat down on his forehead, making himself even more inconspicuous, and his body was relaxed, as if he'd had a few too many, but in reality he hadn't missed a thing going on around him.

"I tell you we can't wait until tomorrow," Jack Hadley was saying. "You heard the sheriff earlier. He said McBride's bringin' men in tomorrow who can clear Heywood. Is that what we want? Paid witnesses comin' in here and lyin' just to keep his neck out of a noose?"

"Who said they'd be lyin'?"

The Kid squinted, moving just enough so he could catch sight of the protestor, and was surprised. It was one of Hadley's own men.

"You stickin' up for him?" Hadley snapped angrily, hands on his gunbelt.

"Hell no! I was just wonderin'." The man shrugged and stepped back into the crowd.

"You heard Hadley," Miles Vance added as he moved over next to the owner of the Circle J. "First of all he and that tramp he calls a lady tried to make it look like my boy was a thief and a murderer, which he wasn't! He was only tryin' to help an old friend whose husband didn't want her no more. Then that connivin' lawyer of his tried to hang Rhetta Heywood's murder on the housekeeper, then Warren Granger, then me. I'm surprised he didn't try to figure out some way to prove the sheriff did it." There were a few angry agreements from the crowd, and Miles went on. "Now, some of his hands are supposedly bringin' in the men they say kidnapped the schoolteacher, if that's what you wanna call her. Personally"—he sneered—"I'd rather call her his whore! And we know that ain't all she is either, don't we, boys?" He waited a few seconds while the men all agreed again, then continued. "And on top of all that, he bought himself a judge." Miles's ruddy face was gaunt, his eyes blazing hatefully. "Now, everybody knows Damian Worth owes Griff, and Damian'll pay the debt back by believin' everything those paid witnesses say, then settin' Griff free. And all those fancy witnesses will get out of it is the money they got paid for testifyin', and about thirty days in jail for kidnappin'. Why, hell, I know more'n a dozen men right in this room who'd be willin' to lie and then spend thirty days in jail just for a coupla hundred dollars!''

Miles had quite an audience, and between him, Hadley, and the whiskey and beer that was flowing, as time went on, the talk became even more malicious, as Warren Granger and some of the men from the Lone Star wandered over to the Golden Cage and joined in. The Kid sat for some time, huddled in a corner near one of the tables, while he watched everything closely, and listened, weighing not only what was said but also who said it, and why.

It was really getting late. He'd been watching for well over an hour now, and although some of the other listeners had slowly filtered out, heading for a place to sleep it off, there were still enough hotheads around that when somebody suddenly hollered, ''I know what we oughta do, we oughta string 'em up!'' the Kid straightened, sliding into a sitting position, but still trying to be unobtrusive.

''Yeah! That's what we gotta do!'' someone else yelled, and one after another, more people started voicing their opinion, clinking beer mugs in agreement and venting verbal abuse not only on Griff but also on Jeanine, until the place was quickly becoming a bedlam of men bent on only one thing, to rid the world of traitors and murderers.

The Kid took a quick look around, making sure he wasn't spotted, then stood up and started making his way toward the door as casually as he could, keeping his eyes on the main body of men at the bar. Miles and Warren were standing right in the middle of the crowd and it was hard to say which one was fueling the flames of vengeance with more zeal as they used just about every ploy they could think of to keep things going, from ''Long live the Confederacy'' to ''An eye for an eye.''

Reaching the swinging doors easily, the Kid slipped out just as the piano player began to play ''I Dream of Jeannie." which brought another round of shouting, cursing, and threats. Then, as the Kid straightened, taking a deep breath of fresh air and tightening the hat on his head, someone behind in the saloon hollered drunkenly, "All right, fellas, who's got a rope?" and without hesitating another second, the Kid took off running, heading for the jailhouse.

"Where's Higgens?" he asked breathlessly as he burst into the sheriff's office, and the deputy, who'd been leaning back in Dave's chair with his feet on the desk, snoozing, almost went over backward.

"Wh-what the hell!" he stammered, swinging his feet to the floor and catching himself by leaning forward. "He's at the house. Why?"

"What's he doin' out there?"

"How should I know?" The deputy was standing now, trying to get fully awake. "Said he needed the sleep."

"He's gonna need more'n sleep," the Kid offered hastily. "He's gonna need guns. The crowd at the Golden Cage is yellin' for a rope."

"A lynchin'?"

"It will be unless somebody starts talkin' sense into 'em, but I don't think they're willin' to listen." He walked to a gun rack on the wall filled with rifles. "You got a key to this thing?" he asked.

"Yeah, somewhere." The deputy turned the lamp on the desk higher and began rummaging around in one of the drawers.

"Where's the other deputy?" the Kid asked as he checked, making sure his own guns were loaded.

"Went home."

"Oh, fine!" The Kid's eyes surveyed the room quickly, taking in every detail. There was no time to ride out for the sheriff. It wasn't really all that far, but if they were really bent on hanging somebody he'd never get back in time to stop them. The deputy found the key and tossed it to the Kid, who started unlocking the glass case.

"Just what the Sam Hill you think you're doin', Kid?" Dave suddenly asked from the doorway, and the Kid whirled around, facing the sheriff, who didn't look any too pleased. The Kid had left the door open when he'd run in, and now Dave stepped through, shutting it behind him. "Well?" he asked again, waiting for an explanation.

The deputy was still a bit rattled, and he rubbed his head, frowning. "I thought you was home in bed."

Dave's dark blue eyes were bloodshot. "Couldn't sleep." He continued to stare at the Kid. "I asked you what you were doin'."

"Tryin' to prevent a lynchin'," the Kid answered anxiously. "Didn't you hear 'em, Sheriff?"

"You mean that ruckus comin' from the Golden Cage?"

"Rukus? When I left they were yellin' for a rope."

Dave's eyes studied the young cowhand thoughtfully. "You sure about that?" he asked.

"I ain't been more sure of nothin' in my life." The Kid was still holding the key to the gun rack, and his fist closed around it. "I been listenin' to them for more'n a couple hours now, and Cory said if they started gettin' outta hand, I should hightail it down here."

"Where is McBride?"

"Headin' toward Fort Belknap to see if he can cut Spider, Luke, and Dustin off so they can bring the men who kidnapped the schoolteacher on in tonight. He said he didn't like the looks of things, and thought maybe if he could get back here in time, he might be able to head off trouble."

Dave glanced over at his deputy. "You seen anything?" he asked.

"Hell, he was sleepin'," the Kid piped in. "How would he know what was goin' on? I'm tellin' ya." His eyes darkened. "They ain't playin' out there tonight, and if somethin' ain't done, somebody's gonna get hurt." Suddenly the Kid cocked his head. "Listen!"

The room grew silent as all three men held their breath, listening for a few seconds; then Dave walked over to the door and opened it, looking out.

"Jesus Christ!" he spat angrily. "What the hell do they think they're doin'?"

The Kid moved over to stand behind him and saw what the sheriff was staring at. There were at least fifty men, maybe more heading down the middle of the street. Some were carrying lanterns, others torches, but it was enough light for them to see that Jack Hadley, Miles Vance, Warren Granger, and a couple of Hadley's hands were leading them, and Hadley was twirling the end of a length of rope that was wound around his shoulder. A few of them looked drunk, but not enough that they didn't know what they were doing.

Dave swore again, then spoke back over his shoulder to the Kid. "You still got the key, Kid, so unlock that case and take out three of them damn rifles," he ordered furiously. "There ain't gonna be no lynchin' in my town!"

The Kid's fingers were steady as he unlocked the case. "They loaded?" he called back, and Dave turned.

"Hell no!" He yelled for the deputy to get the box of ammunition out of the bottom desk drawer, while he checked the guns in his gunbelt. The Kid loaded all three rifles, handed one to the deputy, then hurried over to Dave. "Quick, give me that," Dave said, and grabbed the rifle from the Kid, then bit his lip, taking a quick assessment of how long he had before they'd reach the jail.

He turned back quickly to Griff's young ranch hand. There wasn't a minute to lose.

"Get out of here and go get John Scott," he said hurriedly. "And I want the judge here too. I'll try to hold them off."

The Kid hesitated, glancing back toward the iron door that led to the cellblock. He wasn't quite certain . . . "You're sure you wouldn't do anything foolish, now, would you, Sheriff?" he asked warily.

Dave's eyes smoldered. "I ain't stupid, Kid. If they get by me, it won't be with my permission. Now, beat it, before they get here!"

The Kid took one last look at the throng of men moving toward them, then slipped out the door, turned left, and circled the jailhouse. There was no need to be quiet, because the men out front were making enough noise to drown out a stampede, and he ran past the back of the bootmaker's, then turned left down the side street toward the main street, ducking into the shadows when he reached the corner.

The crowd had attracted a good bit of attention by now, and men were hurrying out of the Lone Star to join in, so the Kid waited for the main body of men to pass, then, before the last few stragglers had finished going by, broke into a run again, heading for John's quarters, upstairs over his office.

John had been restless all evening, and had done so much tossing and turning, the bottom sheet had come loose on the bed. He cursed softly, tugging at the end of it, then rolled over to the other side of the bed, bunched up the pillow, and was just ready to try to get back to sleep again when his head jerked upright and he stared toward the sitting room, where someone was pounding frantically on the door. Quickly slipping out of bed, he didn't even bother with bathrobe or slippers, nor did he light a lamp, but made his way to the door hurriedly, alerted by the urgency of the pounding and fear in the voice of whoever was shouting for him.

"Good God, Kid, what is it?" he asked when he swung the door open and got a good look at the Kid's face.

"You gotta hurry, Mr. Scott," the Kid urged, panting heavily, and he shoved the rifle he was carrying into John's hands. "They're on on their way to lynch Griff!"

"The hell they are!" John hefted the rifle under his arm, starting to leave, then remembered he was in his nightshirt. "Damn thing!" he mumbled, and he handed the rifle back to the Kid just long enough so he could scurry back into his bedroom, pull his pants up over his nightshirt, slipped into his boots, then grab his gunbelt off the chair by the bed, fastening it on as he headed for the door.

The Kid handed him the rifle and they practically flew down the stairs.

"You wake Damian yet?" John asked when they reached the street.

"Haven't had time!" the Kid yelled.

John took a deep breath. "Then get him now. He's in room eight, the top of the stairs," and when they reached the Empire Hotel, the Kid left John, hurrying inside the hotel so he could wake the judge.

Down at the jail, Dave stepped outside, shutting the door firmly behind him. The rifle was halfway into position, with his finger on the trigger, and as the men drew nearer, he raised it, pointing the barrel skyward, then pulled off a shot, letting the loud crack reverberate through the darkness. There was a sky full of stars, but only a sliver of a moon overhead, and it was hard to make out all the faces, but the ones he could see were hostile as they stopped surging forward and stared, flickering lights from the lanterns and torches casting grotesque patterns on the ground around them.

"That's far enough!" Dave yelled, and this time he leveled his rifle right at the crowd.

"We come for Heywood!" Hadley shouted.

"Yeah! Send him out!" another voice cut in, and Warren stepped forward.

"He's gonna hang!"

"Nobody's gonna hang!" Dave answered. "Not tonight anyway. Now, one step closer and you'll be usin' a crutch."

"You can't hit us all, Dave!" Miles yelled.

"No, I can't, you're right there, Miles." Dave lifted the rifle to his shoulder. "So who wants to be first, you?"

"Now, cut that out, Dave," Hadley argued. "You know damn well you feel the same way we do. So why don't you just put down that rifle and let us walk in?"

"You know I can't do that, Hadley."

"We're gonna take him anyway, Dave!" Miles was furious. "He killed my boy!"

"Then the jury'll sentence him!" John shouted from behind Dave, and the sheriff whirled around to see John Scott step out of the shadows only a few feet away, his rifle aimed at the mob. He'd tucked his nightshirt into his pants, and Dave knew he'd been dragged from bed, but John knew how to shoot, and Dave was glad he was wearing his gunbelt as well. "I said let the jury decide whether he hangs or not!" John went on as he moved up next to Dave.

"What jury?" Miles shot back. "There won't be no jury verdict, and you know it, Scott." He straightened, hitching his gunbelt up, then shook his fist at John. "You're gonna bring paid men in here and get him off, and we ain't waitin' for no judge to turn Heywood loose 'cause he owes him a favor!"

While Miles, Dave, John, and Jack Hadley were shouting threats and accusations back and forth at each other, neither Dave nor John noticed Miles's foreman and Hadley's man Mumford working their way to the edge of the crowd, where they slipped into the shadows and made their way to the alley between the bootmaker's shop and the jail so they could circle around back and come up behind John and Dave Higgens, the same way John had arrived.

It was dark in the alley, and the two men almost bumped into some trash barrels, then stayed close to the building, passing just beneath the window of Griff's cell before turning the corner of the building. When they were finally near the front of the building again, they hugged the wall close, and Miles's foreman motioned for his partner to stay back while he took a look. When he turned back to Mumford, his face wore a sinister smile.

"You take Scott, I'll get the sheriff," he whispered. "Only keep them damn spurs of yours quiet, or we'll never get near 'em."

Mumford nodded, and both men stepped cautiously from the shadows and began sneaking up on the two men who were defending the jail.

Miles was right in the middle of a tirade on the evils of letting a sinner like Heywood live, when Dave sensed a movement behind him and started to turn, but he was too late as the foreman's gun butt connected, and it felt like someone had torn off the top of his head.

John saw the movement the same time Dave did, and he swung the rifle up just in time to catch a blow on his temple that took him to his knees. Struggling desperately, he tried to keep from going out all the way, and felt someone grab his arms, wrenching the gun away; then he felt himself being dragged to his feet. He shook his head, trying to clear it, and when he finally managed to open his eyes, all he could see were men all over the place; then he spotted Dave. Two of Hadley's men were trying to get him to his feet, but he was out cold. John tried to break away from the men who were holding him, but couldn't, and he cursed as the mob swarmed into the sheriff's office, shoving, stumbling, and yelling. Dave's poor deputy didn't have a chance. He was a man easily intimidated, and they snatched the rifle from his hands, grabbed a set of keys off the wall; then, still dragging the unconscious sheriff, they shoved the deputy, along with John, until they reached the iron door that separated the outer office from the cellblock, and began unlocking the door.

Griff stood with his hands wrapped around the bars of the cell, staring toward the short hallway that led to the iron door and the sheriff's office. He'd been listening to the crowd now for some time, and no one had to tell him what was going on; he knew. Music and laughter from up the street had been filtering in through the window all evening, and it had been easy to tell when the mood of the crowd started to turn nasty. The noise and laughter had gone from carefree and relaxed to tense and almost fanatically wild, and when the mob began to move down the street, making their way to the jailhouse, the words that had been only a jumble of noise before suddenly became clear, and now Griff's stomach was tightening apprehensively.

He'd heard Dave and John out front trying to talk the men into going back to the saloon or finding a place to sleep it off, only the crowd didn't seem interested; then suddenly it was as if all hell broke loose, and he knew something was wrong. He could hear a commotion in the sheriff's office out front, and as he tried to listen more closely, the hair at the nape of his neck stood on end and a chill ran down his spine. The key was turning the lock in the heavy iron door.

He stared angrily, his hands dropping from the bars as men swarmed into the cellblock. Four men were holding John, who was struggling viciously in spite of the blood that smeared the left side of his face, and two men, each one with an arm locked beneath Dave's armpit, were dragging him behind John, his booted feet trailing across the floor, and he was unconscious.

Griff's jaw clenched as he stared at the two men, but there was no time for sympathy as Hadley, who was carrying the keys, opened the door of the cell next to Griff's, and they threw the two men in, then shoved the deputy in after them and locked the door, then came after Griff.

"You're crazy drunk!" Griff yelled, and he moved over toward the cell where John, Dave and the deputy were.

John had regained his feet and was stumbling toward Griff, wiping the blood from the side of his face with the sleeve of his nightshirt. "We tried to stop them, Griff," he gasped, half-choking, "but they sneaked up behind us."

Griff reached through the bars, trying to reach John to wipe the blood from his face, but there was no time, as Hadley and the others reached him. Griff tried to fight them off, but they crawled all over him, pinning his arms behind him.

"Where's Cory!" Griff yelled at John.

"He went after Burke!" John shouted back; then suddenly Griff felt a gun shoved against his head.

"You're comin' with us, Heywood," Hadley growled close to Griff's ear. "So quit strugglin', 'cause it ain't gonna do you no good."

The men holding Griff pulled him away from the other cell bars, and he couldn't see John anymore as they moved him toward the cell door, pushing him through and on out to the sheriff's office, then into the street.

Every muscle in Griff's body was tense as he stepped off the boardwalk onto the dusty road, his eyes searching the faces of the men around him, hoping fervently that he'd spot a friendly face or hear a familiar voice somewhere in the uncontrollable mob. He didn't want to hang any more than the next man, but there wasn't much a man could do with a gun at his head and two men with viselike grips on each arm, with a dozen other men to take their place even if he did happen to break loose.

Some men began walking in front of him, turning now and then to taunt him, while the rest just strolled along, shouting obscenities and accusations. They were crossing the street now, heading down the side street beside the feed store, heading for the livery stable, and some of them ran ahead to make sure Gus, who ran the livery. wouldn't interfere.

"Now, wait, boys, we gotta do this right," Miles called out when they reached the livery, and he stepped over to Griff, a small length of rope in his hands. Light from the torches and lanterns fell across Miles's face, and Griff stared at him. Miles's eyes were hard, unyielding, his face filled with hatred. "First we tie his hands behind him," he said, and Griff laughed bitterly.

"You finally got them to listen to you, didn't you, Miles?" he lashed out heatedly. "And you too," he went on as he spotted Warren behind Miles. "What lies did you have to make up this time, to finally persuade them to do your dirty work?"

"I didn't have to lie about nothin', Griff," Miles answered. "You tied the knot yourself when you hired that Yankee traitor, then decided you wanted her instead of your wife."

"Hey! That's right," someone in the crowd reminded them. "We forgot about the teacher!"

"Yeah! She's as guilty as he is!" another voice cut in. Then suddenly a shot rang out, and all heads turned toward the street that led behind the feed store, just opposite the livery stable, where Damian now stood, resting his weight on his left leg, his right hand flourishing one of the Kid's six-shooters instead of the usual cane, which at the moment was hooked in the elbow of his left arm.

His hazel eyes were blazing as they scanned the crowd, then settled on what looked like the leaders. "Let Heywood go!" he ordered, his deep voice vibrating in the night air, but instead Griff felt the men who were holding him tighten their grip.

"Why?" Warren shouted furiously. "So you can turn him loose? We know McBride went to hire some men to come here and lie for him and say my sister was gonna kill him! Why should he go free just because you owe him a favor?"

"That's not the way it is and you know it!" Damian answered. "I'm here because it's my job, and for no other reason."

"Bullshit!" Hadley's face was flushed. "You've been bought, judge, and everybody knows it! So put down the gun and we can get on with it." He turned to Mumford and Miles's foreman. "Take a couple men and go get the lady," he said viciously. "We're wastin' time."

"Stay where you are!" Damian shouted, but Miles's foreman started to move anyway.

A shot rang out and the foreman clutched his right shoulder, but before Damian could fire another, a group of men who were standing over toward the side lunged forward, piling into him and the Kid, and although the Kid managed to fire into the air, it did little good except to excite the crowd all the further.

Damian was strong, but no match for the cowhands, who found it just as easy to rope a judge as a fighting calf, and in minutes he was trussed up like a maverick for branding.

"You'll pay for this!" Damian threatened, his eyes dark and foreboding as he watched them manhandling the Kid and wresting the other six-gun from him before tying him up too.

"How's your arm?" Miles asked his foreman, and the man gritted his teeth while one of the other men wrapped his bandanna around it.

"Just a flesh wound," he answered. "The judge ain't too good a shot. Barely grazed the skin." He motioned with his head toward Mumford. "You ready to go get the lady?" he asked.

Mumford grinned.

Down the street in her hotel room, Jeanine heard Dave's gunshot as part of a recurring dream she often had about outrunning a bunch of Confederate soldiers, but Damian's shot brought her out of the dream, and the Kid's shots brought her out of the bed.

It had been warm for sleeping and she put the window up a few inches to get some air; now she raised the window the rest of the way, listening. There were no more shots, but she could hear yelling and cheering, only she couldn't see much of anything from the window because of the balcony. She had to know what was happening.

Not wanting anyone to see that she was up and around, she left the room in darkness while she found her pale blue silk wrapper and put it on, then unlocked the door to the balcony. Her hair was loose and she pushed it back from her face so she could peek out to make sure no one was around. Satisfied that the balcony was empty, she stepped out and made her way to the rail. Most of the town looked quiet, but to her right, down the street toward the jail-house, she could hear yelling and hollering. Only it wasn't coming from the jail. The door to the sheriff's office was wide open, but there wasn't a soul around. The noise and confusion seemed to be coming from the side street near the livery stable.

A chill ran through her. Although light streamed from the windows and through the shuttered doors of the Golden Cage across the street, the usual piano playing and merriment were missing. Even the Lone Star was quiet. Something was wrong, dreadfully wrong.

Shoving aside all the warnings everyone had been giving her all evening, Jeanine hurried back into her room and rummaged around, undressing in the dark, then found her street clothes on the chair where she'd left them and put them on, not bothering to put the green suit jacket on over her white shirtwaist, since she was in a hurry. Still not daring to light the lamp, she sat on the edge of the bed, put on her shoes and stockings, then reached up to her hair. There was no way she could see to fix it in the dark, so instead of twisting it into a bun, she ripped the white ribbon off the front of her shirtwaist and tied it around her hair to keep it off her face; then, straightening hurriedly, she started for the door, and suddenly froze as she heard footsteps outside in the hall. Her heart began to race and she held her breath. Hushed voices could be heard right outside her door, and then the sound of the doorknob turning echoed loudly through the room.

"Damn, it's locked!" Mumford whispered. "Let's get it," and without any warning the door splintered and the two men came crashing through, smashing into Jeanine and knocking her against the dresser.

"It's her! Grab her!" Miles's foreman yelled as Jeanine pushed them aside and bolted for the door. But she wasn't quick enough, and both men recovered quickly, their hands reaching out, and she was pulled back, arms pinned behind her.

"You want I should light the lamp" Mumford asked.

"Nah." The foreman's mouth was against Jeanine's ear. "Just open what's left of the door all the way so we can get her outta here without hurtin' her none." He grinned. "We want her to look pretty for the hangman."

Jeanine tried to break his grip on her while the other man held the door open, but it was useless. "Let me go!" she screamed frantically, but her only answer was to have her arm twisted until she cried from the pain. There was nothing else she could do except go with them. Instead of going down through the front lobby, however, they ushered her down to the end of the hall and down a different set of stairs that went through a dusty storage room, then on outside to the back of the hotel and down the side street, avoiding the main street of town altogether.

Lights were on in a few houses here and there as they went past, and a few people were vaguely visible, hiding in the shadows of some of the porches, but no one seemed willing to try to stop what was happening, even though

Jeanine, seeing them there, screamed at them, trying to get them to listen.

The only response she heard as the men dragged her down the street, fighting all the way, was a shrill feminine voice coming out of the darkness, telling her she was getting what she deserved, and she felt sick.

Griff was furious as he watched Mumford and the foreman emerge from the shadowed side street with Jeanine in tow, and his eyes grew wild with rage. Ignoring the ropes around his wrists, he rammed his body sideways into Miles Vance, hitting the rancher's immense stomach and knocking him into one of Jack Hadley's men.

"Let her go!" Griff yelled, the cords on his neck bulging from the anger that was pouring through him. "You have no right to bring her here!" and he tried to reach her, but they stopped him.

"She's gonna hang too, Mr. Wife Killer," Hadley offered sarcastically. "So shut your yappin'," and he told Mumford to bring her close so they could all get a better look at the woman who'd used her feminine wiles and caused Griffin Heywood to want her so badly he'd kill his wife. The woman who seduced military secrets from innocent men during the war.

Suddenly, as they stared at her, Jeanine's fear turned to indignation, and she became infuriated.

"Innocent!" she screamed at them, tears mingling with her anger. "Oh, what fools you are! The men I stole secrets from weren't loyal soldiers. They were more interested in trying to get me in bed with them than they were in carrying out their orders, you should know that." She laughed bitterly. "They didn't even give one thought to the secrecy of their missions and the orders they'd been given. If they'd been innocently doing their jobs they wouldn't have been such easy prey, can't you see that? You're so eager to blame me, why not them? Their job was to carry secrets, all right. Mine was to learn them." She straightened, her eyes adjusting to the brighter lights from the torches as the men crowded in closer, and suddenly the tears were gone. "Their loyalty was to themselves and their own egos,'' she yelled at them. ''Mine was to my country. If you intend to hang me for that, then I die in glory for a job well done, I'd say!''

She glanced at Griff, and suddenly the tears were there again. ''As for Griffin Heywood . . .'' Her voice broke. ''Yes, I love him, and if I die tonight, that still won't change what I feel.''

Griff's eyes were on Jeanine's and he felt sick inside. Why hadn't she gone out to Trail's End like he'd wanted? There was no one left in town to help them, and he swallowed hard, the insanity of this whole hideous mess driving pain deep into his heart, until he felt like a savage again. Then suddenly that same wild agony that used to engulf him every time he went into battle tried to overwhelm him and turn him into a coward. His jaw clenched stubbornly. He'd have none of it, and without the least bit of warning he threw his thick head of burnt-gold hair back, lifted his eyes to the heavens, and cut loose with a blood-chilling Comanche war cry that caught everyone unawares and made their hair stand on end as it echoed through the darkness around them.

For a brief second afterward it grew so quiet all Jeanine could hear was the crackling of the burning torches and an occasional snort from the horses in the corral next to the livery; then, just as Griff straightened stubbornly, the war cry giving him back his courage, and the shocked crowd began to surge about again, once more beginning to concentrate on what they'd come out here to do, the rattle of a carriage bumping down the road and careening around the corner brought them up short again, and they stared in disbelief as Mrs. Brandt drove a four-wheeled carriage into view with Cinnamon on one side of her and Venable on the other, and both black men were wielding rifles.

''Tell them to put the rifles down, Mrs. Brandt,'' Hadley ordered her as she pulled back on the reins, bringing the carriage to a halt, but the brothers didn't move.

Theola Brandt stared at the throng of men. She'd heard Griff's war cry and had sensed what was happening even before catching a glimpse of Jeanine and Griff, and her face was pale, eyes troubled.

"Why did you come in?" Griff asked angrily. "You were to stay at the ranch!"

"Cory didn't come back," she called to him. "And I knew there was trouble." She looked straight at Hadley, then Miles, and last of all Warren.

"You're hanging the wrong people!" she pleaded anxiously. "Please, you don't know what you're doing!" She spotted Damian, trussed up and propped against a bale of hay, with the Kid next to him. The judge's face was pale, frustration etched on it in the flickering lamplight.

Without any thought of what they might do to her, she handed the reins to Cinnamon, shoved Venable aside as she climbed around him, and jumped down from the driver's seat of the buggy, then hurried to Damian. To everyone's surprise, no one stopped her.

Helping the judge into a sitting position, she began working on the ropes that held his wrists. Hadley started to say something, but before the words left his mouth, she yelled to Cinnamon.

"Drop him in his tracks if he takes one more step, Cinnamon!" she said, and Hadley froze.

"Ain't anybody gonna do nothin'?" yelled Mumford, and Mrs. Brandt straightened, letting Damian finish loosening his own bonds. By now Miles, Warren, and the others had all come to life, and it was Miles who broke the deadlock.

"Griff don't hafta hang, Mrs. Brandt," he hollered sarcastically, "A bullet can do the job just as easy," and he was pointing his gun right at Griff's head.

"You would shoot, wouldn't you, Miles!" she yelled angrily. "Not because of Rhetta, but because of Jarrod. Well, go ahead, shoot Griff and get your revenge, but if you really want to hang Rhetta's murderer, then put the rope around my neck." Jeanine heard mumbling in the crowd as the gray-haired housekeeper's words sank in.

"That's a lie!" Griff yelled, knowing what she was doing, but she silenced him.

"No, it's not a lie, Griff," she said curtly. "You didn't believe it in the courtroom, but believe it now. I killed Rhetta. I hated her, she ruined your life and even tried to kill you!"

Damian was free now, and he stood up on his good leg, leaning against the building. "Mrs. Brandt, do you know what you're saying?" he asked, his eyes troubled.

She nodded. "Yes, I know what I'm saying," she answered. "John was right. I got there before them, hid the buggy alongside the road, then went in to talk to Rhetta. She was all alone and the boy was sleeping, so we came outside, and that's when I killed her. I was afraid to do it inside for fear of waking the boy. Then I heard someone coming so I hurried back to the buggy and pretended to ride in a few minutes later." She straightened, standing erect, head held high, and Jeanine knew now why no one had stopped her from untying Damian. She was a formidable woman of commanding authority, and the chiseled features of her lined face, prominent in the torchlight, left no doubt that she was a woman of dignity.

Hadley stared at her, a little bewildered, and so did Warren. "Griff said you're lyin'," Hadley disputed.

Mrs. Brandt smiled wanly. "Naturally, but what I've told you is true. If you hang Griffin Heywood, you'll all hang for murdering an innocent man."

Suddenly one of the men who had worked for Trail's End and been with the Heywood crew that night, but who had quit after Griff's arrest, moved over close to Hadley's elbow. "She's lyin', Hadley," he said thoughtfully. "Heywood's right, she's lyin'."

Hadley's eyes sharpened. "How do you know?"

"Because I was with his crew that night, and she came ridin' down that road to the mine not quite five minutes after we all heard Mrs. Heywood scream, and there's no way she could have killed Griff's wife, hightailed it on foot back past where we were waitin', then drove the buggy in so it looked like she hadn't been there. We were too far back. It would've taken her at least ten to fifteen minutes just to cover that much ground on foot, even in

the daytime, and it was dark." He looked at Mrs. Brandt.
"No sirree, Hadley, she's just tryin' to save Heywood's
neck, that's all she's doin'."

Hadley was livid. "You connivin' . . ."

He didn't have to go any further, as the crowd once
more took the upper hand, and since Cinnamon and Venable
were the only ones on Griff's side who still had firearms,
they were quickly relieved of them.

"Hey, that's the thing!" Miles yelled as Cinnamon and
Venable were hustled off the seat of the carriage. "Go
bring it over here, Warren," he went on. "We'll have
them stand side by side on the buggy seat. That'll save
saddlin' horses," and the men once more became absorbed
in their task as another rope was found and added to the
one Hadley had, and he proceeded to fashion a noose at
the end of each one, while Warren brought the carriage
over beneath the haylift.

"Can't you do anything?" Mrs. Brandt pleaded with
Damian, tears filling her eyes, but he was helpless, as was
the Kid.

Although they were no longer tied up, they had no
weapons, and men stood at their sides, guns trained on
them, so neither could do a thing without taking a chance
on losing his own life.

Damian shook his head, but his eyes as they looked into
hers said: Maybe, if I get the chance. Hadley saw Damian's
face at the same time Mrs. Brandt did, and Damian frowned
as Hadley warned them they'd be shot if they tried anything, and all three knew the battle was lost.

Heartsick and unhappy, they watched Warren center the
buggy seat directly under the haylift in front of the livery
door; then Jeanine and Griff were ordered to climb up.

Griff glanced over to Jeanine, his eyes probing hers, and
his lips moved slowly. "Forgive me for bringing you into
this, Jeanine," he whispered huskily. "I'm sorry."

She shook her head. "Don't be," she murmured, unable to hold back the tears. "My only regret is that you
never came backstage to see me that day in St. Louis

before the war. If you had, we might have had so many more years together.''

He tried to smile.

"Come on, climb up," Miles ordered, giving Griff a shove, and Mumford laughed.

"Maybe we should have ladies first?"

"Yeah," someone else yelled, then was answered by a voice somewhere in the crowd. "But who says she's a lady!" and the laughing and sniping started again, as Hadley practically lifted Jeanine up, making her stand on the driver's seat; then he climbed up himself, standing on one of the regular seats behind her, a rope in each hand.

"Well, Heywood, I'm waiting," he said viciously, and when Griff didn't move, Miles, his foreman, and a few other men gave him a hand, making sure he had no trouble reaching the driver's seat, where they stood him up beside Jeanine.

"At least I made them work for it," Griff said, his eyes on hers.

She tried to smile back, but couldn't. "I'm frightened, Griff," she said unsteadily, and he swallowed hard.

"I know. Death is easy to take when it's swift and you don't know it's coming, but it's painful when you have time to stare it in the face." He felt the noose hit the top of his head, and closed his eyes as it fell across his face, then opened them again when it reached his neck. He still hadn't looked at the crowd, but kept his eyes on Jeanine as he watched the noose drop down over her head too; then Hadley tossed the ends of both ropes over the haylift and yelled for someone to secure them.

"I love you, Jeanine," Griff whispered softly as he felt the rope tighten.

Tears streamed down her face, and her heart felt like it was breaking. "I love you too," she answered. Then Hadley made sure both ropes were tight. He was just ready to jump down from the carriage when suddenly someone yelled, "Riders!" and all heads turned toward the main road.

Shouts rose from the crowd, and some of the men

moved about, confused, as the sound of a number of horses hung on the night air as they galloped into town, then slowed to an easy trot.

Cory was the first of the riders to spot the open door at the sheriff's office, and he called over to Dustin, riding beside him.

"Go check it out!" he ordered, then urged his own horse a little faster when he saw reflections from lanterns and torches through the feed-store window and on the windows of the sheriff's office and the bootmaker's next to it. The lights were down by the livery, and he dug his horse in the ribs, but moved cautiously, hefting the gun from his holster and ordering Spider and Luke to do the same as they rounded the corner by the feedstore.

He took one look, then rode in close and reined his horse to a halt not more than fifteen feet from the carriage.

"Cut the ropes!" he yelled furiously, and Hadley's eyes narrowed.

"We outnumber you, McBride!"

"That's right, you do. But right now my gun's on you, and I'll bet Spider and Luke have picked out some pretty good targets too. And when Dustin gets over here, we'll see who else wants to eat lead."

"They're gonna hang, McBride!" Miles shouted viciously.

"Why?" yelled Cory. "Because they slept together? Since when is that a hangin' offense?" He motioned with his gun, waving it right at Hadley. "I said cut 'em down!"

Hadley was disgusted. This whole thing was turning into a fiasco. He nodded to Mumford, who reluctantly cut the ropes, then Cory nodded toward Hadley to cut the ropes on Griff and Jeanine's wrists too.

There were other riders behind Cory, but it wasn't light enough to see who they were, and suddenly they parted, letting John and Sheriff Higgens come through, followed by Dustin and the deputy. Dustin had left his horse over at the jail, but he was backing Dave up now with his six-guns.

Once Dustin had released them from the jail cell where the mob had thrown them, Dave and John found their gunbelts in the outer office and strapped them on, and now

Dave was hell-bent on vengeance for what they'd done to him. Dried blood was all over his left ear, and a piece from the tail of John's nightshirt was wound around his head above it, to soak up the blood, and he looked fearsome as he bore down on the leaders of the lynch mob.

One of Hadley's men started to make a move, and Dave didn't even wait to see if he was going for a gun or not, but picked off a shot, and the man swore, clutching his elbow.

"Anyone else wanna ruin their shootin' arm?" he asked, his eyes blazing.

"Now, look, Dave," Hadley began, and Miles started to back him up.

"Shut up, both of you!" Dave screamed at them; then he looked up at Jeanine and Griff, who, with hands free now, were taking the ropes from around their necks. "Get down here, you two," he said quickly, and Griff jumped down, helping Jeanine, and surprisingly, Dave took their place, standing on the seat of the carriage, so he could look out over the crowd.

"It ain't fair," Warren yelled as he stepped away from the others. "He's gotta hang for what he did to Rhetta."

"But not by lynchin'," Dave exclaimed. "Besides, who says he's guilty? We ain't had no verdict yet."

Cory nudged his horse forward alongside the carriage and Griff glanced up at him.

"Where are they, Cory?" Griff asked.

Cory nodded to the riders behind him who were still in the shadows, and it was the first anyone had noticed that they hadn't come willingly. Ropes stretched from Spider and Luke's free hands to the other men's horses, and it was apparent now that the other men's wrists were secured and tied to their saddle horns. There were three of them, and Cory called to Dustin where he stood next to John, who looked bedraggled in his bloody nightshirt and wrinkled pants, a cut near his left eye.

"Bring Burke here, Dustin," Cory told him, and suddenly there was movement in the front of the crowd. "Pack the gun away, Miles," Cory warned the rancher, his own gun pointing at the man, and a smile crossed Cory's face. "Now, I'll show you who killed Rhetta Heywood," he offered, and nodded toward Dustin, who was walking out of the shadows leading Simon Burke, who was riding a horse with a distinctive blaze on its forehead, and a murmuring crept through the crowd.

"That man was hangin' around town most of the summer," someone yelled from the crowd, and other voices joined it, with the same pronouncements, but all remembered seeing him.

"You tryin' to say he's the killer?" Hadley asked, frowning.

"Nope," Cory answered, and the crowd began to grumble.

Suddenly Damian, who'd been watching from near the door to the livery, made his way to the front of the carriage and raised his cane aloft. "Let McBride talk!" he called out, his deep voice echoing through the crowd, and the grumbling quieted as all eyes turned to Cory.

"Go ahead, McBride," Dave urged.

Cory looked down at Griff and Jeanine for a second, then turned in the saddle toward Burke. The man's face was sullen, the scar on it even more prominent in the flickering torchlights, and Jeanine shivered slightly at the sight of him.

"Hey! Ain't that Jarrod's horse he's ridin'?" someone in the crowd hollered.

"That's right," Cory answered. "And that ain't all. If you'll take a good look," he said, pointing to the saddle, "you'll see that the saddle on this horse was special made with saddlebags attached, and they're tooled leather with the initials J.V. on 'em. J.V. for Jarrod Vance. I think most of you are familiar with the saddle Jarrod owned." He straightened again, looking directly at Miles this time, as did Dave and Damian, and Miles's face paled beneath the ruddy complexion, but he stood motionless. He didn't dare breathe as he stared down the barrel of Dave's six-shooter.

The crowd had quieted now, all eyes on the man who was riding Jarrod's horse.

"You wanna know who killed Rhetta Heywood? Tell 'em where you got the horse, Burke," Cory said, and Burke's eyes narrowed as he stared at the owner of Trail's End.

"I got it from Miles Vance," he answered belligerently, and this time Miles did come to life.

"That's a lie!" he shouted.

"You lie, old man!" Burke yelled back as he turned to Miles. Then he glanced over at the sheriff. "Me and the boys were workin' for Jarrod," he went on. "He and Heywood's wife hired us to help get rid of her husband, only we were supposed to make it look like someone was tryin' to stop the cattle drive he was plannin'. That way no one would suspect them."

Miles's face was livid. "That ain't true!"

"Oh yes it is, old man," Burke countered, "and you know it."

"Go on!" Damian said, and Dave's eyes were hard on Burke.

"Do like the judge says. All of it!" Dave ordered. "What about the teacher?"

Burke's eyes were steady on Miles. "We discovered that she and the newspaperman had found out we were hidin' out at the old copper mine, so Vance told us to get rid of her. We couldn't think of any way to make it look like an accident, so we decided to let the Comanche do it for us, only we didn't know that Heywood was friends with 'em. When Vance and his lady friend found out, they was fit to be tied, and had us waylay 'em on their way back from the Comanche camp, only they got away from us again later while we were at the Double V Bar gettin' dynamite."

Burke kept right on talking, telling the crowd about Rhetta bringing the boy to the mine and Jarrod's leaving to get money so he could pay them off, since his promise of jobs running Trail's End had fallen through.

"But he never came back," Burke said, his jaw tightening as he continued to stare at Miles. "At least not alive, he didn't. His old man rode in with Jarrod's body slung over his horse and tellin' some wild tale about Heywood shootin' him."

"He's lyin' through his teeth," Miles screamed furiously. "I never went near that mine. He's the one did it and he's afraid of hangin'. I tell you, I never went near there!"

"It ain't gonna work, old man," Burke yelled at Miles; then he looked up at the sheriff, nodding toward the shadows where his other two men waited. "You need more proof, Red and Chet back there'll tell you the same thing I'm tellin' ya."

"Keep goin', Burke," Cory said, and the crowd that had been ready to tear Jeanine and Griff apart only a short time before were now listening closely, anxious to hear the rest of the story, so Burke went on.

"Well, when Jarrod's old man rode in, we didn't know what to think at first. With Jarrod dead, there wasn't even any money to make the whole damn thing worthwhile, and we'd already spent the money Jarrod split with us after we robbed the Trail's End payroll. We didn't even have no promise of jobs left, either, so the whole thing was all gonna be for nothin' and I guess maybe we sorta looked like we might try takin' out some of our mad on old man Vance, 'cause all of a sudden he claimed he could give us all the money we wanted if we'd just light outta there and never look back for nothin'."

"What was Rhetta Heywood doin' all this time?" Damian asked curiously.

Burke looked at the man who spoke, then glanced over at Cory. "Who's he?" he asked.

Cory explained who Damian was, and Burke looked like he might clam up, but changed his mind and went on.

"She started arguing with the old man and tellin' him if he had that much money she deserved some of it so she and the boy could make it on their own, but he wasn't havin' none of her nonsense and told her to keep her damn mouth shut, that if it hadn't been for her, his boy would still be alive. Well, she lost her temper and slapped his face, only he didn't take that neither, and slapped her back. She swore at him, and started to say somethin' else, but he warned her again to shut up, so she stalked off and sat down on the back step of the old house, just watchin' us. It was too dark to see her face, but I can tell you she was mad. Real mad.'' He hesitated, but just long enough to take a deep breath and shift his weight in the saddle. ''Once she wasn't interferin', I asked old man Vance where he was gonna get the money to keep a bargain like that, and he took me over to Jarrod's horse. He told us Jarrod had robbed the bank in town—''

''That ain't true!'' Miles yelled tearfully. ''I don't know why you're sayin' these things. You know that ain't true. Jarrod didn't do no such thing. You're the one what robbed the bank! My boy wouldn't do that!'' Miles turned to the crowd. ''Don't you see!'' he yelled, trying to discredit Burke. ''He's just tryin' to clear himself. Why, you even heard the teacher tell on the witness stand how Burke took Heywood's guns and hunting knife from him. He's lyin', I tell you . . . lyin'!''

Dave Higgens glanced down at Miles, his eyes smoldering. ''Shut up, Vance,'' he said furiously. ''I think the town's had enough of your caterwaulin'.'' Then he looked over at Burke. ''What about that knife, Burke?'' he asked. ''And when the hell you gonna tell who killed Heywood's wife?''

''Give him time, Dave,'' Cory cautioned. ''He ain't any too happy 'bout this whole thing as it is.''

Dave nodded and looked at Burke, who went on.

''You wanna know who killed Rhetta Heywood?'' Burke asked belligerently. ''Well, I'll tell you. When old man Vance said he'd give us the money from the bank, fine. Who was I to argue? Only it was still in the bank's bag and stuffed in Jarrod's saddlebags, and there was no way we could take time to count it out on the spot, and since none of us had any way to carry a bag full of money with the name of the bank here in Raintree printed all over the sides of it without being conspicuous, we traded horses.

We switched Jarrod's body from his horse here, and put it on my horse; then the boys and I took off, only when we took Jarrod's body from the blaze here, Miles wouldn't let none of us help untie it, insistin' he was gonna do the whole thing hisself. But the knots was too tough, so I gave him the knife I'd taken away from Heywood so he could cut 'em. Now, he never gave that knife back, and when we lit outta there, leavin' him and Heywood's wife behind, that knife was tucked right into the old man's gunbelt just as nice as you please.''

"Lies! All lies!'' Miles shrieked. "There's no way you can prove he's tellin' the truth. I wasn't even there. I didn't kill her! It ain't true!''

Suddenly Warren took a step toward Miles. He'd been listening intently, and had sobered up just enough to start letting his brain work for a change, and now he stared at Miles, his eyes widening, as if seeing the whole thing finally fall into place.

"You!'' he growled viciously. "The man's right, it was you, and all along . . . Now I know why you were so anxious to hang Griff! It was you! I see it all now. The horses . . . How could we have been so blind?'' His gun was still in his hand, and although he'd been holding it down at his side, now he raised it, and before anyone even had a chance to move to stop him, he fired directly at Miles. "You bastard, you!'' he shrieked at the top of his lungs, and his nostrils flared viciously as he saw Miles's eyes widen in shock, the bullet tearing into his side.

Miles gasped, pain shooting through his body, but he was still on his feet, and before Warren could get off another shot, Miles's own finger tightened on the gun he was holding, only Miles was a better shot and Warren's head flew back, his body twisting, and he went down instantly, a bullet in his head.

Warren never opened his eyes again, so he didn't see Miles's gun drop from his hand right after the shot was fired, or see Miles go to his knees, then fall sideways in the dirt.

Griff and Jeanine were beside him in seconds, and Griff

knelt down, then glanced over at Damian, who was standing over Miles too now, but was unable to kneel because of his knee. Damian watched Miles closely as Griff reached out, loosening the collar on Miles's shirt, helping him to breathe a little better, but it was obvious he'd been hit bad. Dave climbed from the wagon, joining Damian; then he knelt in the dirt next to him, shoving his own gun back into its holster.

"Miles, is it true?" Dave asked quietly, and Miles's eyes fluttered a second, then grew steady again, but he didn't answer.

"There's no use covering for your son anymore, Mr. Vance," Damian reminded him, and Miles turned his eyes on Damian Worth, studying the judge's face intently.

The crowd was silent now, only an occasional hushed whisper heard, and Jeanine laid her hand on Griff's shoulder. He reached up, his hand covering hers, letting her know that he knew she was there.

"Did you kill her, Miles?" Dave asked again, and Miles's eyes closed.

"I had to!" he finally choked, tears filling his eyes. "She was no good . . . she ruined my boy's life . . . she didn't deserve to live." Blood began to trickle from the corner of his mouth, and he coughed, splattering it all over the front of his shirt and brocade vest.

"And the money you paid those men with?" Dave asked.

There were tears in Miles's eyes. "Jarrod . . . killed Winslow . . . robbed the bank . . . couldn't let anyone know . . . had to get rid of those men . . ." He coughed again, choking, and his huge body shook. "She paid for Jarrod . . ." He drew his eyes from Dave and they were filled with pain as he looked at Griff. "You . . . you should have paid too," he whispered breathlessly. "I . . . I should have killed you both . . . and the boy . . . Jarrod said the boy . . ." He choked again, only this time he didn't finish the sentence, only gasped, trying to get his breath; then his eyes widened in terror and he let out an agonized groan before they closed again for the last time and he lay still.

Jeanine stared down at Miles Vance. Her heart was filled with so many emotions. In a way she felt sorry for him. For a man to love a son so much . . . Yet it was almost an obscene love. To put the love of a son above the lives of innocent people was a terrible thing to do. He'd been willing to let both of them hang just to protect Jarrod and take vengeance on Griff, and the whole thing wasn't even Griff's fault.

Dave reached down and felt the pulse in Miles's neck, then shook his head, and both he and Griff stood up.

Damian glanced over at Griff. "Well, I guess no one can argue now over who killed your wife, Griff," he said firmly. "Only there are still a few questions to be answered, like how did he leave without you seeing him?"

Cory was off his horse now, and he walked up to stand beside Jeanine. "Burke answered that one on the way here, judge," he offered quickly. "He said that when Miles rode in, he told them he knew Griff was on his way and didn't want him to know he was there, so knowing Griff and his men would be coming down the only road leading into the valley, Miles took his horses around to the back of the house where they wouldn't be seen by anyone approaching from either direction. That's why Warren missed seeing him too."

"But why didn't he leave when Burke and his men left?" Dave asked. "Burke said he came there to let them know Jarrod was dead and Griff was coming after them."

"He also came there to kill the lady," Burke piped in from where he still sat Jarrod's horse. "Just before we left, after he'd come back from taking the horses around back, the lady was trying to talk me into giving her part of the money, and when he heard her, he really got mad. He told her she wasn't gonna need any money where she was goin'. Then told us to get the hell outta there unless we wanted to be hanged for murder." Burke shrugged. "I wasn't about to argue with him, so we left. There's a trail up the back hill and that's where we headed. I guess old man Vance left the same way.''

Griff looked over at Dave. "According to Miles, she paid for Jarrod," he said, his voice raw with emotion. "Now he's paid for Rhetta."

Dave straightened and scanned the crowd that was no longer an angry mob, but a disillusioned, tired group of men who suddenly realized how they'd been used by Miles Vance, and Jack Hadley had been the worst fool of all.

"You satisfied now, Hadley?" Dave asked the rancher. "Or maybe you need more?"

Hadley's face was crimson, and his eyes were downcast as he turned to Mumford and motioned for his men, scattered through the crowd, to join him.

"That's better," Dave said as Hadley began sauntering off with his men at his heels, and slowly, one by one, the rest of the crowd began to disperse too, until the only people left standing next to the carriage with Griff and Jeanine were the sheriff, the judge, Mrs. Brandt, the crew from Trail's End with Burke and his men and John Scott, who, exhausted, was leaning against the side of the carriage, his six-shooter dangling lackadaisically in his right hand.

"Do you think maybe if you have somebody get these bodies out of here, Dave," John said wearily as they glanced over at him, "that it wouldn't be too much trouble, and we could find time yet tonight to get a little sleep?"

All eyes were centered on John, and suddenly Griff smiled as he reached out and put his arms around Jeanine, pulling her back against him, a sense of relief suddenly flooding through him. It was over, finally over, the whole stinking mess was over, and they'd even managed to keep the truth about Gar's real father hidden. Griff glanced down at Miles's body. He had known—Griff was sure of it. Just before dying, he'd almost said it. Thank God he hadn't told anyone. But then, he couldn't. If Miles had told them he knew Gar was his grandson, they'd have to know how he knew, and he'd have been putting a noose around his own neck. Griff took a deep breath and drew his eyes from Miles's lifeless body.

"Well, Dave," he asked, echoing John's question, "am I free?"

"Damian?" Dave asked, turning to the judge.

Damian was staring at the two bodies sprawled on the ground; then he looked up, off toward the main road where the jailhouse stood, and watched the last of the straggling lynch mob disappearing around the corner by the feed store; then he listened to the riders moving out, filtering in all directions from town, some in a hurry, others going slowly. "As far as I'm concerned, the case is closed," he said quietly. "Only there's one thing still bothering me." He turned to Griff. "What did Warren mean before he shot Miles Vance, when he yelled about the horses and about us being blind?"

Griff's arm was still around Jeanine's waist, and she turned, looking up at him. "I've been wondering the same thing," she said curiously.

"He was right," Griff answered. "And I was a stupid fool for not seeing it right away myself." He looked down at Jeanine. "Do you remember what kind of horse Burke was riding when he kidnapped us on our way back to Trail's End?" he asked her.

She frowned. "A pinto?"

"That's right." Then he looked at Dave. "All right, Dave, on the day Miles rode in with Jarrod's body, what kind of horse was his body tied to?"

Dave looked wary. "A pinto," he answered hesitantly.

"Now, Damian," Griff said, "you heard John questioning Miles on the stand, and you heard John say that Miles had his men strap Jarrod's body onto his horse. Onto Jarrod's horse, Damian." He nodded toward Burke. "The one Burke's on right now." Griff shook his head. "We just didn't see it. Miles kept saying he hadn't ever heard of Burke, and yet we were so rattled we didn't even notice that he brought Jarrod's body into town on Burke's pinto, and the only place he could have gotten that pinto was at the mine, after Jarrod was dead, before Rhetta was killed, and before we got there.'' His arm tightened around Jeanine's waist. ''If we'd only noticed it the day he rode in, we could have avoided all this.''

''Well, I'll be damned!'' Dave exclaimed, and reached up, touching the strip of cloth from John's nightshirt that was still wound around his head. He holstered his gun, then straightened. ''Well, now that we have all the answers,'' he said wearily, ''if someone'll go wake up the undertaker and tell him we got a couple bodies down here, I'll take Cory and the men he brought in over to the jail. After all,'' he went on, ''they're still gonna have to answer to charges of kidnapping, attempted murder, and who knows what all,'' and he wandered off with Cory, Spider, Luke, and Dustin at his heels, leading the men they'd brought with them toward the jailhouse, while the Kid said he'd wake the undertaker.

Jeanine watched apprehensively as Cory went by, leading Burke, Red, and another man, whose name she'd never learned. Only three men out of six. Well, it was a start anyway. Someday, somewhere, they'd catch up with the rest of them. She shivered involuntarily.

''Cold?'' Griff asked.

She shook her head. ''No, remembering,'' she answered.

Damian stared at the couple for a minute, then sighed. ''Don't worry, Miss Grayson,'' he assured her thoughtfully, knowing what was bothering her. ''I suspect those three will be coming to trial in a few days, and I have a strange premonition the judge just might decide to send them up for a pretty long stretch.'' He smiled. ''Now, if you'll excuse me, folks, it's been a long day, and like the lawyer said, I think I could use some sleep. How about it, John?'' and he glanced over to where John was still leaning against the carriage.

''Bless you, Damian,'' John replied appreciatively, and he bade everyone good-bye. ''And I swear I'm not getting up until noon,'' he was telling Damian as they walked away, John slumped over wearily and Damian limping along at his usual gait. ''I haven't had a good night's sleep since this whole thing started.''

As Jeanine and Griff watched, the two men disappeared around the corner, and suddenly everything became so quiet. The torches were gone, the lanterns, the shouting and noise, the night had swallowed them up so quickly, and a few minutes later, after the undertaker had left with the two bodies, with Burke and his men safely behind bars, and the Trail's End crew surrounding the carriage, it pulled away from the livery stable with Jeanine, Mrs. Brandt, and Griff inside, and headed out of town.

"But my clothes are still back at the hotel," Jeanine protested to Griff.

"We'll go back for them tomorrow." He glanced up at Cinnamon and Venable sitting side by side in the driver's seat, then smiled when Cory rode by, throwing Griff's hat into the carriage for him. He'd gotten it when he went over to the jailhouse earlier with Dave. Griff set the hat comfortably on his head, then settled back in the knowledge that Cory, Spider, and Luke were leading the way while Dustin and the Kid brought up the rear.

It was a warm night for late fall but there was still a chill in the air and his arm was around Jeanine to keep her warm.

"It won't be easy," Mrs. Brandt was saying from where she sat across from them in the carriage.

Griff nodded. "We know it."

"People will still talk." Her voice was curt, crisp.

"We know that too."

"And they aren't going to forget for a long time, Griffin Heywood," she went on, and he agreed with her again, and for a while there was silence, the only noise the constant clomping of the horses' hooves on the dirt road and the rattle of the carriage. Then suddenly the housekeeper couldn't wait any longer as tears filled her eyes. "Well, for heaven's sake, young man, will you please tell me when the wedding's going to be?" she asked, and Griff laughed.

"The wedding? I haven't even asked her yet." His voice was warm with affection as he turned toward Jeanine. "Miss Grayson," he said, his voice husky as he tried to look down into her face, only it was too dark to see. "Will you marry me?"

"Oh yes, Mr. Heywood," she answered happily, and Griff didn't have to see her face, nor did the housekeeper, as Griff drew her close in his arms, sealing the bargain with a kiss, while across from them Mrs. Brandt leaned her head back against the seat sighing contentedly for the first time in ages. And as the carriage faded into the night, moving steadily away from Raintree, heading for Trail's End, all that was left in its wake was the rattle from its wheels, the plodding hoofbeats, and the faint strains of a spritely spiritual Cinnamon and Venable were singing that floated back toward town on the night air.

About the Author

The granddaughter of an old-time vaudevillian, Mrs. Shiplett was born and raised in Ohio. She is married and lives in the city of Mentor-on-the-Lake. She has four daughters and several grandchildren and enjoys living an active outdoor life.